the Kissing tree

the Kissing tree

PRUDENCE BICE

Sweetwater Books
An Imprint of Cedar Fort, Inc.
Springville, Utah

ISBN 13: 978-1-59955-936-0

Published by Sweetwater Books, an imprint of Cedar Fort, Inc., 2373 W. 700 S., Springville, UT 84663
Distributed by Cedar Fort, Inc., www.cedarfort.com

Library of Congress Cataloging-in-Publication Data

Bice, Prudence, 1967-, author.
The kissing tree / Prudence Louise Bice.
p. cm.
Summary: A young woman returns to her childhood home and discovers that she still loves a young man she had a crush on six years earlier.
ISBN 978-1-59955-936-0
1. Young women--Fiction. 2. Ranch life--Fiction. 3. Colorado--Fiction.
I. Title.
PS3602.I27K57 2011
813'.6--dc23
2011033544

Cover design by Angela D. Olsen
Cover design © 2011 by Lyle Mortimer
Edited and typeset by Melissa J. Caldwell

Printed in the United States of America

10 9 8 7 6 5 4 3 2 1

Printed on acid-free paper

For Carol

. . . a friend for all the seasons of my life

Also by Prudence Bice

The Widower's Wife

Contents

Acknowledgments

SPECIAL thanks to Jocelyn Skousen—for your time, talents, and, of course, never-ending patience. What would I do without you? Thanks to Pam Bice, my amazing sister-in-law, for answering my random phone calls when that one word I was looking for was eluding me and for your encouragement and effort in making this story happen. Thank you, Jelynn Nielsen, for your time and input, and to Joan Cottle for making sure I wasn't full of blarney. Our chance encounter wasn't just chance. Thanks to all of Cedar Fort's talented staff and the excellent job you do, specifically, Jennifer Fielding, Angela Olsen, and my awesome editor Melissa Caldwell. Also, thanks for, once again, giving me the opportunity to share my love for writing with others. To all my family and friends, especially my children, Teila, Natasha, Krista, Kiley, and Joshua; your unconditional love and support buoys me up when I am discouraged, always giving me the strength I need to keep putting one foot in front of the other. And last but never least, to my husband, Ray. Your love and encouragement, devotion, and great romancin' will always be my inspiration.

·Prologue·

GEORGIE ran behind the tree in a fit of giggles, slowly peeking around to see if he had followed her. Sure enough, he was standing not far away watching her curiously.

Her plan had worked. Now she just had to decide what to do next. She needed to get him to come closer so he was officially standing under the tree's low-hanging branches. Georgie took another quick glance at him before ducking behind the tree again. Oh, he was so cute with his wavy brown hair and those big, honey-colored eyes. Even the sprinkling of freckles that adorned his nose were simply adorable.

All of a sudden a sense of shyness came over her. Could she really do it, or would she chicken out at the last minute? Oh, why did Sammy have to go and dare her to lure Ridge over to the kissing tree and kiss him—*on the lips*—before she left town? At almost thirteen years old, this would be her first kiss. Already, she knew she should have gone straight home from school instead of going swimming and fishing with her two best friends. Her mother was probably wondering where she had run off. Besides, Georgie still had to pack before they left for their summer holiday the day after tomorrow.

Her family, which included her mother and two younger brothers, was leaving for a month to visit with her mother's sister, who lived on the east coast. Although she was thrilled for the train ride, her spirits were dampened to know it would be her Aunt Cecelia waiting at the end of such a new and exciting adventure.

Georgie had decided she didn't like her Aunt Cecelia very much. Though she had never met her in person, she had overheard many conversations between her mother and grandparents concerning her mother's controlling sister. From what she had gathered, her grandparents were worried how Georgie and her brothers would be received. Apparently her aunt had a particular distaste for children. "Especially children fathered by a lowly Irish immigrant," she'd heard Grandad exclaim sarcastically. Needless to say, Georgie wished with every bone in her body that something would come up that would prevent them from making the trip.

When nothing seemed to be happening—no chaotic or unforeseen distraction to keep them home—Georgie had done her best to talk her mother into leaving her at home with Grandad and Nana. Although she would miss out on the fun of riding her first ever steam locomotive, she would rather spend her summer vacation at home with them than under the watchful and critical eye of her aunt. Unfortunately, to her great dismay, her mother had insisted they all must go together as a family. Sighing deeply, Georgie resigned herself again to the fact that an unfair amount of her summer holiday was ruined and she would just have to pray the time went by fast.

Suddenly, something rustled at her feet, pulling her from her thoughts. Georgie looked down to see the biggest bullfrog she had seen all year nestled in a small, damp, ivy-laden hollow of the tree's enormous trunk. Ridge and his buddies still raced frogs sometimes, betting on whose would be the fastest. Looking down at the monstrous specimen, Georgiana grinned. This was sure to get his attention. The rest of her plan fell into place.

Inching back around, she looked over at Ridge again. He was still staring at her, though a bit curiously now, like maybe he was wondering if she had bats in her belfry. At least he'd moved a little closer. Smiling secretly to herself, not able to look away from the warm, sweet honey of his eyes, she thought, *He really is delicious. I don't think I'll mind stealing that kiss after all.* Georgie willed away the sudden heat of blush that colored her cheeks at her impulsive and flirtatious thought before stepping out from behind the tree trunk.

"Come closer," she said, beckoning to Ridge, "I wanna show ya somethin'." He still looked a little doubtful but took a tentative step forward anyway. "Oh, come on, Ridge," she coaxed. "You'll miss it!"

Turning back to the tree, Georgie crouched down low as if to get a better look, feigning a great deal of interest in the ugly old spotted frog while frantically motioning for Ridge to follow her lead. "Hurry," she pleaded again excitedly, "before he gets away!" Finally, Georgie could hear the crackling of the undergrowth and then feel his warm breath at her neck as he leaned in close behind her. Goose bumps involuntarily crept down her spine at his nearness.

"Wow, that's about the biggest ole bullfrog I ever did see!" Ridge exclaimed enthusiastically. "Do ya mind if I catch 'im and bring 'im home? This one's even bigger than the one Jeremiah caught down by the crik on Saturday. I'm sure to win the race now."

"Sure," Georgie agreed, not daring to look back at him.

"Great!" Ridge declared and at once leaned in even closer, with his hands at the ready.

Suddenly, before she lost her nerve, Georgie turned toward him and planted a quick kiss right on his lips. The shock of it caused him to fall onto his backside, and his dumbfounded and bewildered look nearly made her laugh out loud.

She hadn't planned on saying anything, just running off. So Georgie surprised herself when, after standing up, she placed her hands dramatically onto her hips and triumphant words came tumbling out of her mouth.

"There you have it, Ridge Carson." She beamed down at him, proud she hadn't lost her nerve. "I've stolen a kiss, and you can never have it back!"

Turning quickly before he could see the blush that adorned her cheeks, Georgie ran off toward Samantha, who was hiding up the way. She grabbed Samantha's hand, and they hurried down the road back toward Georgie's house, both giggling and whispering conspiratorially.

Smiling to himself, Ridge watched them go, still unable to move from where he had landed, the bullfrog temporarily forgotten. As the two girls rounded the bend in the road, he watched as a ribbon tore loose from Georgie's hair and lodged itself in a nearby bush.

·1·

Coming Home

THE stagecoach slowed, turned the corner, and began descending the last low, rolling hill just as the mountains were beginning to cradle the summer sun. The town was awash in the sun's glowing warmth when Miss Georgiana McLaughlin caught her first, long-awaited glimpse. She felt that warmth now envelope her whole body as she recalled the happy memories she had left behind in the dry Colorado air five years ago, memories which now swirled around in her pretty head and turned up the corners of her perfect, heart-shaped lips. The closer the stage drew to town, the fuller her smile became, until finally her face was alight with a look of sheer joy.

She had been away so very long. Georgiana had expected the town to look different. But though she could see a few new additions to the familiar buildings that lined the old boardwalk, the place still looked like it held the same homey quality and feel you could only get from a small town—a town where everyone knows each other intimately, whether you want them to or not. Nonetheless, their knowing is a small price to pay for the acute sense of belonging.

Georgiana had been only thirteen years old when her mother had uprooted the family and moved them to live with her aunt in New York. Aunt Cecelia's house never held any warmth whatsoever, nor did it foster any sense of attachment.

Despite her distress at their move, Georgiana had never been angry with her mother. She understood her mother's need to escape the memories and constant reminders of the love she'd lost. Georgiana's father had been her mother's whole world, and though she possessed a genuine love for her children, she could not bring herself to get past her grief in order to see the hope and promises the future still offered.

Georgiana and her brothers harbored their own heartache concerning their father's death, in addition to missing their home and grandparents. Nevertheless, they had borne the incivility and abuse from Aunt Cecelia for their mother's sake. Georgiana had witnessed enough of her mother's tears during that first year after their father was taken to realize the move might be her mother's only hope of finding peace.

However, that which had bruised Georgiana's heart most of all was the loss of her two closest friends. She hadn't been able to say good-bye when at the last minute their traveling plans were altered. But because at the time Georgiana thought they were only vacationing with their aunt for a month, she hadn't brooded long at not bidding her friends a fond farewell. It was later, when their mother sat all three of them down and told them they would not be returning to Crystal Creek but would instead live with their aunt permanently that her heart had felt the sickening shock of it all.

At first, she questioned whether she had heard her mother's words correctly. Why couldn't she see what a terrible mistake it would be for them to continue at their aunt's home? There was nothing for them there . . . no admiration or favorable sentiment, and certainly no love. The ostentatious house was an empty shell. Staying would feel like they were being sentenced for some reprehensible crime and imprisoned in a dark, cold place that would slowly eat away their souls until they were as empty as the house itself.

For days Georgiana had cried and pled relentlessly to be allowed to return. Grandad and Nana needed her, and it wasn't *fair* to leave them alone. But alas, even the incessant begging from William and Aden, Georgiana's brothers, could not change their mother's mind. She was resolute in her decision. Besides her mother's need to be away from the memories haunting her, Aunt Cecelia had convinced their mother that she could offer them so much more if they stayed in New York. Georgiana and her brothers would attend the best schools and have many more opportunities than they would ever have living on a poorly managed and shabbily outfitted cattle ranch out west. This, Aunt Cecelia had proclaimed in front of Georgiana and her brothers, taking no thought or care as to their tender feelings concerning the matter.

Such harsh and unfounded insults had chafed sorely at Georgiana's pride in her grandparents' livelihood and thus fueled her anger. She had scarcely been able to hide the dismay caused by her aunt's unjustifiable statements. Impertinent and caustic words in defense of her grandparents peppered her young tongue and fought to be set free. They were barely bridled. Georgiana's restraint was only maintained because she hoped she could change her mother's mind if she did not aggravate the situation further. She would yet attempt to make her mother see the disadvantages of such an arrangement.

Finally, after days and weeks of pleading, Georgiana had given up. Despairingly, she accepted her fate. She would one day return, she'd promised herself. She would find a way back to the place where her heart belonged.

The first year passed slowly. Her aunt was never overly generous, but her pride dictated she see her sister's children properly educated, outfitted, and introduced into society. The school they attended was definitely larger and more sophisticated than the one-room schoolhouse back in Crystal Creek, and so were the egos of the spoiled and overprivileged children who attended there. Georgiana chose to keep to herself, often fondly remembering bygone days when she was never lacking for the comfortable companionship of either of her two dearest friends.

When her fourteenth birthday arrived, she had been greatly relieved to quit her aunt's home and move into the Harriet Wilmington's School for Proper Young Ladies as was expected. The school became a haven, a place to be herself and to be free from her aunt's constant nagging and belittling. She'd enjoyed her three years under the security and refined tutelage of Ms. Wilmington's well-regarded institution. The normal length of attendance was two years, but Georgiana had been gloriously offered a position to stay on an extra term. A tutor was needed to attend to some of the more challenged students. She had eagerly accepted. It was during that year, having more free time to herself, she had discovered her love and talent for painting.

Georgiana's fingers twitched as she gazed once more at the beautiful sunset now layering strands of yellow and gold along the rooftops, reflecting a warmth that made the town seem even more inviting. Would that she could stop time this very moment so she could take out her easel and capture this day of coming home on canvas. For surely, this town was the only place that had ever felt like home.

A sudden thought caused a tear to escape and gently trail down her soft cheek. She had not forgotten the reason she had been allowed to return to this place. The warm and loving visage of her Nana McLaughlin passed before her mind—soft gray hair wound loosely into a bun at the back of her neck and a faraway look in her warm, dove-gray eyes as she retold tale after tale of her life back in Ireland. Georgiana, even after these many years, could still remember the sweet, pleasant sound of her grandmother's voice and the music in her laughter.

Taking a deep breath, Georgiana sighed sorrowfully. Her grandmother was gone now. Georgiana had always thought she and her family would return. She had hoped beyond measure even for a short visit. But year after year, they had remained, and now she would never see her dear grandmother alive again on this earth.

Nana, Georgiana thought, choking back the emotion that threatened to overwhelm her, *I am sorry, so very sorry I didn't come home in time.* Pulling a handkerchief from a small, delicately beaded handbag, she dabbed at her wet cheeks.

When her grandfather had written her mother asking if Georgiana could come and live with him at the ranch until he could find more permanent help, her aunt had been furious, ordering her mother to send a note of refusal immediately. Georgiana had been seeing a young man quite seriously for some time, and though she had already decided she could not commit her heart to him as yet, her aunt was pushing for a speedy engagement.

Mr. Dawson Alexander was in line to inherit a great fortune and was indeed a most suitable choice in her aunt's eyes. Georgiana had to admit Dawson was a good man, and she liked him very much. Not only was he considerate and benevolent toward others, he bore no semblance to the other haughty, spoiled aristocrats who shared the selfsame elevated status. He was but one year older than she was, and they had many things in common. In the short time she had known him, she had come to care for not only him, but also the rest of his family. Their generosity and loving nature bestowed so freely upon her attested to the reason Dawson was such a gallant and amicable man.

Much to her dismay and frustration, Georgiana always had a feeling lingering in the depths of her heart and mind that kept her from loving him fully. He was most dear to her, being such the man he was, but she invariably held back. Whatever was causing her to forestall any real commitment to a formal relationship with him stemmed from this feeling . . . this terribly *inconvenient* feeling hidden deep within her.

Georgiana had endeavored to discover and absolve that which troubled her heart and gave her cause to postpone Dawson's repeated attempts at courting her, but she had failed. The only thing she knew for sure was it somehow connected to the pain and loss she had suffered in her tender childhood years. So often she had longed for the home she had once known, for her grandparents she missed so deeply, for the friendships she had been torn from. She had never, in five years, truly become accustomed to living in New York. And though she had learned and experienced many wonderful things, a feeling of contentment and belonging had always eluded her. By returning to Colorado, the only place she'd ever really considered home, she hoped she would finally make peace with all she had lost and free her heart so she could marry Dawson.

After she had overheard her aunt's blatant and insistent demands concerning the matter of her returning, Georgiana had gone to her mother privately and pled her own cause. This time her mother did not deny her. Sensing her deep unrest, her mother knew Georgiana owned an intense emotional need to return to Crystal Creek, quite possibly as strong a need to return as her mother had to escape so many years before. Georgiana also suspected her mother harbored profound guilt for tearing her children away from their grandparents and friends. So, to Georgiana's delight and satisfaction, her mother had given her explicit permission to return and give aid to her grandfather.

Oh, her aunt had ranted and raved and threatened to send them all away. How could Georgiana, after living in the marrow of high society, be subjected to such deplorable living conditions as a ranch house in Colorado with a bunch of uncouth, uncivilized men no less? It was highly improper. And what of poor Mr. Alexander? Was he expected to just wait for her to return?

In the end, her mother had won, insisting it was only a visit and would not be permanent. Besides, her mother pointed out, it was her family's responsibility, as well as Christian duty, to come to her father-in-law's assistance during his time of mourning and need. What was the purpose of teaching responsibility and good breeding if, at the first test of character, Georgiana was not encouraged to take the higher road?

Bravo for Mother, Georgiana thought. She had thrown all of Aunt Cecelia's haughtiness and pomposity back in her face, and the argument had ended. Besides, her mother knew—though she would never let on to Aunt Cecelia—that it would be far from torturous for Georgiana to return to Colorado.

It had taken five years—five long years—but here she was . . . *home* . . . at last.

Finally, the stage pulled to a stop, and Georgiana nervously clutched her valise and handbag and stepped from the coach. Looking one by one into the faces of the few strangers that loitered about the stage depot, her heart at once leapt for joy the moment she caught sight of her grandfather. Forgetting all her well-groomed manners taught by Ms. Wilmington, she dropped her things and ran heedlessly up the wooden steps toward him, throwing herself into his open arms. Both tears of joy at seeing him again and of sadness over the deep loss she felt for losing her grandmother ran unrestrained down her cheeks.

"Grandad . . . Grandad," she managed in between her frenzy of emotions, "I missed you so!" She pulled herself back to look into his weathered yet wonderfully familiar face.

"Georgiana, me darlin' girl," he said, smiling and brushing an aged hand across his wrinkled cheeks to banish his own tears of joy. The sound of his voice brought with it a rush of memories both bitter and sweet. Still, her heart was lightened. "Well then, stand ye back," he continued, "and let me be gettin' a good look at ye, now." But his eyes never left her face. "Aye, 'tis a splendid sight ye are, and my how ye be grown! Were it not fer that golden hair of yar mother's and yar grandmother's eyes, I might've never recognized me wee girl, grown to be a woman." Reaching into his back pocket, he pulled out a handkerchief and handed it to her. "Best ye be moppin' up some of those tears, now. We canna be havin' you wash us both right outta town with 'em." He chuckled, and it made her smile and warmed her heart. She hugged him again before stepping back and dutifully drying her eyes.

When she was finished, Georgiana took a deep breath and looked around her. It was almost as if she had never left. Across the street was Whitaker's Mercantile. Through the window she could see a woman rhythmically sweeping a broom back and forth. She fancied it must be Mrs. Whitaker, cleaning up the store before closing time. A couple of old gentlemen sat out front at a feeble-looking table in a couple of mismatched chairs playing a game of checkers. It was a familiar sight.

Next to the mercantile sat the barbershop. The barber, old Mr. . . . she couldn't recall his name . . . was outside spit-shining his windows before closing shop, just like he'd always done. She had speculated many times why a man, who had no hair whatsoever, would want to spend his days cutting and shaving the heads and faces of those who had plenty.

Mrs. Perkins's dress shop was next. There were a couple of dresses hanging in the windows assuredly meant to display the latest fashions. She would never think of telling Mrs. Perkins that the dresses on display were actually quite outdated from what was now being touted as fashionable in New York. Of course, New York was always one of the first to follow the latest styles coming from Paris. She herself was wearing a tailored traveling suit, which consisted of a pink gored skirt, white ruffled blouse, and a short, pink bolero jacket with perfectly puffed sleeves. Its design was acclaimed to be the epitome of chic among the upper-class socialites, especially when doing a bit of traveling.

Her observations were interrupted when a bout of raucous laughter came bellowing up the street. She didn't have to look to know where it came from. The saloon was obviously still a flourishing business.

Taking in a deep breath, Georgiana let it out slowly as she took another glance up and then back down the boardwalk. She wanted to see everything at once, but it was getting late. It wouldn't be long before all the businesses were closed up for the night, with the exception of the saloon, of course.

"Oh, Grandad." She turned back to him and hugged her arms around her middle. "It feels so good to be home."

Thrusting her arms out, Georgiana spun herself around a couple of times in a moment of pure exhilaration, once again ignoring the assiduous and exacting lessons on how a proper young woman was expected to act in the public eye.

On her second time around, she caught a glimpse of a tall man standing in the road watching her. Startled that she had an attending audience, Georgiana lost her balance and stumbled. She let out a small scream as she started to fall backward off the steps. A look of astonishment was plastered on her grandfather's face, and he tried to grasp her outstretched hand in an attempt to keep her from falling. Almost instantly the look was replaced by a grin and a hearty laugh as Georgiana felt herself being caught from behind by a pair of long, sturdy arms.

"Whoa there, missy," she heard a deep and inherently masculine voice say. "That there is not a proper place to be dancin' and prancin' about." Georgiana gasped. She looked up into the unmistakable yet grown-up face of Ridge Carson. He smiled and continued as if he hadn't a clue who she was. "Though, if you're needin' a lesson or two, I might be willin' to give it a go with ya, but definitely somewhere . . ." He paused, unabashedly winked at her, and pronounced, "More private."

Georgiana fought hard to keep the heat of a blush from her face. This was definitely not the scene she had pictured were she to happen upon her old acquaintance Ridge Carson. In fact, on the off chance he still lived in Crystal Creek, she had played out in her mind an entirely different version of their first meeting. She knew how she would act and what she would say. And of course, they would both be standing a very respectable distance apart.

To her great dismay, he was not only close . . . she was in his arms! His strong and disturbingly comfortable arms! That fact alone was making her aware, and admittedly a little startled, that Ridge Carson somehow had even more of an effect on her now than he'd had so long ago. Since all of her well-planned and scripted words had vanished from her head the moment she had looked into his face, Georgiana continued to silently gaze up at him.

Ridge! Her mind reeled. *It's really you!* Her eyes were drawn to his mouth, and she remembered the last time she had seen him five years ago, a look of shock engraved on his face as she stole a kiss and fled. Now here he was rescuing her from a most humiliating circumstance, and all she could think about was that kiss. *What would Ms. Wilmington say if she saw me now*? Georgiana pondered, even as she continued staring dumbfounded at his lips.

Suddenly realizing how quiet it was, and that he obviously was waiting for her to respond, Georgiana cleared her throat and pulled her attention away from his mouth, only to be captured by his heavenly eyes and the familiar mirth they held. Her heart markedly skipped a beat. She fondly recalled how often she had witnessed that look when he had teased her unrelentingly as a young girl. Again she was struck dumb as a swarm of memories flew through her head.

Without warning, a muffled sound erupted from deep within him, shaking his frame and jolting her back into the present. He was laughing at her, she realized. Not only did she now have to fight harder to keep the blush, which threatened to reveal her embarrassment, at bay, but she was also struggling to keep her temper subdued.

"Pardon me, sir," she began, sounding as flustered as she felt, though choosing to address him formally. "Thank you for coming to my rescue, but if you would kindly . . . please . . . put me down. I . . ." *Calm down,* she told herself. *Speak fluently and with confidence.* The confidence part was difficult because he was still holding her close, and everywhere her body touched his, she felt a heightened tingling sensation. She needed to be free from this sudden rush of confusing emotions.

"Sir, I must insist for propriety's sake, you release me this minute!" she managed to request, pleased her voice finally contained the proper tone and quality expected of a woman with measurable social breeding.

When Ridge made no immediate move to grant her request, she looked over to her grandfather for assistance. Her grandfather had finally stopped laughing, and she begged with her eyes for him to intercede on her behalf.

"Ridge." Her grandfather descended the stairs and stepped forward, taking her free hand and urging Ridge to set her down. He released her slowly, lowering her feet to the ground. "Ye be knowin' me granddaughter, Georgiana, do ye not? Used ta live at the ranch with me and me wife . . . her kin too. Left 'bout five years past and moved east to New York." Georgiana saw a puzzled look cross Ridge's handsome face. Did he really not know who she was?

"Hmm," he answered casually, bringing his hand to his chin while rubbing it thoughtfully. "Think I might recall ya havin' some family livin' with you back a spell, Angus." He then was quiet for a moment as he looked from Georgiana to her grandfather, still rubbing his chin. "Remember a couple of young'uns . . . boys, I think. Must've been your grandsons. Were a bit younger than I was, so we never did get on much together." He continued to look thoughtfully as if he was trying hard to remember who she was. Then dropping his hand from his chin and shaking his head, he added, "Ain't sure I remember any girls."

Georgiana didn't know why exactly, but instantly she was angry. Although proper decorum dictated she keep the infuriated and affronted look from her face, she could not withhold the caustic tone that slipped from her tongue.

"Well, you might not remember me, *Mr. Ridge Carson*," she spat the words, "but I surely remember you! Quite the troublemaker you were, always getting the schoolmaster in an uproar. You made it most miserable for the rest of us as *I* recall."

She wasn't being quite truthful, but he had hurt her feelings by forgetting her so easily. He hadn't really been a troublemaker, mostly just a rascal and a tease. The other children, including her, thoroughly enjoyed the way he kept the schoolmaster hopping with his mischief and tomfoolery. Georgiana hadn't forgotten either, how he had teased her rather exclusively at times and remembered too just how well she had enjoyed it. Ridge had been her friend . . . a good friend. Could he really have forgotten her so easily?

"Hmm." He stood back, and his eyes traveled from the tip of her head down to her toes and back up again. "Maybe I remember a girl after all," he continued. "Seems every school has one," he remarked candidly, and Georgiana could feel her face becoming hot again. Still eyeing her, he walked around her one full circle, coming to stop directly before her. When his gaze at last came to rest upon her face, he added, "Some even have two!"

"And what, may I ask, are you implying with that remark, Mr. Carson?" she countered sarcastically. Her face was really red now. Not from embarrassment but from trying to control her temper.

"Ain't implyin' nothin', *Miss McLaughlin*." He toned his voice to mimic her sarcasm, which did nothing to soften her anger. "Just tellin' it how it was." Now he began walking side to side, looking her up and down again. His face appeared as though he was trying to recall some memory. Suddenly he stopped and faced her once more.

"Ah, yes . . . it's comin' back ta me now. How could I forget such a sassy young thing?" He leaned forward to look deeper into her eyes. Georgiana's heart sped up. Even though she was livid with him, his nearness affected her so. "Yes . . . yes," he went on, leaning even further forward, his lips only inches from hers. She prayed he had no idea how hard she was fighting to keep from closing the gap. "I'm thinkin' she even had the same pert little nose and stormy-colored eyes," he said slowly and then finally stood back up straight. Abruptly, Georgiana's hand came up to cover her nose but only briefly. "I believe," he continued while rubbing an imaginary sore spot on his behind, "that she might've even been the cause of a sound lickin' I got when I played a joke once on Schoolmaster Robinson. Took me quite by surprise her bein' a tattletale an' all. Would've never pegged her for one."

Georgiana remembered what he was referring to, and after a moment of surprise that he had known it was her who had gotten him into trouble, her anger abated and a feeling of shame welled up to replace it.

It really hadn't been her fault. She would have never purposely tattled on Ridge. The schoolmaster had tricked her into answering him during his interrogation of her. She had been so nervous and the schoolmaster so cross. When she realized she had let on to who was responsible, she had begun to cry. Schoolmaster Robinson assured her no one would be the wiser about who had "spilled the beans." This only made her cry harder, causing him to become agitated. He then dismissed her to go home, and she had gladly obliged.

Ridge hadn't acted angry with her then, so she assumed the schoolmaster had kept his word. Had he really known all along it was she who had betrayed him?

Georgiana looked over at him speculatively. He appeared to be trying hard to maintain an angry and irritable persona, but the corner of his mouth kept twitching as if it was determined to break into a half grin. Was he teasing her just now? She had been able to read him almost like a book before she'd left. With so many empty years between them now, she was no longer sure.

Continuing to withhold any response to his accusation, Georgiana took the time to make a lingering observation of him as he had made of her only moments before. *My goodness, he has grown!* she thought. No longer was he the cute, freckle-faced, rascal of a boy she remembered running away from that day so long ago. He was a full-grown man, tall and ruggedly handsome, with a sculpted face and a square jaw that boasted a slight cleft in his chin. No doubt he had been cleanly shaven that morning, but now his face showed signs of manhood. His eyes . . . mmm . . . were still the same warm honey color, but his hair, a deep russet brown, was neatly trimmed. She remembered that he had an unruly tousle of curls as a boy and smiled to herself.

Finally, her eyes traveled to his lips. *Those lips* . . . thick and expressive, accentuated his grin crooked. He had indeed failed to keep it hidden, making it all the more tempting. Georgiana's chest rose and fell with a satisfied breath. Her eyes traveled lastly over his arms and torso. No doubt the muscles beneath his shirt were strong and firm, a mass of strength born of hard work and labor. She could only imagine what a sight he would be to look upon. Her cheeks colored at the thought of seeing him without a shirt. It was most improper for her to be envisioning such things.

Ridge cleared his throat, and Georgiana realized she still was staring at his chest. She was tempted to turn her head to the side to hide her embarrassment, but instead she looked him directly in the eyes, lifting her chin ever so slightly.

"Perhaps you are right about me, Mr. Carson." She noticed how all at once his face fell. He *had* been teasing and for some sentimental reason it pleased her to know he hadn't outgrown his playful manner. "I apologize for insulting you as well as for causing you undo pain in your youth." Quickly turning away from his disappointed look, Georgiana addressed her grandfather, who had been observing their exchange with an amused grin on his face. "I am feeling quite fatigued from my long journey, Grandad. Might we head for home?"

"Aye, me girl, 'tis late and best we be headin' that way now," he answered and then gave her a sympathetic look. "Well then, how 'bout ye go an' wait in the wagon while I be fetchin' yar trunk."

Georgiana nodded and turned back to Ridge once more before walking away.

"Again, I must thank you, Mr. Carson, for rescuing me from a most precarious and possibly dire circumstance. Further, I apologize for any trouble or delay I might have caused you." She nodded her head and added, "Good day to you."

Turning away from him, she gathered her belongings and walked toward her grandfather's wagon in a stately manner, with poise and grace. She had to at least try to somewhat repair the damage to her genteel image. It was a bit more difficult managing to maintain her poised perfection while climbing up into the wagon seat without anyone's help. She hadn't ridden in a wagon in five years. Her hand slipped, and she almost tumbled to the ground before she caught herself. She glanced back to see if anyone had been watching. Her grandfather and Ridge appeared to be deep in conversation while the stagecoach driver unbound the ropes that had held her trunk secure.

Georgiana sat down on the seat, relieved she hadn't been seen. Straightening her back, she sat up tall and looked directly ahead as she waited. Even when she heard her trunk being loaded into the rear of the wagon and afterward grandfather thanking Ridge, she did not glance behind her. A minute later, Grandad seated himself next to her and headed in the direction of home.

At first they rode in silence, her grandfather sensing she was still upset. It wasn't long, though, before he began to whistle. Right away, she felt her mood lighten and found herself smiling as she recognized some of the old Irish tunes.

Her grandfather had taught her how to whistle when she was only four years old. She recalled how delighted and proud he had been at her catching on so fast. With that thought in mind, Georgiana joined him as he started on another tune. The rest of the trip home was spent whistling one song after another. By the time they pulled up to the house, her lips were sore.

Her grandfather smiled at her genuinely as he came around to help her down from the wagon. "'Tis good to be havin' ye home again, darlin'."

"It's good to be home, Grandad," she said, taking his offered hand.

After helping her down, he put his arm around her, and she leaned her head on his shoulder as they walked toward the house. Someone had kept the fire going, so even from the outside, the house appeared warm and inviting.

Immediately upon entering the parlor, a rush of feelings nearly overcame Georgiana, and she stepped away from her grandfather. Hers eyes went to the Irish lace curtains that adorned the windows. They then moved to the mantle over the fireplace. There, upon heavily starched, handmade doilies, were scattered photographs, along with mementos and figurines her grandmother had brought over from the Old Country. Homemade quilts, some she supposed she may have put a childish stitch or two in herself, were draped over the couch and the worn, comfortable-looking parlor chairs.

Home, she thought. *I am truly home.*

Georgiana walked over to one of the chairs, the one her grandmother had always occupied when the family would gather in the parlor on cold evenings to talk and play together while warming themselves by a fire in the great stone hearth. Absentmindedly, she ran her hand back and forth over the Irish rose pattern of the quilt and greedily breathed in the memories, looking around the room.

In a corner sat a small table upon which lay her father's old chess set. The pieces were posed as if someone was still in the middle of a game and had merely stood up and walked away briefly. The only sign that a significant amount of time had passed was the thick layer of dust that had settled on the marble figurines and board. Her father had been teaching her to play before he had been killed. She wondered if the game had been sitting that way since he died. They had lived in the house nearly a year after they had lost him.

She suspected her mother would have insisted it not be touched. Grandad and Nana must have decided to leave it that way after they'd left.

Sighing, she walked over to the mantle and picked up a family photograph that had been taken a year before her father's death. They all looked so happy. She ran her finger along the faces in the glass. She remembered that day when the traveling photographer had come to town. Her mother had been overjoyed and insistent about needing a family photo done. Her father hadn't shared her mother's sentiment. Yet he had willingly dressed in his Sunday best and drove them into town. Drawing her finger back over her father's face, she chuckled softly. She recalled the argument he had gotten in with the photographer. Father wanted his arm around their mother's shoulder for the photograph, but the photographer insisted everyone's hands be neatly folded in their lap. They were told they had to remain very still while the photograph was being taken or it wouldn't turn out. Three times Father had moved and put his arm around Mother before the exposure was finished, ruining the picture each time. Finally, the frustrated little man had given up and taken the picture the way Father wanted. Georgiana was glad. The photograph was evidence of how much her father had adored her mother. She could only hope the man she married would adore her half as much.

Georgiana lovingly placed the old photograph back on the mantle and turned to gaze contentedly about the room once more. *Home*, she thought again. She couldn't think it enough. Though the furniture was perhaps old and worn, the decorations out-dated and unfashionable, the room emitted a feeling of welcoming, of belonging. It was as if while standing there she was being wrapped in a soft, loving embrace.

Everything was so different from the parlor in her aunt's home in New York, with its brocaded draperies, mohair settee, and Queen Ann chairs, stuffed hard and uncomfortable with horse hair. It was fashionable, to be sure . . . fashionable and *sterile*!

Georgiana sighed deeply once again. It had taken so long for her to return, but finally here she stood. Closing her eyes, she wrapped her arms around herself and breathed slowly in and out, allowing the feeling of contentment to wash over her in waves.

Grandfather cleared his throat softly, breaking her from her reverie.

"Are ye wantin' a bite to eat before ya turn in?" he asked thoughtfully. She was too tired to eat and too full of both memories and regrets, so she shook her head no, her eyes still closed. "Would ya like me to bring yar trunk in fer ya then?" he added as he walked to stand beside her.

"Don't trouble yourself, Grandad. I'll make do for tonight," she answered wearily, opening her eyes and leaning forward to kiss him on the cheek. "Thank you for picking me up from town." She brought her hand in front of her mouth to hide a yawn. "It was a long trip, and I fear I'm quite fatigued," she added, slightly embarrassed.

"Awk! Don't ye worry yar pretty little head, now. A good night's sleep and plenty of this blessed Colorado air will have ye as right as rain in no time at all." His eyes were alight as he looked at her.

She suspected he was right. Some sleep and a little time and her heart was sure to settle. "Good night then, Grandad." She gave him another kiss.

"Good night, Georgie," he answered, "and sweet dreams ye be havin'. I'll expect nothin' less." He grinned and winked before she turned and went to her room.

·2·

Temper, Temper

As the morning sun filtered through the Irish lace on her windows, Georgiana rubbed the sleep from her eyes and sat up on the edge of her bed. The blankets fell from her shoulders, and the chilling morning air assaulted her bare skin. Her muscles were tender and sore from the stagecoach ride, so she rubbed them and her lower back a moment to relieve the aches.

Georgiana had slept soundly once she had fallen asleep. At first, her mind had been kept awake with thoughts of Ridge Carson. She hadn't expected to see him so soon after arriving, though she had often wondered what had become of him. She'd presumed he still lived nearby her grandparents because every so often Nana would mention the Carson family in one of her letters, even mentioning Ridge specifically a time or two. She hadn't realized he lived so close, and then Grandfather informed her on their ride home last night that Ridge was his foreman. That meant he most likely lived on their ranch, and she would be seeing him every day.

Rubbing her arms to warm them, Georgiana briefly considered the bothersome goose bumps he had caused when he'd held her the day before. She would need to keep her distance until she could sort through the confusing emotions he had stirred within her.

Annoyed at herself, Georgiana stood up and walked to her vanity. Withdrawing a brush from the small valise she had brought for the journey, she sat down and began vigorously brushing out her hair.

She wasn't going to waste any more time thinking of him. There was a copious amount of work to be done. Even in the dimness of the firelight last evening, she could see evidence of neglect brought about by her grandmother's passing. She wasn't going to fritter away any more time pondering her old school friend. Besides, he was probably married or at least courting some girl by now.

Georgiana laid her brush down and pinned her hair into a loose bun with some frustration, still contemplating Ridge. They had been close once, but that had been long ago. Still, the idea of him married or even engaged unsettled her slightly. *What girl might have finally caught his eye*, she curiously wondered, trying to recall some of the girls they'd gone to school with. Many had doted on Ridge. She endeavored now to picture one of them grown up and snuggled in his arms. Instead, her mind kept going back to a picture of herself in his arms. How alive her senses seemed to come at his mere touch!

"You're acting like a silly girl!" Georgiana reprimanded herself. She paused to scrutinize her reflection in the mirror. She couldn't imagine why she was allowing the man to so thoroughly dominate her thoughts. It was a stupid schoolgirl crush, a simple naiveté, and it had been years since she'd swooned at the prospect of one day being *his* girl. Besides, she had many suitors vying for her attentions back in New York, aside from Dawson. She had only to show just an inkling of interest and they would throng around her. In fact, many of her peers thought it a game to see how many men they could keep dangling at one time. Yet, although it was flattering, Georgiana did not want to unfairly garner their attentions. She didn't believe in giving false hope to any man or flirting unabashedly in public. She felt it cruel to trifle with the feelings of another. That was why she wouldn't commit to Dawson without being completely sure of her heart.

Looking around the once familiar room, Georgiana noticed her trunk sitting on the far wall. Excitedly, she walked over to it. Her grandfather must have brought it in this morning while she slept. Relieved she would not have to don her dusty riding outfit again, she opened it in earnest.

Having never done any long distance traveling, with the exception of her trip to live with their aunt when she was thirteen, Georgiana was shocked to see the condition of her clothing. Wishing now she had indeed allowed her grandfather to bring her things in the night before, she frowned slightly. If she could have hung up a few articles of clothing last night, some of the wrinkles at least would certainly have been loosened.

Well, there was nothing she could do about it now. Pulling a pale yellow dress out, she shook it several times in hopes of making it more presentable. There wasn't much change in its condition, and she shook her head in dismay. *Well, it will just have to do*, she considered optimistically. *Grandad won't mind, and surely the cowhands will be too tickled to have a woman who can cook about the ranch that they won't notice either.* At least she hoped that would be the case.

Slipping the dress quickly over her head, she began the tedious job of doing up the small buttons. It was then she realized her foolish mistake in choosing this particular dress to wear. It had too many buttons on the back. Had she remembered, she would have left the useless thing back in New York. There had always been servants to help her with it at her aunt's home, or at least her mother. Perhaps her grandfather wouldn't mind for today. Determined to be finished dressing and begin her day, Georgiana quickly exited her room, heading toward the kitchen.

"Grandad, are you here? Would you mind terribly doing up these last buttons for me?" she called as she walked through the parlor.

"Um-hmm," was the answer, and she felt him come from behind and begin buttoning the last of her dress.

"I don't know why I even brought this silly thing. It's shameful when a woman can't dress herself. I am most grateful for your assistance."

"Oh, believe me, the pleasure is all mine," came the teasing reply.

Just as she realized that this voice did not belong to her grandfather, he appeared in the doorway of the kitchen in front of her with a hot drink in his hand.

"Aye, what was it ye were needin', me girl?"

With a look of shock frozen on her face, Georgiana spun around and came face-to-face with Ridge, who was smiling mischievously at her.

"Good mornin', Miss McLaughlin," he greeted and tipped his hat to her as if nothing out of the ordinary had just occurred. Georgiana's face turned three shades of red.

"Mr. Carson! How *dare* you take such liberties with me! Why of all the . . . you . . . you . . ." Her grandfather laughed heartily and interrupted before she could finish.

"Awk, Georgie, what could be wakin' that Irish temper of yars so early in the morn, now?"

"Why he . . . I thought that . . . you . . . oh, never mind." Frustrated, she gave Ridge a venomous glare and stormed off into the kitchen.

They could both hear the immediate clanking dishes and slamming of cupboard doors.

"Well now, lad, ye sure managed to get me girl fired up again, didn't ye?"

"I'm a thinkin' it don't take much to do that," Ridge spoke, still grinning.

"Aye, ye be right about that." Angus chuckled. "Her darlin' grandmother, ma dear Shannon, 'twas the same, all fire and flame. Truth be known, some days it's what I miss the most."

"Then I 'spect you're glad to be havin' Miss Georgiana back home with ya."

"That I am, lad . . . that I am." He walked over and slapped Ridge on the back. "Best we be gettin' to work then, now. Let the girl cool her head a bit. Them fences won't be buildin' themselves."

Both men walked outside through the front door, avoiding the kitchen, and crossed the field to where a couple of cowhands were already working on a new fence.

From the kitchen window, Georgiana watched them go. *That Ridge Carson may look like a grown man, but he is ever still a boy,* she thought to herself. *Imagine the nerve of him*, she continued to ponder. *Why, if Ms. Wilmington knew I had allowed a grown man to button my dress . . . to see my camisole . . .* The thought caused a crimson blush to color her face again, and she began to knead the bread she had started making with more vigor.

It didn't take long before the dough was smooth and ready to rise. She was glad her mother had insisted she learn to cook, even at the risk of Aunt Cecilia's disapproval. As far as Aunt Cecilia was concerned, Georgiana would choose a suitor with great financial means. She would have more important duties to perform on a daily basis than ever having to set foot in the kitchen, except of course when she, on occasion, would have need to instruct the staff. The same had been expected of her mother when she was young.

However, her mother had fallen in love with her father, a poor Irish immigrant, and had married him secretly against her family's wishes. Shortly after they'd wed, they headed west to Colorado. They had decided to live with her in-laws, where her husband could work the cattle ranch with his father. She had no homemaking skills other than embroidery and basic sewing. It had been an embarrassment and a shame to her that she could not even cook a simple meal for her new husband. That's why she had insisted on Georgiana having weekly lessons in the kitchen with her aunt's cook. Georgiana had developed a love for cooking, and it was a comfort now to know she would be able to take care of her grandfather and the others on the ranch more than adequately with her acquired skills.

Covering the dough with a cloth, she set it aside to rise. It was then she finally looked around at the disheveled state the kitchen was in. Obviously her grandfather had been doing most of the cooking since her grandmother had passed. She lifted the lid of a grimy pan and peered into it. Ugh! She had better spend her first few days cleaning and organizing. Georgiana shook her head in amazement at how much damage one man could do to a kitchen in such a short time. So, after pouring a glass of fresh milk and quickly eating what looked to be a sort of biscuit her grandfather had made, she got to work.

She was not used to such physical labor, and Georgiana knew she would be feeling the aftereffects for the next few days, but for today, it felt surprisingly good to be working her muscles. As an added bonus, her vigorous cleaning was effectively keeping her mind off a certain incorrigible cowhand. When she was done, she sat down and examined the results. Her grandmother would be proud of her kitchen once again.

Grabbing a pencil and some paper, Georgiana began jotting down a list of supplies she would need to get in town. When lunch-time rolled around, she had rooted about for something she could fix the men to eat. There were plenty of eggs and milk, but not much else, other than some flour and a small bit of sugar. She'd decided there wasn't much of a choice other than to make them hotcakes and eggs for lunch.

The men eagerly consumed the food. She could only imagine what her grandfather had been feeding them.

Seven men were present at lunch, including Grandad and Ridge. They were refreshingly polite and courteous, and since she hadn't really known what to expect, it had pleased her immensely. All in all, they seemed a happy lot, and she'd decided she liked each and every one of them.

Roddy was the oldest and Irish like her grandfather. She learned both Roddy's mother and her grandfather's mother had been good friends in Ireland. Then there were the Johnston brothers. Jeremiah and Jonas were a couple of years older than Georgiana and she remembered them from school. They were twins and had an odd habit of finishing each other's sentences. Next was Pete, whose nick-name was Tiny, though he was anything but small. Standing well over six feet tall, he was a burly man and looked to be as strong as an ox. Last, but not least, was Jimmy. He was the youngest, not yet sixteen. He didn't look much like a cowhand, and Georgiana figured he struggled with much of the required work. But he seemed to pos-sess a determined spirit, and she admired that. Grandad would have had a good reason for hiring such a boy. On the whole, the cowhands seemed to thoroughly enjoy one another's company, despite a little good-natured teasing.

In the afternoon, Georgiana picked up the bunch of vegetables Tiny had brought in after lunch. It seemed the big burly fellow had a knack for growing things and had been caring for her grandmother's vegetable garden. Her grandfather had brought in some meat a little while ago, something never in short supply on a cattle ranch, and it was already stewing on the stove.

Happily, Georgiana started to whistle one of Grandad's Irish melodies as she washed the vegetables and began chopping them up for the stew.

After only a moment, she stopped whistling. Smiling to herself, she recalled the somber look Ridge had worn on his face all through lunch. She had been attentive and forthcoming with all the other men but had ignored him completely. *It serves him right,* she thought. *I am a grown woman now, not a little girl he can tease mercilessly. He'll find it a greater challenge to best me in the future.* She laughed conspiratorially and began whistling again as she scooped the vegetables into her gathered apron to carry over to the stew pot.

"Well, ya seem to be in a better mood."

Georgiana jumped, letting go of her apron and sending vegetables flying everywhere. Immediately she knelt down, gathered her apron up, and began haphazardly throwing vegetables back into it. She was grateful she had just finished scrubbing the floors pristinely clean less than an hour before.

Not daring to look up, she made no response to Ridge's comment. Nevertheless, he came over and began helping her gather the vegetables. When they were finished, they both stood up and after giving the vegetables a good rinse, Georgiana dumped them into the waiting pot. When she turned back around, he was grinning at her.

"I'm beginnin' to think I have quite an effect on ya, Miss McLaughlin," he bragged. A smile tugged at the corner of his mouth and the mirth was back in his eyes.

"Oh, don't flatter yourself, Mr. Carson. You only startled me. I didn't expect anyone back at the house for another couple of hours."

"Ah, well your grandfather sent me up to tell ya he had ta leave for a spell but would be back in time for supper."

"Well then, if that's all you came here to say, you've said it. Now you may go." She turned away from him but not before she saw Ridge raise one eyebrow slightly.

"Dismissin' me, are ya?" he asked, his voice sounding surprised.

Georgiana was flustered. That wasn't what she'd meant. She didn't know why she had said it that way. She was just still so irritated with him. Maybe it was because she'd hoped he had come to apologize for this morning. She deserved that much, didn't she? Even so, why couldn't she keep from being so clumsy around him and always saying the wrong things? It was damaging her pride terribly.

"I didn't mean . . . I wasn't . . . oh, would you stop looking at me that way!" she exclaimed in frustration.

"And what way would that be?" he asked, feigning ignorance.

"I don't know. Like . . . well . . . like you're waiting for me to do something to make you laugh." She couldn't help but glare at him as she answered. He was having fun once again at her expense. Why did he have to agitate her so? And where had all her controlled and proper training gone?

"Is it so bad to laugh?" he asked, a small chuckle escaping.

"Well, that depends, I suppose, on whether you're being laughed with or laughed at," she quipped.

He really laughed then, and it only made her glare more intensely.

"I 'spose I need ta be gettin' back to work anyways," he said while trying to keep a straight face but not succeeding very well. He turned away from her to leave, reaching for his hat that he had tossed on the table when he'd bent down to help her. After putting it on his head, he turned back around, reached toward her hair, and plucked a piece of carrot out that had found its way there. Grabbing hold of her hand, he put the carrot into her palm. "You missed one," was all he said before tipping his hat to her and walking to the kitchen door. Before going through, he stopped and turned back again, another smile tugging at his mouth. "By the way, I see ya still don't like wearin' shoes."

Georgiana glanced down at her small pink toes peeking out from under her skirt. Her face turned pink to match. She had taken off her shoes earlier and had forgotten to put them back on. The truth was she loathed to do it. Ridge was right. She hated wearing shoes, had hated them ever since she was a small child. She might as well rip up her certificate from Ms. Wilmington's school right there. She looked up from her feet to Ridge. He winked at her, chuckled, and shook his head back and forth as he went out the door. She could still hear him laughing as he crossed the yard to where the men were working on the new fence.

Later that night, Georgiana sat pondering the day's events as she methodically took the pins from her hair and began to brush out its soft, golden strands. She angled her face slightly away from the mirror so she did not have to look at herself any longer. Her normally vivid gray eyes were dull, and her long, dark lashes were matted from her profusion of tears, even though she had finally stopped crying. She knew from experience her eyes would remain red and swollen and the skin on her cheeks and forehead would be splotchy and uncomely for a long time still. The thought had occurred to her earlier in the day, when Ridge walked out of the kitchen door humored at her expense, that things couldn't possibly get any worse. Of course that was before her grandfather had revealed a fact that had made her humiliation utterly complete.

Everyone was sitting around the table, and she was beaming from all the compliments she had received for the meal. Between the bread and the stew, she had been surprised at how much the men could eat. She was excited to see what their reactions would be when she procured enough ingredients to begin making some pies and other desserts.

They all had taken turns thanking her grandfather abundantly for bringing her here and then thanked her for agreeing to come. It reminded her that she had forgotten to thank her grandfather for his thoughtfulness earlier that morning on her behalf.

"Grandad, I neglected to thank you for bringing my trunk into my bedroom this morning."

Her grandfather smiled rather coyly and took a quick look at Ridge before turning to her.

"Truth be told, me girl," her grandfather began, sheepishly, "I can't in good conscience be acceptin' yar thanks fer that, now. 'Twouldn't be right if I did. Ya see, me old back just ain't what it used to be. I s'pect it's Ridge here who would be deservin' of yar gratitude. 'Twas he who carried yar trunk in for ya." Ridge had not dared look up from his bowl of stew and so had not seen the utter look of shock and humiliation cross Georgiana's face.

"Grandfather Angus McLaughlin!" she scolded, standing up from the table. She quickly tossed her napkin down and put both hands on her hips. Georgiana had never before spoken to him with such formality and anger. He immediately wore a look of chagrin. "How could you?" She felt the heat rising up from her neck. "How could you allow a man into my room while I was sleeping? It's utterly improper and . . . and . . ." Her eyes got as big as saucers as she recalled she had not even worn a nightgown because all of her nightclothes had been packed in her trunk. The heat reached her face, turning it beet red from both embarrassment and anger.

The room was deathly quiet as Georgiana stood glaring at her grandfather. She didn't dare to venture a glance at any of the other men to see the looks on their faces or contemplate what they might be thinking of her. She was already determinedly fighting the tears that threatened. She couldn't hold them back much longer. Finally, she turned away from the table, hurried to the door of the kitchen, and paused.

"I suppose you can manage the dishes," she pronounced while keeping her back to them. "I am suddenly not feeling very well. If you'll please . . . excuse me." Her voice broke from her pent-up emotion, and she rushed to her room as the tears began to stream down her face. Flinging herself onto her bed, she had cried until she'd fallen asleep.

An hour later, she woke up, dressed in her night clothes, and sat down to begin removing the uncomfortable pins from her hair.

Georgiana paused in her brushing and looked directly into the mirror, scrutinizing her reflection. *What must he think of me?* she asked herself. *Oh, why do I care? He's nothing but a boy who looks like a man.*

She turned away from the mirror again. *Maybe I shouldn't have come home!* The unbidden thought popped into her mind. She discarded it immediately. She knew she couldn't have stayed away. Ridge or no Ridge, this was where she was needed, where she belonged.

At least when I woke up this morning, I was still snuggled under my bedding, Georgiana contemplated, trying to console herself. She had an awful habit of kicking off her blankets during the night and was forever having to get up and retrieve them from the floor before morning. *Thankfully*, she considered further, *with full-grown men such as Ridge Carson wandering about my room, at least my modesty was preserved. A gentleman—humph—he most certainly is not!*

Georgiana turned her thoughts from Ridge and instead thought about Dawson and their last meeting before she left for the train station.

She already felt the loss of his companionship. They were comfortable together, and he rarely gave her cause for annoyance. Often, they were seen walking arm in arm through central park or attending the theater. Whenever a gallant affair or party worthy of attendance was held, Dawson was her escort. It was assumed by most that it was only a matter of time before their intentions were officially announced.

When he arrived that morning to bid her farewell, she feared he would once again renew his sentiments and endeavor to convince her to make a commitment. She hadn't been wrong. Scarcely had he stepped foot into the garden, where she was awaiting his arrival, than he had rushed forward and begun pleading his cause.

"I can't bear that you're leaving me." Dawson took both her hands in his. "Why must you go? Please stay. I will do anything . . . just marry me."

"Dawson, I . . ." Her heart was filled with guilt at leaving without committing to him one way or the other. "I told you why I must go. My grandfather needs me. My mother can't possibly leave William or Aden here alone. Aunt Cecelia would never approve of interrupting their education, even to visit their grandfather they haven't seen in five years," she added bitterly.

Dawson placed his hands at her waist, closing the distance between them. She allowed him to do so, despite Ms. Wilmington's rules and her own reservations. She sincerely cared for Dawson.

When he pulled her even closer, encouraged by her allowances, Georgiana still did not push him away. She had not permitted any intimacies between them thus far because she did not want to lead him into falsely believing she had made her mind up concerning their relationship. When he laid his head to the side of hers and nuzzled it lovingly against her cheek, she secretly hoped she was not allowing her guilt to cause her to falter.

"Georgiana," he whispered into her hair, "you must promise you will return to me. I cannot bear to let you go otherwise." She felt a tear escape her eye and travel down her cheek. "Promise you will return and then we can be married."

"I cannot make that promise, Dawson. As much as I would like to, I cannot. It would not be fair to you."

He pushed her back and looked into her eyes.

"I don't care if it is fair or not, make me the promise anyway." His eyes begged her. "It's unfair that you are leaving me. So lie to me, tell me you love me, that I may have but a little hope you will one day be mine."

"I do care for you, Dawson . . . deeply. I just . . ."

Her explanation was lost as his lips came crashing down upon hers. At first his kiss was desperate, but slowly it became almost soft and pleading. Her heart ached for him, and she allowed his kiss to linger, though she made no move to return it . . . or his embrace. She began tasting the bitter salt from her own tears as they mingled with his kiss. When at length Dawson ended their exchange, he leaned back and gazed into her eyes. She saw the flame of hope burning brightly there now, and she was suddenly fearful she had allowed him too much.

"Will you write to me?" he asked hopefully. She smiled and nodded, not trusting herself to speak. His arms tightened again around her waist. "I will write you too . . . every day. And if you take too long in coming back, I will go and fetch you myself."

Just then Georgiana's mother had called out from the entrance of the gardens that she needed to make haste, for her carriage had arrived.

"I must leave." Georgiana turned quickly to walk away, needing an emotional reprieve, but he grabbed her hand once more and pulled her to him for one last desperate kiss. This time she ended his kiss quickly. "Dawson, I really must—!" she began. She pulled her hand from his grasp and fled from the garden while a torrent of tears finally broke free.

Inhaling deeply, Georgiana laid her brush down. She would write a letter to Dawson in the morning. He would be waiting, and she *had* promised. Standing up, she walked over to her bed, crawled in, and sank deep under the covers. The late summer days were still warm, but the nights were getting cooler. It was just the way she remembered. She sighed in pure contentment knowing she would sleep well.

·3·

Ribbons of Blue Remind Me of You

RIDGE Carson leaned up against the outside wall of the bunkhouse and looked up into the velvet night sky. Somehow the stars seemed to be a little closer and a little brighter these last two evenings. He smiled to himself. *Could it be because one Miss Georgiana Anne McLaughlin has returned to Colorado? My "Georgie," as I used to call her?* he mused.

She was different than he recalled. He smiled at the thought of how she had felt in his arms. Not a young girl anymore, but a fully-grown woman, and more beautiful than he ever remembered. Pigtails, ribboned braids, and a stolen kiss was what had come to mind when her grandfather had told him she would be coming for an extended visit. Not anymore! Her hair was as long and glorious as he ever remembered it being. When they'd had their little escapade at the stage depot, it had been piled atop her head. But that next morning when he'd brought her trunk into her room, he had stopped to admire her as she'd slept. Her hair was, of course, let loose and spilling in magnificent waves across her shoulders and pillow. Though her hair was blonde, her eyebrows and long curly lashes were darker, complimenting her soft and creamy skin. It was all he could do to restrain from running the back of his hand along her cheek, slightly flushed pink from the cool morning air. A vision she was, serene and peaceful.

She would be horrified if she knew that he had picked up her covers from the floor and gently laid them back over her as she'd slept. She would also be horrified if she knew he'd seen the little rose-shaped birthmark on the back of her left shoulder. He had seen it before, a time or two, but had forgotten, probably because he possessed the good sense not to tease her about it when they were young. Women never liked such little imperfections. Personally, even then he'd found it endearing. He would never have seen it this morning, though, had the sleeve of her camisole not slipped slightly off her shoulder when she sighed and shifted in her sleep. Likewise, he would never have stopped to look had her modesty been compromised. He was a gentleman, despite what she might think. All the ribbons and lace adorning her undergarments kept her covered up quite sufficiently. Though after this morning's tirade, he suspected her opinion might differ strongly on the subject.

When they were young, Georgiana, Samantha, and he swam in the lake together quite often on hot summer days in only their underclothes. Of course, they were innocent young girls and he a naïve young boy. Well, she wasn't a little girl any longer, and the feelings she stirred within him were those of a man. But he was ever honorable, though she threatened to bring out the rogue in him.

Ridge chuckled quietly to himself as he recalled the happy memory of her running hand in hand with Samantha Wallace. He, of course, was on his rear end where she had knocked him down after stealing a kiss from him under the old oak tree in the center of town. He hadn't realized it would be the last time he would see her for a very long time. If he had known, he might have run after her that day. She had stolen his heart long before she had stolen his kiss. Maybe that was why, at almost twenty years of age, he had never even courted a girl.

Plenty of women had made their desires toward him known, and some he found attractive enough, but something seemed missing . . . something they lacked. Some were too serious and didn't have any sense of humor . . . or any sense at all, for that matter. A few talked way too much or too little, and yet others thought too highly of themselves, and he knew they would be impossible to please. Every time he got close to a gal, there was always some fault or hidden trait he discovered that would cause him to back off.

His thoughts returned to Georgiana. Dash! The gal had a temper, that was for sure. She'd always had one, and he remembered it well. He recalled the way she had stormed off this morning and at dinner tonight. When they were young, he liked to do nothing better than to tease her and—boy, oh, boy—would she get angry. He chuckled. She never would stay mad at him for too long though, always forgiving him by the next day. That is, except the time he had tied her braids together around the stair railing of the schoolhouse.

Georgie had the longest blonde hair of any girl he had ever seen. She always wore it in either pigtails or braids, which hung down almost to her waist. *Yes*, he thought, *I will never forget that day*. He could picture it as if it were yesterday.

"Ridge, look," one of his classmates called out to him.

It was Jeremiah Johnston, and he was pointing over to where Georgiana was sitting on the steps to the schoolhouse, concentrating on untangling her boot laces.

Georgiana was always taking her shoes off. He knew she never liked wearing them much. While waiting for school to begin, she had taken them off and left them beside the steps before running off to play with Samantha. One of the boys in their class had tied her laces together in a million knots when she wasn't paying attention. She'd gone to put them back on after a while, knowing Schoolmaster Robinson would never allow her into class without her shoes. Realizing what had been done, she'd immediately sat down on the steps and quickly began untangling the knots. She looked upset and frustrated.

"I dare ya ta tie Georgie's braids 'round the stair railin'." This time it was Jonas, Jeremiah's brother, talking.

"She's tryin' so hard to untangle them laces, she'll never know ya did it," Jeremiah spoke again.

Ridge remembered looking over at her. She already looked pretty unhappy. He didn't know if it was wise to push her any further.

"She looks pretty mad already," he told them nervously, not really liking the idea anyway.

"Ah, come on, Ridge. It's been a long time since ya pulled a good prank," Jonas chided.

"Yeah, you're not losin' your touch, are ya?" Jeremiah teased.

"Course not," Ridge answered. Then he smiled wickedly and added, "She'll never know it was me."

Carefully, so as not to be noticed, Ridge snuck around to the back of the school and made his way cautiously up the shaded side. As he neared the landing next to the porch, he crouched down low and inched up to it, cautious not to make a sound. When he got to the railing where Georgie's back rested, he looked over his shoulder to see if Jeremiah and Jonas were still watching. He was still a little nervous about pulling the prank, and if they had wandered off, he didn't intend to go through with it.

No such luck, however. They were keeping a close eye on what he was doing, and Jonas had given him an okay sign when he had looked back.

Reaching down, he very carefully lifted each end of a braid, bringing them together around one of the wooden posts. He had planned on just tying her ribbons together, but today she hadn't worn any, so instead he took small strands of the ends of her hair and tied them in individual, intricate little knots so they would hold.

He was just finishing when Schoolmaster Robinson stepped out of the schoolhouse door and began to ring the bell. He froze for a moment and then ducked lower into the shadow of the porch. Georgiana didn't even flinch when the bell rang out. She just kept working frantically on the knots in her laces.

Ridge looked over his shoulder again. The Johnston brothers were poking their heads around the corner of the schoolhouse, motioning for him to hurry away while both the schoolmaster and Georgiana were still distracted. He made his way over to them and back around the corner. After slapping him on the back and congratulating him, all three boys hurried around the schoolhouse and began casually walking up the steps.

As he walked past Georgiana, she looked up and smiled, unaware of what he'd done. He smiled back, a sense of guilt welling inside him. She'd just finished untying the knots and had slipped on her shoes. Quickly tying the laces, she tried to stand up to walk next to him. The smile froze on her face when she realized her predicament, and he watched as her expression changed into a hateful scowl, her eyes narrowing into pointed slits as she glared at him.

Ridge stood stock-still. She knew it was him. He should have known better than to think he could hide it from her since he was the only one brave enough to pull off such a prank. He regretted what he'd done instantly, but what could he do now?

"Come on, Ridge!" Jonas and Jeremiah called to him from the door, motioning for him to hurry inside.

He looked up in their direction, but he couldn't move. Why had he listened to the twins anyway? He liked Georgie a lot better than he did either one of them. But they'd *dared* him! If word leaked out that he'd chickened out on a dare, he would have never heard the end of it. Looking down at Georgie's face, he wasn't so sure he cared about what everyone else thought. Unfortunately, he realized too late, he did care *a lot* about what she thought of him.

"Mr. Carson," Schoolmaster Robinson said, startling him from his inner debate, "go take your seat."

Ridge still made no effort to move.

"Mr. Carson!" This time the schoolmaster's voice meant business.

He hastened up the steps past the schoolmaster but paused in the doorway, waiting. Everyone had gone back into the schoolhouse except Georgie and him—and, of course, Schoolmaster Robinson. Ridge watched as she reached behind her head and tried desperately to loosen the knots.

"Miss McLaughlin, get up off those steps and make haste this minute!" Schoolmaster Robinson yelled down to her.

"I can't," she cried.

"You can and you will," the schoolmaster ordered.

When she made no move to get up, but instead put her face in her hands, the schoolmaster walked down the steps and stood angrily in front of her. She did not lift her head, so he reached down and yanked her arm up, trying to force her to stand. When he did, she cried out as her hair was pulled at the roots of her tender head. The sound of her cry made Ridge cringe. The schoolmaster realized the situation and walked down the steps and behind her to see what could be done. Ridge still stood frozen in the doorway when the schoolmaster looked up at him.

"Mr. Carson," Master Robinson spoke angrily to him, "bring me the scissors from my desk." Ridge didn't move, looking at the horrified expression on Georgiana's face. "Mr. Carson," Master Robinson shouted this time, "bring me my scissors at once!" Georgiana jumped. Even though the schoolmaster's voice once again left no doubt he was to be obeyed, Ridge couldn't seem to move his feet nor tear his eyes away from Georgie's face.

Just then Samantha peered around the opening of the door.

"What's the matter with Georgie, Ridge?" she whispered to him.

Upon seeing Samantha, the schoolmaster called to her.

"Miss Wallace, I need you to bring me the scissors from my desk at once!" Samantha gave Ridge a confused look before quickly running to obey the schoolmaster. When she came back with the scissors in hand, Ridge reached out and caught the end of her dress, knowing what would happen if she succeeded in delivering the scissors.

"Ridge, what are you doin'? Let go of me!" She yanked her dress out of his grasp and hurried down the steps to the schoolmaster. Ridge cringed for the second time as he heard Samantha cry out.

"Oh, Georgie, who did this to you?" Georgiana said nothing but continued to cry as the schoolmaster took the scissors and cut the ends of her braids off. Samantha knelt down by her and put her arms around her.

"Miss McLaughlin, you're excused to go home if you like. Miss Wallace, come with me inside."

Samantha made no move to leave her friend's side, so the schoolmaster grabbed her arm and pulled her up. She reluctantly let go of Georgiana and headed into the schoolhouse. Georgiana looked up at Ridge one more time before turning and running home.

"Mr. Carson, go to your seat immediately. I'll deal with you later," the schoolmaster scolded as he brushed past.

Samantha narrowed her eyes at him, suspecting he was the one responsible. Ridge followed them into the classroom, ignoring the snickering coming from Jeremiah and Jonas. He sat down in his seat, fearing he may have made the biggest mistake of his life.

Ridge knew he had been terribly wrong to pull such an awful prank on Georgie. He knew he had to make it up to her, but it took him a whole week to get up the nerve to formally apologize. She hadn't spoken a word to him or even glanced his way since it had happened. The guilt was eating him alive. So when he saw Samantha and Georgiana walking home one week later, he mustered up the courage and ran to catch up with them.

"Hello, Georgie. Hello, Sam."

"Now you just ignore him, Georgie, and keep walkin'," Samantha ordered. "We'll pretend he's not even there." She took her friend's arm, coaxing her to walk faster.

"Oh, come on, Georgie. I really am sorry. I should've never done it," Ridge pleaded sorrowfully.

"Ridge, will you just go away?" Samantha snapped. "Can't ya see she doesn't ever want to talk to you again?"

"Ever?" Ridge asked.

"Ever and ever," Samantha repeated, ". . . and ever!"

Aghast, Ridge suddenly stopped walking, but when he did, Georgiana did too.

Turning to Samantha, she spoke, "Sammy, go on without me." Samantha looked like she couldn't believe what her friend had said. "It's all right. I need to talk to Ridge . . . alone." That made Samantha's eyes go big.

"Are ya sure, Georgie? I could walk a few feet behind or in front of ya. You know, just to make sure he doesn't try anything," Samantha offered earnestly.

"Sammy, I'm sure." Georgiana smiled at her friend reassuringly. "And if my mother's outside when ya pass by, tell her I'll be home shortly."

"Well, I guess . . . if you're sure." She looked at Ridge. "You'd better not try any stupid pranks, or I'll get my brother Theo to teach you a lesson or two." Ridge held his hands up in surrender, and she glared at him one more time before hurrying off ahead.

"Thanks." Ridge looked at Georgiana gratefully. Suddenly a sense of shyness came over him. He looked at the ground and stuck his hands in his pockets as they started walking again.

"For what?" she asked.

"For givin' me a chance ta apologize." He looked up into her face so she would know he was sincere.

"Well, I know you're feelin' bad, but it was a very mean thing to do . . . even for you, Ridge," Georgiana admonished him.

"I s'pose you're right," he admitted. "Well, you'll be glad ta know I've decided ta give up pullin' pranks," he announced.

"And teasin' too?" She looked stunned.

"Nah," he said, shaking his head. "It would be too hard ta give up the teasin'. Usually teasin' don't harm no one, as long as it's all in good fun." He smiled over at her, and she smiled back. *Boy, she's pretty,* he thought, *with those gray eyes and all that blonde hair.* He studied her golden hair for a moment and how it was noticeably shorter than it was a week ago. "Pranks are different," he began again. "Ya never know when someone is gonna get hurt." He stopped and turned to her, picking up the end of one of her braids. "I'm sorry ya got your hair cut 'cause of me. I've always kinda liked your long hair." Her cheeks turned slightly pink, and he let go of her braid.

"Well, to tell ya the truth, Ridge, I think ya did me a favor. I like it better this way. Its lots easier to brush out at night, and 'sides, it's not that much shorter."

He could tell she was trying to make him feel better, but it actually made him feel worse. After school was out that fateful day and he had been scolded by Schoolmaster Robinson for failing to bring him the scissors, Ridge had walked to the railing where it all had happened. The ends of her braids, at least four inches long each, lay forgotten on the ground.

It hadn't been necessary to cut so much, but Schoolmaster Robinson was mean by nature, and Ridge bet he had cut that much on purpose.

"Anyway," Ridge said, feeling the shyness returning, "I bought somethin' for ya, ta sort of show ya I really am sorry."

Georgiana's eyes lit up immediately as he reached into his pocket and retrieved a small brown paper package. He handed it to her and waited for her to open it. As she tore the paper away, two long, bright blue ribbons fell to the ground. She quickly bent to pick them up and examined them lovingly.

"Oh, Ridge, they're perfect."

"I was thinkin' maybe they would match that blue dress you're always wearin'," he nervously added.

He noticed her cheeks glow pink again, so he turned and started walking once more so she wasn't embarrassed. She folded the ribbons up, putting them in her apron pocket, and hurried to catch up with him. When they got to the turnoff to her family's ranch, she stopped and turned to look at him.

"I forgive you, Ridge, for bein' a rotten apple to me, but I will say one thing." She took a step closer to him so her face was mere inches from his. His heart began to race. She was so cute, and he wondered what it might be like to kiss her, in a year or two anyway. But then she narrowed her eyes at him. "If you ever . . ." She poked her finger into his chest then and tapped it with each syllable she spoke. "I mean, if you ever try to pull a prank like that on me again, Ridge Carson . . ." She paused for emphasis while she stared into his eyes. "I can promise ya, you will wake up the next mornin' shaved as bald as the day you were born."

Stepping back, she gave him a broad grin before turning and skipping down the road to her house.

Ridge smiled at the memory again. The girl had a lot of spunk, and he believed she'd do exactly what she had threatened that day if he crossed the line again. He hadn't pulled another prank. Jeremiah and Jonas had pestered him for months before they finally started to believe he had been reformed.

He really did possess a bushelful of fond memories from his childhood. They had been good friends, Georgiana and himself, after she'd forgiven him. When Samantha finally forgave him too, they became an inseparable threesome and had spent many fun times together. After Georgiana's father had been trampled and killed, both he and Samantha had been there for her. Then, suddenly one day, her family was gone.

Ridge pulled a blue ribbon out of his pocket for a moment and stared at it. The color had faded some, but it still felt soft between his fingers.

"Well, hello there, lad."

Ridge was startled from his thoughts when Angus walked up and leaned against the bunkhouse wall beside him. Discreetly, he folded the ribbon and slipped it into his pocket again.

"Thought it might be ye standin' out here all alone," Angus said.

"Figured everyone had hit the hay long ago. What brings ya out so late this evenin', Angus?"

"Ginger should be birthin' her new colt any day now. Thought it'd be best if I looked in on the old gal once more tonight before I turn me old bones in."

"Wouldn't mind keepin' a closer watch on her, if ya like. I seem to be up a bit later these days," Ridge offered.

"Been havin' trouble sleepin', have ye now?"

"Seem to be."

"Wouldn't have anythin' to do with that pretty girl of mine, now would it?"

Ridge looked over at the old man, who wore a grin on his face and a twinkle in his eye.

"Aye, she's been gettin' to ya, hasn't she, now? I may be old, but I ain't blind. Been seein' how ye set me girl off huffin' more than yar fair share." He let out a soft chuckle. "If there be one thing that girl of mine inherited from her da and old Irish grandparents, it be her Irish temper." He chuckled again and continued, "And you, me lad are right grand at flarin' that temper of hers easily enough."

Ridge gave Angus a forlorn look. "That can't be good, can it?"

"Awk, don't be so certain, lad." Angus grinned and gripped Ridge's shoulder, squeezing gently. "There be an old Irish tale me good da told me once. Said his own old da told it ta him as a young lad. Don't know who told it to me granda, but if it be true, ye still have hope. Well then, if I can just be rememberin' how it goes." He looked thoughtful for a moment. "Aye, I remember now."

When Irish born, then Irish blood
Runs through a lass's veins,
The truth of where her true love lies,
Be how her temper flames.
If when first ye steal a lover's kiss,
She warms within yar arms,
Her heart will not be given true,
Ye are not the one she loves.
But if when that kiss be stolen,
Her anger burns like fire
She'll bind her heart and soul to ye,
And none but ye desire.
Mark me words and listen well,
T'were not mere legend ye be told.
Take heart, me lad, she's yar true love,
If her flame with ye be bold.

"Me Shannon were like that, and she was the great love of me life." He sighed deeply, and they stood in silence for a moment. "Well, lad, best be gettin' off to me bed now and ye best be doin' the same. Mornin' comes early on a cattle ranch. Good night, then." He turned and ambled back toward the house.

"Night, Angus," Ridge called quietly after him, "and I thank ya . . . for the advice, I mean."

"Anytime, lad . . . anytime," Angus called over his shoulder.

Ridge stared into the night, pondering. A few moments later he heard the door to the ranch house close. If Irish tales were true, maybe she did like him a little. He smiled thoughtfully at the idea of stealing his own kiss from Miss Georgiana McLaughlin. After another moment of pondering, he headed into the bunkhouse to try to get some sleep. If he was going to be able to keep his wits about him around that woman, he'd need it.

·4·

Reunited

GRANDAD," Georgiana addressed her grandfather as she served the men their breakfast, "I have a list of things I need from town. Is there one of the men who can drive me there? I haven't yet learned to drive the team myself." Her grandfather looked about the table into the hopeful faces of the men before his gaze settled on Jimmy.

"Jimmy, me lad . . . how 'bout ye take me granddaughter into town today?"

Jimmy's face beamed with the luck of being chosen.

"Yes, sir, I'd be right pleased ta do it."

Georgiana smiled at his enthusiasm and then sat down at the table.

"When would ya be wantin' ta go, Miss McLaughlin?" he asked after she had placed her napkin properly in her lap.

"Just as soon as we're through with breakfast Jimmy, and I've cleaned up." She smiled again at his eager look. "I'll need to change into something more suitable. I imagine about an hour will be an ample amount of time."

"I'll go fetch the horses and hitch up the wagon right away," Jimmy said eagerly, standing up promptly. Grabbing his hat, he hurried out the door. Georgiana stood up from the table, gathered his plate, and brought it to the sink, briefly wondering at his untouched meal, but flattered at his eagerness. Once he was out of hearing range, the rest of the men at the table burst into laughter. Georgiana spun back around to face the men.

"He ran out of here so fast . . . ," Jeremiah began as the laughter finally died down a bit.

" . . . that he hardly ate a thing," Jonas finished the statement.

"He'll sure be hungry come lunchtime," Tiny added sympathetically.

"Think that was wise?" Ridge asked her grandfather. "The boy's terribly smitten already. Walks around moon-eyed most of the day as it is." Ridge paused and rubbed his chin in contemplation before adding, "In fact, since your granddaughter arrived, that boy has been happier than a pup with two tails."

A fresh bout of laughter made its way around the table at Ridge's comment, and Georgiana narrowed her eyes at him.

Roddy sobered a bit and then offered his opinion. "I think ye made a good choice. The lad has been lookin' a might worn out of late."

"That's 'cause he can't sleep . . . ," Jonas snickered.

". . . 'cause he's always thinkin' 'bout Miss Georgiana here and hopin' she'll spark with him a bit . . . ," Jeremiah added.

". . . out behind the barn," Jonas finished. The men burst out in laughter yet again.

Georgiana couldn't believe they were talking about her like she wasn't even in the room. She turned bright red and fought to keep her temper in check. Purposely, she cleared her throat loudly to get their attention.

"Well, it seems to me you men are finished here," she announced and began stubbornly picking up their unfinished plates and tossing their remains into the compost bucket. The men were stunned. "I'm sure you need to be getting off to your work," she added, smiling inwardly, satisfied at the shocked looks on their faces. "Oh, and since I'll be spending the better part of the day in town . . . *with dear Jimmy,*" she turned to her grandfather, "I'm afraid it will be your responsibility to fix the men both their lunch and supper."

At that, all the men groaned. They remembered well their boss's skills in the kitchen, or rather his lack thereof. Georgiana wasn't done yet. After making sure all of the food, even the portion she hadn't served, was discarded in the compost bucket, she stripped off her apron and hung it on the peg beside the sink. Walking toward the parlor door, she stopped and turned to face the men once again.

"Since Jimmy will probably be finished hitching the wagon soon, I'd better hurry and make myself presentable. I'm sure you boys wouldn't mind cleaning up the kitchen for me. After all, I wouldn't want to keep *dear Jimmy* waiting." She walked to the door that led to the parlor, paused, and turned. "But mind you do it well," she warned, remembering its condition when she first arrived. "If I find it in a poor state when I return and it becomes necessary to spend the evening hours cleaning it again, I might just sleep in tomorrow. Of course I'm sure none of you will mind." She smiled innocently, immensely enjoying the way they were squirming, "Only Grandad here would have to cook your breakfast too." With her head held high, she turned sharply and walked the rest of the way to her room.

"Now look what you've done." Jeremiah swatted at his brother, who ducked just in time.

"Me?" Jonas asked innocently and became the aggressor, attempting to pummel his brother in return. "You said as much as I did."

"Fellas." They both stopped when Angus stood up. "Why don't ye go and get to workin' on finishin' them fences, now. We're needin' to be headin' up the mountain. That storm last week will have brought them cattle down to the winter gate, to be sure. Those fences need finishin' before we can bring them the rest of the way in."

Angus tried to keep the worried look from his face at the mention of the cattle. He was none too happy that the cows would have to be brought in almost two months early, but with the early snowstorm covering their winter grazing lands in the higher mountains, they had no choice. Thankfully, they had harvested a good crop of hay that would likely last for winter feed. He might be wise to buy some extra feed to store in the loft in case the winter ran long. Angus turned his attention back to the men.

"Well then," he said, looking around the table. He suddenly had an urge to laugh at the miserable looks on their faces. His granddaughter had put them all in their place. They would likely think twice next time about opening their mouths until after their food was eaten. Angus again suppressed his desire to laugh and instead motioned toward Ridge. "Ridge and meself will see to cleanin' up the kitchen."

Nodding their agreement, the boys scrambled out of the kitchen still bellyaching over the loss of their breakfast. They didn't want to be stuck cleaning up after the meal they hadn't been allowed to fully partake of.

Angus turned to Ridge and spoke. "Best we be gettin' to work afore me granddaughter be comin' back through here." He smiled and shook his head. "Aye, she be all fire today, that is fer certain."

Ridge walked over to the sink, grabbed a pot to fill with water so he could heat it on the stove, and began gathering the dishes. Angus grabbed a broom and started sweeping the floor.

They had been working for about twenty minutes when suddenly and without warning Ridge burst out laughing and Angus couldn't help but join in.

"Did ya see the look on her face, lad, when Jonas and Jeremiah mentioned the boy's daydreamin'?"

"Never saw that shade of red before on a woman," Ridge marveled.

"Aye, but you better be gettin' used to it. If she be like me own Shannon, ye ain't seen nothin' yet."

"How much worse can it get?" Ridge asked, a look of worry contorting his face. Angus laughed blithely at the boy's expression.

"Don't ye be worryin' your head about that, now. Though 'tis true that sometimes the arguin' can be hard, I can assure ye, lad, the makin' up is worth it." Angus gave Ridge a wink and laughed again.

"Well, I see at least you two men are getting something done in here despite all the chatter going on," Georgiana suddenly burst into their conversation.

Both Ridge and her grandfather spun around to see her standing in the kitchen doorway. She watched with satisfaction while Ridge's eyes wandered from her head to her toes and back again. She'd chosen to wear a lavender gown that she knew complimented the color of her hair and eyes while following her curves almost sinfully. Frankly, she had chosen it on purpose. She had also pinned her hair up in a stylish manner, leaving a few curled strands loose about her face. She could tell by the look on Ridge's face she had made the right choice.

"It's best I hurry along," she continued as she pulled a pair of lace gloves over her slender hands. "I'm sure Jimmy is eager to begin our day, and it would be rude of me to keep that delightful boy waiting." Walking to her grandfather, she gave him a kiss on the cheek and headed toward the door, brushing past Ridge as she did. She meant to unsettle him, but it was she who became unsettled when goose bumps shot up her arm. She was thankful he couldn't see her surprised expression.

Jimmy was sitting on the porch steps waiting for her with his hat in hand. He stood quickly as she walked out and offered her his arm. As she slipped her arm into his, his face pinked up.

"Ya look mighty perty in that dress, Miss McLaughlin," he complimented, grinning bashfully.

"Why thank you, Jimmy, but please, you may call me Georgiana." She squeezed his arm affectionately, causing the pink in his face to creep to the tips of his ears. "I do appreciate your willingness to drive me into town today. I'm sure you'll be good company." Georgiana didn't have to glance back at the door to know Ridge was still watching her. She could feel his eyes on her back, and she smiled complacently to herself.

When they reached the wagon, he released her arm, and she held her hand out to him so he could assist her up onto the wagon seat.

"Thank you, Jimmy." She smiled as he released her hand.

Although she tried to fight it, her eyes were drawn back to the house. However, instead of catching one last glance of Ridge, she unexpectedly saw Jimmy doing a little jig as he came around the back of the wagon. Quickly, she turned forward again so he would not know she had witnessed his jovial dance. A second later, he climbed onto the seat next to her. She continued facing ahead, trying to hold back her grin and smothering the desire to giggle.

Georgiana liked sitting atop a wagon in the fresh air better than in some stuffy carriage. The slight wind playfully tugged at her hat. She glanced at Jimmy. He really looked nervous. She decided to try to make him feel more comfortable.

"Jimmy, how did you come to be working for my grandfather?"

"Hired me last spring when my pa died," Jimmy answered solemnly and continued explaining. "When it happened, Pa dyin' I mean, my oldest brother Phil moved back home with the family to help keep the farm goin'. I never did care much for farmin', and so I decided I'd stay on only long enough to help Phil plow the ground and get the crop seeded. After that I figured I'd find me some work on a ranch somewhere. No one 'round these parts was needin' help, so I decided to take the stage to Castle Rock and see if I could find me a job on a ranch over there."

"You changed your mind then?"

"Your grandfather changed it for me." He smiled at her. "There I was standin' at the station awaitin' the stage when Angus happened along.

"'Jimmy Hutchins,' he says ta me 'is that ye lad?'

"'Yes, sir,' I says back.

"'Why, I haven't seen ye since ye were nigh to a hitchin' post.' He laughs and asks, 'Where ye be headin', now?'

"'Out to Castle Rock,' I tell him. 'Lookin' to get hired on as a ranch hand.'

"'A ranch hand is it? I thought ye be a farmin' boy.'

"'No, sir,' I says. 'Farmin' may be in my blood, but it isn't in my heart.'

"'Well, the saints be praised,' he shouts and then says, 'If I ain't the lucky one. I've been lookin' for another hand, and here ye be. How would ye like workin' for old Angus, now?'

"At that, I could have jumped for joy right then and there, 'cause even though I ain't got the heart for farmin', my ma was achin' real bad that I was leavin'. I didn't have much of a heart for hurtin' my ma any more when she was already a-grievin'. So that's how I come to work for your grandfather." Jimmy smiled sincerely. "He's been good to me too, payin' a good wage and all," he added, his gratitude for her grandfather clearly evident.

"Do you have any other family besides your mother and brother living nearby?" Georgiana continued to question him. Their conversation was clearly helping him to relax.

"Sure do. My sister Lizzie is married to Reverend Stevens," he answered proudly. "Figured I'd go pay them a visit while ya did your shoppin'. She just had her a little boy a month past, which means I'm an uncle again. 'Sides, your grandfather sent some beef to give 'em. He is a right generous man, your grandfather."

Georgiana was smiling now. She remembered well her grandfather's generosity. It was one of the things that had always made her feel so proud to be part of his family.

For the remainder of their trip, she asked Jimmy general questions about town. Did the Whitaker's still own the mercantile? Who was the sheriff now? What were the new buildings she saw as they came into town? She noticed Jimmy becoming more and more comfortable the more they talked, and she was glad of it. In no time, it seemed, they had arrived.

"Would you like me to drop you off at the mercantile, Miss McLaughlin?"

"Actually, I need to post a few letters and inquire about an old friend first. If you would please stop at the post office, I will walk over to the mercantile from there." She didn't know quite how long it would take. "Why don't you pick me up in front of the Whitakers' store in about an hour? Afterward, we can have something to eat together over at the café and maybe peruse some of the shops along the boardwalk before heading home."

"Sure thing, Miss McLaughlin . . . I mean, Miss Georgiana," he said enthusiastically. She could tell he was pleased at the prospect of sharing their noon meal and spending some extra time together. Pulling to a stop in front of the post office, Jimmy quickly jumped down and hurried around to the wagon's other side.

"Thank you, Jimmy." She smiled and squeezed his hand lightly as he helped her down. He immediately turned red all the way to the tips of his ears again. "I'll see you in a little while," she added, turning quickly to suppress a laugh.

Poor Jimmy. Unconsciously, she feared she had undone anything she had accomplished on the way over to make him feel more comfortable in her presence. She would have to be careful not to encourage him though, if indeed what the other ranch hands had said was true.

The bell on the door rang out announcing her as she entered the post office, and a pleasant-looking elderly woman came through the door of a back room to the counter.

"Hello, dear." Her smile was warm and friendly. "You must be Angus's granddaughter. I had heard tell you were coming to stay for a spell. Miss Georgiana, isn't it? Why, I remember you when your ma was still carryin' you on one hip. Suppose you don't much remember me. I reckon I don't look as young as I used to."

Georgiana knew exactly who she was, for indeed she looked the same as she had five years ago. She couldn't recall Mrs. Swansen ever looking young, per se. She had the same gray hair she'd always had and still wore it in the same style, braided and then wound in a bun at the back of her neck. To her credit, though, she looked as fit and as healthy as ever. Happily, the woman still seemed to possess the same pleasant and kindly demeanor that Georgiana remembered.

"Nonsense, Mrs. Swansen," Georgiana began, wording her response carefully as to duly flatter the post mistress, "you look the same as I ever remember and not a day older!" The elderly woman's eyes brightened, and she smiled bashfully.

"Well, you're still the sweet thing I remember too." She chuckled softly, and the pleasant sound of it made Georgiana wonder why the woman had never remarried after she lost her husband so long ago. "Angus must be overjoyed to have you back home. And are you glad of it yourself?"

"Yes, I've missed him and this town very much," Georgiana replied thoughtfully.

"I'm sorry your grandmother isn't here to see you. She so often talked of the day you and your family would return." Mrs. Swansen shook her head sadly. "Poor Angus, he grieves more than he lets on, you know. Your grandmother was a good woman. She has been sorely missed since her passin'." She shook her head once more and wiped at a tear before suddenly brightening up again, as though it was her duty to be cheerful. "Oh, I'm sorry to be goin' on about things, dear. What can I do for you today?"

"I would like to post a few letters, if you please." Georgiana laid her letters down on the counter.

"Certainly dear, and will you be expectin' a return reply soon?"

Georgiana smiled. She was sure she would not have to wait long for Dawson's reply.

"Yes, I believe so," she predicted.

"Would you like me to hold your mail here for you," Mrs. Swansen queried, "or would you rather I send any letters home when someone from your grandfather's ranch picks up the mail?"

She didn't think it would be of any consequence if Grandfather or any of the other ranch hands picked up her mail. Besides, she didn't know how often she would get to town.

"It would be fine to send any return mail I receive along home," Georgiana informed her.

"Good then, your letters will be on the next dispatch. Is there anything else I can help you with, dear?" Ms. Swansen asked sincerely.

"I wonder if you could tell me where I can find the Wallace home," Georgiana asked hopefully. "My grandfather told me they sold their farm and moved into town several years back. I am particularly interested in Miss Samantha Wallace. We were good friends before my family moved."

"As I remember it, you two were almost Siamese twins, you were together so often." She chuckled again, and once more Georgiana wondered why the woman was still single. "When Mr. John Wallace inherited a rather large sum from his grandfather back east, he sold their farm and purchased the bank, movin' the family to town. Bought the old Grantsville place and fixed it up right smart. Truth be told, he makes a much better banker than a farmer. He never was much good at farmin'. Though, don't you ever tell him I said so. Good family, the Wallaces. Not high and mighty like the last banker, Mr. Carl Jamison and his wife. That Eliza Jamison put on such airs! She really got my goat. I wasn't sorry to see them leave town. 'Course they only moved a little south to Westchester. Not far enough, if you ask me." She paused for a moment as something outside the window caught her eye. "Why, there's Miss Samantha now, comin' out of the mercantile with Miss Cordelia." Her face puckered slightly. "Watch out for that one, mind you. Never could understand how Miss Samantha could stand the likes of her or why she came back to town in the first place." She shook her head and continued muttering, "Livin' over at the boardin' house, orderin' people around like she's somethin' special. Well, I suppose I should just be grateful she didn't bring that awful mother of hers back with her."

When Mrs. Swansen had pointed out Samantha, Georgiana was immediately lost in a flood of memories and didn't hear anything the woman had said afterward.

"Thank you for everything, Mrs. Swansen. You've been a wonderful help," she called over her shoulder as she hurried out the door.

"My pleasure, dear, and do tell Angus I hope he's doin' well," Mrs. Swansen called after her.

Georgiana paused before stepping into the street, suddenly unsure of herself. She had been gone a long time. Even though they had been such good friends for so many years as children, Georgiana had left without even saying a real good-bye.

When her mother had told them they would not be going back, she had written Samantha a letter explaining what was happening and that she would always be her best friend, no matter how far apart they were.

She had never received a letter in return.

Georgiana had continued to write letters anyway, had sent letters to Ridge too, but it was as though her friends were no longer there.

Now, as she stood watching Samantha speaking so animatedly to the woman standing next to her, Georgiana felt a profound sadness overcome her. Maybe Samantha had never valued their friendship as she had.

"Oh, Sammy," she spoke quietly to herself, "I've missed you so."

At that same moment, Samantha looked across the street and their eyes locked momentarily before she turned back to her companion. Georgiana let out a sigh of despair. Suddenly, Samantha looked at her again and realization washed over her features. She immediately dismissed her companion and walked in earnest across the street. Georgiana timidly descended the steps and began walking toward her as well.

"Georgie . . . Georgie, is that you?" Samantha called out, and Georgiana smiled and nodded affirmatively. The rest of the distance between them was closed quickly as both young women ran and excitedly threw their arms about each other squealing and laughing in delight. "Georgie, I can't believe it's really you!"

"I'm home at last!" Georgiana exclaimed. "Look at you, Sammy. You're beautiful!"

"Me? Look at you. I knew you'd grow up to be the picture of perfection." Sammy leaned slightly away and observed her closely.

"Oh, Sammy, it's been so long. Are you still angry with me?"

"Angry? I was never angry," Samantha's smile waned slightly. "Only hurt that you never wrote. What happened to you?"

"Never wrote? Why, of course I wrote you letters—dozens of them. After the first year, I stopped writing as much, but I still sent you letters on your birthday and at Christmas." A puzzled look crossed Samantha's face.

"I've never received any letters, not one. Your grandmother gave me your address, and I wrote to you too. When you never wrote back, I thought maybe you had made too many new sophisticated companions in New York and no longer needed a backward, small town friend like me," she explained, a hurt and bewildered expression on her face.

"I don't understand," Georgiana said, looking as upset and dazed as Samantha. "What could have possibly happened to all those letters? Moreover, how could you think I could forget you so easily? We were sworn sisters, remember?"

"I remember," Samantha answered softly. "But you moved so

far away, and I could imagine all the wonderful things around you. I didn't blame you, really. If I had moved to such a brilliant city, with all the fashionable ladies and dashing young men, well, I might have wanted to forget too. Besides, with your father dying like he did and your mother so lonely, you deserved it!"

"I never wanted it!" Georgiana declared, frustrated as buried feelings surfaced. "I begged to stay, and then I begged to be allowed to return."

"I'm sorry," Samantha apologized. "I should have kept writing."

"No," Georgiana said. "It wouldn't have mattered. You did the right thing. You moved on." She glanced at the woman on the boardwalk who was glaring impatiently in Samantha's direction. Samantha seemed to understand what Georgiana was inferring.

"No, Georgie. I didn't replace you. I can't explain what happened—why I never received your letters or why you didn't get mine. But I still always thought of you as my dearest friend."

"Me too," Georgiana affirmed. Both girls hugged again.

Suddenly Samantha's face brightened. "Let's not dwell on the letters right now. I want to know everything that has happened to you since we saw each other last." She grabbed both of Georgiana's hands affectionately in her own. "What have you been doin' all these years? Do you just love living in the city?"

"Well, if I must confess the truth of it, I'd much rather be living here in a small town."

Her friend gave her an incredulous look. "But all the parties and glamour, the museums and exhibits, surely they are exciting," Samantha exclaimed, releasing Georgiana's hands and clasping her own at her bosom, a dreamy look in her eyes.

"Yes, they're exciting, to be sure, but . . ." Georgiana tried to think of how to explain to her friend how she felt. "I don't know . . . it's just . . . well, maybe it has more to do with living with my Aunt Cecelia. She has all the warmth and comfort of a frozen porcupine." Both girls giggled.

Suddenly snatching up Georgiana's left hand, Samantha made a quick observation. "Well, you're not married, but do you have a beau? The men there must be ever so dashing and cavalier, not boorish and clumsy like boys out here. Is there someone special you are seeing?"

Georgiana blushed slightly as she thought of Dawson.

"There is someone," Georgiana confessed. That was all she managed, but the small revelation still made Samantha squeal with delight and give her yet another hug.

"Is he handsome? I bet he's just divine to look at. Oh, Georgie, I am so excited for you. What is his name?" While she and Samantha talked, they had slowly drifted over to the side of the street. Now they both stood in front of the mercantile, oblivious to everyone around them.

"Ah-hem." Georgiana looked up when she heard a woman loudly clear her throat. "I'm awfully sorry to interrupt your little . . . well . . ." She didn't finish whatever she was about to say, nor did she look to be very sorry. Instead, she wore a somewhat peaked expression that disturbed her otherwise flawless features. Her skin had the look of ivory, which was complemented by perfectly formed strawberry curls that hung in ringlets from under her hat. Before she spoke again, she sighed loudly as if about to scold a child she was tired of correcting. "Samantha, dear, we haven't finished discussing our plans for the social. I have a twelve o'clock appointment at Miss Matilda's salon, which I absolutely cannot reschedule. If I'd any idea I would be standing on the boardwalk frittering away my valuable time, I would not have agreed to a meeting today."

Samantha instantly appeared to be flustered. This woman was obviously the domineering factor in their friendship, but Samantha quickly regained her composure.

"I'm sorry, Cordelia. Of course we may finish our discussion, but first let me introduce you to a dear friend of mine." She grabbed Georgiana's arm and pulled her a little closer. "This is Miss Georgiana McLaughlin, my bosom friend from long ago."

"Pleased to meet you, Miss McLaughlin." The woman nodded and smiled politely as she said it, but again Georgiana got the impression her civil attitude was more forced than genuine.

"Georgie," Samantha said, turning to her, "this is Miss Cordelia Jamison. We are planning the town social together for next month. It is going to be a glorious event. You can't miss it," Samantha coaxed. "Surely you'll still be in town?"

Georgiana did not overlook the way Miss Jamison's eyes had narrowed slightly when Samantha mentioned the social. She wondered if the woman shared any relationship with the previous bankers since they shared the same surname. Samantha began coaxing her again, and Georgiana turned her attention back to her friend. "Of course it will probably be nothing compared to what you're used to," Samantha added apprehensively, "but, Georgie, I know you'll have fun. Please say you'll come."

Georgiana smiled warmly at Samantha.

"Samantha, dear, don't pester her so," Miss Jamison piped in. "I am sure Miss McLaughlin will have returned to wherever it is she came from, long before the social. She is probably extremely anxious to get back to her home and her *city friends*."

Miss Jamison had purposely emphasized the last two words. Samantha looked stricken. Georgiana had more than an inkling that she wasn't going to befriend this Miss Cordelia Jamison, no matter how long her visit lasted. She ignored the woman's last comment and gave all her attention to Samantha.

"Oh, Sammy, of course I'll come. I wouldn't miss it for the world!" Georgiana smiled at Samantha assuredly and added, more for Miss Jamison's benefit than Samantha's, "I'm actually on an extended visit until my grandfather can hire some more permanent help. The social will give me something to look forward to."

Samantha threw her arms around Georgiana's neck excitedly. As she did, Miss Jamison made no pretenses to hide her disgust this time. Pulling away, Samantha clasped both Georgiana's hands again and squeezed them gently.

"We'll get together soon so we can talk," she said excitedly. Leaning forward, she whispered, "I want to hear all about this man of yours."

"Samantha," Miss Jamison began tapping her foot irritably on the ground, "we really must—"

"Yes, yes . . . I know." Samantha winked at Georgie, giving her hands a final squeeze before releasing them. "I'll see you soon."

As Georgiana looked into her friend's eyes, an overwhelming feeling came over her. It had been so many years since she'd felt so endeared to another girl her age. They had been apart for so long, but after sharing only a smattering of words and a few fond affections, she could already feel the time gap closing shut.

"Good-bye, Sammy," Georgiana whispered, her voice suddenly thick with emotion. She was sorely disappointed to be ending their conversation so soon.

Samantha walked over to Cordelia, who quickly grabbed her arm and led her across the street toward the café.

Georgiana sighed and walked up the steps to the mercantile. Before she walked through the door, she glanced back just as the two women disappeared through the café's entrance. Though still disappointed, she was content. Despite the long empty years between them, she and Samantha were still friends. It was more than she'd hoped for so soon. *Thank you*, she prayed silently before pushing through the mercantile door.

·5·

Bit o' Blarney

Angus watched as Ridge took his hat off and got a drink of water from the pump. Walking over to the porch, the lad tossed his hat onto the steps and sat down next to it. It was an uncommonly hot day, and Angus couldn't blame him for needing a break. However, Angus suspected that it wasn't the heat getting to Ridge, but rather the vision of his granddaughter in that fancy dress. Angus chuckled. The look on the lad's face when she'd come prancing in the kitchen all dolled up reminded him of the first time he'd seen his Shannon sporting her Sunday best. Bet Ridge was wishing he was the one driving his granddaughter to town instead of Jimmy. Not for his sake, of course, but for Jimmy's. Angus chuckled again. Either way, both Jimmy and Ridge were sure to be impossible to live with now.

After a while, Angus walked over to Ridge and leaned against the porch railing. He removed his hat and laid it on the step next to Ridge's. For a few minutes, both men remained silent. Shortly, Angus pulled a pocketknife out and began chipping away at some worn paint. "Been thinkin' the house could do with a new coat of paint," he observed.

"Might could," Ridge answered, his mind obviously elsewhere.

"But I suppose it can wait 'til spring," Angus added.

"Yep," Ridge replied.

"Heard the old Clayton ranch might be goin' up fer sale this next year," Angus said offhandedly.

"Mm-hmm."

"All three hundred and fifty acres, prime cattle land," Angus bated Ridge. "Hear they be askin' only twenty dollars for the whole of it," he teased, hoping to get a reaction.

"That's nice," Ridge mumbled.

"Awk!"

"What?" Ridge looked up, noticing Angus for the first time.

"Lad, ye are a million miles away," Angus accused as Ridge ran his fingers through his hair and sighed. "'Tis me granddaughter again, ain't it?"

By the look on his face, Ridge didn't need to answer.

"Well, now, I canna be blamin' ye for that. She sure did a bit o' growin' up since I'd last laid me eyes on her. And that dress she be wearin' today." Angus shook his head. "She's a sure to be turnin' heads in town."

Angus saw Ridge tighten his fists, but the lad didn't comment.

"Well then," Angus said, putting his hat back on. "Best we be finishin' up our work so I can fetch me shillelagh."

"Your what?" Ridge asked, looking puzzled.

"Me stick, lad . . . me fightin' stick," Angus explained. "I'll be needin' it fer certain to be beatin' off all them young fellas that'll be comin' around, now."

"Don't count on it with that temper of hers," Ridge huffed, shoving his hat back on his head and stalking angrily to where the other men were still working in the heat.

Angus chuckled softly to himself as he watched Ridge storm off. The lad had it bad, far worse than Jimmy, even.

He was a good sort, Ridge Carson, and truly Angus wouldn't mind having him steal the heart of his girl. He came from a good family too. Angus was sorely disappointed when Ridge's father, William, had given up cattle ranching, sold his land, and moved back to Wisconsin to help his brother run a dairy farm. He thought Ridge would be leaving too.

Ridge was a cowboy though, through and through, and cattle ranching was in his blood. When Ridge had told him he was planning on staying behind, Angus had offered him a permanent position as his right-hand man. Ridge had accepted, and hiring the lad had turned out to be the best decision Angus had made in a long time. The lad had a true talent for the work. Not only was he cattle smart, but he also worked harder than any cowboy he had ever known. Angus remembered the day when the lad left a note on the doorstep for his Georgiana, sadly a little too late.

It was the day Charlotte left with his precious grandchildren to New York to live with her sister. They weren't supposed to leave for two more days, but that morning Charlotte had received a telegram from Cecelia saying she had changed their tickets from the Friday noon train to the Thursday train leaving at five a.m. from the Castle Rock Station. There were no explanations as to why there was a change.

The earlier departing train meant they would have to ride to Castle Rock that night. He could see the stress on his daughter-in-law's face as she read the telegram. Not only would they have to rush to finish packing, but she dreaded telling the children, especially her daughter. He knew she wouldn't dispute her sister's change of plans, even for the sake of the children. She no longer held any of the strength and conviction that had given her the courage to love Angus's son so powerfully to forsake her family and follow him here.

He and Shannon worried about their grandchildren living in the same house as that vixen. Charlotte told them they were only going for a visit and would be back in a month. When he had looked in her eyes though, he knew they would not be returning.

Charlotte was still grieving terribly over the death of her husband. They all grieved sorely, but his daughter-in-law could not find even a measure of peace. At that time it had been almost a year since Michael's passing, and, sadly, he knew that even his own manner of speech—because it so resembled his son's—grieved her sorely.

Charlotte had found Michael that terrible day. What the girl had truly suffered he figured he would never really know. But he would remember that day well, for good or for ill.

There was a barn raising happening over at the Claytons'.

Charlotte needed to check on their neighbor, Mrs. Thompson, who was expecting a wee one any day. Michael told the rest of the family to go on ahead. He'd stay behind and finish tending the horses until Charlotte returned. They would ride on over together later.

Angus, Shannon, and the grandchildren had gone on up to the Clayton's, and Charlotte had headed over to the Thompsons'. When two hours had gone by and neither Michael nor Charlotte ever arrived, Angus started to worry and decided to ride home to see what was keeping them.

As soon as he drove the wagon up to the house, he knew something was wrong. The gate to the corral stood open, and the horses were out. Looking at the ground, he saw a trail of blood leading away from the gate. His heart beat savagely against his chest when he figured out what he would find at the end of the trail. There was just too much blood.

Setting the brake, he'd hopped down from the wagon and quickly followed the trail, which led him to the side of the house.

When he turned the corner, the scene before him immediately stopped him in his tracks. His son lay on the ground, his head in Charlotte's lap. She had ripped a large piece of cloth from her petticoat and was repeatedly dipping it in the water barrel, trying frantically to wash the blood from his body. She'd looked up at him when she heard him approach. Her eyes were swollen and hollow, her pale face streaked with blood and tears.

He knew his son was dead. He could see by his wounds he had been trampled to death. How Charlotte had been able to drag him this far, he would never know.

"Father McLaughlin," she'd pled with him as he came forward and stood next to her, "help . . . me . . . help me wash away the blood . . . the children . . . they must not see him like this. It will frighten them, and that would make him sad."

So with a bleeding heart of his own, he had helped her clean the blood from his son's body and also wiped the tear-stained dirt and blood from her face. Charlotte had never again spoken of what had happened that terrible day, but she had been changed forever.

And so she had run away. Away from the painful memories that surrounded her.

Angus thought again about the night his daughter-in-law and grandchildren left.

It was late, and he had only returned from Castle Rock a half hour before. He was in the kitchen making some herbal tea for his Shannon. She'd been crying all day, and he was hoping a warm drink might help her to relax and fall asleep.

He was surprised when he heard a knock at the door. Walking to the window, he peered out just in time to catch a glimpse of a young lad running around the corner of the barn. He walked to the door and opened it, anxious to know what the young prankster was up to. He stopped short when he saw a note tied to a sunflower lying on the steps. He bent down, picked it up, and brought it in the house, closing the door behind him.

The note had Georgie's name written on it. Since he knew she wouldn't be coming back, he decided he ought to see what the boy had wanted. The note simply read,

> *I have something that belongs to you. Meet me under the old oak in middle of town tomorrow at noon so I can give it to ya.*
> *Ridge*
> *P.S. I think you know which tree I'm talking about.*

What is that boy plannin' on givin' my granddaughter under the old tree? Angus had thought. He knew the old oak was affectionately nicknamed "the kissing tree" by the young'uns and had been for years. Its branches hung low like a canopy, and at night you could hardly see anyone standing beneath it. There was no other tree like it anywhere around these parts. How it came to grow there, no one knew. During town socials and picnics, many a lad and girl would hide under its cover to steal kisses. *Well, no matter what the lad is planning, 'tis not going to happen, because my darling girl has already left.*

Out of kindness, he decided to ride into town tomorrow and

explain to the lad his Georgie had gone and probably would never return.

And that's what he had done.

After tying up his horse in front of the mercantile, he walked over to the old oak. The lad was sitting under the tree, holding something in his hand, but when he saw Angus approaching, he quickly shoved it in his pocket.

"Good day to you, lad," he called to the boy. "What ye be doin' sittin' under this tree for, now?"

"Just sittin'," the lad answered.

" 'Tis a fine day to be sittin' in the shade, I suppose. Mind if I join ye?

The boy looked around a little nervously before replying.

"I'm kinda waitin' for someone."

"Well then, I won't be stayin' long," Angus replied, and he eased himself down and looked at the boy. "What was that ye was fussin' with when I walked up, now?"

The boy fidgeted a bit before answering.

"Nothin'," he fibbed. With a hopeful look on his young face, he asked, "Did Georgie come to town with ya?"

Angus stared straight ahead, knowin' he was about to break the lad's heart.

"Well now, I'm afraid she's gone and left town already." He felt the boy stiffen beside him. "Aye, 'twas a surprise for her grandmother and meself too, them havin' to leave so sudden like." Angus looked over at the lad. "I came by to tell ye she'll not be comin' back." The look on the lad's face saddened him even more than he was hurting already. "I am real sorry for ye, lad. I know ye and Georgie were mates." They sat for several minutes in silence, and then Angus stood up. "Well then, best be makin' me way home, now. Me Shannon will be wonderin' where I've got off to. If yer wantin' to be sendin' her a letter or two, I'll give ya the address when I be receivin' it."

A few weeks later, the lad had come over to his home asking for the address. He never knew whether his granddaughter and Ridge had ever corresponded.

He looked over at Ridge now hammering at nails with a force ten times more than necessary. He had seen the woman folk batting their eyes at him each time they went to town for supplies. He'd been wondering why Ridge hadn't taken much of a notice to any of them. *Most of the other lads around these parts have taken wives already and have a wee one or two under foot. Could it be Ridge has never gotten over me granddaughter?* he thought. Angus shook his head in wonderment. *If that be the case, the lad deserves his girl. Just maybe he could be helping things along.* Angus bent down, picked up his hat, and plunked it onto his head before heading back over to the boys. Hopefully, his granddaughter would return from town in a better mood than Ridge. Already he was having to cook lunch and supper. He didn't want to be fixing breakfast too. Even he didn't care for his own cooking!

·6·

Contemplation

Georgiana pulled the piping hot pies from the oven and set them on the windowsill to cool. The men had finally come back from bringing the cattle off the mountain last night and had been forced to endure Grandpa's cooking for lunch again today. She wanted to reward them with her cinnamon berry apple pie for dessert tonight. She had spent the afternoon visiting with Samantha at her house, and just before Georgiana headed home, Mrs. Wallace had given her a basket of ripe apples from their small orchard out back. Tiny had also, that very morning, brought her fresh blackberries he had picked down by the creek. Her mouth watered, remembering the last time she had baked the delectable dessert. The men would be pleased.

She could hardly believe she had already been there three weeks. Since renewing her friendship with Samantha, the time seemed to be flying by. They had yet to figure what happened to the missing letters. Georgiana had mentioned the subject to her grandfather, but he was just as puzzled as they were. Despite the unsolved mystery, their friendship amazingly seemed to pick up right where it had left off so many years ago. They had spent hours catching each other up on the things they'd been doing since parting last.

After Samantha had finished thoroughly questioning her about Dawson, Georgiana learned Samantha had once been engaged to a man named Mitch Tyler. He had come over from Denver to work on his uncle's farm for the summer. Samantha and he had met at a barn raising, and they had instantly been drawn to one another. After announcing their engagement a few short months later, Mitch had gone home to tell his family about his plans to marry and gather the rest of his belongings. Samantha's father had offered him a job at the bank, so they would continue living at her parents' home until they could save enough to purchase a piece of land on which they could build a house of their own. That was two years ago. Mitch had never returned.

Two of Samantha's brothers, Theodore and Caleb, had ridden to Denver that first fall after Mitch's disappearance, their confidence in Mitch's good character assuring them the man would never profess undying love and devotion to their sister and then for no reason abandon her. Mitch's family was devastated when Theodore and Caleb finally located them and explained the reason for their visit. Apparently, Mitch had sent a letter sharing the news of his engagement and informing them he would return home for a brief visit to gather his belongings. But he hadn't told them exactly when he would be returning. When a few months passed and they hadn't seen or heard from him, they naturally assumed his plans had been changed or delayed somehow. They'd never even considered writing a letter to find out if he might be in peril or have come to some harm. Mitch's father spent the next two weeks making inquiries and searching the outlying lands with Theodore and Caleb in hopes he might discover the fate of his son. Their searching unearthed no answers, but Mitch's father wouldn't give up.

Theodore solemnly returned home to his sister with no hope to soothe her aching heart. She continued to be tormented with unanswered questions. In fact, her anguish and misery seemed to increase for a time.

They finally concluded that Mitch must have been injured while traveling and died from his wounds, or if his fate wasn't an accident, he was most likely killed by either hostile Indians or outlaws. That summer, there had been more than one reported incident between their town and Denver.

Georgiana could see Samantha still grieved for him terribly but was well practiced at hiding it most of the time. She wished she had been around to comfort her dear friend. They had missed out on so much together. It all seemed so unfair.

After dusting the tops of the pies with sugar, Georgiana stood at the window and looked at the Colorado Mountains in the distance. She'd stolen away to paint almost every day the men were gone and had finished two paintings completely. A third was more than halfway done. She planned to send one to her mother in New York for her birthday the following month. She knew her mother would appreciate seeing the mountains again. It would remind her of the land she and her father had loved so dearly.

The most recent letter her mother sent came to mind. Her mother sounded particularly lonely, and guilt washed over her. Aunt Cecelia was probably wearing on her mother's nerves. With the boys at school most of the time, and the fact that her mother didn't venture out much, the only one to keep Charlotte company was her sister. The two were so very different. It was hard to believe they were even related. Aunt Cecelia was brash and demanding, selfish and haughty, whereas her mother was warm and kind, most often putting others' needs before her own wants and desires. Georgiana sometimes wished she had known her mother's parents so she could compare their personalities to those of their offspring. Sadly though, both of her mother's parents had died during a cholera outbreak shortly after her mother had married and moved to Colorado. Aunt Cecelia had been left the house and the estate since her mother had been disowned. Georgiana sighed heavily. How tragic it must have been—her mother so far away, missing her parents and hoping they would one day reconcile all that had come between them. What unimaginable devastation she must have felt when they both succumbed to a terrible disease before that reconciliation could happen. Georgiana placed a hand over her heart as she continued staring into the distance, pondering what her mother had suffered.

She was startled when the kitchen door slammed shut, surprised that she had been so deep in thought she hadn't even heard anyone come in or go out until then. She was equally surprised to see the wagon in front of the barn. She hadn't heard or seen it drive up.

When she caught a glimpse of Ridge walking across the yard to the barn, she deduced he must have been elected to go into town today. Georgiana watched him open the barn door and go back and forth from the wagon to the barn, unloading supplies. Before he'd begun, he'd stopped and rolled up the sleeves of his beige cotton shirt. She admired the way the muscles in his forearms flexed as he easily picked up the heavy bags of horse feed and carried them inside the barn. Indeed, the very sight of him was breathtaking. As a boy he'd been cute . . . as a man he was rugged and handsome.

A satisfied smile crept across Georgiana's face. They had somehow found themselves left in each other's company often over the past few weeks, especially the few nights before the men had gone to the mountains to bring the cattle down. She suspected it was her grandfather's doing, but, truthfully, she hadn't minded. He had somehow managed to keep from teasing her—well, enough that she could handle anyway—and she had kept her temper in check. It had actually been quite pleasant, feeling some of the familiarity returning as they reminisced about old times and the more unforgettable adventures from their youth. It was also a bit unnerving, the way his nearness seemed to constantly affect her so.

Watching him work now, she admitted to herself she had been thinking of him more than she ought to, especially these last two weeks, since she had found his letter.

After the men left for the mountains, besides painting each day, Georgiana was taking the time to catch up on the rest of the housework, cleaning what had been ignored since her grandmother's passing. She marveled at the amount of dirty clothing her grandfather had accumulated and wondered if he had taken to purchasing more than a few new items in order to avoid doing the laundry. It had indeed taken her a whole afternoon to wash his things.

After the clothes had dried and been folded, she took them into his room to put them away in his bureau. That was how she'd found the note. It was sitting in his top drawer. A yellowed, folded piece of parchment bearing her name, tied up with what appeared to be an old, dried up sunflower. Figuring it wasn't a breach of privacy because the letter clearly had been intended for her, Georgiana sat down on his bed, laying the clothes down beside her, and began reading.

The letter turned out to be from Ridge, probably written the same day she'd stolen a kiss under the old oak. It mentioned he wanted to return something to her. She puzzled as to what it could be.

Apparently, he must have delivered the letter after she had already left town, for she had never received it. The same as Samantha, she had never received any letters from Ridge. As a result, she had spent many nights crying herself to sleep, her young and tender heart broken.

She really couldn't blame him. It wasn't his fault she had nurtured a crush on him, loved him even, as much as a girl could love at such a tender age. But still, they were friends and had actually become quite close after she had forgiven him for the mean prank. She had been almost closer to him than she had been with Samantha. That was the reason it had hurt so badly when he hadn't written. She should never have taken that kissing dare. It had ruined their friendship, and living in her aunt's house, she had needed her friends so much.

Now, as she watched him work, she wondered just how deep those feelings for him ran. She had been so young, and it was so long ago. Was it possible that this boy, grown to be a man, could still have a hold on her heart? And was that hold growing stronger with each passing day, with each look he gave her or each time he accidentally brushed past her, causing her senses to thrill?

Shaking her head, Georgiana turned back from the window, walked to the cupboard, and began retrieving the old earthenware plates, setting them out for dinner. She then noticed the pile of letters sitting on the corner of the table. *That must have been what Ridge was doing in the house*, she thought. Georgiana picked them up and quickly shuffled through them. There was a letter from her mother, one from her younger brother William, and five from Dawson! Last week there had been three from him . . . but five? When he had said he would write daily, she hadn't really believed he would. She had only written him three letters, one the morning after she had first arrived, and two since.

What was she going to do about him? Georgiana buried her

face in her hands in exasperation. It wasn't that his letters weren't sweet, but he constantly wanted to know when she would be returning home. She did miss him, truly she did. However, as far as she was concerned, she'd just barely arrived and was quite far from being ready to leave. Especially since, from the moment she'd come, she had felt a peace she had not known in a long time. The constant longing for something else no longer nipped and tugged at her. If it weren't for the sake of her mother and brothers, she would send a letter tomorrow announcing she planned to stay in Colorado permanently.

Suddenly Georgiana was shocked at her own admission. She cared for Dawson more than that . . . didn't she? Of course she did. He was everything she could want in a man *and* in a husband. She would be foolish not to recognize her good fortune. Yet . . . she was painfully too conscious of the knowledge that when he'd held her hand, she didn't feel any special impulse or awareness other than complacency. Additionally, when he had put his arms around her and pulled her close at their parting . . . her heart had not sped up with frenzied and delightful titillations. Finally, when she had allowed him to kiss her, an allowance she did not consider trivial, his lips had not awakened any fervent or burning desires.

Still, the kiss had been nice, hadn't it? Even though she had not returned it? True, there had been no fireworks, no heated passion—but so what? What was wrong with being comfortable and content with a man? Not all lovers shared rapturous kisses and spellbound moments of euphoria. It would be a good life with Dawson. Didn't he adore and love her enough for the both of them?

Georgiana turned back to the window where she could still see Ridge working. Her heart warmed at the sight of him, but it also caused a sense of guilt to overcome her. She had not come back for Ridge. She had returned to help her grandfather in his time of need, hoping to free her heart for Dawson. She must stop thinking about Ridge or at least pondering anything other than friendship.

Georgiana quickly slipped the letters into her apron pocket and continued setting the table. The men would be in shortly, and they were sure to be hungry.

She had been right. In less than thirty minutes, the men were all seated around the table, cleaned up and as hungry as a pack of wolves in the winter. All her dawdling at the window earlier had made it necessary for her to scramble a bit in order to have dinner ready on time.

She had cooked roast beef with mashed potatoes and gravy, along with sweet fresh corn and biscuits. Again, she was awed at how much food a few men could consume in such a short period of time. When she placed the two pies and a bowl of fresh whipped cream in the center of the table, the men began to whoop and holler like a bunch of schoolboys who discovered their lunch pails contained nothing but fresh baked cookies and cinnamon rolls. The evening had been perfect—that is, until she stood up to clear the table.

Noticing she had neglected to hang up her apron, Georgiana picked it up from the sideboard, proceeding to vigorously shake off the crumbs before hanging it on the wall peg. The forgotten letters she had placed in the pocket started flying about the room in every direction.

All conversation at the table ceased as the men caught the letters in mid air or retrieved them from off the ground. Georgiana froze.

"Who's all this mail for?" Jonas remarked, looking at one of the letters. Suddenly, everyone was holding a letter in front of him, looking at the inscription—everyone except Ridge, that is. He just laid the one he had caught on the table before him. Try as she might, Georgiana still could not will herself to speak.

"This one's for you, Miss Georgiana. It's from your mother," Jimmy remarked with a smile and handed her the letter. She numbly took it from him, mumbling a polite thanks.

"This one's fer ye too, Miss," Roddy spoke up. "It be from yar brother William." He handed her the letter he held.

"Well, this one . . . ," Georgiana instinctively cringed as Jonas began his remark, "ain't from someone related at all, but rather, I would bet, someone who wants ta be." He snickered softly, and she could tell he was trying hard not to laugh heartily at his own cleverness.

"And what would be the name on that letter ya have there, Brother Jonas?" Jeremiah asked, his voice laced with the same poorly controlled humor. "Would it perchance be from a Mr. Dawson . . . ?"

". . . Alexander?" Jonas finished.

"Why yes, Brother Jonas," Jeremiah said dramatically. "I do believe we have a match."

"This one's from Mr. Alexander also," Tiny chimed in.

"Aye, and this one here as well," her grandfather added.

Then all heads turned to look at Ridge, who sat eagerly finishing his pie, seemingly ignoring the conversation altogether.

"Well?" Jeremiah asked him.

"Well, what?" Ridge answered in a monotone voice.

"Is that there letter in front of ya from Mr. Alexander too?" Jonas asked.

"The letter ain't addressed to me, so it's none of my business who it's from," Ridge answered matter-of-factly. He washed down his pie with the last of his milk.

"Hogwash!" Jeremiah replied, reaching across the table and snatching the letter up. He did not need to say anything, for the triumphant expression on his face told everyone that indeed the final letter was from the same originator.

"Well, Jimmy, looks like ya might have a little bit of competition." Jonas slapped Jimmy on the shoulder. Poor Jimmy, he turned as red as a tomato.

Everyone's attention then turned back to Georgiana. Jonas gathered up all the letters and handed them to her with an exaggerated bow.

"I believe these belong ta you, my dear Miss Georgiana McLaughlin, for that assuredly is your name clearly written on 'em," he spoke with exaggeration, lending his voice to the dramatics of the moment.

Still no one dared laugh. Not until her grandfather, who obviously could not hold it in any longer, let out a loud guffaw. That was all it took to break the ice, and all the men, with the exception of Ridge, laughed simultaneously. But even he was struggling to hold back a chuckle.

"Dearest girl . . . ," her grandfather began, pausing to wipe away tears born of merriment from his eyes. "I think ye have quite the admirer," he finally managed to say after the laughter had died down a bit. "Five letters in but a week! The lad must be writin' to ye 'bout every day. If I didn't know ye better, I'd be thinkin' ye had the lad's heart attached to yar sleeve." His comment only served to cause another round of hearty laughter from the men.

"How many letters did he write last week?" Jeremiah quizzed her.

She wasn't sure, but she thought Ridge might have attempted to thwart Jeremiah's questioning because he let out a howl and threw Ridge a dirty look. Finally Georgiana found her voice.

"That's not any of your business, Jeremiah Johnston. In fact, you all should be ashamed of yourselves. Does not one of you have any sense of propriety? These letters are addressed to me, and, as such, are of no concern to any of you. So . . . ," she said, crossing her arms across her chest and taking a moment to eye each man individually, "in the future, I would ask that each of you mind your own business where my personal life is concerned. Unless, that is, I choose to seek your opinion. Though I think that after such an ungrateful show of appreciation for all my attentiveness to each of you, and for your obvious display of bad manners, it is highly unlikely." She felt guilty for lumping Ridge in with the rest of them, for at least he had tried to abstain from mocking her. Maybe that was only because he already knew who the letters were from. After all, he had brought them from town.

"Now, now, Georgie," her grandfather spoke up again. " 'Tis been a long day, and the lads and I mean ye no harm. There be no doubt, ye being the beauty that ye are, many lads would be rivalin' after yar affections. Hold not these here boys' failin's against them this night." He turned to the men. "Now, I be expectin' each of ye to apologize to me girl fer not respectin' her privacy 'bout her lovesick lad and teasin' her thoroughly for it."

One by one, the men brought their dishes to the sink, offered their apologies, and thanked her for dinner before heading out to the bunkhouse. Last of all, her grandfather gave her a kiss on the cheek and, looking very chagrined, stood before her.

"Why don't ye go to relax a bit, me girl, and be lettin' me clean up fer ye tonight." His kind offer softened her anger a bit, as had each of the men's heartfelt apologies. She knew her words had been harsh, but they had struck a nerve with her, teasing her about the very thing she was frustrated over.

"That's kind of you, Grandad, but I'd like to stay up for a while. Besides, you're the one who needs to take it easy. You're not as young as you used to be." She patted his cheek and gave him a kiss.

"Aye, ye be right about that. One day, I'll be sellin' this old ranch and puttin' me old bones to rest." For a moment he got a faraway look in his eyes. "Maybe then I'll be takin' me a trip back to the Old Country and gettin' me one last, long look before I go to be with me Shannon."

"That would be a nice holiday, Grandad." She dabbed a tear and smiled at him affectionately, then abruptly shook her finger at him. "But don't you be thinking of leaving me too soon. I want you around for a good long time, all right?"

"Aye, 'tis been grand havin' ya here, darlin' girl." He took his aged, roughened hands and placed them on both of her cheeks, looking lovingly into her eyes. It was something he'd always done when she was a child. The last time had been just before she'd boarded the train to New York five years ago. She couldn't remember what he'd said, only that his eyes had glistened with the same raw emotion. His tender gesture made her tear up again even before he spoke. "Ye have been a blessin' to me . . . a blessin' from heaven." He paused for a moment to add emphasis to what he'd said, released her face, grabbed one of her hands, and held it lovingly between both of his. "Aye, I canna tell ye how much it be easin' the ache in me heart ta have ya home again." He then released her hand and turned to go.

"Good night, Grandfather . . . sleep well," she called after him softly, wiping the tears from her face. She slowly turned and began putting the remains of supper away.

A short while later, as Georgiana washed up the dishes, the kitchen door opened, and Ridge appeared. He made no immediate move to come in the rest of the way, but just stood there, quietly watching her. It unnerved her slightly, and she only dared glance at him for a moment, though it was enough to start her heart racing. Slowly, he walked up beside her, grabbed a dish towel, and began drying the dishes she was washing. Neither of them said anything to each other, just worked in comfortable silence. Yet each time he accidentally brushed up against her, it sent a thrilling sensation up her arm. That spoke volumes. When the kitchen was clean, Ridge turned, opened the door, and headed outside.

"Ridge?" Georgiana called softly before he shut the door. He stopped and turned toward her. It bothered her that she couldn't read any emotion in his eyes. "Thank you . . . for your help and . . . ," she took a deep breath, trying to slow her heartbeat, ". . . and for earlier at dinner, for being respectful of my feelings."

He didn't say anything to her, simply nodded his head, and turned again to leave.

"Ridge," she called again, and once more he turned back, but this time he refused to meet her eyes. She could sense something was bothering him. "Is everything all right? Did I do something to . . . ?" she asked, fumbling over her words. "I mean . . . you just seem different tonight . . . somehow. I thought . . . well . . . before you left to the mountain it was like we were finally . . . um . . ." She was about to say "friends" again, but for some reason the word *friend* suddenly didn't seem enough. But that's all they were to each other, wasn't it?

Instead of answering, Ridge turned and leaned his forearm on the doorframe and looked up at the night sky. "There ain't goin' to be much of a fall this year. Too bad, 'cause I know how much you always liked the fall leaves and such. Winter's already beginnin' to set in," he commented bleakly. Then he added more tenderly, "Ya shouldn't sleep with your window open tonight. There'll be frost in the mornin'."

Feeling compelled to do so, Georgiana walked to him. When she was but a step away, she reached up and laid her hand on his shoulder. She felt him immediately stiffen at her touch, but she did not pull back.

"Ridge . . . maybe we should talk. There are things we need to—" she began.

He cut her off by shrugging her hand off his shoulder. "It's late," he said abruptly, "and I still have some chores to finish up." Catching her eyes briefly, he gave her an almost imperceptible nod before turning away and quietly mumbling, "Good night, Georgie. Best be gettin' to bed. Mornin' comes early . . ." That's all she caught before he was too far away to hear anymore.

Georgiana walked to her room and sat on her bed. The easy-going feeling between them had once again disappeared, leaving only awkwardness in its place and making her wonder what had changed.

Frustrated, Georgiana turned her thoughts instead to the letters she'd received. She eagerly read the letters from her mother and brother. The boys had a few days' break from their classes, and having them around the house seemed to have brightened her mother's mood. She was glad of that.

Looking down at the stack of Dawson's letters beside her, Georgiana decided she was just too tired to read them tonight. She gathered them up, walked over to her dresser, and put them in her top drawer. She would read them tomorrow when she got a break in the day.

Before heading back to her bed, she walked over to the window and pushed it closed. *Ridge was right*, she thought as a shiver passed through her. Her room was already notably cooler than it had been the night before. Quickly, she slipped beneath her covers. It wasn't much warmer at first, but before long the heat from her body warmed the blankets and she was content.

Sleep did not come right away, though. Her mind was troubled. When had everything gotten so complicated? Of course the answer to that lay five years in the past. Closing her eyes, she forced herself to think of younger days when life had seemed so carefree and easy, days when she hadn't a care in the world. Days before her father had been killed and when her mother had worn a smile. She remembered how they had danced about the parlor as Grandad whistled and Nana tried to clap in time with the beat while balancing Georgie's giggling brothers, William and Aden, on her lap. A deep smile, born of joy-filled memories, graced Georgiana's face as sleep finally claimed her and her dreams temporarily took her away to a different time. Always though, while she laughed and played with her family, she was conscious of a boy with curly brown hair, smiling and laughing with them, the warm honey of his eyes dancing with mischief and mirth.

❦ ❦ ❦

Ridge still didn't feel like turning in after he finished the last of his chores, so even though the evening was uncomfortably cool, he found himself once again leaning up against the bunkhouse wall looking at the stars. A name was tumbling about in his mind over and over, and he couldn't seem to make it stop. Ever since Mrs. Swansen had called him over to the post office on his way out of the feed store and had handed him the bundle of letters for Georgiana, his mind had been troubled.

"That gal must have a beau back home," Mrs. Swansen had commented, "and he must be smitten for sure." She smiled as if she were revealing a great secret. "I've never seen a man write so many times to one woman in a matter of just a few weeks. By golly, he sent her three last week. Things must be serious between those two lovebirds. I sense a weddin' not too far in that girl's future." She had then winked at him conspiratorially before hurrying back into the post office.

Ridge sighed in frustration.

The thought had occurred to him when she had returned that she might have someone waiting for her. But still she had awakened old hidden feelings in him he thought he had ridded himself of years ago. He should've known she'd long since fallen in love with another man. Old Angus had been right when he'd pointed out at supper there must be lots of men trying to catch her eye. Well, obviously at least one had succeeded. How could he have been so foolish as to allow himself to start wondering what it would be like to hold her in his arms, to taste a sweet kiss upon her lips?

On the mountain, he had hardly been able to keep his head out of the clouds, and he was beginning to worry he would be accused of acting like a lovesick pup right along with Jimmy. Of course the other hands didn't know he had feelings for Georgiana. Only Angus, he knew, had guessed at it.

Well, at least he hadn't made a fool of himself in front of her.

He'd be better off without her and that Irish temper. In fact, he should feel sorry for Mr. Dawson Alexander. The man probably didn't know what was in store for him.

Glancing over at the ranch house just in time to see Georgiana's light go out, Ridge was surprised. He figured it would take her hours to read through all them letters, and even longer if she answered the man right back.

Ridge sighed deeply, his shoulders slumped low. Leaning deeper into the wall behind him, he suddenly felt weary. It was late, and the lack of sleep he was getting lately was wearing on him. If only he could just stop thinking. Walking around to the door of the bunkhouse, he quietly let himself in. Most of the men were already fast asleep. Only Jimmy lay awake on his top bunk. Ridge cringed inwardly. The boy was almost assuredly waiting up for him, and there was no avoiding it. Ridge slept on the bed directly beneath him.

"Night, Jimmy. Best you be gettin' to sleep. Remember, mornin' comes early on a cattle ranch." Ridge lay down on his bed, not bothering to undress and only kicking off his boots.

"Hey, Ridge?" He could see the bed move as Jimmy rolled onto his side.

"Yeah, Jimmy." Ridge really wasn't in the mood to talk.

"Do ya think Miss Georgiana is in love with that city boy who wrote her all them letters?" Jimmy all but whined.

"Now, how would I know a thing like that, boy?"

"Well . . . I thought you two were sorta . . . ya know . . . good friends."

"And just what made ya think that?" he asked Jimmy, pondering the fact that he really didn't know what he and Georgiana were anymore.

"Don't know. I guess 'cause ya seem ta spend so much time helpin' and talkin' to her." he answered. And then with more exuberance, he added, " 'Sides, Jonas and Jeremiah told me you two was friends when you was younger, afore she moved away and all. They said she was the reason ya got all the fun knocked out of ya." He paused for a moment as if contemplating his next question. "Did ya really tie her braids 'round the stair railin'?"

"Yep," he answered honestly. "Weren't one of my best moments, I'm afraid."

"Boy, I bet she got all fired up at ya. That girl could bite the head off a rattlesnake with that temper of hers."

"You're right about that." Ridge chuckled softly, remembering he'd thought the exact same thing several times.

"I kinda like it when she gets all fired up, though. Have ya ever noticed how when she does her eyes turn from gray almost to violet?"

Ridge had noticed . . . noticed that very thing when he first moved to town at the age of ten and started teasin' her. He was not about to admit it to Jimmy though.

"Jimmy, stop thinkin' 'bout Miss Georgiana and get some sleep."

"I s'pose you're right." He heard Jimmy roll over onto his back, and he was silent for a while before he spoke again. "Hey, Ridge, ya still awake?"

"Mmm . . . hmm."

"How come ya haven't ever got married?" Before Ridge could answer, Jimmy started laughing. "I know why Jonas and Jeremiah ain't—who would want'em? Ya wouldn't get one without the other, and, boy, they would drive any girl crazy. But you're a good guy, Ridge, and you're always turnin' the ladies' heads. Why haven't ya found some nice gal and settled down?"

Ridge groaned audibly. Jimmy had him thinking of Georgiana again with all his questions, and now this new line of questioning was bound to have him thinking about her more. It was all too frustrating.

"Ah, Jimmy, go ta sleep, will ya? Remember . . . "

"I know . . . I know," Jimmy cut in. "Mornin' comes early on a cattle ranch. Night, Ridge."

"Night, Jimmy."

Ridge lay in bed thinking for a long time after Jimmy had fallen asleep. He envied the boy's ability to drop off so quickly. Only minutes had passed before Jimmy's breathing had become soft and even.

Frustrated, Ridge stood up, undressed, and climbed back into bed. It was still a while, though, before he was finally able to fall into a dream-filled sleep. One woman dominated those dreams—one woman and a faceless man.

·7·

The Old Oak

GEORGIANA paused in the doorway to watch her grandfather for a moment. He was sitting at the table, staring out the window while absentmindedly twirling a delicate piece of fabric in his hands. Taking a closer look, it appeared to be a lace-trimmed handkerchief. He appeared to be deep in thought, but he must have sensed she was standing there because he slowly glanced over at her.

"Good mornin', darlin girl."

"Good morning, Grandad." She walked over and kissed him on the cheek. "What is that you are holding?" she asked as she casually walked over to the cupboard. She began removing the items she needed to make breakfast.

"Belonged to yar grandmother," he said thoughtfully. She had figured as much. "Found it in one of me saddlebags on top o' the mountain."

She turned at his revelation, hearing the poignancy in his words. His hands were shaking slightly. She could tell he was fighting to hold back his emotions. With a voice stronger than he appeared, he continued speaking.

"Yar grandmother was ever the romantic, even 'til the day she died." He breathed in deeply for a moment. "Whenever the fellas and me went out on a drive or a trip somewhere, she'd tuck one of these here hankies, doused with that flowery scent she liked so much, in me pocket when she kissed me good-bye. 'For luck,' she'd say, and then she would wink at me and add, *'and to be remindin' ye who yar heart belongs to.'* I must have left it in me pack on the last drive." He lifted the cloth to his face and breathed in deep. "Still smells of me dear one." She could see that his eyes were moist.

Georgiana went over and sat next to him, taking the hand that wasn't holding her grandmother's handkerchief in hers. He squeezed it gently in appreciation.

"I miss her too, Grandad," was all she managed to say as her own eyes filled and threatened to lose their burden.

They sat for another few moments in silence before he stood up and released her hand. He carefully folded up the hankie and put it in his shirt pocket.

"Awk, enough of this here. Best be gettin' back to work. Do ye need me to be doin' anything fer ye this mornin'?"

"Would you mind too terribly seeing if Jimmy, or one of the other men, would be willing to drive me into town today after breakfast? I'm in need of a few things from the mercantile and I have some letters to post."

"Aye, Jimmy will be all too glad to be takin' ye into town again. I'll go make his day a grand one by givin' him the news." He smiled as he leaned down and kissed her on the top of the head. "Well then, I suppose I'll be seein' ye shortly for breakfast." He took his hand and patted his stomach. "Ye are too good of a cook fer me own good. If I don't stop eatin' so much, I'm goin' to have ta be sendin' ye into town to be buyin' me some new britches." He chuckled softly for a moment and added, "Course, even if yer fattenin' me up, I wouldn't have ye anywhere else but here."

"I love you, Grandad." She reached over this time and laid her hand on his arm. He laid his own hand over hers. "I wouldn't want to be anywhere else."

"Aye, 'tis good to hear it, and I love ye as well, me girl . . . more than ye will ever know." He smiled as he turned to leave.

Georgiana stayed sitting for a minute, watching him out the window as he walked toward the barn, his head hung low. Finding her grandmother's handkerchief, as he'd done, surely must have been a shock. They had loved each other dearly. She had known it was so, even as a young child. The way her grandmother's eyes would light up every time he'd enter the room and the way he had to always be near her, holding her hand or touching her in some small way. It was almost as if there was some unseen magnetic force always pulling them toward each other. She had felt something akin to the same whenever Ridge was around lately.

Startled at her admission, Georgiana stood up quickly and started the task of making breakfast. Since the men had returned from the mountain, their appetites seemed to have doubled, if that was even possible. If she wanted to get to town before too long, she needed to spend less time thinking about a certain person and more time getting things done.

After arriving in town, Georgiana was pleasantly surprised, not to mention relieved, when upon entering the mercantile she found Mr. Whitaker tending the store instead of his overly nosy wife. She hadn't yet seen him since she'd returned, not even at church where his wife tried to corner and bombard her with questions each Sunday. Thankfully, her grandfather most often came to her rescue.

Mr. Whitaker looked nearly the same as he had five years ago, except for the speckling of gray at his temples and a slightly rounder midsection. She smiled genuinely at him. She had always liked Mr. Whitaker, ever since he'd talked her father into letting six-year-old Georgiana have one of the new pups he was giving away. In his honor, she had named the pup Benny, since Mr. Whitaker's given name was Benjamin.

"Good morning, Mr. Whitaker. It's a pleasure finally seeing you again." She quickly looked around to see if he was the only one she needed to greet.

"If it isn't little Miss Georgie, all grown up!" he laughed enjoyably.

"Where have you been hiding out these last few weeks?" she inquired.

"Well, do you remember my brother who used to run the livery stables?"

Georgiana nodded, faintly remembering the man.

"About three years back he moved to Nebraska, where his wife's family hails from. Their youngest daughter, Eliza, finally found herself a beau. She was always a good girl, mind you, just not the best looker."

Georgiana had to fight to suppress a grin. She did remember Eliza. She'd been a year older than Ridge and for the longest time had made him the object of her affections. She could still remember the look on Ridge's face every time he saw her headed his way.

"When John wrote and told me the boy had proposed," Mr. Whitaker continued, "I told the missus we ought to go to the weddin'. It was high time we paid him a visit anyway." He paused to straighten the candy jars lining the counter. "The missus was sore pressed to have to close up shop for two weeks being it's a good time of year for the store and all, so she told me I should go alone." He grinned somewhat guiltily. "I wasn't going to argue with that." Leaning forward, he lowered his voice to a conspiratorial tone. "Got me some good huntin' and fishin' in while I was there." With a wink, he stood back up. "There's a surprise comin' for the missus in a few weeks, maybe less if I'm lucky. Shot me a twelve pointer and had the tanner stuff it. I was thinkin' it would look good right there." He pointed to the wall above the counter. "I'm gonna give it to the missus for her birthday." A mischievous look alighted his eyes as he added, "In front of a few witnesses, that is. She can't make me get rid of it that way. It would not only be rude, but unchristian-like if she did. She's got her reputation, ya know." He smiled gingerly. "She'll probably be mad at me for years, but boy, will it be worth it!"

Georgiana almost laughed out loud picturing the look on Mrs. Whitaker's face when her husband hung a stuffed deer head above the counter.

Mr. Whitaker's face turned all business. "Now, enough about me. What is it you're needin' today?"

Georgiana handed him her list, and he started gathering her things. When he was finished, he carried them out to the wagon, which Jimmy had left in front of the mercantile.

"Thank you, Mr. Whitaker," she said graciously.

"It was my pleasure, Miss Georgie," he answered heartily. But before he went back into the store, he leaned in close and whispered, "Now, I trust my secret is safe with you. Don't want the missus's surprise ruined or anythin'."

"Why of course, Mr. Whitaker," she promised, trying to look serious. "I wouldn't dream of ruining what is sure to be the best gift at your wife's birthday celebration."

Mr. Whitaker grinned proudly, then, giving her a wink, headed back into the store.

Georgiana looked about to see if she could spot Jimmy. When he'd dropped her off at the post office this time, he said he needed to pick up a few things at the feed store and was then off to visit his sister. There were several items and bags of feed stacked in the back of the wagon, so she assumed he was still at his sister's house.

Well, she thought, *I'll just wander about town a while until he returns.*

Looking up the boardwalk, Georgiana decided maybe she would pay a visit to Mrs. Perkins's dress shop, but when she walked up to the store, she could see from outside the window that Mrs. Perkins had customers she was waiting on. She would have to pay the woman a visit another time.

Not too much farther up the street was the saloon. Even during the day, the loud, obnoxious vaudeville music drifted into the road.

Disdainfully, Georgiana turned and walked the other way, when something down the street caught her eye. Unconsciously, her step hastened until only moments later she stood a few feet from it. It was still as grand and as glorious as ever. Standing at the edge of the wide, low hanging branches, she looked around furtively to see if anyone was watching. When she saw no one, she quickly ducked underneath.

A flood of memories assaulted her at once, and she walked hesitantly toward the trunk of the ancient tree. Reverently she placed her hands up against it and with her fingers began tracing the names that had been carved into weathered bark over the years. Some of the names were familiar, others were older that she did not recognize, and still some she could tell had been written in recent years. One inscription in particular caught her eye and tore at her heart. It read *Mitch and Samantha . . . Forever.* She crouched down and ran her fingers over the inscription lingeringly, her heart pained for her friend's loss.

Just as she was about to stand up, another inscription farther down caught her eye. She moved closer to read it. Her breath caught in her throat as she saw what it said. The letters were all capitals and carved deeply into the bark: RIDGE LOVES GEORGIE. A faint line of a heart shape encircled the words. *When did Ridge carve this?* she thought, running her now trembling fingers along the deep grooves. A tumultuous wave of raw emotion rose up within her and ebbed its way to the surface. For a moment she was a young girl again, experiencing all the thrill and excitement of her first crush, and in the next moment she felt beaten down and hopeless.

All of a sudden, the sound of leaves crunching on the ground behind her caused Georgiana to jump up and almost lose her balance. Grabbing the trunk with both hands to keep from falling, she quickly turned and leaned against it to further steady herself. As she finally looked up, there he stood.

"Ridge!" her voice registered her shock at seeing him standing there. "What are you doing here?"

He didn't answer right away, just stared at her. He seemed to be deep in thought. She fidgeted nervously.

"I could ask you the same thing," he finally answered, his eyes still boring into hers.

Realizing he would have seen her examining his inscription, she instantly became self-conscious and looked away from him. Oh, why had she walked over to the tree in the first place? Because she had somehow felt drawn to it, she admitted to herself. The last time she'd stood under this tree she was happy, truly happy. With the exception of having lost her father, she had felt grounded. She knew where she belonged. She felt loved. Her home, her family, her friends . . . everything had been almost perfect. She'd missed it all so much.

A feeling of déjà vu washed over her as she looked at Ridge

standing there—the same wavy brown hair and big honey-colored eyes. She was taken back to that day, her nervousness . . . her excitement. She feared if she stared up at him much longer, with him looking at her the way he was, she just might walk over to him and steal another kiss. This time though, she wouldn't be able to run away. She imagined she would lose herself in his arms and confess her growing feelings.

Just then, Ridge took a few steps forward and stopped directly in front of her, his eyes never leaving her face. At once, she knew he meant to kiss her, and her eyes were drawn to his lips. Her heart beat rapidly against her chest.

Is this what I want? she thought. *What of Dawson?*

When Ridge reached over and took her hand in his, her body warmed as a surge of excitement ran through her senses, straight to her very core. But just as quickly, her brain began flinging out questions as it fought for control of her emotions. Her senses became confused as her mind continued to battle with her heart.

"Ridge . . . please . . . I . . ." Georgiana knew she needed to get away now, fast. She couldn't think with him being so near. Stepping to the side, she tore her hand from his and started to move past him. She hadn't gone far when he turned and grabbed her arm this time.

"Georgie, wait . . ."

Her mind willed her legs to keep walking, but her heart willed them to stay. The inner turmoil gave cause for moisture to well up in her eyes. In the end, her heart won out, and she turned to face him.

"Ridge, I . . . I just can't . . . It wouldn't be right," she finally managed to say.

"How could it be wrong?" he asked gently.

She shook her head, not wanting to reveal her thoughts. She definitely didn't want to bring up Dawson. They quietly stared at one another again. She was very conscious of the fact that his hand still held her by the arm. Neither of them moved as he waited for her to reply.

"I just think," she began, not knowing whether she could explain fully the way she felt, "that the past should remain the past. There was a time when I thought . . . I mean . . . even though sometimes I still think that . . ." She was having a difficult time. To add to that difficulty, her heart kept trying to compel her forward into his arms, but thankfully her mind kept her feet planted firmly where she stood. Finally, she just blurted out, "I've decided I'd like to be your friend, Ridge . . . but *only* your friend. Do you think that's possible?"

Georgiana couldn't decipher the look that came to his face, but he didn't hesitate to question her.

"Is that *really* what you want?"

She nodded her head, and he immediately released her. At once, Georgiana wrapped both arms around her own body because her hands were trembling as her heart shouted its disapproval. She didn't want to give herself away as to how hard it was to say what she'd said, when what she really wanted to do was beg him to love her. She had to put some distance between them.

"Look, Ridge, I really need to get back to the wagon. Jimmy's probably wondering where I've gone."

As she turned to leave again, he unexpectedly grabbed hold of her once more, this time with both hands.

"Stay . . . please," he asked, his voice tinged with pleading.

She struggled to free herself. He was making this harder for her. She didn't want to break down in front of him. In frustration, she felt her temper rising.

"No, Ridge . . . I really must go," she said harshly, but he continued to hold her arms.

"Stay?" he asked again as she struggled to free herself.

At the almost desperate sound of his voice, Georgiana stopped struggling and turned back toward to him. When she looked up, his eyes were soft, warm, and her heart lurched forward. For some reason, her body's reaction only fueled her anger. He was too handsome, too tempting. It wasn't fair play!

Her eyes fell to his lips, and she felt herself weakening.

Quickly she tore her eyes away from his face, and they chanced to glance at the carving on the tree. If only her family had never moved away . . . if only. A flash of anger surged through her as she remembered lonely nights and tear-stained pillows.

"Ridge, release me!" she insisted.

Instead of listening to her, he drew her close to his chest, resting his cheek against hers.

"I'm sorry, Georgie, but I can't," he countered.

His breath was tickling her hair, and the sensation that ran down her body made her knees feel weak. She couldn't resist him much longer. Oh, why was he doing this to her?

Georgiana brought her hands up to his chest as best she could and tried to force him away, but instead he wrapped his arms around her body and held her even closer. She was fighting against something she wanted entirely too much. She was sure to be undone at any moment.

When she felt his lips brush tenderly against the skin of her neck, she couldn't help the sigh that escaped her lips. He pulled back momentarily to look into her eyes. Slowly his head began to descend to hers, and finally she found her voice, though it sounded weak and breathy.

"No, Ridge, you mustn't. Please . . . I can't explain, but . . . you must let me go," she begged, her voice breaking with emotion.

He released her then, suddenly, and stepped back, her emotion having triggered something deeper inside him than his desire.

He looked torn, and she was instantly sorry. If only she wasn't so confused! Georgiana shook her head and looked at the ground. Things had happened the way they did, and it had caused them to grow apart. She would never stop caring for him—loving him even—but that didn't mean they were meant to be together. Maybe he would always own a small piece of her heart. Maybe she just needed to understand that and accept it so she could be with Dawson. She sighed deeply.

"I'm so sorry," she mumbled as she turned, ducked, and stepped out from under the cover of the oak's branches. Looking around, she was glad the street seemed to be deserted, at least from where she stood. She glanced once more back at the tree, sighed again, and began walking toward the mercantile. From what she could see ahead, Jimmy still wasn't waiting for her. *Where could he be?* she thought impatiently.

Georgiana was almost to the mercantile when she felt someone grab her wrist and swing her to face the direction from which she had just come.

"Ridge!" she exclaimed, pulling her wrist out of his grasp.

He reached forward again, took her by the hand, and quickly led her halfway down the alleyway that ran between the store and the warehouse next to it.

Despite everything she had just said, her heart sang as he pushed her against the wood planks of the store and took her face in both of his hands. His lips at once found hers and began weaving a spell in the form of a passionate, driven kiss. She felt her defenses crumbling, her desire for him growing stronger as each second passed, when suddenly a sense of guilt seized her. She was being selfish, ignoring her duty to her esteemed companion back in New York, who'd been patiently and faithfully waiting for her to accept his proposal. She must end Ridge's kiss before she became lost in her desire and there was no turning back. Besides, how dare he take such liberties when only moments ago, she'd emphatically told him she only wanted to be his friend. There was too much at stake, too many hearts at risk to allow this! He should have listened. Now, having been kissed by him, her heart would suffer even more. Her temper ignited immediately. Using all the strength she could muster, she managed to push herself out of his arms and smack him soundly across the face.

At first his face registered shock, and then curiously, of all things, a wide grin spread from ear to ear.

"Thank you," Ridge remarked, his grin widening even more. "That explains a lot."

She was bewildered, but before she could ask his meaning, he had secured her in his arms once more and was kissing her again!

This time his kiss was softer yet fervent—gentle, yet rousing. She had only ever imagined being kissed in such a way. She was surprised at how quickly her temper quelled, and her heart took control as her own arms instinctively entwined themselves about his neck and her fingers found themselves lost in the soft waves of his hair. He pulled her even closer, and she returned his kiss eagerly and without restraint.

In that moment, she cared for nothing at all except the feel of being in the arms of the man she loved—had loved for so long—feeling his heart beat in time with her own, fast and fierce.

Too soon, he ended the kiss, but before stepping away, Ridge whispered in her ear, "You owed me that, you know." His voice was deep and husky from their impassioned exchange. He pulled away slightly to look into her face, one corner of his mouth turned up into the half grin she loved. He added, "Now we're even."

He released her then and, tipping his hat, turned and walked back to the boardwalk.

In shock, Georgiana watched him as he left. Jimmy was standing in the street staring at her with his mouth hanging half open. Ridge tipped his hat to Jimmy in greeting as he walked past. Jimmy mumbled something inaudible in return and watched Ridge mount his horse and ride off. Jimmy glanced back to stare at her again. It was all too easy to read the shocked and hurt look on Jimmy's face.

Embarrassed, Georgiana hurried out of the alley and looked around to see if anyone else had witnessed the kiss she and Ridge had shared. Directly across the street, the curtain in one of the upper boarding house rooms fluttered like it had just been let down. She stared a moment in that direction but looked away abruptly, choosing to dismiss it. Adjusting her posture and lifting her chin slightly, Georgiana walked over to the wagon and climbed up without assistance.

Thankfully, Jimmy didn't say a word to her on the way home.

·8·

Wishful Thinking

RIDGE slowed Storm to a trot and veered off the path toward the stream that ran along the ravine at the foot of the low-lying mountains.

He tied his horse to a tree that had access to a small pool of water divided from the stream by a deserted beaver dam. Once his horse began drinking, Ridge turned and walked farther downstream, where the water curved slightly and offered a familiar and inviting place to sit.

He bent down occasionally along his way, picking up a variety of small, flattened stones. When at last he sat down, he laid the stones beside him.

Examining one of the stones a moment, Ridge tossed it into the middle of the stream, watching the ripples until they slowly faded away. A soft wind swept through the long wispy grass that grew along the water's edge, and above him it whispered through the birch trees. Occasionally, a leaf would tear free from a branch and drift slowly down to the water.

Usually the stream had a very calming effect on him, but not today. His mind was racing, and his thoughts were tumbling over themselves.

He had gone into town today on the pretense of needing a new pair of boots. Glancing down at his shoes, he felt guilty for his deception. Though they showed a little wear, he was sure he hadn't fooled

Angus. Ridge had been working for the man quite a long time now. Angus knew he wasn't wasteful, and his boots would certainly last him through another winter at least. Besides, he'd never even made it over to the mercantile. Instead, he had followed Georgiana and found himself standing beneath the old oak, watching her as she ran her delicate fingers across the words he had painstakingly carved long ago.

The nostalgia at once took him back to the day he'd carved the inscription, the day she'd stolen a kiss. It had been the most incredible day of his young life. Of course he had fallen in love with her long before, but that day had been the one he'd realized she loved him back, or so he'd thought.

He hadn't seen it coming, he remembered, thinking of her wide-eyed grin after she'd kissed him. The three of them had spent most of the day fishing and playing down at the creek. When they were packing up their things to go and see what they could find to do in town, Samantha had pulled Georgie aside and whispered in her ear. He really didn't think anything of it. They were girls, after all, and girls were always doing that sort of thing.

When they got to the edge of town, Georgie handed her fishing pole and bucket to Samantha and turned toward him.

"Hey, Ridge, I'll race ya to the old oak," she'd challenged.

"Nah, I'm already tuckered out, and besides, I always win. If I beat ya while I'm tired, you'll feel even worse."

"How do ya know I just haven't been lettin' ya win ta boost your male ego?"

"Because ya wouldn't do that, Georgie. *You* like ta win too much."

When he looked over at her, she raised an eyebrow at him, giving him a look that made him doubt whether he knew what he was talking about.

"Oh, all right," he gave in and started laying his things on the side of the road. "Just give me a sec to . . ."

"Ready, set, go!" she chimed quickly and took off running before he had even finished speaking or emptying his hands.

He immediately dropped everything in one heap and took off after her.

Less than five minutes after that, he was sitting square on his bottom, watching as she and Samantha took off giggling hand in hand up the road.

Ridge's thoughts came back to the present as he slipped his hand in his pocket and made sure the soft satin was still there. He had seen it fly into the bush that day and fetched it out before he'd headed back home. It was one of the blue satin ones he had given her himself. She'd worn them often.

Ridge pulled his mind away from his memories and picked up another stone. Instead of throwing it, though, he worked it back and forth between his fingers.

When he first saw her standing under the oak today and had looked into her troubled eyes, he knew she needed to know how he felt about her, how he'd *always* felt. He'd promised himself right then and there she would not walk away from him until she knew one way or another.

Well, if she didn't know now, she'd never know because he finally kissed her . . . kissed her soundly too. Oh boy, had she been mad! When he'd kissed her again though, she'd melted in his arms, and her kiss had been the sweet confection of his dreams.

His last thought before he stood up to fetch his horse and head back to the ranch was of the old Irish tale Angus had recited to him.

Take heart, me lad, she's your true love,
If her flame with ye be bold.

Ridge rubbed his cheek where the skin still burned slightly, and smiled.

·9·

Regrets

CHARLOTTE McLaughlin refolded the letter from Georgiana and sighed peacefully.

The lighthearted tone of her daughter's words reminded her of a time when Georgiana was much younger and full of exuberance and zest for life, before they had come to New York. She missed her child dearly but once again felt a deep confirmation she had made the right decision in letting her go.

Painfully, Charlotte recalled how quickly her sweet young daughter had accepted her lot and settled into a dull existence in New York. Crippled by her grief, Charlotte wished she had possessed the strength to remedy the mistake of running from their life in Colorado. But she had not and watched helplessly as her vibrant daughter became more and more introverted. Georgiana spent her days either reading or wandering aimlessly through the gardens that bordered the estate instead of laughing with friends and exploring the world around her.

When Georgiana had come of age to attend finishing school, Charlotte was overjoyed. When she'd attended the same school, she'd made so many friends and had thoroughly enjoyed herself. She hoped for the same for Georgiana. Much to her delight, Georgiana seemed to thrive there, even though she kept mostly to herself.

Throwing back her coverlet, Charlotte rose from her bed and picked up the oil lamp she had been reading by. She was drawn to her dresser, where a small photo of Georgiana sat. She picked up the photo and carried it to the blue velvet wing-backed chair sitting near the hearth. The fire was almost out, but a steady warmth still radiated from the coals that burned red and gold. It seemed she was always cold as of late, and she feared her health was failing. She'd suffered more illness in the last five years than in the first twenty-nine of her life. The pure Colorado air had definitely been more beneficial to her health.

Charlotte spread the small crocheted blanket lying on the arm of the chair over her legs and looked lovingly down at the photo she held in her hands. Georgiana was no longer a child, that was for certain, and Charlotte well understood that all too soon her daughter would find herself as both a wife and a mother. If the honorable and companionable Mr. Alexander had anything to say about it, it would be soon indeed.

She found Dawson Alexander to be a gentleman in every form of the word and was pleased to have such a man so taken with her daughter. Georgiana was a prize as well, having grown into a great beauty whose looks were only rivaled by her inner strength and maturity. Charlotte wasn't fully convinced her daughter's silent demeanor wasn't anything more than a façade, and inside there was still a lost and lonely child.

A loud knocking pulled Charlotte from her musings.

"Yes," she called out softly, her voice raspy from lack of use. After Cecelia's last tirade, Charlotte decided avoidance would be the best avenue to take, at least until her sister's mood was placated. So she had spent the better part of the week in her room, even having her meals brought up.

"Charlotte, dear, it is late. You should go to sleep now."

Cecelia's voice bore a distinct note of authority, as always. Even after so many years, her sister still treated her like an imprudent child. It hadn't always been this way between them. Though Cecelia was nearly six years her senior, there was a time when they were close, a time when she'd looked up to her elder sister and longed to be just like her. Charlotte smiled at the memories. They were few and so long ago, but she held them dear. Such memories of how her sister used to be gave her the courage and the compassion to continue living with the hard, unfeeling woman Cecelia had become.

If only Cecelia had never met Lionel Bradley! Charlotte shuddered even thinking the man's name. He had deceived her sister in the worst way—had deceived them all! Again Charlotte shuddered, wondering how such cunning and wickedness could be hidden under the guise of a seemingly upstanding and honorable gentleman. Cecelia had fallen for him almost immediately, with all his lavished attentions and magnetically handsome face. So had many of her friends, but Mr. Bradley only had eyes for Cecelia.

One night, as Charlotte was sitting on the stairs absentmindedly petting their rather overindulged cat, Cecelia came floating through the door, giddy after returning from an evening with Mr. Bradley. When she spotted Charlotte, she sat next to her and pulled the reluctant animal onto her lap.

"Oh, Charlotte!" she exclaimed blissfully as she scratched their cat's belly, forgetting he hated that and barely missing an encounter with his sharp claws, "he makes me feel as if I am the most beautiful woman in the world!"

Charlotte had smiled at the look of love evident on her sister's face while stealthily lifting their pet from her sister's lap and setting him down out of her sister's reach. It wasn't until she was dressing for bed that night she recalled a conversation she had heard months ago that made her sister's joyful exclamation take on a deeper meaning.

"The poor thing," her mother's chambermaid had commented. Charlotte had just reached the top of the stairs. The two servants were standing in front of the window at the end of the hall, looking down on the courtyard as they conversed. Charlotte stepped back onto the stairwell, pressing her back against the wall so she could listen unnoticed. "She'll have a hard time finding a good one, she will. And her mother so beautiful! A cruel twist of fate, she having taken her looks from her father instead. 'Tis a shame!"

"Hush, Bridgette," Midge, the old housekeeper, scolded. "You shouldn't say such things."

Charlotte smiled; she always liked Midge the best.

"Besides," the housekeeper continued. "Plain or not, at least she has a good dowry, which is more than you'll ever have. Some man will come along. I hope he'll be worthy of her heart."

Midge was right. Cecelia had always been especially kind and thoughtful of her family and friends. This, to Charlotte, made her beautiful.

Then Mr. Lionel Bradley had come to New York, and Cecelia fell in love. When Mr. Bradley apparently returned those affections, many couldn't believe her good fortune, and for the first time, her friends were jealous of her.

A wedding date was set, and all was going as planned. They were to be married at the end of April and would spend four months honeymooning in Europe. It had all been such an exciting time for Charlotte. Cecelia had included her in everything. The dresses, the flowers, the decisions regarding what foods they would entertain their guests with. Charlotte had never seen her sister so happy. Mother and Father were deep in all the preparations as well. Everything was in perfect order until disaster struck.

It was a week before the wedding when things began to go awry. Many of their out-of-town guests had already arrived, some even coming from as far as London, from which Mr. Bradley hailed. His widowed father had arrived two weeks previously, expressing an interest in relocating to America.

He had brought servants with him who would continue working for the young Mr. Bradley in their new home. The servants all immediately set about helping with the wedding preparations. However, one serving girl in particular carried an air of disdain and refused duties not assigned directly from her employer's son. After the first week, Charlotte's mother became exasperated with the servant and requested an audience with Cecelia's fiancé concerning the obstinate girl. Much to her dismay, Mr. Bradley made excuses for the girl's behavior. His actions, as well as the snide, knowing look the girl gave her, made her mother suspicious of what the girl's real role would be in Mr. Bradley and her daughter's new household. Being the shrewd woman she was, Charlotte's mother thought it prudent to enlist one of her own servants to watch the comings and goings of Mr. Lionel Bradley.

It was because of her mother's intuition and zeal that his true nature and intentions were exposed. That very night, her mother awoke Cecelia and bade her come with her to the stables. Their servant informed them that the young Mr. Bradley was, at that very moment, entertaining a guest in the hayloft. It was perhaps a cruel thing to force Cecelia to discover them, but her mother feared she would not believe it otherwise.

Needless to say, Cecelia was heartbroken, and Mr. Lionel Bradley and their guests were asked to leave immediately. When the shame should have been all Mr. Bradley's for his deplorable actions, Cecelia was hit with a cruel and undeserving amount of ridicule. Later it was found out that Mr. Bradley had lost his family's fortune in an unscrupulous business venture. He had needed an heiress to save his family from humiliation.

Cecelia went to Europe, taking only her personal maid. If for no other reason, the time away would free her from the seemingly endless hushed voices and pitiful looks that incessantly followed in her wake. When she returned home, she was different. At first the change in her seemed subtle: she chose to eat alone in her room and avoided people whenever possible. Mother allowed it because she knew Cecelia was still heartsick and anguished over the whole affair. But after being home two months with nothing seeming to improve, Mother insisted Cecelia eat her meals with the family and attend church on Sunday. That's when the true damage became noticeable. Cecelia was by far no longer sweet and thoughtful but instead cynical, controlling, and abrasive. She had allowed the heinous actions of one person to rot inside her and spoil that which was good.

"Maybe she can't help being so cruel," Charlotte whispered as she ran her hand across Georgiana's photo. She knew in her heart Cecelia had allowed what happened to damage her soul. It was much like how she had allowed her grief to overrule good judgment time and time again. *Well*, she thought suddenly and with conviction, *a change is certainly overdue.* Quickly she placed the photo back on her bureau and climbed back into her bed. Before she drifted off, she said a prayer.

"Please, Father, watch over my children. Bless my dear daughter, so far away. I pray she has found the peace she seeks and the answers she is looking for." She paused for a moment and repeated her familiar nightly plea. "Bless Cecelia, Father, that she can one day find a way to forgive. Amen." With that, Charlotte drifted off to sleep, determined that tomorrow would be a new beginning.

·10·
Rescued

GEORGIANA laid her paintbrush down on the lip of her easel. Dark clouds had rolled in and changed the lighting on the mountains she was painting.

Standing up, she stretched her back and looked around her. This place was perfect. She had found the meadow when the men had gone to gather the cattle, and she had already painted more than one picture here. Since the snowcapped mountains pleased her so much, she was once again drawn to this same meadow to paint from a slightly altered viewpoint.

Wrapping her arms around her middle, she took a moment to gaze at the surroundings. The meadow was small, but still wide enough so that while sitting in the middle, she could see over the low-growing pinyon pines to the majestic mountains behind them. An old felled tree lay in the center and provided a suitable if not adequately comfortable place to perch with her easel set up in front of her.

Still admiring the beauty around her, Georgiana spotted a rather large stone to the east side of the clearing and walked over to it. Climbing on top of it and hugging her arms around her knees, she warmed her bare feet on the stone's surface.

The air was starting to cool quite a bit, and a strong westerly wind was just beginning to blow. Her instincts told her she should pack up and head back to the house, but she pushed her nagging senses aside and made no move to leave. There were still so many things swirling around in her mind that she wanted to take a moment to sort them out.

Another two weeks had flown by already, making it an even five since she had arrived from New York. It had taken her a week to finally get around to reading all of Dawson's letters. By then she had been presented with another bundle from Jeremiah after he had gone into town to pick up some nails. Having finished the new fences, the men had been busy making sure the old ones were repaired and secured in anticipation of the coming winter storms. It seemed Mrs. Swansen had made it a priority to make sure Georgiana got all her letters, especially those from Dawson, promptly. Tiny had ridden into town again today, and she feared what would be at the ranch when she got back.

Georgiana let out an exasperated sigh. Not only was it starting to get ridiculous trying to keep up with Dawson's letters, but it was also difficult reading his increasing desperation for her return. While she did miss him, she dreaded leaving the peace and sanctity she felt living here in this beautiful land nestled amongst such majestic giants. Furthermore, since first arriving, she'd felt needed and appreciated. She lived her days purposely and with lucidity, always knowing what tasks lay before her and enjoying the fruits of her labors. There was a comfort in knowing what was expected of her, while life offered plenty of other surprises to keep her happy.

She sorely missed her mother and her two younger brothers. Her love and devotion for them was what had kept her from losing herself completely while living with her aunt. Her time at Ms. Wilmington's had been a blessed respite but had ended all too soon. At least when she had returned, she had her painting and drawing to derive pleasure from. Still, her aunt's home was such a contrast to the bright chattering halls of the school. Her aunt's home felt even more oppressive than before, so she began devoting a good part of her day to sitting in the park sketching. That was how she had come to know Dawson.

It was the first of summer, and the air was warm but still not too humid to be enjoyed. She'd found a place to sit under the shade of a big oak tree.

She had noticed him the first day she'd come. In fact, she'd spent an inordinate amount of time admiring the way he played uninhibited with his younger brother, who obviously adored him immensely.

He had brought his brother back to the park the next day, and she watched as he once again played with the young boy, this time along the water's edge, catching frogs and pollywogs and skipping stones along the lake's placid surface. Once, she looked up and thought he had been staring at her, but he had looked away too quickly, and she couldn't be certain. She took a moment then to fully admire him. To say he was attractive would be putting it mildly. He was quite tall, with broad shoulders and a chiseled, handsome face. She couldn't be sure from the distance whether his eyes were green or blue, but his hair was as black as the night and boasted a soft natural curl many women would envy. All together, his looks were quite agreeable indeed. The following day, he introduced himself.

She was sitting by her usual tree sketching a pair of swans that had ventured unusually close to the water's edge, when a voice above startled her.

"Good afternoon, lovely lady."

Glancing up, she was aghast to see him perched casually and looking quite comfortable on a tree limb not too many feet above her head. She couldn't help but smile. Who was this handsome stranger that not only sailed play boats and caught pollywogs, but spent his days climbing trees as well?

"Good afternoon to you, sir," she had replied.

"Would you mind terribly if I came down and indulged in the pleasure of your company for a spell?"

"Well, seeing as I'd rather indulge you than have to rescue you when you fall down and break your leg, I'm inclined to concede to your request."

"Rescue me?" In one fell swoop he swung down from the tree and was sitting at her side. "Why, it is I, lovely lady, who intend to rescue you."

"And what, pray tell, will you be rescuing me from, kind sir?" she asked, raising one brow curiously.

He lowered his voice to a whisper and leaned slightly toward her. "From that rather odd, robust-looking man over there." He made a slight gesture with his hand off to his left. Georgiana leaned forward to look past him when he suddenly cried out, "Don't look, milady! He will suspect we are speaking of him."

Quickly, she turned her head in the opposite direction.

"Who is he?" she asked, her curiosity now fully piqued.

"I'm not sure exactly, but he has been here two days in a row and . . . ," he paused for effect, "I saw him looking at you yesterday. Then earlier today he seemed to be studying you quite assiduously." She was having difficulty keeping her eyes from searching out the supposed man.

"Do you think I have cause to worry then . . . to fear his intentions?" Georgiana shivered slightly as she posed the question.

Instead of answering, he slowly turned his head to gaze at the man. She made to do the same.

"No, don't look!" he warned, and again she abruptly turned away. "I'm only checking to see if he's staring even now," he explained. He was quiet for a moment, and she became impatient.

"Well?"

"A moment ago, before I came to your aid, it appeared he might be getting up the nerve to request an audience with you."

"And now?" she asked earnestly.

"Now, he is looking rather disappointed. I believe he thinks you and I are companions of some sort, which is exactly what I had intended." He turned back to face her and flashed a candid smile. "Only to save you from him, of course."

"Of course," she mimicked. She had a sudden feeling he was playing a game, but she was presently inclined to play along. He suddenly gave an exaggerated sigh of relief.

"I do believe the worst is past and that he was only enamored with your beauty and your grace. I have surely saved you from some unknown catastrophe this day."

"And what makes you think I need saving, Mr. . . . "

"Alexander . . . Dawson Alexander." He quickly took up her hand and kissed it graciously.

"Well then, Mr. Alexander . . . I ask you again, just what triggered your heroic actions?"

"He is most certainly not your type, Miss . . . Miss . . ." He gave her a questioning look.

"McLaughlin . . . Miss Georgiana McLaughlin." She eyed him while speculating how he had, not so unwittingly, secured an introduction from her. "And what is my type exactly?" she continued.

"Well, Miss McLaughlin, I have an inkling you would prefer a more . . . prepossessing gentleman, one not quite so rotund, and certainly with a better sense of fashion."

Georgiana was suddenly startled when a dark bundle fell from the tree above, bringing a branch full of leaves down with it and landing on the grass in front of them. The "bundle" stood up and grinned from ear to ear.

"Dawson, did you see that?" the boy declared proudly. "I have never jumped down from so high before." He was a perfect miniature of his older brother.

"I'd be more impressed, Thomas, if you hadn't terrified Miss McLaughlin here."

The boy turned his eyes to her, seeming to notice her for the first time.

"I'm sorry, miss. I didn't mean to startle you." He looked duly penitent.

"I'm quite all right. No harm done, see?" She quickly brushed the leaves from her dress and smiled up at him to ease his worries. "Especially since I have only just been rescued by your gallant brother here."

"Rescued?" Thomas glanced perplexedly over to his brother. "From whom?"

"Why, from that man right over there." She pointed vaguely in the direction Dawson had indicated moments before without actually looking. Thomas started to turn his head that way.

"Oh, don't look!" she exclaimed. "We wouldn't want him to know we're discussing him."

Thomas gave her a doubtful look and glanced over anyway.

"Why, that's only Mr. Weathereby. He owns the sweet shop around the corner. Why would you need to be rescued from him?"

Georgiana looked over to Dawson and raised an eyebrow at the sheepish look on his face. For the first time, she glanced over at her would-be admirer.

The man was indeed robust, with an ample paunch. Though he wasn't wearing a look of utter disappointment as Dawson had surmised but rather seemed to be quite cheerfully enjoying what appeared to be a very large and satisfying meal. She looked again to Dawson.

"Mr. Weathereby, is it?" Georgiana queried. Thomas answered instead.

"Sure, he comes to the park every day to eat his lunch." Glancing at the man again, this time with a hopeful look, he added, "Sometimes he even hands out free peppermint sticks."

As if on cue, Mr. Weathereby packed his things back into his basket and withdrew a bulging sack. Immediately, he was converged upon by a multitude of children. Thomas looked over to Dawson hopefully.

"Dawson, may I?"

Dawson nodded his head, and Thomas immediately ran to join the thronging crowd of children all vying to be a recipient of one of the tasty treats.

Georgiana laughed softly at the memory.

She and Dawson had become fast friends after that, spending most of the remaining summer days together either walking in the park or taking rides through the countryside. It was a poultice to her heart to have a dear friend once again.

He had been patient, not forcing his desires to further their relationship upon her. She had known since the beginning his ardor for her had been the greater, but she cherished their developing friendship and hoped in time her feelings for him would grow stronger. Near the time of the annual Masquerade Ball had been a turning point in their relationship, a turn which brought them even closer.

One evening, two weeks before the ball, she and Dawson were

sitting in the gardens at his family's estate. They often spent time at his house rather than her aunt's. She could feel the love in his home. Each room was filled to the brim, enough to spill out from the windows, crowding her heart with remembrances of a similar feeling she left behind in her grandparents' home so long ago.

Today was her grandmother's birthday, and she'd sent her a birthday card, along with a letter to Samantha only that afternoon. As it always did, sending letters to her friend when she knew she would receive no answer had put her in a somber mood. She didn't even know why she still continued to write. She supposed she only did so out of habit and maybe out of some misguided longing. It was as if she were writing her thoughts down and then tossing them, sealed in a bottle, into the sea. Though they were likely never to be read, the simple act brought a measure of peace for having released the words from her mind.

Dawson suddenly startled her with his question.

"What was your home like back in Colorado? You never talk about it. I've seen you sending letters I presume are for family and friends there, but like today, the letters don't seem to bring you much joy."

He reached over and took her hand. He had never held her ungloved hand before, and it surprised her how soft his hands were.

"There's not much to talk about." She turned her head slightly to the side and watched intently a small sparrow gathering some broken twigs into its beak under a nearby bush. Her emotions were mounting, and she didn't wish to subject Dawson to a distressing display of feminine sentimentality.

"I know you were still young when you moved, but surely you left some friends behind. You lived there eleven years, did you not?"

"Yes," she answered, noticing a slight tremble in her voice. Try as she might, she feared she would not be able to hold the tears at bay threatening to be released if he kept asking her questions.

"Well, besides your grandparents, who else have you still kept in contact with?"

A single rebellious tear trailed hidden down the far side of her face as she kept her head turned from him. It didn't stay hidden for long. In the next instant, he released her hand, laid his gently on her warm cheek, and turned her face toward him.

He looked stricken to discover the tear and wiped it away with his thumb.

"Georgiana, I'm sorry. I didn't mean to . . ." He drew his hand gently away.

"No, it's all right, Dawson." Maybe if she talked about it, shared her feelings of rejection and frustration, she would finally be able to move past . . . her past. So she told Dawson of her two friends and how they hadn't ever written back.

"Strange," he commented when she was through. "Maybe it's not what you think." Georgiana shook her head back and forth.

"Maybe you're right," she agreed, though she couldn't see how. "Come, you promised to show me your mother's new pair of swans," she said, standing. "Let us go to the pond before Thomas has them in such a fright they'll never come out of hiding."

Dawson stood, took her hand, and laced his fingers through hers. It felt warm and comforting. She smiled up at him as they walked toward the pond. They hadn't spoken of her friends again after that, but she'd somehow felt closer to him.

Dismissing thoughts of Dawson, Georgiana turned her musings to Ridge.

She hadn't seen much of him lately. He had taken Jeremiah with him over to the land office in Castle Rock to conduct some business for her grandfather. It was more than that though. It was as if he was purposely avoiding her, skipping meals and spending most of his free time either out in the barn or in the bunkhouse so he didn't have to see her. Today at breakfast was the first time she'd laid eyes on him in more than a week, and still he had avoided looking her in the eyes.

He must regret having ever kissed me, she thought. *Why else would he be acting the way he is?*

Georgiana contemplated his kiss. She knew she would never regret it. An excess flood of moisture came to her mouth just thinking of it. Would that it had held as much meaning for him as it had for her. A now familiar tingling sensation spread through her limbs whenever she so much as pictured his face. He didn't even have to be physically near anymore to affect her in such a way. She knew no other man could ever awaken in her such longing . . . such depth of emotion. If she ended up marrying Dawson, would she be content to live her life without ever again experiencing such a deep stirring within her? She may not have a choice. She was suddenly unsure in which direction her life was headed, but that didn't stop her from pondering on Ridge's kiss further. Georgiana sighed.

Meals were tense for a while with Jimmy. He had brooded for days after witnessing their passionate exchange. Unfortunately, it hadn't discouraged him enough to stop him from vying for her attention. Actually, it seemed quite the opposite. Between Ridge's kiss and her sudden barrage of "love notes," as the men had started calling them—no thanks to Jonas—Jimmy had become even more persistent. He had somehow deduced that if he didn't make his move quickly, either Ridge or the doting and persistent Mr. Alexander would secure her heart.

Poor Jimmy. She'd felt bad, and the situation was out of control. A week ago, she had asked him to go for an evening walk with her. It had been difficult, but she finally found the words to explain to him that though she adored him and considered him most amiable, she did not possess any feelings for him beyond friendship. When his face still appeared hopeful, even after all that, she assured him she wouldn't be changing her mind in the future.

She felt a huge sense of relief when Jimmy finally seemed to accept what she was saying. Surprisingly, he only sulked for a few days before returning to his normally cheerful self. His demeanor became more confident and relaxed, and she began to truly enjoy his friendship.

Abruptly and without warning, a huge gust of wind hit Georgiana square in the chest, almost knocking her backward onto the ground. Quickly, she glanced at the sky and saw that dark, ominous clouds now covered the meadow completely. She had been too deep in thought to notice the changes occurring about her. A twinge of regret at having pushed her instincts aside made her nervous, and a powerful sense of foreboding rose within her.

Hastily jumping down from the stone, Georgiana forgot her feet were still bare until she felt something sharp pierce through the tender flesh of her left foot. She cried out in pain. Immediately sitting back on the stone, she lifted her foot to examine it. A sharp, jagged piece of shale was embedded deep into her skin. She winced before grabbing the protruding edge of the shale and looking away. Quickly, she pulled the treacherous piece of rock from her foot. Blood instantly oozed from the gash.

Using the hem of her dress, Georgiana pressed the cloth tightly against the wound to stop the flow of blood. The wind was now starting to tear feverishly past her, and she knew she needed to make haste. She waited only a few moments before releasing her foot and attempting to stand.

As she limped back to her belongings, Georgiana felt the first few drops of rain. Trying to hurry, she made her way over to where her canvas now lay on the ground. Removing her shawl, she wrapped it around her painting as best she could. She hurriedly gathered her scattered tubes of paint and brushes, haphazardly tossing them into her satchel.

Just as she reached out to grab her easel, another powerful gust of wind ripped through the meadow, successfully knocking her and the easel over and throwing them against a fallen log.

For the second time, Georgiana cried out in pain as she came down hard on her wounded foot. How would she ever make it back in this storm with her injury? She needed to find where she had left her shoes and put them on. By now, the wind was blowing so hard, both dirt and debris were flying aimlessly through the air, and the rain was beginning to come down in sheets.

Getting down on her knees, Georgiana crawled around, trying to find her shoes and stockings. Mercilessly her hair became tangled in some brush as the wind whipped it about. She chastised herself for having even taken it down. It took forever to set herself free, but when she did, she hastily stood up, not wanting it to become entangled again. Glancing around her frantically, she wished for somewhere, anywhere, that looked safe. She needed to find some shelter fast.

As Georgiana tried to decide which direction to go, she heard a loud crack from behind her. Turning around, she watched as a large branch broke free from a tree across the meadow and began flying through the air directly at her. In shock, she stood frozen.

Just before it reached her, Georgiana closed her eyes. Something hard rammed into her side, knocking the breath out of her. The side of her head slammed into the ground, and she momentarily lost consciousness. When she came to, she could hardly breathe for the weight that was upon her, but at least she was alive. As she tried to push off the object, her fingers felt the texture of fabric, not tree bark. She realized it wasn't the weight of the tree branch pinning her down, crushing the breath out of her, but a man. For a moment she panicked, but then she heard him shout above the chaos going on around them.

"Georgie, are ya hurt?" He leaned back, and she looked up into Ridge's face.

"Ridge?" Her voice was barely audible because she could hardly gather enough air to speak "How did you . . . ?"

"Later," he growled, a worried look etched on his features. "Right now we need to get outta here. We're sittin' targets here in the open. Didn't ya hear me callin' your name?" His face was directly above her, but most of his words were whipped away with the wind. She lay there, injured, frightened, the very life being squeezed out of her, but even in their precarious state, her heart raced because of his nearness.

She shook her head. "It's too loud to hear you," she whispered with great effort. As if he suddenly realized he was crushing her, Ridge shifted his weight and sat up. Georgiana immediately and eagerly sucked in big gulps of air. Ridge reached over and helped her to a sitting position, putting his arm around her shoulder protectively. Georgiana had often wondered what it would feel like to be cuddled beneath one of Ridge's arms. How ironic that it would take a wicked storm to compel him to do it. Still, she found herself leaning in a little closer.

"Do you think you can stand?" he asked loudly. It was easier to hear him as they sat side-by-side, huddled close.

"I'm not sure. I've cut my foot pretty badly."

Ridge released his arm and moved opposite her, grabbing her foot to examine it.

"Confound it, woman! Where are your shoes?" Ridge grumbled loudly when he saw her damaged foot. He took his handkerchief from his pocket, and with the aid of the rain, began wiping the dirt and blood gently away. As he worked, he muttered under his breath in frustration. Curious, she leaned closer to him to hear what he was saying. "Blasted female, always taking her shoes off," was all she managed to hear.

When he was finished examining her foot, he grabbed onto her petticoat and tore a small section from it, wrapping the piece securely around the wound. Afterward, he pulled a bandanna from his back pocket and tied it over the top for extra protection.

"The cut is bad. We need to get your shoes back on so your foot doesn't get hurt further." This time he grasped her shoulders and pulled her closer to him as he spoke.

"I can't seem to find them," she cried out. He was less than happy with her new revelation, and it didn't help that another branch, though much smaller this time, flew over their heads, barely missing them again.

"Where is your coat then?" he shouted. The noise around them was getting louder and stole the sound of his voice away. She shook her head confused as she felt herself starting to panic, her heart rate increasing.

"Georgie," he grabbed her shoulders and pulled her close this time so his mouth was next to her ear. "Your coat . . . where did you leave it?" Despite the cold rain and wind beating down on them, his warm breath still managed to tickle her neck. She could feel goose bumps forming, and her heart raced even faster. She couldn't blame it all on the storm.

"I didn't bring one . . . only a shawl." She leaned her head against the side of his as she shouted back.

"Georgie! Have you completely forgotten how fast the weather can change up here?" He looked angry now as he pushed her back to study her face. "Well, where's your shawl then?"

Sheepishly, Georgiana pointed over to her painting. It was not doing any good protecting her work anymore, and her shawl was rendered useless, being soaked with rain and covered with paint.

Ridge shook his head, took off his own coat, and began helping her into it.

"Please, Ridge. I'll be fine," she protested, but he shook his head again and looked at her sternly.

"Hush, woman, we need to get outta here . . . now!" he said harshly. "I left my horse tied up there," he continued, pointing to the trees that bordered the meadow on the right. He was worried. She could hear it in his voice and see it in his face as she watched his eyes scanning the trees for the exact spot his horse waited, even though it was near impossible to see anything through rain and flying debris around them.

Ridge stood up and gently helped her to her feet. Without warning, he scooped her up into his arms and began running in the direction he had just pointed. Georgiana gasped when another loud crack thundered behind her. Closing her eyes, she held onto Ridge more tightly.

When they reached the trees, the force of the wind immediately lessened and the sheets of rain were replaced by a hard drizzle. She spotted Ridge's horse right away.

Ridge lifted her up into the saddle, careful not to hurt her foot, and climbed up behind her. He held the reins tightly in one hand and wrapped his other securely around her waist. Georgiana tried hard not to think of the affect it was having on her to be so close to him. She was sure he could feel her heart pounding. She worked hard to steady her breathing in an attempt to calm herself.

It didn't take much encouragement to get Storm moving. The horse seemed to be as eager as they were to get out of there, and consequently they made good time getting back.

Once home, Ridge hopped down, opened the barn door, and led

them through. He eased Georgiana back into his arms and sat her down on a bale of hay while he removed his horse's saddle and put him into his stall. Walking over to Georgiana, he lifted her into his arms again and carried her to the house.

Setting her down on one of the kitchen chairs, Ridge lit a lantern and quickly went to work stoking the fire and putting water on to boil. He dropped a threaded needle into the pot. Next, removing his wet coat from around her, he hung it by the door and fetched a quilt from one of the parlor chairs, wrapping it securely around her shoulders.

"Ridge?" she called his name softly, but he didn't seem to hear. Instead, he walked to the cupboard, withdrew a bottle of whisky and some clean strips of linen, and laid them out on the table.

By this time, the water had started to boil, and Ridge dipped a clean wash rag into it. Grabbing the soap from the sink, he brought it and the pot with him to the table. Finally, he pulled up a chair in front of her and sat down.

He gently lifted her foot onto his lap and unwrapped the bloodied bandanna and cloth. Her cut was still bleeding, but not as profusely. Ridge cleaned it thoroughly, first with the soap and then with the whisky. Both stung her raw skin, but she tried to hold her foot still, managing to wince only a time or two.

When at last he retrieved the needle and thread from the pot, he paused. For the first time since making it back to the ranch, Ridge looked into her eyes.

"This will hurt," he warned, all harshness gone from his voice, "but it is a deep wound and will heal faster if it is stitched." Georgiana nodded but said nothing.

He had been right about it hurting, and she was grateful she had been able to keep from crying out. However, she couldn't keep the tears from her eyes.

When the last stitch was completed, he took the clean strips of linen and wrapped them around her foot. Leaning back in his chair, he let out a weary sigh. She could visually see the tension releasing from his body as he relaxed.

The house was so quiet, so peaceful, that it made the storm outside seem even more brutal. It was then she realized that all this time they had been alone. She hadn't seen her grandfather or the others.

"Where is everyone?" she asked thoughtfully. "And how did you know where to find me?"

"A large birch tree in the west pasture was blown over by the wind and breached a portion of the fence. Some of the cattle got through. I 'spect everyone is still out either gatherin' the cattle or movin' the tree and fixin' the fence." He lifted her foot from his lap and placed it on the floor before he continued. "Your grandfather was worried 'bout ya when the storm started and sent Jeremiah to the house to warn ya to secure the windows and be prepared for a bad one. That was 'bout the time the wind really got wild. We headed over to check on the herd and spotted the felled tree. When Jeremiah came ridin' up with the note ya left about headin' out to paint for a bit before supper, your grandfather asked me ta hurry and find ya."

"But how did you know where I was?"

"From your paintings," he replied. "I was hopin' you'd gone off to the same place today. I've seen them mountains before. Storm and I like to get out by ourselves once in a while. That there meadow was a particular favorite spot a summer ago. Though after today, I'm thinkin' I might be inclined to avoid it permanently."

On an impulse, Georgiana leaned forward and grabbed one of his hands, holding it between both of hers. At once goose bumps broke out on her skin and her breathing increased. She tried hard to ignore her body's reaction.

"Thank you, Ridge. Thank you for saving my life out there." Then, surprising herself, she lifted the palm of his hand to her lips and kissed it.

"Georgiana, I . . ." He didn't finish the sentence but instead stood and took a small step forward so he was directly in front of her. She let go of his hand. Leaning forward, he placed both his hands about her waist and lifted her up to stand before him.

The quilt fell from around her shoulders to the floor.

Releasing her waist, he lifted a hand slowly to her face, brushed a strand of her long blonde hair to the side, and tucked it behind her ear. His fingers then delicately traced her jawline until his hand came to rest beneath her chin. Tilting her head up slightly, he looked deeply into her eyes.

"Georgiana," he spoke her name softly, the sound of it so tender and loving, its intonation resounded in her heart. She was spell-bound, staring into the warmth of his eyes. As his lips neared her own, she instinctively closed her eyes and eagerly awaited his touch.

"Georgie girl?"

Georgiana was startled when she heard her grandfather call out her name from the other side of the door. Then, instead of feeling the anticipated touch of Ridge's lips, she felt herself being gently but firmly pushed back into the chair she had just been so beautifully drawn out of. She watched as Ridge barely missed stumbling over the chair standing behind him and scrambled to the opposite side of the room.

"Georgie?" her grandfather called again, but this time the door slammed open from the force of the wind behind it. Georgiana jumped from both the sound and the sight, because there in the doorway next to her grandfather, looking like a drowned city rat, stood Dawson.

·11·

Surprise!

GEORGIANA stood up for a moment, sat back down, and stood up once again. She couldn't believe Dawson was here, but there he stood, dripping wet and smiling from ear to ear. He made no move to step forward but waited politely to be invited in. Even with the rain beating hard against his back, he was ever a gentleman. Sadly, she was having trouble finding her voice. Her grandfather came to her rescue.

"Look who Tiny found in town today."

Georgiana still said nothing. He came into the house and beckoned Dawson to follow him. "Come on in out of the rain, lad. If ye stand any longer in that there storm, ye will surely be blown away."

Dawson came inside, and Angus took his overcoat while Georgiana stood gawking. What was he doing here? Had he written to say he was coming? Admittedly she still hadn't read the last batch of letters.

She quickly glanced at Ridge, aware he was monitoring her reactions closely, and turned her attention back to Dawson. He was smiling at her tentatively. It was good to see him, despite the shock and the fact that his timing was extremely bad.

Her grandfather cleared his throat loudly. They were all staring at her, waiting for her to speak, and here she stood, still gaping at them in silence as she sorted her thoughts. From somewhere in her memory, she heard the voice of Ms. Wilmington saying, "A lady never gawks, but rather, when caught by surprise, she exercises the utmost control in both her facial expressions and her mannerisms, thus quickly gaining the upper hand in any situation." Encouraged by that thought, Georgiana finally found her voice.

"Dawson . . . ," she began. Ridge continued to watch. Feeling the weight of his stare was causing her mind to have trouble forming cognitive thoughts. "Dawson, I . . . I . . . " Suddenly Dawson hurried forward and gathered her up into his arms.

"I've missed you too, Georgiana, most terribly. I warned you I would come to fetch you if you stayed away too long."

"But Dawson . . . how . . . when did you—"

Before she could finish her sentence, his lips were upon hers. She was so stunned, so taken aback, she couldn't think how to respond until she heard the front door slam shut.

She managed to push Dawson off just in time to see her grandfather follow Ridge out the door.

"Dawson, what are you doing here?"

"What do you mean, love? I told you . . . I missed you and I couldn't stand to be away from you a moment longer." She had freed herself from his embrace, so he reached down and took her hands. "Didn't you miss me?" His eyes seemed to be pleading with her to answer in the affirmative.

"Yes, of course I've missed you," she answered, feeling a twinge of guilt. "It's just that I'm surprised to see you. So much has happened today. I'm afraid you're the last person I expected to see standing in the doorway in the middle of this wicked storm." She let go of his hands and sat down again in the chair, clasping her hands conveniently together so he couldn't grab them. "When did you arrive?"

Dawson sat down in the chair opposite her that Ridge had been sitting in moments before.

"On the afternoon stage. It was pure luck I happened upon one of your grandfather's cowhands." He stopped to smile charmingly, and she couldn't help but return his smile. "Especially since I loathed wasting any of the time I have to spend with you. I promised my father I wouldn't stay longer than two weeks. That reminds me, Mother sends her love and asked me to tell you she misses your visits immensely."

"Your mother is very kind."

"Alysa also wanted you to know the leaves are just beginning to turn, and if you hurry home, you won't miss painting them." Alysa was Dawson's ten-year-old sister. Georgiana adored her.

"And how are Thomas and Viviana, and, of course, your father?"

"They are all in good health, but they miss you terribly as well."

When he finished speaking, his eyes fell to her lips. Georgiana worried he might try repeating his earlier unexpected greeting. Suddenly, her mouth became very dry, so she stood up and limped over to the sink.

"Can I offer you any refreshment?" she asked, reaching for a cup from the cupboard. "I could make some herb tea if you like."

"Still the gracious hostess, I see," Dawson teased, a smile alighting his face.

Georgiana had almost forgotten his playful manner and how it was so endearing.

"It might do well to take the chill off," she suggested.

"I believe you might be right, so yes, my lady, I graciously accept your offer."

He continued to talk about his family while Georgiana took down the kettle, pumped water into it, and placed it on the cook stove, which was still warm. She didn't bother stoking the fire. She knew Dawson liked his tea warm, not hot. She took down another cup and filled it with water for herself, being careful not to splash any on the floor as she hobbled back over to her chair.

It was then Dawson finally noticed she was limping.

"My dear, you've been injured." Dawson leapt to his feet to aid her the rest of the way to the table. "What has happened to your foot?" he asked, helping her into the chair, and sat back down across from her.

The sincere look of concern on his face touched her. She did miss this man. She had been lonely for such a long time before they had become friends. She had reveled in the fact she had found a confidant and friend in Mr. Dawson Alexander.

"I am afraid my foolishness resulted in a rather unfortunate accident, that being a rather bothersome cut to my foot."

Dawson jumped to his feet once again, his look of concern deepening.

"We should fetch the doctor. I will ask your grandfather to lend me a horse, and I'll—"

"Dawson, I'm fine . . . really," Georgiana interrupted, motioning for him to sit back down. "It has been cared for properly, I assure you."

"But you can't be too careful," he warned, the worry evident in his voice. "I couldn't bear the thought of anything happening to you."

"It's not that serious and will mend itself in no time," she reassured him.

When she took a drink, a tangled lock of her hair fell forward. At once, she realized what a fright she must look with her hair down, damp, and disheveled from the storm.

Embarrassed, she quickly ran her fingers through it, untangling it as best she could before nimbly working it into a braid and rolling it into a loose bun. She secured the bun with the few pins that thankfully had remained in her pocket. When she was finished, she stood up and carefully walked back over to fetch the kettle and finish preparing Dawson's tea. He never took his eyes off her the whole time she'd reworked her hair in silence, and when she got up, he followed over to help.

"Let me finish this, Georgiana. You need to rest."

"Nonsense," she chided him. Surely she was not so hurt she couldn't prepare a cup of tea. Besides, she had responsibilities to the men, and she didn't intend to ignore them because of a little wound. They were all still working out in this beastly storm and would no doubt be cold, tired, and hungry when they came in.

She began hastily taking down pots and pans. Georgiana had promised the men fried chicken tonight with potatoes, and that's what they were going to get.

"What are you doing?" Dawson asked, looking shocked.

Georgiana turned to face him, placing a hand on each hip. "What do you think I'm doing? I'm fixing dinner," she replied sternly.

"But surely you can't with—"

"I can and I will." She narrowed her eyes at him, and he put his hands up in mock surrender. Dawson was not ignorant of her Irish temper. She had never tried to hide it from him. If she had succeeded in doing so, surely that would mean they weren't nearly as close as she thought they were.

"But how can you? You can barely stand," he said, an incredulous look on his face.

"With your help," Georgiana announced. Reaching over and grabbing her apron from its peg, she threw it at him. The look on his face made her laugh. She knew he wouldn't put it on. Wearing an apron was always where he drew the line. Dawson had joined her in the kitchen back home a number of times while she was trying out some new recipe or technique she had learned. At first she figured he had devised it as a way to spend more time talking with her, but after a bit of coaxing on her part for him to participate, he seemed to enjoy himself. He would never admit it though.

All of their kitchen rendezvous had, of course, been on the sly. Had Aunt Cecelia ever found out, she would have put an end to them immediately. Never would she have tolerated such a breach of etiquette. It was already a stretch for her to allow Georgiana to continue cooking and sharpening her skills. Nevertheless, Georgiana had not once seen her aunt push aside a dessert or crumpet she had baked.

Dawson looked back at the door and then at her injured foot. She assumed he was weighing in his mind the repercussions of being caught cooking, by a bunch of cowboys no less. Would it damage his reputation too entirely? He must have decided to take the chance because he removed his town coat, hung it on a chair, and began rolling up his sleeves. When he was finished, he walked over to her side and smiled.

"Where would you like me to begin?"

Georgiana motioned over to a sack of potatoes leaning against the door to the pantry.

"If you wouldn't mind peeling a few potatoes for me, I'll start frying the chicken. I prepared most everything before I left earlier to paint. If we hurry, we can probably be done before any of the men return." Before he walked away to begin his given task, Georgiana stood up on her toes and kissed him on the cheek, ignoring the pain that shot through her foot.

He grinned a little wider.

"Thank you, Dawson, for risking your reputation to help me," she teased, but having to feign her smile. Her foot was hurting her more than she would admit to, but with Dawson's help, she would no doubt be able to get off it more quickly.

While they cooked, Georgiana told Dawson about what had happened in the meadow that led to her injury. She could see the grateful expression on his face when she told him how Ridge had saved her from being struck. Afterward, she dared not look at him directly. When she talked about Ridge, even as she said his name, her body warmed and a blush came to her cheeks. She worried Dawson would notice.

Her thoughts were instantly drawn back to the moments before Dawson had arrived. Ridge had almost kissed her again. She imagined she could still feel the warmth of his hands on her waist and the tender way he had held his hand against her chin as he looked into her eyes.

Guilt washed over her. Here, directly beside her, stood Dawson. A man she knew loved her dearly and one she greatly admired—maybe even loved back. He must have gone to great lengths to come out so far to see her. Dawson was a city man, through and through. He had no hidden or repressed desires to live on the frontier, and she knew him well enough to know he didn't particularly enjoy being unclean for very long. The stagecoach ride was probably a great sacrifice, as dirty and dusty as she remembered getting. Now here she was being unfair to him—unfair to both of them, actually. Could she be in love with both men? How would she ever choose between the two?

It was Ridge, though, who seemed to be dominating her thoughts and affecting her so much lately. So much more than Dawson ever had or possibly could, she was beginning to realize. What did that mean for her and Dawson? Could that be her answer? Yes, she couldn't deny it. She knew now that Ridge was the reason she had never been able to give her heart to Dawson. But now that Dawson was here and had kissed her in front of Ridge, what was she to do?

Letting out a frustrated sigh, Georgiana turned her thoughts from both men and put her energy instead into the meal she was preparing.

❧ ❧ ❧

Ridge stormed into the barn and shook the fresh rain from his coat and hat. Then, grabbing a currycomb, he went over to his horse's stall and began brushing him down vigorously.

"Confounded, fickle women," he swore under his breath, and Storm twitched his ears. "Why do they have ta be so . . . so . . ." He didn't finish his sentence but instead kicked a bucket lying at the foot of the stall. The sound startled the horse, and Ridge gently rubbed Storm's side and murmured a few soothing words to calm him down before continuing to brush him.

When the barn door opened and closed, he didn't have to guess who had come in, and soon Angus stood leaning up against the door of the stall.

"Evenin', Ridge."

"Evenin', Angus," Ridge replied without looking up.

"I'm here to be thankin' ye for findin' me girl and bringin' her home."

Ridge nodded his head that he accepted his thanks, but he didn't say anything.

"Surprised I was to see Tiny a totin' that city lad of Georgiana's out to the west field with him where we was workin'. Havin' a tough time of it, we were, when they arrived. That there birch was no wee saplin'. If we tried haulin' it out of the way with the horses, it would've fer certain taken another portion of the fence down with it. So I sent Roddy back to be gettin' a couple of cross saws. Jonas and Jeremiah were searchin' for the cattle. When Roddy returned, there was just the three of us, not countin' Mr. Alexander." He stopped to shake his head and chuckle softly. "Shocked out of me skin I was when the lad grabbed one end of a saw and started workin' right along with us." He looked up at Ridge and watched him for a second. "Never stopped or complained, just kept workin' till we were done, even helped with fixin' the fence. I 'spect he might be a pretty good lad after all."

Ridge was finished seeing to his horse, so after he hung the currycomb back up, he walked over and picked up his coat and hat where he had haphazardly tossed them. After putting them back on, he grabbed a lantern.

"The storm's let up quite a bit. I think I'll walk around ta make sure there isn't anythin' else that needs tendin' to."

"Awk! Don't ye be troublin' yourself about that lad. 'Tis a chore that can wait 'til morn," Angus argued.

"I'd feel better 'bout doin' it now," Ridge insisted.

As he opened the barn door, Jonas, Jeremiah, Tiny, and Roddy all rode up together. The storm indeed seemed to be passing. The wind had died down considerably, and only a light drizzle fell.

"Good, yer back," Angus called to the men. "Have any trouble findin' them runaways?"

"Nah, we got 'em under control," Jonas called as he dismounted his horse and headed in their direction.

"Didn't need Tiny and Roddy's help," Jeremiah added and followed suit.

Tiny and Roddy dismounted and walked their horses over. They looked a bit more worn for all the sawing they had done on the big old birch tree.

"Well then, lads, I thank ye for all yar hard work tonight. Take care of yar horses, get cleaned up a bit, and I'll see ye in the house." He turned to Ridge, who had begun walking off. "How long are ye expectin' ta be gone, lad?"

Ridge looked up at the sky. As he stood there contemplating an answer, the rain ceased to fall.

"Seein' as it has stopped rainin', I think I'll do a more thorough check of things." He walked off again. Calling over his shoulder, he added, "Don't wait supper for me." Suddenly remembering something, he turned around. "By the way, Angus . . . thanks for the warnin' earlier." He tipped his hat at his boss's knowing look and walked away.

⁂

Angus shook his head as he watched the lad go. What a day! At least he had been able to head off what could have been a bad scene only moments before.

When he had first sent Ridge to find his Georgie, he was hopin' they could find a minute to talk. Ridge had only returned from Castle Rock that mornin'. Angus had sent him there out of pity mostly, figurin' it might give him a little peace to get away for a few days.

He knew Ridge was driving himself crazy worrying about Georgie having a beau back in the city. He'd been working and keeping himself busy enough to avoid being around her, and that was making him even crazier.

His granddaughter hadn't been acting much better. What feelings she had for this Mr. Alexander, he didn't know. But he knew, as sure as the dawn, she had feelings for Ridge. Besides, Jimmy had told him what had happened in town between the two of them.

When he and Mr. Alexander had headed back up to the house, Angus started to worry what they might be walking into. He decided it was best to call out to his girl. From the commotion he heard on the other side and the look on Ridge's face when they entered, he figured he had made the right decision.

Angus shook his head and headed back up to the house. Yes, what a day this had been already, and this was only the beginning. Things were going to be lively around here, for a few days at least, he was sure. He was glad Jimmy had gone home for a few days to help his brother with the harvest. Even though Georgiana had seen fit to put the lad in his place, it would be one last thing to add to the drama.

⁂

By the time dinner was prepared, the storm seemed to have passed. Georgiana's grandfather came in and began engaging Dawson in a conversation about his family. It was then Georgiana excused herself to change and freshen up for dinner.

As she closed the door to her room, she let out a deep and weary sigh.

At least her surprise and apprehension at Dawson's unexpected arrival had begun to dissipate somewhat. For now, all she had to do was get through dinner.

Georgiana slipped out of her tattered dress and sat down on the edge of her bed, drawing her foot up to take a look. She had begun to worry it had started bleeding again. She was pleased when she could see no sign of blood coming through the bandage. Ridge must have done well with his stitching, even though it throbbed relentlessly.

Lying back on her pillow, a sense of fatigue overcame her all at once, and she found herself struggling to keep her eyes open. *Maybe I can rest for just a few minutes,* she thought. Emotionally drained and having lost quite a bit of blood in the meadow before Ridge had bound her foot, her body was fighting exhaustion. So closing her eyes to rest, she fell unexpectedly into a deep sleep.

Startled, Georgiana sat up in her bed and looked around, her blanket falling away. Some night sound outside her window must have woken her, and for a few minutes she remained motionless, confused at the consuming darkness of her room. *What time is it*? she thought, shivering violently as the cool night air seeping in through the window pricked at her bare skin. She was wearing only her undergarments, but someone had thrown a quilt over her. It was the one that usually lay folded at the end of her bed. Georgiana pulled the quilt, still warm from her body heat, up and around her shoulders. She must have fallen asleep before she'd finished getting dressed. After the scolding she'd given her grandfather her second day back, she was confident he would never have allowed anyone else into her room. He must have checked on her and covered her with the quilt before going to bed himself. Snuggling deep into the comforting warmth, she laid back down on her pillow.

The moonlight filtered in through the window across her room, highlighting small particles of dust that danced around in the soft light as if to some reticent melody. Outside, a multitude of stars peeked out from behind a few wispy clouds. The storm had passed.

Georgiana lay in bed another moment debating which was worse, the pain in her foot or the pain in her stomach. She had eaten only a slice of buttered bread for lunch and had completely missed dinner. Either way, she would never get back to sleep if she didn't at least try to appease her appetite. Besides, she was curious what had happened in her absence. There would be no one to ask, but the state of the kitchen would surely hint as to how everyone had gotten along at dinner.

Throwing back the quilt, Georgiana swung her legs over the edge of the bed. The throbbing became exceedingly worse as blood rushed to her injured foot. Nevertheless, she stood up slowly, limped over to her bureau, and retrieved her nightgown. As she slipped it on, Georgiana shivered again until the heat from her body, trapped in the heavy fabric, warmed the chill from her skin.

Leaving her room, Georgiana felt her way down the poorly lit hallway, grateful to the walls for support as she fumbled awkwardly. It would be a little more difficult to cross the parlor without upsetting some unseen object, but she didn't want to risk stumbling with a lighted lamp.

When finally she hobbled through the kitchen door, having managed without incident in the parlor, there was enough moonlight coming through the two large windows that she could see fairly well.

Everything in the kitchen seemed to be in perfect order, and she felt an immediate sense of relief. She decided a slice of bread and a glass of milk would be sufficient to stave off her nagging hunger, or at the very least, it would get her through the night.

After pouring the milk and slicing a large piece of bread, she turned to head over to the table but then jumped with a start. Recovering quickly, Georgiana immediately smiled. Ridge was sitting at the table eating a plate of cold chicken. They had obviously been thinking alike.

Georgiana felt her heart begin to race. Oh, how being near him thrilled her senses! And now she wouldn't have to wait until morning before they could talk. *Besides*, she thought hopefully, *we have unfinished business.*

Georgiana limped a few steps toward Ridge and slowed to a stop when she remembered she was not only wearing her night clothes but also her hair hung loose, trailing wildly down her back. The gown was modest enough, she supposed, but just being near a man in her bedtime attire with her hair unbound felt entirely too intimate. She wouldn't even consider what Ms. Wilmington would say. Shamelessly choosing to ignore her sense of propriety, she began walking toward him again.

"Georgiana . . . ," Ridge spoke her name tenderly and leaned slightly forward into the light streaming in from outside.

She froze. He'd only whispered it, but she could hear in his voice the same timbre that earlier had spoken so completely to her heart. Her pulse quickened even more. She couldn't help that her eyes were drawn to his full lips, which were now bathed in the moon's soft glow. The disappointment of being deprived of his kiss earlier was still fresh in her mind. Forcing herself to look at his eyes instead, she saw a flaming hope that he might kiss her still this night. But instead of coming to her and taking her in his arms, his expression abruptly changed to something she couldn't read. Next, his shoulders sagged, and she heard him sigh deeply as he turned his eyes away from her to stare out the window.

"What are you doing up in the middle of the night?" Georgiana finally asked when her heart rate slowed enough to trust herself to speak. She limped the rest of the way over and sat down across from him, wincing slightly because her foot was now throbbing. He looked back at her when she spoke, and she saw a sympathetic look flit across his face before it was once again unreadable.

"Same thing you're doin' in the middle of the night, looks like." He attempted a grin, but it ended up looking more like a smirk.

"Hmm," was all she could think to say as she stared at him. Georgiana knew now was the time she should explain about Dawson's kiss . . . tell him it was a misunderstanding. "Ridge . . . about earlier . . . I . . ."

He stiffened immediately and sat up straighter. "Ya don't need to say anythin'. I understand."

"What is it you understand, Ridge?" Georgiana was suddenly nervous about the direction their conversation was heading.

"Look, Georgie." He leaned further back in his chair, the shadows once again obscuring his features. "Before ya came back, we hadn't seen or talked to each other in five years . . . *five years*," he emphasized. "Ya been gone a long time, and . . . we grew up." He only paused slightly before adding, "You're different, Georgie. I'm different. It's not the same as when we was kids. We've been livin' in two separate worlds . . . both goin' opposite ways." Once more he halted his speech. When he spoke again, his voice was tinged with what sounded like defeat. "I'm sorry . . . 'bout the other day. I mean, I should never have—"

"Please don't," she hastily interrupted. He was about to apologize for kissing her, and her heart couldn't take that.

Nervously, her stomach tied itself in knots. Ridge needed to know how she felt. Nothing was going right. She thought she had sensed he shared similar feelings with her. Maybe she'd been wrong? Maybe she'd been wrong about a lot of things. Tears gathered in her eyes, threatening to spill over. It was now her turn to stare out the window as she garnered enough courage to speak.

"Ridge, please. I know how it looked, but I . . . ," she finally managed even though her words were barely a whisper.

"Ya moved away," Ridge suddenly broke in, his voice tinged with frustration, "made new friends." He paused, but when he spoke again his voice was softer. "Don't ya see, Georgie? Ya've changed. You're a city girl, now. That fancy school did a right good job of it too. Why, if I hadn't grown up with ya, I'd never have known it was you, walkin' and talkin' the way you do."

She cringed at his words. She wasn't a city girl . . . and she never would be. This is where she belonged. But before she could defend herself, he spoke again.

"I'm a simple cattle rancher; it's all I ever wanted. I don't reckon I'll ever leave Colorado." He stood up then, picking up his glass and plate. "Go back to New York, Georgiana," he added with a note of finality as he walked over to the sink. "It's where you belong. You have—" He stopped abruptly and sighed before finishing the statement.

She heard him set his dishes down, and for a long moment he didn't say anything, just stood there quietly. It was her chance to speak. To shout out that he was wrong. She hadn't changed, not really. She hated New York, and the last thing in the world she wanted to do was return there. In fact, she'd dig her heels *and* her fingers deep into the Colorado soil and hang on for dear life if anyone tried to drag her back. Though her mind raced with all the things she should say, an underlying fear kept her mouth closed tight.

Still, she wanted to go to him. Put her arms around him and tell him he was who she wanted and that her life had always been here with him. If it wasn't meant to be between her and Ridge, her heart had somehow failed her. Yet, she couldn't bring herself to turn around. He had said she was different . . . she'd changed. Was he really just saying he didn't want her? So, instead of running into his arms, she sat numbly staring at the empty chair sitting across the table. Suddenly she noticed the coat hanging on it and a thought jumped into her mind.

"Dawson!" He was here. Somewhere. She'd nearly forgotten about him. She'd left him with her grandfather earlier, promising to return as soon as she changed for dinner. Where was he? Had he gone back to town? Surely not, especially with the storm flooding the roads. Her grandfather would have found a place for him to sleep, but where?

"Yes . . . Dawson," she heard Ridge repeat.

Georgiana was at once confused. Why had Ridge said that? It didn't make sense. What exactly had he said to her a moment ago? She contemplated. He'd told her to go back to New York . . . but then didn't finish his statement. Ridge must think she had chosen Dawson over him. *Maybe he does care?* she wondered hopefully and turned quickly in her chair to explain, but Ridge was already gone. She watched helplessly as the kitchen door swung closed.

Standing up, Georgiana hobbled over to the door to call him back, explain to him the misunderstanding. But when she opened the door and took a step through it, she saw the bunkhouse door swing closed too.

Sighing, Georgiana made her way back to her room, leaving the milk and bread at the table, forgotten.

·12·

Pillow Talk

RIDGE left immediately, not daring to even look at her face when Georgiana had confirmed his suspicions. He feared he would take her into his arms and, with a kiss, try to convince her to change her mind . . . to choose him. He hurried quickly to the bunkhouse. She'd made her choice. He would have to learn to live with it somehow. Maybe he would find some respite in his sleep, though he sincerely doubted it. Surely his dreams would be of her—holding her close, smelling her skin and her hair, her eyes reflecting the longing evident in his own. Would he be able to hold himself back from tasting her sweetened kiss once again, even after her admission that it was Dawson she wanted to spend the rest of her life with?

Disappointment weighed heavily on him. *Angus had seen to that*, Ridge thought, annoyed, even though he knew the old man's intention had only been to fend off a possible scene. All the same, the thought had occurred to him that perhaps it would have been better if Mr. Dawson Alexander had witnessed Georgiana wrapped in his arms, instead of the other way around. Maybe it would have caused the man to turn around and run right back to New York. Georgiana would then be his.

Shaking his head, Ridge wearily leaned up against the inside of the bunkhouse door he had just closed behind him. *She'll never belong to me*, he thought, sighing deeply as his shoulders sagged with the weight of defeat. It had been hard saying all he had, but the last thing he wanted was for her to feel trapped or obligated to stay in Colorado. He could sense she'd been struggling for weeks trying to choose between the two worlds she lived in. He wanted to make it easier for her. If she'd felt differently, she'd had her chance to say so. In the end, she had made her decision, and he couldn't argue with that.

Ridge stopped to listen for a moment to the quiet breathing of the men, all except Roddy and his incessant snoring. Thankfully, he was used to it by now. It no longer disturbed his sleep like other things did lately.

Walking to his bunk, he unrolled the bedding he had brought in earlier that day when he and Jeremiah had returned from Castle Rock. He was tired, both physically and emotionally, so he failed to notice the lump lying on Jimmy's bunk above him. He was glad the men were all asleep and he wouldn't have to endure the chatter and speculation about the unexpected arrival of Dawson Alexander.

Lying down on top of his bedding, Ridge put his hands behind his head and stared up at the bed above him. He was shocked to see it move as if someone had rolled onto his side. Had Jimmy returned already? Surely not with the storm.

"You must be Ridge," he heard a vaguely familiar voice say.

Startled, Ridge realized who the voice belonged to and was glad the man could not see the look that crossed his face.

Although Ridge didn't say anything in return, it didn't stop Mr. Alexander from resuming the conversation.

"Georgiana told me how you rescued her in the storm this afternoon and doctored her injured foot." He paused for a moment. "Miss McLaughlin means the world to me, and I am exceedingly in your debt."

"Ya owe me nothin'," Ridge answered, trying to keep his voice sounding normal. He took his hands from behind his head and began massaging his temples. His head was starting to pound, and he had no desire to have a late night chat, especially with the present company. "Should try to get some sleep, Mr. Alexander. Mornin' comes early on a cattle ranch," he advised, hoping to end the conversation.

He heard Dawson roll onto his back, and for a while there was only the familiar silence once again. Relieved, Ridge figured the man had fallen asleep. However, as soon as he thought it, Dawson began talking again, softly this time, and Ridge wasn't sure whether the man was talking to him or to himself.

"I remember the first time I ever saw her." Ridge wasn't sure he wanted to be listening to this, but what choice did he have? Maybe blessed slumber would find him soon, if he could only be so lucky. "I had promised my younger brother, Thomas, I would take him to the park so he could show off the new boat he had been given for his birthday. We were running to keep up with it as it sailed along the edge of the lake when suddenly there she was." He paused, and Ridge could hear him breathe in deep. "The sight of her was like Christmas morning. She was sitting on a blanket, leaning up against a tree, sketching some young children as they played at the water's edge. One corner of her mouth was turned up slightly in a sort of half smile like she couldn't decide whether to be amused or amazed at something she saw before her. As I stood there watching, an oak leaf floated down from a branch above and came to rest on her lap. She laid down her sketchbook, picked up the leaf, and began twirling it between her fingers as a look so sad, so forlorn spread across her face. I knew in that moment, if I accomplished nothing else in this life other than to keep such a look from ever torturing this lovely woman's face again, I would have truly accomplished a great task indeed."

He laughed softly before he continued. "It took me three days to get the nerve up to speak to her, much to Thomas's delight at being taken to the park each day. I was lucky she made a habit of sketching daily, or I might have had to spend an entire lifetime looking for her again." He sighed and took another deep breath. "The first time she looked up at me with those lovely, thoughtful gray eyes, I knew she was unlike any other woman I had ever known."

This time when he paused, Ridge could imagine the look on Dawson's face. It may have even resembled his own expression, as he could picture exactly how looking into Georgiana's eyes made him feel.

"I was right," Dawson continued. "I've never known anyone so kind and unselfish, especially one as beautiful as she. Not only is Georgiana generous with her time and her talents, but she is also the most genuine, caring woman I have ever met. For some reason, just being near her makes you feel like you're the luckiest man alive." He paused briefly. "That was a year ago.

"I'm afraid I must confess I was unsuccessful in keeping her from ever experiencing another painful moment like she did in the park that first day. Try as I might, every once in a while, when she thought no one was paying attention, I would see the look again. It's a sort of deep and mournful sadness lurking just behind the smile in her eyes. Have you ever seen it?" When Ridge didn't answer right away, Dawson answered for him. "No, of course you haven't. Before I came here, I had noticed the look was never really ever gone, only that she was expertly skilled at hiding it most of the time . . . her mask only occasionally falling away."

Dawson stopped speaking, and Ridge pondered what he'd just said. Dawson was wrong. He had seen the same look when she had first arrived, but it hadn't been long before it disappeared and was replaced by a look of contentment. It was as if Dawson read Ridge's mind as he began speaking again.

"I did not see it in her eyes tonight—not a trace. She's happy here. Maybe she has finally made peace with what was causing her sorrow." Ridge wondered at that. "I had hoped to convince her to come back with me." Ridge felt his heart constrict. "I have sorely missed her. All the color seemed to leave my world when she left." Ironically, Ridge could relate to that very thing. "But . . . maybe she's not ready to return just yet. Maybe she has only just begun to make peace with what has pained her for so long. I would never want to undo any good that has been done here."

Ridge was surprised at Dawson's last words. He expected him to be selfish, acting all high and mighty, but instead Dawson was acting as if he truly cared for Georgiana. Perhaps Angus was right, and he was a pretty decent man. This new revelation was painful to consider. No wonder Georgiana liked him so well. Maybe Dawson was more deserving of her than he could ever be. Ridge was deep in thought when Dawson spoke again.

"I have asked her to marry me . . . more than once, actually." This time when he sighed, it sounded tinged with frustration. "I don't know what's holding her back. I know she has feelings for me."

After hearing Dawson's newest revelation, Ridge questioned why he had come to the bunkhouse. Ridge was tired, clear to his very bones. He didn't want to think of Georgiana any more tonight. He didn't want to think of anything. He just wanted to sleep.

He had assumed Dawson would have been put up in the guest room of the ranch house. What had possessed Angus to have him sleep in the bunkhouse instead? Surely the city boy would have protested, wouldn't he?

Even as he thought it, Ridge knew the answer to both questions. Angus would not have allowed a man so clearly enamored with his granddaughter to sleep in the guest room, which bordered her own, even if the man appeared to have impeccable morals. Also, from what Angus had told him about Mr. Alexander, he knew the man was of good character, not haughty and self-absorbed as he had been expecting . . . or maybe as he had been hoping. Truth was, Ridge knew if it weren't for the fact that Dawson was obviously the man Georgiana had chosen and desired, he would likely have befriended Mr. Dawson Alexander of his own accord. Ridge was surprised when he heard himself speak.

"Give her time," he advised Dawson. What was he saying? Was he actually giving advice to the man who wanted to marry and take away the woman he loved? But this man was who Georgiana chose, Ridge reminded himself, and he sensed the man's feelings for her were genuine. Dawson would make her happy, and Ridge desired Georgiana's happiness above all else. So he continued, "I 'spect she's had a hard time of it comin' back after so long. Though it was never her doin', she feels guilty for leavin' and never returnin' to visit. She and her grandmother were close. Mrs. McLaughlin oft spoke of the day Georgie would return." In the few days before they had gone to bring the cattle down, Georgiana had confided in him her sadness for not coming home until after her grandmother had died. "She'll make her peace eventually, if she hasn't already."

Ridge heard Dawson sigh, and the sigh sounded to be one of relief.

"Thank you, Ridge . . . for being there for her today." He sincerely added, "If I can repay you somehow, it will be an honor."

"Just doin' my job. No thanks needed." The statement sounded too blunt, but how else could he respond, considering?

"Well, thank you again just the same," Dawson proffered once more, and Ridge could see him roll onto his side again.

When the room remained quiet for some time, Ridge was deeply relieved the conversation finally seemed to be over. His emotions were raw at this point, having felt he had relinquished his claim on the only woman he would ever love. Then Dawson once again broke the soothing silence.

"I was jealous of you at first."

"Hmm," was all Ridge dared respond.

"We'd known each other for about six months when I was finally able to convince Georgiana into talking about her life here in Colorado." Ridge perked up a little, long ago unanswered questions awakening in his mind. "I thought it strange she never referred to anything before moving to New York. She'd lived here for more than half of her life, and except for very rarely mentioning her father or grandparents, it was like this life never existed. I could sense, somehow, it was something that pained her terribly. I thought if I could get her to talk about it, maybe I could discover the hidden sadness about her. It was then she told me about you, her friend, Miss Wallace, and the friendship you three had shared. I could see by her expression how much it had cost her when she couldn't return."

"Samantha took it pretty hard too, I remember." Though he didn't mention his own pain, he also had been devastated.

"I thought at first, maybe you were the reason she wouldn't commit to me. Some childhood crush she'd never gotten over. After she said your name that day, she looked away from me. I suspected she was trying to hide the emotion on her face. When she told me she was returning to Colorado for a visit, I have to admit I was a bit worried."

Ridge thought of Georgiana's admission earlier. Dawson had no need to worry. He'd won the battle, and Ridge would be licking his wounds for a long time.

When Dawson spoke next, his voice sounded more confident. "I was relieved though, when after disembarking the stage, I overheard a pleasantly attractive woman mention your name in conversation. She was discussing with her companion what they would be wearing to the town social come Friday. She was speaking in that overly excited way that some women do. I am sure you know what I mean," he chuckled softly. "She obviously thinks highly of you," Dawson added, his voice pleased. "Though I can imagine why, since she went on to confide in her companion you were soon to be her intended."

"She did, did she?" Ridge was immediately fighting to keep his anger in check.

"Yes," Dawson agreed, obviously missing the irritation in Ridge's voice. "When she turned and saw me standing there, she introduced herself. Miss Jamison, isn't it? She seemed quite amiable."

Ridge didn't trust himself to speak since he was gritting his teeth so hard. He was not, nor would he ever be, anything to Miss Cordelia Jamison. The woman was truly incorrigible. If it weren't for his ma's patient hand insisting Ridge be taught good manners despite being raised alongside cows and horses, Cordelia would know exactly what he thought of her. Obviously, avoiding her wasn't enough. He would have to take a more drastic approach.

"You can't believe everything you hear, Mr. Alexander," Ridge finally said, trying hard to keep his anger in check, "especially in a small town. Sometimes folks can't find anything better to do than wag their tongues. Though I must admit, that little tidbit comes from a different source altogether."

"You sound angry. I fear I have said something to upset you," Dawson remarked, sounding genuinely apologetic.

"It ain't no fault of yours," Ridge answered, his anger softening a bit.

"Was she not speaking the truth then?" His voice sounded a little anxious.

"Not exactly." Ridge suddenly felt sorry for the man. "But you needn't worry about me, Mr. Alexander." *As of tonight, at least*, he thought to himself. "Miss McLaughlin and I are just friends."

"I must say, that is good to know," Dawson said, sounding a little too relieved. Ridge supposed the man was more worried than he'd let on. "But please," he continued while stifling a yawn, "call me Dawson."

Ridge was reminded how tired he was himself.

"Good night then, Mr. Alexander—er . . . I mean, Dawson.

Best ya get some sleep. Mornin' comes early on a cattle ranch."

"Thank you, Ridge, and good night to you."

Ridge heard him roll over onto his back and then a few moments later onto his side again. *He must have another question*, Ridge surmised and waited patiently until Dawson spoke.

"Don't be offended, but . . . ," Dawson began finally. *With a beginning like that*, Ridge thought, *no wonder it took the man so long to get to the question.* He hoped at least it was something he could answer honestly. "You know that thing you keep saying about getting some sleep?"

"Mm-hmm," Ridge responded both relieved and curious.

"I've read a number of published works and have heard that phrase before. Doesn't the saying actually go, 'mornin' comes early on a farm'?"

"Yep," Ridge agreed as he thought of the saying they had all adopted from Angus. "Mornin' does come early on a farm." He let a few seconds go by before adding, ". . . and a cattle ranch."

Dawson chuckled softly. "I think for the first time in a very long time, I might sleep well."

The conversation finally ended.

Ridge lay in his bed and listened to Dawson's breathing as the man eventually fell asleep. He wasn't so lucky. Dawson had given him a lot to think about.

Fate surely was on Dawson's side as far as Georgiana was concerned. He needed to stop wishing and read the signs. Or at least reread them. His thoughts gravitated briefly to the stack of unopened letters hidden in the bottom of his trunk, all addressed to Miss Georgiana McLaughlin 725 West Glenwood Rd., New York City, New York. All of them—each and every one—stamped with a big red "Return to Sender" on them.

It was time he concentrated on forgetting the girl he'd fallen in love with and the woman she'd become. He should never have allowed himself to begin dreaming of a life with her again. It was going to cost him dearly. She would be going back to New York, and it wasn't fair to his heart to be broken twice by the same woman.

When sleep finally claimed him, he was thankfully too tired to dream.

·13·
Alterior Motives

GEORGIANA woke when she heard a soft knock at her door. Her room was bathed in the bright sun, and after looking out her window briefly, she could see it was already high in the sky. *It must be almost noon*, she thought, surprised she had slept so long. As she quickly sat up in her bed, her stomach groaned an angry plea. She had slept through another meal. Surely, the men couldn't have been happy about that!

Georgiana heard the soft knock again, this time followed by her grandfather's voice.

"Are ye awake, Georgie? May I come in now?"

Georgiana quickly grabbed the quilt from the floor and pulled it up around her.

"Yes, Grandad," she called out to him. He opened the door tentatively and stepped inside.

"How ye be feelin' this mornin'? Ridge told me 'bout that there cut on yar foot. Do ye think it wise to be goin' into town?" His face showed his worry.

"I'll be fine, Grandfather. It seems to have stopped throbbing." *At least for the moment*, she thought. She'd promised Samantha she'd come over today. "I'm sorry I missed dinner . . . and breakfast. Are the men awfully angry at me for having to eat your cooking again?"

Her grandfather laughed heartily. "To be tellin' ye the truth, it weren't none too bad this morn. Seems that there city lad of yers knows his way around a kitchen a bit. Offered to help me out, he did. The fellas actually seemed to be pleased well enough with their meal. Though the lad made me swear not to be tellin' a soul who 'twas done the cookin'."

Georgiana smiled. She'd have to make sure and thank Dawson when she saw him.

"Where did Mr. Alexander sleep last night, Grandad? Surely you didn't send him all the way back into town." Georgiana looked questioningly at her grandfather.

"Nah, I wouldn't be doin' that to the lad, now, and fer certain not after he be helpin' out the way he did. 'Twas out in the bunkhouse he bedded down," he announced unceremoniously. Georgiana was instantly horrified.

"Grandfather! The bunkhouse? How could you? He's our guest!"

"An unexpected one, I be addin' to that," her grandfather answered, obviously not at all worried about her reaction. "And what's wrong with the bunkhouse? 'Tis good enough for the other lads, mind ye, and besides . . . 'twas either that or the barn."

She was shocked he'd even suggest the barn, and she knew her face showed it. He continued his explanation, this time more sternly. "I'll not have some lad, crazy in love with me only granddaughter, sleepin' in the same house, in the very next room, no less."

"Grandfather! How could you even think—" Georgiana exclaimed again, shocked that he would imply Dawson was capable of anything so unthinkable.

"Don't 'Grandfather' me, girl," he interrupted sternly. "I was a lad once too!" Georgiana's face went from shocked to indignant, but as her grandfather's expression softened, she realized how silly she was being. Dawson was surely not any worse for wear from sleeping one night out in the bunkhouse. When her grandfather spoke again, his voice was gentle and pleading. "Now don't be angry with me, Georgiana. I just woke ye up to tell ye that if yer still planning on going into town, the wagon's hitched up and ready to go. Asked that city lad of yars if he'd ever driven a team, and he said he could manage it. He's a wantin' real bad to get ye all to himself, he is. Been pacing back and forth all mornin', worryin' his head about ye ever since breakfast. 'Bout worn the planks clean through on the parlor floor." Georgiana smiled, picturing Dawson, but then his face was suddenly replaced by Ridge's.

"Where will the men be working today?" Georgiana asked innocently.

"Well now, mostly just securin' up the fences some more and checkin' on the herd. Makin' sure none of them were injured in the storm. Ridge checked most things out real good last night, so I gave him the day off. The lad headed into town first thing this mornin' to take care of some personal business." Georgiana stood up instantly and tossed the quilt back up on the bed, all modesty forgotten.

"Well, if you'll excuse me, Grandad, I best hurry and get dressed. I don't want to keep Dawson waiting."

"Fer certain, lass. I'll get out of yar way." He quickly exited the room and shut the door.

Georgiana readied herself quickly and met Dawson in the parlor. Dawson seemed to relax as soon as the wagon was going and kept up a steady flow of conversation. Georgiana found herself easily distracted as her mind kept wandering. Before long, Dawson pulled the wagon up in front of the mercantile and brought the team to a halt. Georgiana had been impressed. He was actually quite efficient at driving them.

Hopping down, he came around and helped her from her seat.

"Where to first, milady? The mercantile?"

She nodded her head as he linked his arm in hers, and they headed together toward the entrance.

The instant they walked through the door, Mrs. Whitaker converged upon them, introducing herself and inquiring as to how she may assist them. The whole town knew about Mr. Alexander's arrival and was eager to make his acquaintance. Truly, Georgiana had expected no less. This was a small town, after all.

When they were through answering questions and purchasing the needed items, Dawson carried her things—along with two new pairs of Levis, a couple of cotton shirts, and a pair of sturdy leather gloves and work boots—and placed them in the wagon. Mrs.

Whitaker took advantage of the time alone to beleaguer Georgiana with a few more intimate inquiries.

"Have you announced the engagement yet? My, he must be such a romantic. Just imagine . . . five letters in one week and so many since! And to think he came all this way just to see ya. Better hold on to that one, Miss Georgiana. Don't turn your head for a minute or some sweet thing might come along and snatch him up from under your very nose." She gave Georgiana a brief warning look before sighing again. "Not all women are so lucky, you know. My Robert doesn't have a romantic bone in his entire body." The woman's eyes inadvertently looked up above the counter. Georgiana's eyes followed in the same direction. There, proud as pie, hung Mr. Whitaker's twelve-point deer head. Georgiana tried to stifle the giggle welling within her by concentrating hard on Mrs. Whitaker's next question. "Will you be going back to New York with him soon? Your mother must be so thrilled. He looks as though he comes from a fine family," she gushed. Putting a hand to the side of her mouth, she added more conspiratorially, "And wealthy too, by the way he's dressed."

Dawson returned to get her before she had a chance to answer or dispute any of the woman's assumptions, nor could she deny anything in front of Dawson. It might embarrass him horribly to know he was already the subject of the town's local gossip circle. So she quickly excused herself and said good-bye, allowing Dawson to take her arm and lead her toward the door without setting the record straight to Mrs. Whitaker that she was *not* engaged.

Before they exited, Mrs. Whitaker called after them again, "Thanks for coming in, my dear, and you too, Mr. Alexander. And, Georgiana, you must come back soon—alone—so we can have a good long talk."

I must avoid the mercantile at all cost, Georgiana noted as she hurried Dawson through the door.

"What was all that about?" Dawson queried, purposely slowing her quick pace to a leisurely stroll.

"Nothing really," Georgiana answered, thinking it best not to go into too much detail. "Mrs. Whitaker leads the town gossip circle. She likes to be the first one up on the local news." He raised an eyebrow at her, but she ignored it. "Let's hurry over to Samantha's house. I'm so excited for you to meet her," she urged, walking quickly, despite a slight limp.

Of course, Dawson knew who Samantha was. She had explained to him in one of her recent letters before he came out to Crystal Creek how they had come to renew their friendship. He was happy for her and seemed genuinely interested in acquainting himself with her friend.

As they crossed the street, Georgiana stopped abruptly when Ridge walked out of the bank with Miss Cordelia Jamison. One of her hands held tightly onto his arm, while the other played flirtatiously with the lapel of his coat. She was smiling demurely up at him. By chance, Cordelia glanced her way, and Georgiana could have sworn she glared at her threateningly as if to say, "He's mine—hands off," but she quickly turned back to Ridge, smiling again. Why would the woman feel threatened by her? She knew nothing of Georgiana's feelings for Ridge. How could she?

Ridge walked over to his horse with Miss Jamison still attached to his arm. Miss Jamison leaned in very close to him, certainly breaking a number of Ms. Wilmington's rules. The woman obviously lacked a sense of propriety. Leaning in even more, she coyly whispered something into his ear. Georgiana was watching Ridge closely for his reaction, so she jumped when Dawson spoke, startling her.

"Seems you and I aren't the only two lovers out for an afternoon stroll."

"What do you mean by that?" Georgiana asked, annoyed by his comment, hastily turning her head in the direction they were walking and pretending she was unaware of anyone else's presence but his.

"Well . . . nothing," he answered, too content to notice her irritated demeanor. "Other than it's a beautiful day and love is obviously in the air."

"Love?" She gave him a dubious look.

He laughed and stopped walking before turning to face her while simultaneously taking both her hands in his.

"Yes, *love*, my dear Miss McLaughlin. For I most definitely am in love with you and hope you return my affections."

He looked over to where Ridge and Miss Jamison stood. Obviously he'd just witnessed Miss Jamison's brazen attempts at garnering Ridge's attentions too. She was about to make a comment along such lines, rebuking such a display of audacious behavior when he began speaking again.

"Though I can't say exactly what Ridge's intentions are toward Miss Cordelia, I am pretty certain she has romantic intentions toward him."

Georgiana was confused by his comment. He was speaking as if they were sweethearts. How did he know Cordelia and what feelings she might have for Ridge? And more important, why did he think Ridge might have feelings for Cordelia? Dawson's face suddenly lit up.

"That reminds me, I hear tell there is a grand social planned for tomorrow night. You do remember how much I love to dance?" Theatrically, he lifted one of her hands and put his other hand at her back as if they were about to begin the waltz. "Might I have the honor of being your escort?" Dawson smiled encouragingly down at her.

The social! She had totally forgotten—and she had promised Samantha she would attend. Georgiana looked up at Dawson. He looked so happy, so hopeful.

A sense of guilt washed over her. What should she do? It had only been last week that she had been daydreaming of what it would feel like to be held in Ridge's arms as he spun her about the room.

Apprehensively, her attention was drawn back over to Ridge. Miss Jamison was still pawing at him. Obviously, he must have been dreaming about being in the arms of someone other than herself. Quickly, her mind saw his face again as he had been about to kiss her the other night. She was so sure of what she had seen in his eyes. How could she have been so dead wrong?

Miss Jamison laughed and leaned toward Ridge again, her strawberry curls brushing up against the side of his face. When she stepped back this time, she stumbled slightly as if she were about to lose her balance. Ridge's hands were immediately at her waist to steady her. Miss Jamison took advantage of the opportunity to place both of her hands on his shoulders.

Georgiana pulled her own hands away from Dawson and turned around. Her stomach tightened, and her arms encircled her waist where she could still recall the feel of Ridge holding her. Instantly, the thought of attending the social seemed daunting. She suddenly wasn't feeling very well at all.

"Georgiana, are you all right?" Dawson asked, concern evident in his voice. When she looked up at him, the encouraging smile plastered on his face was gone. His brow was now creased with worry, any semblance of cheerful demeanor vanquished.

She took a deep breath to calm herself and turned back in the direction they were headed. One quick glance told her Ridge had now noticed her and Dawson, but Miss Jamison was still standing awfully close.

Well, if that's how he wanted to play it, she would give him an eyeful! Pushing away her guilt and suppressing the thought that she was acting no better than some of her more deplorable female friends back in New York, she turned to Dawson at her side.

"Yes, Dawson. I'm fine. It's just this foot. It's beginning to throb again." She looked up at him, forcing a shamefully helpless expression, and slipped both arms around his waist. "Do you mind?" she asked innocently, leaning her head against his shoulder as they began walking once again toward Samantha's.

"Don't mind at all," he proclaimed readily.

Georgiana felt a deep, sharp pang of guilt as he wrapped a supportive arm around her waist and began to whistle cheerfully as they walked.

After they'd traveled a ways down the street, Georgiana snuck one final peek over her shoulder. Ridge was gone, and Miss Jamison was standing in the street glaring at her again.

·14·

Women!

As soon as Ridge was out of sight of the town, he urged his horse into a full gallop. He wished to get as far away from those two women as fast as he could. It wasn't long before he found himself sitting at his favorite stream again. Reaching over, he picked up a couple of stones lying conveniently where he had piled them on his last visit. Methodically, he began tossing them into the water. He let his mind wander back to Georgiana and the day before, despite all his concessions to Dawson the previous night concerning her.

For those few moments that he'd held her after he had tended to her foot, the ache in his heart had totally disappeared. It felt so right, her being there, so close. If only her grandfather and Dawson Alexander hadn't shown up!

The man was clearly enamored. It was written all over his face as he stood there in his fancy clothes, dripping wet, not able to tear his eyes away. She'd hardly got two words out before Dawson had gone to her, and in the next moment, instead of the sweet nectar of her kiss belonging to Ridge, the city boy had claimed it. How could she have kissed Dawson, when only moments before she'd been in Ridge's arms?

Last night, he promised himself he would stay away, not interfere. Why then could he still not get her out of his head? Seeing them together was proving to be too much. Then there was that insufferable woman, Miss Jamison. What a day it had been so far!

When Angus had given him the day off, he decided to take care of some business in town. He'd been needing to make a deposit at the bank for a while now, and he wanted to make a few inquiries at the local land office.

When his father had sold his ranch and moved back east, he had given Ridge half the sum of the ranch's value to go toward purchasing his own place. Even though he had told his father he didn't need it, his father had insisted it was the right thing to do. Ridge had been a partner with his father in their business ever since he was barely more than a boy and could pull his own weight. Ridge had also been tucking away his earnings from Angus.

With Mr. Wallace's help, Ridge had invested some of the money his father had given him, and it had grown considerably. By now he had quite a large sum. It was more than enough to purchase a substantial piece of property, start up his own cattle business, and live rather comfortably in a nice home. Ridge enjoyed working for Angus though and had been putting off the inevitable. Maybe the time had come at last. If Georgiana convinced Dawson to stay out west instead of returning to New York, he didn't think he could continue working for her grandfather. He knew he couldn't, and he wanted to be long gone before that ever happened.

Involuntarily, a vision of Miss Cordelia Jamison's face quickly flashed before him. That woman never ceased to surprise him with her nerve. When he'd gone to the bank to take care of his business, she was sitting outside. He had pretended not to notice her and hurried through the doors, but she proceeded to follow him. Mr. Wallace, realizing the situation and taking pity on him, called him into his office straightaway. Mr. Wallace closed the door authoritatively, barring Miss Jamison from following Ridge in, insisting their business needed to be conducted in private. As soon as they were safely inside, Ridge thanked Mr. Wallace profusely for the interference on his behalf.

"I'm afraid, dear boy, she has been watchin' for you for days now. I think somehow she got wind you're thinkin' about purchasing some land and startin' up your own ranch." He snorted his disgust. "She's lookin' to find herself a rich husband, Ridge. Best you be avoidin' that woman for your own good. That father of hers had no business runnin' a bank any more than I did a farm, though at least I was honest. I hear tell he spends most of his days in the saloon down in Westchester. There he sits gamblin' and drinkin' away what little money his wife makes workin' in the hotel there seven days a week. I'm sure the only reason they have a place to live is 'cause her boss takes pity on her. I don't know how Miss Jamison can even afford to be stayin' over at the boardin' house. Heed my words, Ridge: steer clear of that filly."

"Thanks for the warnin', John," Ridge said gratefully, even though the bank owner hadn't divulged any information he wasn't already aware of. "She's not my type anyway."

That made Mr. Wallace laugh.

"Well, I hear Miss Georgie is back in town," he said, smiling encouragingly. Ridge pretended he didn't notice. "Hard to believe she's been here five weeks already, and I haven't so much as said two words to her. Did see her out in front of the mercantile one day, though." He let out a slow whistle. "Grew up to be a beauty, she did. Apparently she has some city boy head over heels for her too." Ridge was starting to wonder if it would be better to take his chances outside with Miss Jamison rather than listen to Mr. Wallace go on about Georgiana and Dawson. The man continued to ramble. "She's been to my house a number of times, but you know how all my time is spent here." He chuckled again. "Thought the two of you would always end up together, if truth be told, but then her family up and left like they did." He looked thoughtful for a moment. "Did you keep in touch? Never got one letter from her at our house. It broke my dear Samantha's heart. Never saw those two hardly apart in all the time Miss Georgie lived here."

"We didn't keep in contact," Ridge answered matter-of-factly. *Though, not for lack of trying,* he thought ruefully.

"Seems strange, if you ask me . . . strange indeed," he said, shaking his head back and forth. "Never did like that aunt of hers, Ms. Cecelia Harrington. I met her once, you know, when Michael McLaughlin first brought his new bride home to live with Angus and Shannon. That Charlotte was a beauty, not unlike her daughter. Those golden locks and that figure . . ." Mr. Wallace whistled again and then rolled his eyes. Ridge had to suppress a grin at the man's besotted expression. "Now I was married already, mind you, so don't be tellin' the missus, but there weren't a man in this here town that wasn't envious of Michael McLaughlin about his woman. Besides," he lowered his voice as if suddenly worried he would be found out. "it don't hurt none to look."

"No, sir," Ridge replied, and Mr. Wallace chuckled again before his face became serious once more.

"Wasn't more than a mere two weeks after the weddin' when that sour-faced Ms. Harrington showed up on the stage throwing dirty looks and insults at anyone who came near. Hired a wagon and driver, then rode straight out to Angus's ranch and insisted Charlotte leave poor Michael and come home with her." He slammed his fist on the desk for emphasis, and Ridge jumped. "Charlotte was a good girl, though, and wouldn't leave, even when that sister of hers threatened to disinherit her if she didn't return at once." He shook his head sadly. "Hard to think of poor Miss Georgie and her two brothers havin' to grow up in the same house as that woman. What could have possessed Charlotte to ever move back? I can only guess her grievin' led her to it."

Mr. Wallace was still shaking his head when Ridge stood up to leave.

"I suppose I best be getting' on." He reached over to shake the man's hand. "Thank ya for your time, John." He paused a moment and nodded his head toward the door. "And for the warnin'. I can assure you I don't plan on gettin' hooked on that line!"

Mr. Wallace stood up and grabbed Ridge by the hand, giving it a firm shake. Instead of releasing it right away, he leaned forward and spoke in a low voice. With his other hand, he pointed out the window just as Dawson was helping Georgiana down from the wagon in front of the mercantile.

"Just so you know, I'm still bettin' on you." He smiled and chuckled at the shocked look Ridge gave him. "And just a reminder, boy," he added, looking Ridge straight in the eyes, " 'cause I think you're in need of a little advice. Before you go runnin' off some place, tail between your legs, lickin' your wounds, you remember . . . all bets are still on 'til the preacher says 'man and wife.' "

Ridge was stunned for a moment, not knowing what to say. When Mr. Wallace released his hand and became all business-like again, Ridge opened the door to the office. He groaned inwardly as he saw Miss Jamison was still in the bank lobby chatting with the teller. As soon as he stepped out the door, she was at his side.

"I thought you'd never get done in there," she exclaimed ceremoniously. "I was about to give up and leave." Ridge wished she had. "But I'm glad I didn't because I really needed to talk with you, Ridge."

"Miss Jamison . . ."

"Cordelia, please. Must you be so formal, Ridge?"

"Miss Cordelia." She smiled up at him, obviously pleased. "I haven't finished my business here, if you wouldn't mind . . ."

"Oh, I don't mind waitin' at all, Ridge dear. You go ahead, and I'll just wait over there."

She pointed to a corner by the door, but as he walked to the teller to make his deposit, she didn't budge. He decided he would just have to ignore her.

"Good afternoon, Mrs. Johnson."

"Afternoon, Mr. Carson."

"Would you please just deposit this into my savings account?" He handed her the money he'd brought, along with his bankbook. When she was finished counting the money and making a notation in his book, she handed it back.

"There you are, Mr. Carson. Is there anything else I can help you with?"

"No, thank you, Mrs. Johnson. That's all I needed," he replied, tucking the bankbook into his inside coat pocket.

"Well, you have a good afternoon then." She smiled sweetly at him.

"Thank you, ma'am." He reached up and tipped his hat to the woman politely. "And you do the same. Good day."

"Good-bye, Mr. Carson." She smiled again, lifting her hand in a small wave.

Walking toward the doors, he tipped his hat to another woman who'd just entered the bank. "Ma'am," he greeted.

The woman smiled. "Good afternoon, Mr. Carson."

Ridge headed out the door, but not before Miss Jamison attached herself to his arm again. No chance he was going to have a good afternoon. Not at this rate anyway. He stepped out of the bank and into the bright sun, wishing zealously that the woman had an aversion to sunlight.

He was not that lucky. Not only had he not been able to rid himself of her, she had been so bold as to ask him to escort her to the social the next evening. He told her that after taking today off, he wasn't sure he wouldn't have to spend the day tomorrow catching up on his work. He would not feel good about accepting her invitation without knowing what his boss had in mind.

"But, Ridge, you must at least come," she pouted, running her fingers up and down his lapel. "I bet there isn't anyone else in this town that dances as well as you. Besides, you're the only one *I* want to dance with."

Ridge walked over to his horse, hoping she would release him.

"I'm afraid I can't make any promises," he insisted, hoping to deter her.

Just then she leaned in close to him, too close, and made a pretense of brushing something from his shoulder.

"There," she said and stood back up again. "I dare say you've been playin' in the hay today."

He hadn't stepped foot in the stables this morning. When he had gone out to fetch his horse and get it saddled, Tiny had come out with the work already done. Ridge smiled at the big man's thoughtfulness.

Miss Jamison beamed up at him, thinking his smile had been for her. He quickly let the smile drop. He surely had no desire to encourage the woman.

Suddenly she laughed, for no reason at all, and leaned closer to him again. This time when she took a step back, she stumbled as if she were going to fall. Instinctively, his hands shot out to steady her. He knew it had been a ploy to have him hold her when she'd coyly put her hands on his shoulders.

That was when he'd seen them.

Ridge picked up the last stone and threw it as hard as he could toward the water's surface, then he stood up and walked back toward Storm. After today, it would be a long time before he allowed Angus to give him another day off. It just wasn't worth the trouble.

·15·

Confessions

Georgiana watched Dawson from Samantha's bedroom window as he helped young Matthew Wallace get a kite into the air. A moderate breeze was blowing, and Dawson hadn't stepped more than two feet up the Wallace's walk before he was converged upon by Matthew, who pleaded for him to assist with the kite flying adventure before the wind died down. They were having a difficult time dodging the trees, and twice already Dawson had fallen onto his behind while running backward. She couldn't help but laugh when after each tumble, he spent an inordinate amount of time brushing himself off.

Dawson was out of his element here in Colorado. He never did like getting dirty, even for all his playing in the park with his younger brother. The problem was that his benevolence was forever getting him into situations that contradicted his need for cleanliness. She had spied him earlier looking woefully at his hands and nails. Even though he purchased some gloves, with all his help in the storm, they were probably in pretty poor condition.

Now she, on the other hand, even after five years of being pampered, didn't mind getting her hands dirty at all. She'd grown up playing in the mud, scaling trees, swimming in murky ponds, and fording streams after she and her friends had tired of fishing. Chuckling to herself, Georgiana tried to picture Dawson baiting a worm on a hook. Try as she might, she just couldn't fathom it. Even after countless kitchen rendezvous, Dawson was still squeamish about some things. It wasn't his fault, she admitted freely. He'd just grown up differently.

Turning somber, Georgiana admitted this new realization was more evidence against their sharing a future together. The truth was, Dawson loved New York, with its pristine houses and manicured lawns. Though he had a deep appreciation for all walks of life, he especially thrived in a crowded room and reveled in attending one glorious event after another. If she asked him, she knew Dawson would stay here in Colorado just to be with her, but the light would go out of him. He'd still be a wonderful man, but he'd never truly be happy.

Georgiana despised New York and almost everything about it. Being in a crowd was stifling, and the parties and dances seemed to be nothing more than excuses to flaunt one's title and wealth. Her aunt's house certainly hadn't helped her adjust to the change. Though even in Dawson's home, where she'd been embraced as part of the family, it never once compared to the innate comfort of her grandmother's parlor. There was also something about the open expanse of the land in Colorado that made her spirit feel free, not trapped as it had been for many years.

Georgiana chuckled when Dawson became wrapped up in the kite string he was trying to untangle from a tree branch. He scrunched his face, and Matthew fell to the ground laughing. Even with his ridiculous expression, he was still so charming. Amazingly, and much to his credit, he was even more appealing on the inside. Dawson was a more than worthy catch, to be sure.

As Mrs. Whitaker had insinuated, there were all sorts of women waiting back in New York, more than ready to pounce at the first given opportunity. *Maybe even his soul mate*, Georgiana thought despondently. Shamefully, she realized just how selfish she'd been in keeping him to herself all this time when she knew in her heart they could never marry.

"He's really going to be a good husband and father for some lucky girl someday."

The words were out of her mouth before she could take them back. Georgiana glanced over her shoulder to see if her friend had been paying attention. Instantly, Samantha set the big satin bow she was fiddling with down on the bed. She and Samantha had spent the last couple of hours tying bows to adorn the baskets of flowers, which were part of the social's decorations. Her bed was covered with them.

One look at Samantha's face, and she knew she wouldn't be going anywhere until she explained herself. Turning away from the window, she walked over to Samantha's bed, pushed a few of the bows aside, and sat down.

Tears sprang to her eyes, and before she could even open her mouth, they were trailing down her cheeks. Immediately her friend's arm encircled her shoulder consolingly.

"Oh, Samantha . . . I don't know what to do!"

"Why don't you start by first tellin' me what you meant? I thought *you* were going to marry Dawson." Samantha took hold of both her hands. "Georgie, you love him, don't you?"

"Of course I love him." Georgiana swallowed hard. For the first time, she was about to say aloud the doubts her heart had been harboring for so long. "What's not to love?" she added wistfully, not daring to look up into her friend's face as her tears continued to fall. "It's just that . . . that I've finally accepted what I've known for a long time. I love him more like a brother, a friend. How could I have been so . . . so selfish? I've . . ." Georgiana chewed on her lip for a moment, not wanting to continue. Finally she blurted out, "I've been so unfair to him!" Speaking the words out loud was so much harder than thinking them, and feelings of shame and guilt poured over her, causing a tumult of emotion that wracked her body with sobs. When after a while her sobbing subsided, she curled up on the bed and laid her head in Samantha's lap. Samantha stroked her hair soothingly, brushing it off her tear-streaked face.

"Oh, Georgie. I'm so sorry," Samantha spoke sympathetically. "You were just confused. You didn't know."

Samantha was wrong—Georgiana did know. Deep down, the

answer was there. She'd just been too afraid to look. Dawson had become her lifeline, and she hadn't known how to give him up.

Forcing herself up, Georgiana walked back to the window. Just as she did, Dawson looked up at her and waved. Taking a deep breath, she forced down another swelling of emotion and tentatively waved back.

"He's such a wonderful man . . . and a dear friend," she said, watching him resume his play. "How can I bear to hurt him?" Georgiana turned away from the window to look at her friend. "Many times I've contemplated marrying him anyway. I know I'll grow to love him more like a wife should love her husband with time." She turned to look at Dawson once more. "It could work," she added, trying to convince herself. She absentmindedly traced a heart with her finger on the glass. "He deserves better though." She looked down at the handsome man entangled once again in the kite strings. "He deserves a woman who swoons at his touch and whose heart begins to race whenever he is near. A woman who longs for the feel of his lips against hers and is eager to be held in the warmth of his arms . . . a woman who will feel the things Ridge makes me feel." Georgiana quickly stopped speaking. Once again her thoughts betrayed her openly. She looked over at Samantha and sighed.

* * *

Samantha looked into the eyes of her friend and struggled to hide the sudden desire to smile. She had suspected long before Dawson had shown up that Georgiana was still in love with Ridge. Ridge, she knew without a doubt, was still in love with Georgiana. Over the last five weeks since Georgiana had returned, she could see something in both of them come alive. She was actually quite surprised when Dawson arrived. She'd almost forgotten about him since she'd first peppered her friend with questions about her city beau.

Unexpectedly, Samantha felt a familiar pain clench her heart when it suddenly called upon her memories of Mitch. Talk about unfair! Here was Georgiana, faced with the dilemma of choosing between two worthy men who adored her, and she had none. A measure of jealously fought hard to find its well-deserved place in her heart, but she suppressed it. She wouldn't give in to it now. Her friend needed her. She would wait to feel sorry for herself until later, when the dark, lonely hours found her exhausted and spent from the tears that were her nightly ritual.

Samantha forced her thoughts toward more pleasant things. At last, Ridge and Georgiana would be together! She knew somehow, someday, everything would work out. She almost couldn't contain the joy in her heart for her two friends. Still, she kept her face neutral. Now was not the time. Georgiana was confused, afraid, and harboring a profound sense of guilt about the man outside her window who loved her. She opened her arms, and Georgiana immediately came forward again to be comforted.

As her friend cried softly in her arms, Samantha continued contemplating Georgiana and Ridge. After Georgiana had all but disappeared, she had remained friends with Ridge. At one time, she fantasized she might be falling in love with him herself. But that had been the summer she'd met Mitch Tyler. She had been drawn to Mitch immediately. That was when she knew she never really had any romantic feelings for Ridge. Mitch was everything she'd ever wanted.

Samantha felt another pain pass deep through her heart. If it hadn't been for her friendship with Ridge, she might have never made it through the last two years. For a long time she had held out hope that Mitch would ride up one day and take her in his arms. She wouldn't even care why he'd stayed away so long, if only he'd return. It had taken her over a year to finally admit what she had felt in her heart that first week, the week Mitch had left, was the *real* truth. Something had happened to him. Something cruel and unfair had ended his life, and she would never see him again.

Ridge had been with her that day when she had at long last taken off the ring Mitch had given her. Oh, how she had cried. They'd sat on her porch swing together for hours as he'd held her, tenderly caressing her hair, never saying a word, just offering comfort.

Samantha was startled from her thoughts when Georgiana pulled away from her and stood up, once again walking to the window.

"Oh, Sammy, how can I still love him after all these years? When he never wrote me back, I was so angry and hurt. I swore I'd never let him do that to me again." Fresh tears began to trickle down her cheeks. "He's been avoiding me since Dawson arrived. He won't even look at me." Georgiana swiped at the tears on her face. "Why is everything so mixed up? Dawson is in love with me, but I love Ridge, and now Ridge, I fear, may be in love with Cordelia Jamison."

"Cordelia?" Had Georgiana really just suggested Ridge might be in love with Cordelia Jamison? "No, Georgie, certainly you must be mistaken. Ridge would never fall for Cordelia! Why she . . ." All at once everything about Cordelia, especially her strange behavior, started to come together.

Samantha stood up and walked over to Georgiana. She looked down absentmindedly at the man below playing with her brother as she considered Cordelia's actions further.

It was strange that she abruptly moved back to town and the way she had so quickly latched onto her for some reason. Since Cordelia had arrived almost six weeks ago, Samantha could hardly find any respite from her endless questions. Questions about the bank and its investments, who she thought were the wealthiest families in town, and so on.

When she had somehow found out Ridge was considering buying his own land, she began asking questions about him. How much did she think it would cost to start your own cattle ranch, and were she and Ridge just friends?

At first Samantha thought she was just curious about how the town was doing since her father had been practically run out for mismanaging the town folks' money. Now she wasn't so sure.

Cordelia's questions concerning Ridge hadn't really set off any warning signals. Ridge was one of the handsomest men around these parts, and eligible too. All the young girls swooned over him and made regular plays for his attentions. But Samantha knew Ridge. He wasn't interested in any of them. He continued searching for the right woman, but she'd known he would likely never find what he was looking for. At least not until the day Georgiana returned.

Then, miraculously, Georgiana did return.

When that happened, Cordelia had, of course, begun a new line of questioning. How long had she and Samantha been friends? Did she think her friend would really stay very long? One afternoon, she seemed especially irritable, and her questions became even more personal. What did Ridge and Miss McLaughlin think of each other? And had there ever been a romance between them?

How had she known about Ridge and Georgiana? Samantha wondered. She surely would never have divulged such personal information, especially to Cordelia. Samantha would surely be glad after tomorrow night when the social was finally over and done with. Cordelia had definitely been more of a hindrance than a help.

Looking down, she noticed Dawson and her brother were winding up the string to the kite. Dawson would be expecting Georgie to come back down to be with him. Quickly, she turned to Georgiana and took both of her hands in her own.

"Georgie, listen to me." Her friend's eyes were swollen from crying. She needed to quickly help her friend repair some of the damage so she looked presentable. "I don't know what you saw or what makes you think Ridge has any feelings for Cordelia, but I can promise you that you needn't worry about that."

"But Sammy . . ." Georgiana shook her head sadly and kept her eyes to the ground.

"Look at me, Georgie." Samantha waited until Georgiana finally looked up. "I've known Ridge a long time. We stayed friends after you left. I know only one girl, or rather woman, who will ever be the one for Ridge."

"But I told you, he never bothered to write," Georgiana complained.

"Do you know that for sure?" Samantha questioned her. "I wrote to you, and you wrote to me. Where are those letters? Maybe he wrote you dozens of times. Until we find out what happened, we can't assume anything."

Georgiana still didn't look convinced. She'd have to worry about that later. "Now listen, Georgie, we'd better hurry. If you don't want to have to explain to Dawson why you look the way you do, we need to fix you up a bit."

Samantha quickly walked over and poured some water from a pitcher onto a washcloth. Directing Georgiana to sit at her vanity, she handed her the cool cloth.

"Now, hold that over your eyes while I straighten your hair. It won't take the redness and puffiness totally away, but it certainly will help." For a minute Samantha feared Georgie was about to start crying again, so she put her arms around her friend's shoulders and they both looked silently into the mirror for a moment. "Don't worry, Georgie. Everything will work itself out." *Even if I have to help it along*, she thought. She added out loud, "I promise."

As she stepped back and reached for the brush, Georgie grabbed her hand again for a moment.

"Thank you, Sammy. Thank you for being here for me."

"What are best friends for?" Samantha asked, smiling.

·16·

Lost and Found

"Grandad!"

Georgiana walked over to the edge of the corral on the south side of the barn. Her grandfather looked up from his examination of the new colt. Georgiana smiled. Two new colts had been born in the last several weeks, one just shortly after she had arrived, and now this other one barely a week ago. Both were fillies, a blue roan and a black. She knew her grandfather was pleased. She watched as he sauntered over to the fence to greet her. Though he wore a smile, she could tell by the faraway look in his eyes that he had been thinking of her grandmother again.

Nana McLaughlin had possessed a great love and skill for working with horses. In Ireland, her father had raised and trained champion bloodlines and Shannon had inherited his great talent. Though they hadn't made it their livelihood, her grandmother had continued breeding and training horses when she and Angus began the cattle ranch. Those she bred had good bloodlines too and were proven stock. They were well sought after in the area for many years. These two colts would be the last her grandmother had a hand in breeding.

Georgiana watched as her grandfather brushed a few loose strands of hair off his forehead. Even at his age, it was still thick, showing only a sprinkling of gray. Grandmother had always been the one to cut his hair, and it was long overdue for a trim. He'd either have to make a trip to the barber soon, or she'd have to try her hand at cutting it.

She imagined he'd been a considerably handsome man in his youth. Her father had been a younger version of this wonderful man, and surely her father's good looks bore testament to the truth of it. Even though Granddad was soon approaching his sixty-fifth birthday, he was more than a fine specimen in any woman's eyes. She wondered if he would ever take a fancy to one of the widows in town. She didn't doubt a few had already taken a fancy to him. The pleasant sound of Mrs. Swansen's voice came to mind.

It hadn't really been long enough, though, since he'd lost the love of his life, and she suspected it would be some time before he could look at another woman with any romantic notions. Georgiana was grateful she was with him now to offer whatever comfort she could.

She smiled as he finished ambling over to where she stood waiting.

* * *

Angus warmed at the sight of his granddaughter.

"Hello, Georgie girl. What brings ye out in the wee hours of the mornin'?"

"I went to bed too early last night, Grandad, so I woke up restless long before the roosters did. I thought it would be a nice change to take a walk before breakfast." Georgiana pulled her shawl a little tighter around her. "I didn't think about it being so cool out," she said, shivering slightly.

"It'll warm up soon enough. Take heart," Angus replied optimistically.

He knew a certain cowhand that could warm his granddaughter up well enough if she was willing. At that thought, a plan took root in his mind.

"Any of the men up yet?" she asked casually.

"Surely, ye haven't forgotten that mornin' . . ."

". . . comes early on a cattle ranch."

He chuckled softly as she finished his sentence. "I haven't forgotten," she assured him.

Angus reached down, picked a blade of sweet grass, and began chewin' on it thoughtfully. "Lookin' for anyone in particular?" he questioned her.

"Why would you think that?" she answered, eyeing him curiously.

"No reason. Just wonderin' what ye have on yar mind."

"What I have on my mind is taking a walk. What's on your mind, Grandad?" she replied, needling him for an answer. She suspected he was up to something. When he stared at her innocently, she changed the subject. "Incidentally, one of the men told me you weren't planning on coming to the social tonight." As he nodded, she added, "There's sure to be more than a few disappointed ladies if you don't make an appearance, at least."

"I'm feelin' a bit too old these days to be a dancin' and a socializin'. Besides, I never really liked them shindigs much. Only went to be pleasin' yar grandmother."

Georgiana was quiet for a moment, and he waited patiently. Suddenly she asked, "Where's Dawson about this morning? Is he up yet?"

Angus quickly hid his disappointment. He had hoped she'd been wondering about someone else altogether.

"To be sure," he replied. "Good lad, that fella. Been helpin' out 'round here as much as he is able. When he isn't with ye, that is." He was indeed a good sort. Would do right by his girl were he the lad she were to be choosing. "Headed out 'bout an hour ago with Tiny," he finally told her.

"Well," Georgiana said, looking at him purposefully. He was certain she was contemplating inquiring about Ridge's whereabouts, but she didn't ask. "I suppose I should be on my way or breakfast will be late," she finally announced, sounding somewhat unsure. Turning away from him, she walked in the direction of the meadow.

"Georgie," he quickly called after her. Grabbing the empty bucket he had just fed the horses oats in, Angus held it out to her and tried not to grin. "Why don't ye take a walk over by the crick this mornin'? Saw me some bushes of wild berries plum overloaded last week not too far down. I 'spect they ought to be about ripe by now. If the critters haven't got to them, that is. Would make an awfully tasty pie, come Sunday," he added, looking hopeful.

She smiled at him endearingly and took the bucket from his hand. He quickly suppressed the sudden guilt he felt as she kissed him on the cheek and headed toward the creek whistling merrily. It had not been much more than a half hour ago he had talked Ridge into heading over to the creek to catch him a few trout, since he'd been assigned lunch duty again.

Georgiana had offered to spend the day helping the Wallaces get everything finished up for the social tonight. If he was going to have to cook lunch, he was going to fill his hankering for grilled trout. Leastways, it was something he knew how to cook. After watching his granddaughter until she turned from his view, he walked back over to the new colt.

"Oh, Shannon, she is a beaut, ain't she? Just look at her." Glancing briefly back down the lane, he snickered for a moment. "Now ye can't blame me for meddlin'. Those two lovesick pups need a little nudge. That there Dawson's a good lad, but I've felt a long time Georgie and Ridge were belongin' to each other. 'Tis a match made in heaven, just like ye and I were." Suddenly he sighed, deep and long. "'Tis missin' you I am, Shannon, me dear. Havin' our bonnie girl home this last little while has surely been easin' my pain a bit, but the nights are so long without ye in me arms."

Giving the colt one last pat, he watched her trot to her mother. He headed back toward the house, pondering further on his granddaughter. When Jonas came back down from town yesterday, he'd handed him a post from Ms. Cecelia Harrington herself. She had demanded to know when he would be sending her niece back home. When he'd written Charlotte asking her to send Georgiana until he could find some permanent help, he hadn't held out much hope. To his everlasting surprise, he'd received a return post from Charlotte saying she would send Georgiana as soon as he sent the funds for the trip, since her aunt had refused to pay for it. He had mailed it that day. He was supposed to be trying to find a permanent cook and housekeeper, but none of that mattered anymore. Angus smiled secretly to himself, remembering the telegram he'd received over a week ago. *At last,* he thought.

His mind quickly returned to Charlotte's sister, and his smile fell away. Cecelia Harrington had never forgiven Charlotte for running off and marrying his son. *The poor son of an Irish immigrant,* she would call him in her letters. It was true he was an immigrant. He and Shannon had come to America when Michael was but fourteen years old. They had all traveled across the ocean together, his young family, father, mother, and brother Brody with his young wife. When they arrived, the war between the North and South over slavery had just ended. They saw much destruction as they worked their way across the states. When they reached Colorado, Angus's mother said it was as green and lovely as the rolling hills of Ireland, so Angus's father purchased enough land to run cattle on. Angus, his father, and his brother had worked hard to build it up and make it into a successful working ranch, and they'd made themselves a pretty decent living.

After their parents passed on, Brody decided to head farther west to California. On their way, the wagon train had been attacked, and his wife and two young daughters had been killed. Brokenhearted, Brody had gone back to Ireland.

Angus was the only one left here in America, except Charlotte and his grandchildren, and up until now, Cecelia had managed to take them away.

Well, Angus had half a mind to write her back, give her an earful—a written one anyway. He had a few hard questions for the woman. From what he could tell, she had been less than honest with both his daughter-in-law and his granddaughter. Angus stopped to calm his raging emotions before opening the door to the house. He would bide his time a little longer and see what would become of this new development. Maybe when all was said and done, he'd finally be able to forget Ms. Cecelia Harrington for good.

* * *

It didn't take Georgiana long to find the wild berry bushes her grandfather had spoken of. The bushes had indeed been filled with big ripe berries, more than she could fit in her bucket. She would have to return on Monday and pick the last of them. She would make them into some jam her grandfather and the men could enjoy during the winter months.

Popping a plump berry in her mouth, she walked over to the creek, took off her shoes, and sat down on a large stone that overhung the water's edge. Easing her feet slowly into the water, she sighed contentedly as the water rushed over her bare skin. The temperature had been dropping steadily as fall set in, so the water was cool, but it felt especially good on her wound. She pulled her hurt foot out and examined her cut. It was healing nicely, though it was still painful to walk on. She figured she wouldn't be able to do much dancing tonight. Dawson was sure to be disappointed.

The thought of Dawson made her think back to her discussion with Samantha the day before. It had certainly given her some things to consider concerning both Dawson and Ridge.

When she had come down from Samantha's room to meet back up with Dawson, she tried not to look at him directly. She didn't want him to notice the redness of her eyes and the splotchy tone of her face. He had noticed anyway, but when he questioned her about it, she had brushed him off by mumbling something about missing her mother and two little brothers.

After supper, she had gone straight to bed. She was exhausted, more emotionally than physically, and was certain she would not sleep well, for the troubled thoughts that plagued her. Surprisingly, she had fallen asleep quickly and slept soundly.

Georgiana put her foot back in the creek. Reaching up, she unpinned her hair and began running her fingers through it absent-mindedly as she watched a cluster of colorful leaves that had fallen in the water float downstream. If only she had time to get her easel and paint the scene. She would have to remember this spot for later.

The water was so clear she could see the fish swimming around on the bottom. When a rather large trout got spooked and swam off, something shiny wedged between a couple of rocks caught her eye. She pulled her feet out of the water and crouched on the edge of the stone to get a closer look. The water made the stone rather slippery, so she braced her hands tightly onto an edge that was not wet.

It almost looked like . . . a chain of some sort. *It couldn't be, could it?* she thought incredulously. She had lost it so long ago. Quickly standing up, she looked about her for a stick to help her fish it out. Finding one she thought would do, she crouched down on the stone again. Her foot slipped slightly, but thankfully she caught herself.

Reaching down with the stick, she carefully poked at the shiny thing until she managed to get the end wrapped around the stick a little. Holding her breath, she slowly began to lift it from the water. Just before it broke the water's surface, it unfortunately slipped back off the stick and fell to the bottom again.

"Blast!" The word was out of her mouth before she could think. She didn't make a habit of swearing, and even though she was alone, she couldn't help but look around self-consciously to see if she'd been heard.

Working the stick again, she managed once more to wind the chain around its end. This time, when she lifted it toward the surface, she reached out with her other hand ready to snatch it should it begin to fall.

"Steady," she coached herself. "Just a little farther . . . almost." It was starting to unwind itself. Quickly she tried to bring the stick toward her outstretched hand before it fell. She almost had it when suddenly her foot began to slip. She tried to stand up to right herself, but that only put her further off balance, so she crouched back down, attempting to grab hold of the edge of the stone.

It all happened so quickly.

Just as she thought she had secured herself, her foot slipped back once more, propelling her head first into the creek. Her face met the cool water, shocking the breath out of her. Next, her legs and feet flew over and down, resulting in a none too graceful somersault. As her backside hit the creek bottom, her head popped back out of the water, just above the surface.

Her long hair now hung tangled and wet in front of her face, so she was startled when she heard something come splashing toward her. Next thing she knew, someone had grabbed her by the arms and lifted her up to stand on wobbly legs.

Still coughing and sputtering, she brushed her hair back from her face and looked up to see Ridge standing before her in the water. He was soaked almost to the waist with a concerned look on his face.

Immediately upset that once again she had humiliated herself in front of him, she roughly shrugged her arms out of his firm grasp.

"What are you doing here?" she asked him angrily.

Quickly his face went from concerned to one she was sure could rival her own.

"Confound it, girl! What were you thinkin'? You've succeeded in scarin' away any trout I planned on catchin', that's for sure!"

* * *

Ridge looked at Georgiana standing in front of him. She was soaked through from head to toe. A moment ago he had been concerned, but when her temper flared, he had become instantly angry too.

Would he ever be free from this woman? He had vowed he would steer clear of her until she went back to New York with Dawson, which he was fairly certain would be soon. But even though he managed to avoid being near her most of the time, he couldn't seem to banish her from his thoughts. She'd plagued his dreams all night. Now here she was again, making him think about her some more. He was tired and in a foul mood.

When Angus had asked him if he wouldn't mind seeing if he could catch a few trout for lunch today, he'd jumped at the chance to get away. He planned on staying away until after breakfast. Didn't figure he'd have much of an appetite anyway, watching her and Dawson make eyes at each other.

Ridge was taken aback and a little annoyed when he saw her wander over to the creek carrying a bucket of berries. He'd walked by the very bush he was sure she had picked from, before heading up the creek a bit to cross the bridge. He always seemed to have better luck fishing on the far side. He had just relaxed under the shade of his favorite tree with his pole, waiting on his first catch.

So he'd watched her silently, knowing she couldn't see him from where she was—until she'd tumbled into the water, that is. He would have laughed out loud if his concern for her hadn't been greater.

Knowing there were often sharp rocks embedded in the creek bottom, he'd jumped to his feet and plunged directly into the water, shoes and all, and crossed to the other side to help her.

Now as he looked at her, all danger gone, dripping water and hair hanging in her reddened face while she glared at him with those gray and violet eyes, he couldn't help himself. Throwing his head back, he laughed, loud and hard.

"What are you laughing at?" She narrowed her eyes at him even more.

"If you could see yourself, you wouldn't be asking me that," he countered. Even drenched and angry, she was beautiful.

Sharply turning from him, she waded over to the creek's edge, nearly slipping again on the rocks and falling back down. He followed closely behind.

Grabbing onto the branch of a tree that hung over the water, she began pulling herself out onto the bank. But the bank sat high, and the water was low. When she nearly fell a third time, he reached out to steady her.

"What are you doing?" she snarled.

"I'm *trying* to help ya. Ain't that obvious?" Ridge snapped back.

"I most certainly do not need your help, Mr. Carson, so if you don't mind, I would appreciate it if you would go back to wherever it was you came from."

"Just doin' my job, Miss McLaughlin. Your grandfather wouldn't be too pleased with me if I let ya injure that foot of yours again."

She let go of the branch and turned back to look at him, placing her hands firmly on her hips.

"I am most certainly not part of your job description, Mr. Carson, despite what you think my grandfather would want.

Now, if you won't go away, at least turn around. This is difficult enough as it is, let alone trying to preserve my modesty."

Ridge turned away from her as she had asked, but he couldn't hold back the chuckle that escaped or his retort. "I'm afraid your modesty has already been compromised after that near flip you did into the water." He didn't turn to look at her, but he could imagine the expression she wore.

She didn't answer back, but he could hear she was still struggling to get out.

"What are you doin' out at the crick this early anyway?" he asked curiously.

"It's my business where I am and at what time." He heard her feet splash back down in the water. "But if you must know, my grandfather suggested I come and pick some wild berries before the critters got to them."

Ridge shook his head knowingly. He had suspected for a while what old Angus was up to.

"What are *you* doing here?" He turned around after she asked because he could tell by the sound, or lack of it, that she had given up.

"Your grandfather asked me to catch a few trout for lunch," he answered, and she raised an eyebrow at him.

"Well, if he would have told me that, I . . . I wouldn't have come and dis-disturbed your p-precious fishing spot," she exclaimed, giving him an annoyed look, despite the fact she was becoming obviously chilled.

"I think that's exactly what he had in mind," Ridge mumbled to himself softly.

"Ex-excuse m-m-me?" Georgiana asked, narrowing her eyes.

"I said ya might as well let me give ya a lift from behind before we both catch a chill." She looked at him doubtfully, but by this point she had begun to shiver quite uncontrollably.

"I'm . . . I'm afraid I'm going to have to . . . to accept your help," she began, trying terribly to keep her voice from trembling, "I . . . I fear I have been living in . . . in the city to-too long. I'm not as nimble as I used to be." Georgiana narrowed her eyes and looked at him sternly. "But pray, you . . . you watch where you place your hands, Mr. Carson. We . . . we may b-b-be alone out here, but I'm sh-sure if I *am* part of your job description, my gr-grandfather would want you to preserve what's left of m-m-my modesty at . . . at all costs. Especially, since y-you have just informed me that it has b-b-been compromised already."

Ridge was finding it almost too difficult not to laugh again at the indignant look she wore, especially since she couldn't keep from stuttering her words. Pushing aside his worry, he playfully took a step forward and bowed graciously before her.

"Ya have my sincere promise, Miss McLaughlin, that I will truly endeavor to be ever the utmost gentleman as I help rescue you from this crick." He chuckled softly and stood to meet her eyes. For a moment he thought he caught a brief look of amusement, but she turned from him quickly and once again grabbed hold of the branch.

Ridge waded over behind her and placed his hands on her waist, hoisting her up until she was able to secure her feet on the creek's edge. She was then able to pull herself the rest of the way up.

Ridge was surprised when she turned, leaned toward him, and extended her hand as if to give him aid. Her other arm she wrapped securely around the trunk of a tree. He had no choice but to take her hand if he didn't want to offend her again. So, grabbing the same tree branch with one hand and her hand with the other, he began pulling himself out of the water.

When he was almost out, Georgiana's face abruptly changed from soft and serene to one of mischief, and he knew immediately he was in trouble. Before he could even register his disbelief, she took her uninjured foot and wedged it against his chest. Then letting go of his hand, she shoved him back into the water.

When he had run across the creek to rescue her, he had only become wet from the waist down. Now as he unexpectedly fell back into the water, his whole body was submerged. Quickly, he sat up and stared at the satisfied, smug look she wore. He glared back.

"Now, don't you . . . you look at me like that, Mr. Ridge Carson. You de-deserved that and you . . . you know it." The corners of her mouth curled up slightly. "You have had your laughs at me more than once today already, and it's m-m-my turn to laugh."

With that, she turned and walked away, stopping only to gather her shoes and her bucket of berries. As she headed up the lane back home, he heard her begin to whistle, interrupted only by a stutter and a giggle now and then.

As he listened to her a moment, he smiled at the sound of her laughter. The sound brought with it a healthy sampling of memories waiting to be indulged in. Regretfully, he pushed them away. Just then a thought occurred to him. *What was she tryin' to get out of the crick?*

Looking around him, it didn't take him long to spot the chain in the water. He instantly knew what it was and why she was so earnestly trying to fish it out.

Standing himself up, he reached down and grasped it. He took a moment to examine it. Its condition showed it had been in the water a long time. Slipping it into his pocket, he waded back to the other side to gather his pole and head back to the house. Angus was sure to be disappointed, but there wouldn't be any fish caught in the creek this morning, the gal had seen to that. 'Course it served Angus right, meddling like he was.

Thinking back to the mischievous look that had spread across her face, Ridge couldn't help but grin. His Georgie still had a little spunk, just like the old days, though soon, he reminded himself, she wouldn't be "his Georgie" ever again.

❦ ❦ ❦

Georgiana couldn't keep the smile from drifting back every time she pictured the look on Ridge's face as she'd pushed him back into the water. She really hadn't planned on doing it when she'd first extended her hand to help him out. What had possessed her, she didn't know, but she had to admit it felt good to, for once, have the upper hand.

Ever since she'd returned to Crystal Creek, she had been subjected to one humiliating situation after another. Her pride was suffering greatly. Now, thinking of her appearance as she approached the house, she girded herself up for another knock to her ego.

Grandfather and Roddy were out on the side of the house inspecting the fire pit. Jonas and Jeremiah weren't far away, cleaning up by the water barrel. Tiny and Dawson sat on the porch stairs intently discussing something. Dawson had a stick and was working the dirt and mud from off his new boots. Jimmy had finally returned from helping his brother, but he was nowhere to be seen. Maybe he'd ridden into town.

The men were probably hungry by now, but she suppressed the feelings of guilt. She hadn't meant to be so long, and she certainly hadn't planned on falling into the creek.

Grandfather noticed her first and walked forward. She knew she looked a fright, barefoot, soaked, and still dripping water. She must have unconsciously given him a "Don't say a word" look because he cringed noticeably. His interference had backfired, and he knew it.

Next, Jonas and Jeremiah turned toward the house, then stopped and stared.

"Good mornin'," Jonas suddenly piped out.

"Miss Georgiana," Jeremiah added quickly.

She nodded her head as she passed by. "Jonas . . . Jeremiah . . . I trust you're both having a good morning?"

"Yes, ma'am," they both said in unison.

As she walked to the bottom of the porch stairs, Tiny stood up and removed his hat.

"Mornin', Miss McLaughlin," he said, stepping aside to allow her access to the stairs.

"Good morning, Tiny."

Dawson jumped up too but didn't say anything, only stared with his mouth gaping open, forgetting to brush himself off as he stood.

"Good morning, Dawson." She smiled at him, climbed the stairs, and went in the house door, straight to her room.

They were still gaping after Georgiana when Ridge came walking up the road. Jonas saw him first.

"Ridge, what have you done to Miss McLaughlin this time? If I miss breakfast because of you, I'll—"

Ridge headed straight for Angus.

"You're placin' blame with the wrong man this time, Jonas."

He stopped in front of Angus and handed him the fishing bucket. Angus took the bucket excitedly and looked sorrowfully down at the empty bottom.

"Fish weren't bitin' today, lad?" he asked innocently.

"Yep, they weren't bitin'." Ridge fairly glared at him. "I figure ya just must've sent me the wrong kind of bait."

The man immediately wore a look of chagrin, and Ridge knew Angus realized he'd been found out.

"Now, Angus . . ." Ridge took a deep breath in an effort to hold back his anger for he respected this man immensely. "I know she's your granddaughter and all, but that doesn't give you the right to—"

Before he could finish, Angus glanced over at Dawson. Ridge followed his gaze. Dawson was watching them, listening intently. Ridge felt sorry for the man. It wasn't his fault Angus had gotten the fool's notion that he and Georgie were meant to be together. The man was in love with her, probably near as much as he was. Why else would he have come so far to bring her back?

Ridge sighed, and Angus suddenly looked encouraged that he had escaped a severe tongue-lashing. Though Ridge would never have disrespected him in front of the others, he wasn't letting him off the hook that easy. Georgiana had a right to make her own choices, and he certainly didn't want to win her by default.

"You and I will talk later," he said to Angus, giving him a look that said he meant it. "For now, I'm needin' to get out of these here wet clothes." As he walked to the bunkhouse, he felt at least one set of eyes boring into his back.

·17·
Secrets to Ponder

SAMANTHA came running out to the wagon even before Georgiana had time to set the brake and climb down. She was tired of having to rely on the men to drive her around, so after breakfast she insisted Dawson show her how to drive the team herself. It had been rough at first when she'd started out on her own, but her determination had overridden her feelings of nervousness, and soon she was able to get the team under control.

"I'm so glad you're here," Samantha said, out of breath from her mad dash. "We still have so much to do. I just know we'll run out of time. Oh, why did I have to go and volunteer to head up this year's committee?"

Georgiana leaned over and gave her friend a reassuring hug.

"You're doing a fine job, Sammy, and I'm sure this year's fall social will be the best one ever, all because of you."

Samantha finally cracked a smile.

"Oh, I hope you're right, Georgie." Her face lit up, and Samantha took Georgiana's hand, dragging her toward town. "You've got to come and see the decorations so far. They are absolutely wonderful, and I know you'll love them. Ridge and Tiny volunteered to help and spent all morning, since after breakfast, hanging streamers and . . ." Georgiana stopped and pulled her hand from Samantha's grasp when she'd heard Ridge's name mentioned. He was the last person she wanted to see right now. She'd done a lot of thinking on the wagon ride over and had decided that after this morning's incident, she was foolish to think things would ever work out between her and Ridge. Every time they were together, she found herself getting so frustrated and angry about the simplest things. Maybe if she finally let go of Ridge, her feelings would change toward Dawson.

Samantha had grabbed her hand again and was once more coaxing her toward the town social hall, which was really an old abandoned warehouse.

"Wait, Samantha, I don't want to . . ."

"Georgie, please . . . don't be such a stick in the mud. It's not like Ridge is going to bite you or anything. Besides, he's not even there right now."

Georgiana relaxed and allowed her friend to continue dragging her along. While she did, her thoughts turned to Dawson once again.

He'd hardly said two words at breakfast, and when Georgiana had coaxed him into teaching her to drive the team, he had seemed so distant.

On the wagon ride over, she'd spent the whole time contemplating their relationship. She decided she wouldn't be hasty in giving up on Dawson, despite everything she had confessed to Samantha. She truly cared for him. Wouldn't it be better if she made sure of her feelings before she broke his heart? Georgiana pushed the nagging feeling aside that the answer to that question had already been given to her.

"Georgie!"

Samantha was talking to her. Startled, she looked around. They were standing at the door to the social hall. Georgiana looked at her friend's beaming face.

"I asked if you're ready."

Georgiana nodded her head yes.

"Okay, but first you have to close your eyes."

"Sammy . . ."

"Oh, come on, Georgie . . . I want it to be a surprise," Samantha pleaded.

Georgiana still wasn't sure about all this, but she couldn't bring herself to disappoint her friend.

"All right," she conceded, "but I'm warning you, Sammy, if this is any kind of trick to get me and Ridge—"

"No, no, I promise . . . I told you, Ridge isn't even here right now. He told me earlier he needed to run some errands and he'd be back later this afternoon."

Georgie could tell her friend was sincere. So she closed her eyes and allowed Samantha to lead her into the center of the hall.

"Okay, now open your eyes."

Georgiana opened her eyes and could hardly believe what she saw. They were standing in the middle of the dance floor. Streamers, made from colorful strips of fabric, were strung back and forth to create a false ceiling. Randomly, bright-colored balls hung at different lengths intermittently and more streamers hung down the walls. On tables waiting to be loaded with every imaginable treat, were brightly colored cloths. In the center of each table was a big basket filled with the last of the summer flowers and adorned with bows. Every corner or wall in the room was decorated. The transformation was astounding. Ridge and Tiny had certainly got a lot accomplished in a short amount of time.

Georgiana turned and looked adoringly at her friend.

"Well?" Samantha asked.

"Sammy, it's absolutely wonderful!" Georgiana exclaimed, and Samantha beamed again.

Grabbing each other's hands, both girls shrieked excitedly.

* * *

Ridge was up in the loft when he heard some commotion below. He had to come back to fetch his toolbox he'd forgotten so he could make repairs to the widow Swansen's roof. Leaning the ladder on the outside wall, he had climbed in through the open window. If he dragged the ladder back inside, he'd risk knocking down the decorations he and Tiny had hung that morning. Worried someone needed help, he looked over the railing to the dance floor below.

Samantha and Georgiana were standing in the middle of the room, hand in hand, while Georgiana gazed about her in amazement. He felt a slight twinge of jealousy of how the two women had quickly reignited their friendship, but quickly pushed it aside. Of course, he couldn't expect it to be the same between Georgie and him.

Assured nothing was wrong, he turned to leave but nearly jumped out of his skin when both girls squealed loudly again. Setting his toolbox back down, he leaned over the loft to make sure none of his carefully hung decorations had come crashing down on them.

Samantha and Georgiana were now waltzing around the room. Feeling foolish for worrying, he watched them for a moment. He should have realized it was a woman thing. They were always squealing and making funny noises when they were excited. The problem was they made the same sort of noises when they were in trouble. They sure knew how to keep a man on pins and needles sometimes, trying to figure out if they were happy or needed to be rescued.

After a few minutes, both women tumbled to the ground in the middle of the dance floor, giggling and laughing as women do.

Then they both became suddenly quiet.

Ridge had a sense the conversation was about to turn intimate, and his conscience told him to leave, but curiosity got the better of him. He turned and sat down, leaning his back against the short railing of the loft. He was well hidden from sight by all the hanging decorations.

Samantha spoke first.

"Oh, Georgie, I'm so glad you came back. These last weeks have been so much fun, almost like you never left." Samantha paused for a moment, then asked. "How much longer do you think you'll be able to stay?"

Ridge held his breath as he waited for her to answer.

"I really don't know for sure. It depends on a lot of things, I suppose."

On how long it takes Dawson to convince her to return with him,

Ridge thought sarcastically but quickly turned his attention back to the women when Georgiana started speaking again.

"Grandfather got a letter from Aunt Cecelia. When I came back from my walk this morning, I saw it sitting on the edge of the table. I asked him what it was about, but he told me not to worry. It had made him angry though, I could tell right away. Nothing good comes from Aunt Cecelia."

"I'm sorry you were forced to live with such an awful woman."

"Well, for three years I didn't have to live there. I can be thankful for that. You would have loved the Harriet Wilmington's School for Proper Young Ladies." She pronounced the name in the tone he imagined Ms. Wilmington did herself, and it made Samantha laugh.

Again he felt a twinge of jealousy. They were so comfortable with each other.

Ridge called to mind the few days before they'd left for the mountain. When she began confiding in him some of her feelings, he'd felt a closeness returning. Then all those letters arrived, and he remembered that she had a life without him hundreds of miles away. He began to doubt himself and the solidarity of their returning friendship. He knew things would never really be the same. However, it hadn't done him any good to try avoiding her. The more he forced his thoughts away, the more powerful his thoughts of her became.

Ridge heard the two women giggle, and he sorely wondered what he'd missed when his thoughts had run off.

"Remember the spring social when we were nine and we talked your parents into letting you spend the night over at my house?" Georgiana asked. "They never did let us stay at the socials very late. It was always so awfully unfair."

"Yes, they'd send us home to bed and then stay and have all the fun," Samantha bemoaned.

"It was a good thing they'd decided on old Mrs. Wickers to babysit us that night. I never knew a woman as senile as she was." Georgiana laughed.

"How old was she then anyway?"

"I don't know. I was amazed to hear she's still around, but even back then she was so . . ."

"Old!" they both said it in unison and laughed.

"We told her we were going to bed, and we promptly climbed out my bedroom window and snuck into the back of the wagon under a blanket."

"That's right," Samantha exclaimed. "Your grandpa had gone to check on that old pregnant mare for your grandmother before he headed back to town." Samantha added, "Were you as scared as I was?"

"Probably more than you!"

"Nah, you were always the brave one, Georgie."

"No, I was just better at pretending."

Neither one of them said anything for a while. Finally, Georgiana spoke again. "It was worth it though, wasn't it?"

"Yeah, it was worth it . . . all except the part of seein' Agnes Fitzgerald kiss Harvey Hancock under the kissin' tree."

"Eeew!" They both spoke in unison again, and they both laughed, harder this time.

"You know, we only thought it was disgusting because we were nine." Samantha pointed out. "It wasn't too many years later you kissed Ridge under that same tree."

"You dared me!"

"You never took dares, Georgie. You only took that one because you wanted to kiss him," Samantha accused.

Both women were silent for a moment, but when Georgiana spoke again, her voice was almost a whisper.

"That was a long time ago." Georgiana said thoughtfully.

"Yeah, I suppose it was . . . but . . . but was it worth it?" Samantha asked.

There was silence again, and Ridge wondered if she would answer. Did Samantha know that wasn't the only kiss they had ever shared?

"Oh, Sammy, it doesn't matter anymore anyway. Call it fate . . . call it destiny . . . but that very day, I unknowingly walked out of his life for good."

Ridge sighed deeply at her admission.

"Don't say that, Georgie . . . I know you still love him."

Ridge's heart began to beat faster as he awaited her reply. This was the moment he was hoping for.

"It doesn't matter," Georgiana finally blurted out.

Ridge sighed, his disappointment sinking deep.

"Of course it matters," Samantha argued. "Why ever would you say it doesn't?"

"Because I've already made my decision, Sammy."

"And?"

"And what?"

"Have you decided to follow your heart or follow your head?"

"I've decided to do what hurts the least, for everyone involved."

"Everyone but you?" Samantha accused.

"Listen, Sammy, I really don't want to discuss this right now." He heard her sigh of frustration. "Look, we really should get back. We have lots to do, remember?"

"But, Georgie . . ."

"Come on, Sammy . . . let's go," Georgiana said firmly.

A second later, he heard the doors open and close.

Ridge didn't move for a while, just sat contemplating everything they had talked about and what it all really meant. He had to admit it didn't sound very encouraging.

Before he could think any more about it, another thought suddenly turned up the corners of his mouth.

She really had wanted to steal that kiss.

·18·
Shall We Dance?

Dawson sat with Samantha on her front porch, waiting for Georgiana. She had known she'd be helping Samantha for most of the afternoon and had asked him to pick her up here for the social. He had arrived a little bit early, so he couldn't fault Georgiana for making him wait. Besides, Samantha had come out to keep him company while he waited.

He glanced over at her for a moment.

She was pretty. Her hair wasn't quite as blonde as Georgiana's, but it boasted the softest hint of red, which gave it highlights and complemented the ivory color of her skin. Her eyes were a deep emerald green and matched her dress perfectly. He had always been partial to the color green.

Looking at her more intently, he thought, *She isn't as stunningly beautiful as Georgiana, but nevertheless, I have to admit she is quite comely.* In fact, if he weren't already in love, he had a feeling this woman could easily steal his heart.

Samantha looked over at him and smiled. By the way her cheeks turned red, he realized she had been mindful of his staring. He smiled back and quickly turned away.

"So are you enjoyin' your stay?" she asked all of a sudden.

"You have a lovely little town. I find it quite refreshing," he answered honestly.

"I'd have to agree with you because I am quite partial to it myself.

I wouldn't mind seein' a big city one day, though. I don't think I've ever been farther from this town than right there." She pointed to the large outcropping of mountains not too far in the distance. "Is it exciting living in New York? I've always dreamt of going to the theater."

"Well, if you're ever out my way, I promise I'll see that you get there."

She smiled again, and he was genuinely glad to see it.

Georgiana had confided in him what her friend had gone through. He could only imagine what she had suffered.

"Maybe I should go and see if I can help Georgie with anything," Samantha offered.

"No, I don't mind waiting. I was early, after all," he reassured her.

"Yes, I suppose you were . . . and we unfortunately finished up late," she said, slightly embarrassed.

Standing up, he looked down at her.

"Why don't you show me around your home? I thought I saw a pond out back when your little brother and I were trying to fly that kite."

"All right." She stood up, and he offered her his arm. "I'm afraid it's not much of a pond, though," she said, taking his arm and giving him an amused look as they began walking. "Father had it put in. It wasn't here when the house was built."

"Is it for decoration then?" he asked. "My mother had one put in last summer."

"Not quite." She laughed softly before continuing. It was a pleasant sound, Dawson noted. "When Father gave up farming and bought the bank, we moved to town. He told Mother the only thing he missed was 'ye olde fishin' pond,' as he called it," she said with an animated tone. "Banking takes almost as much time as farmin', except of course, he has Sundays off."

"Of course!" he repeated. "That's the best part of the job!"

She smiled at his playful banter and then went on.

"Sadly, mother won't let him fish on Sundays because there's church and family time, and Mother usually entertains guests. So, with no hope of ever making it out to visit 'ye olde fishin' pond' . . ." She stopped as they came around to the back of the house, "he decided to bring the pond here."

Dawson looked over to where she was pointing and smiled.

Indeed, there it sat, complete with rocks, an overhanging tree, and an old wooden bench seat, in the middle of their pristinely manicured backyard.

"Mother was horrified at first, but I think it's finally grown on her."

"So does your father actually fish in it?" Dawson asked, genuinely interested and somewhat amused.

"Most certainly, but not as often as he would like. He keeps it well stocked with trout though, just in case he finds the time. Mother says she's going to order a pair of swans, to make it look more . . . um . . . elegant?" This time when she laughed, her smile finally lit up her eyes.

For a moment, Dawson was taken aback as his heart skipped a beat. Abruptly he let go of her arm.

"We probably should go check on Georgiana," he said quickly.

"Yes," Samantha answered, appearing a bit flustered herself. "She might be concerned where we've wandered off to."

When they came around to the front of the house, Georgiana was sitting on the porch swing. Dawson hurried up the steps to her.

"There you are. I'd wondered where you two had gone," she said, smiling.

Dawson looked at her appraisingly. She was a vision in her blue gown. When she stood, he offered her his arm. Turning, he offered his other arm to Samantha.

"Well, ladies, shall we go?" He smiled at each of them. "I think I just may be the luckiest man alive tonight, and I *know* I will be the most envied when I walk into the dance with you two angels on my arms." Both women laughed as they descended the porch steps and began strolling toward the social hall.

In no time at all, they had arrived.

❦ ❦ ❦

Ridge watched intently as Dawson entered the room with both Georgiana and Samantha. He had been leaning against the far wall for ten minutes now, not so patiently awaiting their arrival.

Georgiana was wearing a blue dress, his favorite color. He loved her in blue. He remembered well the blue calico dress she often wore when they were young, the one he had bought the blue ribbons to match. This blue dress could easily become one of his favorites too. The neckline was modest, though flattering, resting just wide enough to show off a hint of her soft, creamy shoulders. The rest of it complemented her figure almost too well. It made him wish he was the man standing next to her right now.

Gazing at her reminded him once again how long she'd been away. Gone were the ponytails and ribbons. They had been replaced by . . . Ridge suddenly smiled broadly. Upon closer examination, he realized she was wearing tiny blue ribbons scattered in her hair amid her mass of cascading locks. She looked beautiful!

The dance was already in full swing, and the band was playing a lively tune. Immediately, Dawson turned to Georgiana and appeared to ask her for a dance. Ridge watched as she shook her head and pointed over to a bench. He walked her over and helped her to sit. She'd been on her foot all day, he guessed, and the deep cut, still so new, had probably started giving her pains.

She gestured for him to come closer, and as Dawson leaned in, Ridge thought she was going to kiss him. Instead, she turned her head slightly to the side and whispered something into his ear.

Dawson stood back up and looked to where he'd left Samantha at the door. Georgiana nodded her head encouragingly, and he turned and walked back to Samantha.

When Dawson leaned forward to whisper into Samantha's ear, she smiled and followed him to the dance floor.

Ridge turned back to watch Georgiana just as she reached up and began playing with the chain that hung about her neck. He hadn't noticed her wearing it when she'd come in. It must have been tucked in the bodice of her gown.

He smiled to himself, happy that she'd found where he had put it.

When he had pulled it from the creek, he had recognized it immediately. It was the gold chain her father had given her for her tenth birthday. It had come all the way over from their family in Ireland. Her great-grandfather had given it to her father when he had turned ten. A medallion hung from it, engraved with the McLaughlin family crest.

He hadn't even realized she'd lost it. It must have fallen from around her neck that morning when they had been playing down in the water, the day before she had moved away.

He was amazed it had been lying at the bottom of the creek these last five years and he'd never seen it, probably because he always fished on the other side. He was further surprised it had never washed downstream. It must have somehow become lodged under a rock that had secured it where it had fallen all this time.

After lunch, he had taken it to the jeweler, Mr. Hobbs. He was able to polish it up somewhat and fix the latch while Ridge waited.

When he had returned to put up the last of the decorations, he decided he would get close enough to Georgiana to slip it into her pocket. The task had proved difficult indeed. Obviously part of her new decision involved staying as far away as she could from him.

When Samantha called him over to the heavily laden dessert tables to hand him a note that had been delivered for him, he knew it was his only chance. So, leaning forward between the two women, he snatched a piece of cake with one hand and slipped the chain in Georgiana's pocket with the other. From Samantha, he got a playful swat . . . and of course the cake. Georgiana had only given him a glare.

Frustrated, Ridge recalled the note Samantha had handed him. It had been from Cordelia. She had written to tell him that due to some unforeseen circumstances, she would be late this evening. She sent her apologies and asked that he save her a dance. He'd wadded up the note and threw it away, secretly praying her unforeseen circumstances would keep her from the dance altogether.

After Ridge watched Georgiana from across the room a little

longer, he stood up from the wall and began walking in her direction. *She may be avoiding me*, he thought, *but I'm not avoiding her—not any longer, anyway*. He'd made his own decision this afternoon. As he passed the refreshment table, he grabbed two glasses of punch and walked the rest of the way to where she sat.

"Ya looked like you could use somethin' to drink," he said, smiling down at her.

He handed her the cup and was pleasantly surprised she accepted it without any protest.

"Thank you, Ridge. You're very thoughtful." As she spoke, the song that was playing ended and another one began immediately. Dawson and Samantha continued dancing.

Ridge gestured to the seat next to her.

"Do ya mind if I . . . ?"

"Of course not," she answered and politely moved the folds of her dress to one side to allow him ample room to sit.

Inwardly relieved, Ridge sat down next to her. He was two for two, and he hoped his luck would hold. Turning to watch the dance floor for a while, he found himself staring at Dawson and Samantha. He knew Samantha was a good dancer, but apparently Dawson was as good, if not better. They were certainly dominating the dance floor and having a good time doing it.

Ridge glanced over at Georgiana. She was watching them as well.

Suddenly he felt sorry for her. She probably wasn't enjoying herself so far. He was contemplating what he could say to her when she starting speaking, almost duplicating his thoughts from a moment ago.

"I had no idea Samantha could dance so well. I know how good Dawson is. They look like they're really enjoying themselves."

"Yes, but what about you? You don't seem to be havin' much fun," he commented.

"I'm just fine," she informed him, then added, "really," when he looked at her doubtfully. "I knew I wouldn't be able to dance much with this foot of mine. I've been walking on it way too much."

"How is it healin'?" he asked but turned back to the dance floor briefly when he heard an enthusiastic applause. A crowd had assembled around Dawson and Samantha as they danced.

"Amazingly well, thanks to you."

Ridge turned back to look at her when he heard the emotion in her voice.

"By the way," she began, her eyes searching his, "I want to thank you for this." She touched her father's chain with one hand and laid her other hand on his arm. Ridge shook his head. "Don't try to deny it, Ridge. I know it was you. You're not as sneaky as you may think."

When he didn't answer either way, she removed her hand and turned her eyes back to the dance floor. The song ended again, and a slow one began. When it became apparent that Dawson wasn't coming for her, Ridge stood up and offered her his hand.

"Shall we dance?"

She smiled up at him and placed her hand in his. After helping her to stand, he led her to the dance floor.

Before they started dancing, he cautioned her. "If your foot begins to pain you too much, let me know right away."

She nodded her affirmation, and taking the proper position, they slowly began the waltz.

He struggled with the desire to hold her closer than was proper. Angus wasn't here to scowl at him, and Dawson was temporarily distracted. But, despite what he wanted, Ridge was also determined not to cause her any discomfort, though her very nearness was nigh to causing him to falter.

"I must say, Ridge, you dance very well too," she complimented him sincerely.

"I have Samantha to thank for that," Ridge admitted honestly. "She grew tired of me always stepping on her toes, and so she made it her goal one year to teach me."

* * *

Georgiana felt a sudden twinge of jealously when she thought of Ridge and Samantha dancing together. For the first time, she wondered if Samantha and Ridge had ever had feelings for each other, and an even larger wave of jealousy washed over her. Suddenly she felt an angry swell ebb its way in, and she fought to keep it at bay. How could she have missed out on so much? She should have been here. When they'd moved to New York, she'd left too much behind. Looking up into Ridge's face, she concentrated on suppressing her jealous feelings. She was determined not to be annoyed with him tonight.

When she had begun changing her clothes at Samantha's home to get ready for the dance, something fell out of her pocket onto the floor in front of her. She had immediately picked it up and inspected it. It was the chain her father had given her—the one she tried to retrieve from the creek! It had been recently polished. There was no question as to who had placed it in her pocket. When Ridge had leaned forward to snatch a piece of cake earlier, she had felt his hand brush up against her. She distinctly remembered getting angry at the thrill that had warmed through her body. He must have dropped it in her pocket then.

Watching him now, his eyes suddenly caught hers. She blushed to be caught staring, though she did not look away. The same thought kept spinning and spinning around in her head.

She loved him—fully, and without reservation. She could no longer deny it. His name was etched upon her heart, and it had forever been so. If he could not love her in return, she was doomed to live a life forever longing for the one man who touched her soul and owned her so completely.

The dance came to an end, and Ridge slowly released her and offered his arm as they walked to the edge of the dance floor. Dawson was instantly at her side, and Ridge stepped back. Dawson placed his hand at her waist and nodded to Ridge.

"Good evening, Ridge."

"Dawson," Ridge nodded back.

Dawson turned his attention to Georgiana.

"I wondered where you were until I spotted you on the dance floor. I went to get Samantha some refreshment after our dance, and when I returned, you were gone." He paused, then asked, "Is your foot feeling better?"

"Yes, a little," she admitted, feeling slightly guilty for denying him a dance and accepting Ridge's offer.

"I hadn't intended on leaving you so long." Now he wore a look of chagrin. "Samantha is a very good dancer, and you know how I enjoy dancing."

"I'm glad you're enjoying yourself. The both of you looked wonderful out there. Besides, I was fine. Ridge here kept me company." She turned toward Ridge, smiling. "By the way, I didn't thank you for the dance."

"The pleasure was mine."

And mine, Georgiana thought. She felt Dawson draw her possessively closer.

"Where did Samantha run off to?" Georgiana turned to Dawson, gently forcing his hand to fall from her waist.

"There was an incident at the refreshment tables that needed tending to." As he spoke, another dance began, and Dawson turned toward her and held out his hand. "May I?"

"Of course." She smiled up at him and took his hand.

"Excuse us, Ridge," Dawson said as he led her onto the dance floor.

Georgiana glanced over at Ridge when she passed by but couldn't decipher the look on his face.

"I wanted to apologize about earlier today," Dawson began immediately as they started to dance.

"Earlier?" Georgiana's mind had still been contemplating Ridge's expression.

"Yes, I was a little out of sorts this morning, and I'm afraid I may not have been as cordial as I should have."

Georgiana's mind was still trying to catch his meaning when it dawned on her that he was talking about his somber demeanor when he was teaching her how to drive the wagon.

"You do yourself a discredit, Dawson. You are always gracious company no matter what your mood."

He smiled and endeavored to hold her a little closer. They danced in silence for a while before he spoke again.

"Georgiana, I've been thinking."

She instantly felt apprehensive.

"I can only stay another four or five days, at most. I promised Father." Dawson looked away from her a moment, as if he were stalling, but when he looked back, he seemed more determined to say what was on his mind. "We haven't had too much time to talk . . . privately. Not as much as I had hoped." He now looked nervous, and her uneasiness increased. "I was wondering . . . if perhaps you have had enough time to consider my last proposal?"

"Dawson, I . . ." She looked away, trying to gather the right words to say.

"If you need more time . . . ," he hastily added, "I understand. I know you've had a rough go lately with your grandmother's passing and returning here, as well as your responsibilities helping your grandfather." He gently turned her face to look at him. "It's just . . . that I had hoped . . . to bring you home with me."

An unexpected jolt made her instantly tense. She was not ready to leave! She knew that much for sure. In fact, she was fairly positive she didn't ever want to go back to New York. No matter how things turned out.

"Dawson, my grandfather still needs me. I don't know if I can . . ."

"So you're not saying no to me, just that you can't come home yet?" he gushed, not giving her a chance to answer before he let out a relieved sigh and leaned his head against the side of hers. "Oh, Georgiana . . . I don't know what I'd do without you."

Georgiana groaned inwardly. This was going to be harder than she thought. She had once again inadvertently given him false hope, and she could not abide hurting him any longer. She opened her mouth to speak frankly, but before she got out a word, the dance ended, and he began walking her back off the dance floor. When they reached the edge, Samantha walked up to them. Her face shone with delight, and Georgiana couldn't help but smile.

"How are things going?" Georgiana asked her friend.

"Splendidly . . . well, except for the mishap over at the

refreshment table," she explained. "A few plates got jostled and a few drinks spilled when Clyde Pickering found his two young sons Phillip and Miles hiding under the table sneaking treats when they were supposed to be home in bed.

Georgiana looked at Samantha for a moment trying to keep a straight face, but soon both girls broke out in giggles.

* * *

Ridge smiled as both women broke down in merriment. He could barely keep from laughing with them as he recalled overhearing both women's earlier recollections about when they had done something similar. He couldn't help but wonder if they had shared a similar hiding place as the two wily boys.

He looked over at Dawson. The man wasn't laughing. However, he couldn't help but notice the worried expression Dawson had worn earlier was replaced by something else, relief maybe, or perhaps hope.

Thinking back to the intimate manner in which Dawson had been holding Georgiana only moments ago, Ridge tried to speculate what their intense-looking conversation had been about. His stomach tied in knots thinking of the man's earlier confession that he had proposed marriage to Georgiana already, at least twice. Looking to Georgiana, he tried to discern if there was some secret she could be hiding.

When she glanced up at him, mirth still evident on her face, their eyes locked. *She may look happy*, he pondered, *but it is only a façade. Something is bothering her.* As the music started up again, she turned to Dawson.

"I'm afraid I must sit again for a while." She glanced away from Dawson's disappointed look.

"I'll stay and keep you company," Dawson offered solicitously.

Georgiana shook her head, still looking down. "Please, Dawson. Take Samantha out on the dance floor once again. I so much enjoyed watching the two of you before."

Ever so slightly, Georgiana turned her head toward Samantha and winked. Dawson didn't notice. Instead, he looked sideways over to Ridge, trying to appear nonchalant. Ridge could tell he had no intention of leaving Georgiana alone in his care again, so he politely excused himself and went to ask the widow Swansen to dance. The night, he feared, was going to be a long one. At least to his good fortune, Miss Cordelia Jamison had not yet arrived.

The thought had not yet even passed through his mind when he spotted her entering the hall and looking about, presumably for him. Gracefully, he maneuvered Mrs. Swansen to the far side of the dance floor. The older woman smiled and seemed to be enjoying herself.

"I haven't seen you in town much this last little while, Mr. Carson, not since you picked up the post a few weeks ago. Been keepin' to yourself lately? You know that's not fair to all us women folk."

He smiled down at the woman. Though he gave no response, she continued. "Of course, you were a dear to mend my leaky roof today. It has been worryin' me ever so." A quick glance about the room gave her another avenue of conversation. "My, that Samantha Wallace did a splendid job with this year's social. That girl just has a knack for this sort of thing. Remember last winter when they put her in charge of the Christmas pageant? Why, that was the best one I'd seen since, well . . . since ever, I reckon." She stopped only to catch her breath and started up again. "Why there's that sweet Mr. Alexander over there dancin' with Miss Wallace right now. Don't they make lovely looking dance partners? If that young man wasn't so far gone on Miss McLaughlin, I would encourage that Wallace girl to snatch him up right fast. It was so tragic what happened to her. I pray she doesn't hold herself back too long because of it though. The longer a woman waits, the less her chances. All the good ones are gone." She looked up to Ridge. "What about you, Mr. Carson? Why haven't you found yourself a nice girl, settled down, and had a few young'uns to bounce on one of them strong knees? Miss Wallace is sure a handsome girl, don't ya think?"

"Samantha? Yes . . . yes she is, but we're just friends," he told her, glancing over to where Samantha was dancing with Dawson.

She raised an eyebrow at him. "Seems to me you used to say that about Miss McLaughlin, but I know you was sweet on her for a long time."

Ridge looked over to where Georgiana sat idly playing with her father's chain. She looked troubled, not like a woman who had just accepted a proposal of marriage. As he watched her, Miss Jamison sat down beside her and began to engage her in conversation. Ridge worried as to what could possibly be the subject of a conversation between the two women. As he was thinking, Georgiana looked over to him, horrified. Miss Jamison had obviously said something that had caused that look. He needed to get over there. *Dang!* When was this blasted dance going to end?

He watched helplessly as Georgiana stood up and made her way to the door of the social hall. Turning back to Cordelia, he stared at the smug look on her face. She caught him staring and smiled brightly over at him.

When the dance finally ended, he thanked the widow Swansen and walked her back to her friends. Turning, he immediately headed to the door. On his way, he noticed Dawson looking for Georgiana, and avoided him. He wanted to get to Georgiana first. He had a sneaky suspicion whatever Miss Jamison had said to her to make her leave was directly related to him.

·19·

Returning Home

"Ridge!"

Before he could reach the door, he was stopped by Mr. Wallace. "I've been looking for you, son. I hope I don't ruin your evening if I mix a little business with pleasure, but I need to discuss a financial matter with you."

"Mr. Wallace, can it—"

"Now I promise it will only take a moment," Mr. Wallace added quickly. Reluctantly, Ridge turned to the man and gave him his attention, though not undivided. "The Wells Fargo stage will be by first thing in the mornin' to pick up a deposit and transfer it to Denver. You know ever since Mitch Tyler went missin' a few years back, it makes me nervous every time I have business up that way. There's been too much talk about Injun trouble, and if it's not them, it's the outlaws. The law around here isn't what it used to be, and too many incidents have gone unsolved. Seems every gamblin' Jesse James copycat is tryin' his hand at thievery." He made a disgusted sound. "I've been thinkin' . . . since you've got about as much invested into seein' the money arrives safely in Denver as any of us, that you might be willin' to round up a few men to follow the stage for a while and make sure at least no one 'round these parts has a try at robbin' it. Those Wells Fargo guys are sharp shooters, but the way I see it, an ounce of prevention is worth a pound of cure."

Ridge agreed to ask a few men tonight if they would be willing to meet Mr. Wallace at the bank come sunrise. He knew Angus wouldn't mind him helpin' out. It was the right thing to do.

Finally able to end the conversation, Ridge hurried through the door. He did not see Georgiana anywhere. Sighing, he leaned up against the side of the building to think.

What could Miss Cordelia Jamison have said to upset Georgiana? As far as he knew, the two women didn't even know each other. Georgiana had been gone two years when Mr. Jamison and his wife had come to work at the bank. When tragedy killed old Mr. Potter, the bank's owner, Mr. Jamison had taken over the running of it. Unbeknownst to the town, the man hadn't a clue how to run a bank, and it wasn't more than two years later he had nearly put the town into financial ruin. If Mr. Wallace hadn't used his inheritance to buy the bank and shore up its financial creditability, many innocent people would have suffered great financial losses. The town had seen to it that the Jamisons found another place to reside. A little less than two months ago, Miss Cordelia Jamison, their daughter, had shown up and moved into the boarding house.

His thoughts quickly reverted back to Georgiana. His hand warmed at the thought of holding her tonight, even for one dance. He wished he could read what she was thinking behind those confusing gray eyes. Sometimes when he looked into them, he could see all his love and longing for her reflected back as though she too felt the same. Other times they told another story entirely. Then there was Dawson. Had Dawson been able to convince her to return with him? He didn't know if he could bear to see her leave again.

"Ridge, dear, there you are. Where did you run off to in such a hurry?"

It was Cordelia. She fairly sauntered up and leaned up next to him against the building, closer than was comfortable. "You still owe me a dance, you know."

"Don't know that I'll be stayin' much longer," he replied, inching a little farther away. She slid closer to him again, and once more he scooted away. Boldly, she moved to stand directly in front of him.

"Oh, come on, Ridge. Don't be such a stuffed shirt. All I want is one dance." Leaning forward slightly, she reached her hand out and coiled a finger in a strand of his hair. The scent of her perfume was so strong, it immediately made his head pound.

"Cordelia, please . . . don't," he warned, his anger starting to mount. Why couldn't this woman leave him alone? Couldn't she see he was not interested in her? It was time he made his intentions toward her plain. "Miss Jamison, it's obvious that ya have taken an interest in me, but I need to let ya know that—"

Before he had a chance to finish, she threw herself forward, put her arms around his neck, and began kissing him. Ridge was stunned. Never before had he witnessed or been the recipient of such a brazen act perpetrated by a woman. It took him a moment to gather his wits about him before he reached up and grabbed hold of her wrists. Forcing them from around his neck, he brought them down to his chest and pushed her body away from his. She gasped as he forced her lips from his, and he looked directly and harshly into her eyes.

"As I was sayin', Miss Jamison," he spoke between clenched teeth, "I need to inform you that I do not return your affections."

Fire flashed in her eyes, but despite his obvious rejection, she smiled demurely.

"Would you mind releasin' your hold on me, Mr. Carson?"

At once he released her wrists and let his hands fall to his sides. He felt guilty for causing her discomfort, despite the salaciousness of her actions.

"Thank you," she spat as she rubbed them a moment before continuing. "Well, I think you've made yourself clear, I'll not be bothering you anymore." She moved to step away but turned back around. "Ya know I had to give it one more chance. When I saw you kissin' that woman the other day in the alley, you have no idea what a thrill it caused me to see a man so capable of lovin' a woman like that. I had hoped that I could persuade you . . ." She paused for another moment, fairly smirking. "No matter . . . I can see it would never work out between you and me. We're much too different." Reaching into a pocket, she pulled out a set a gloves and began putting them on. When she was finished, she reached forward and ran one long, gloved finger along the side of his cheek. "Well, good-bye, Ridge Carson." Her touch made him cringe, and she smiled at his reaction. "I can honestly say I hope to never see you again." As she pulled her hand away and made move to leave, she flippantly added, "Oh, by the way . . . that woman you prefer was inside lookin' for you a moment ago. I can't be quite certain, but she seemed to be terribly upset about something."

Smiling wickedly, she gave him one last long look before turning and walking up the street. Ridge only watched her for a second before hurrying back into the social hall.

* * *

As soon as Georgiana saw Ridge's form disappear through the doors, she sank to the ground. She felt as if the life had been knocked out of her. When that woman had approached her, endeavoring to slander Ridge's good name, she hadn't believed a word of it. Samantha had assured her Ridge wanted nothing to do with Miss Jamison. But her eyes told her another truth.

She'd come outside to get away from the woman and to think. Cordelia said she'd come over to warn her not to get mixed up with the likes of Ridge Carson. She said she'd been watching out the window of the boarding house that day he had forced his kisses upon her and was shocked because Ridge had purposed marriage to her only the week before. She told Georgiana she had been waiting to meet up with him that morning to accept his proposal. Just as Georgiana had begun to digest what she was saying, the woman had laid a hand across her midsection and all but told her outright the marriage was one of necessity.

It couldn't be true! Everything she knew of Ridge, every feeling that she got about him, told her he was a man of the highest and utmost moral character. But then she had just seen them together with her own eyes!

Georgiana swatted at the tears cascading down her face and crumbled to the earth as her knees gave out. Those lips that had given such resplendent joy to her own only a few weeks before had betrayed her! Had it all been a ruse? What game was being played and where did she fit in? Georgiana was still sitting on the ground when Samantha walked up.

"Georgiana, is that you?" Samantha asked, peering through the shadows.

"Yes," Georgiana answered in barely a whisper.

Her friend came closer.

"Where did you go? Everyone's been lookin' for you. Dawson and Ridge are both . . ." It was then Samantha saw the emotional condition she was in. "Georgie, what happened?"

When Samantha put her arms around her, she could not respond, only weep.

"Has someone hurt you? Look at me, Georgie. Tell me what's wrong."

Georgiana shook her head.

"I . . . I . . . can't."

"Yes, you can. Now look at me, Georgiana McLaughlin, and tell me what has made you so upset."

"I . . . I . . . saw them . . . together."

"Who, Georgie? Who did you see?"

"Ridge . . . Ridge and . . ." She almost couldn't say the woman's name.

"Ridge? Ridge is inside looking for you."

"No, Samantha, I saw them. They were kissing and . . . and Miss Jamison told me earlier, when you were dancing with Dawson that . . . that . . ." She couldn't say to Samantha what the woman had inferred. "Oh, Samantha, I've been such a fool. I was beginning to think maybe we really did have a chance. Sometimes when he looks at me I'm so sure he feels the same. I'm still the same foolish girl in love with a boy who will never return my affections." She stood up and smoothed the wrinkles in her dress. "I need to get out of here, and I don't want anyone seeing me like this, especially Dawson. I can't go back to Grandfather's tonight. I just can't face either one of them." She reached out and took one of Samantha's hands. "Would you mind if I stayed at your house?"

"Of course not. I'll take you home and get you settled, but I'll need to come back after a while and take care of some things."

"I understand." Georgiana nodded, relieved she would have somewhere else to stay tonight. "Thank you," she said gratefully, reaching forward and taking Samantha's hand. Samantha gave it a squeeze.

"First, let me go inside and talk to Dawson and Ridge. I'll explain to them you are not feeling well and that I'm going to take you to my house for tonight. Then you and I will sit down and get to the bottom of all of this. I know you haven't told me everything, but I have a strong feeling that things really aren't what they seem."

Georgiana nodded in agreement, and Samantha hurried back inside.

Georgiana fidgeted while she waited, hoping that Samantha wouldn't be very long. Thankfully, it was just a few minutes later when she returned.

"May we go now?" Georgiana asked anxiously.

"Yes, I let them both know we were leaving. Dawson seemed a bit worried and told me to make sure you knew he hoped you were feeling better." A concerned look crossed her face. "Ridge acted pretty upset. I've never seen him so agitated."

"If I were in his shoes, I'd be pretty upset too." Samantha gave her a puzzled look before they headed in the direction of her house.

They were walking in silence, each lost in their own thoughts, when Samantha suddenly cried out, startling her. "What was that?"

"What?" Georgiana asked.

"There," Samantha said, pointing to the bank, "I thought I saw a light. It couldn't be Father because when I finished talking to Ridge, I saw him and Mother dancing."

Georgiana thought Samantha must have imagined the light until she saw it too.

"Who would be there without your father?" Georgiana asked, starting to worry.

"I don't know," Samantha contemplated. "Let's go over to see if we can tell who it is through the window." As she began heading over in the direction of the bank, she added, "What's that wagon doing parked there?"

Georgiana felt a little uneasy. People at the social had parked their wagons over by the social hall. So it was strange that there was a wagon parked in front of the bank. It would be better if they went back and got Samantha's father or someone else to help, maybe even the sheriff, but she couldn't bear to face Ridge. So even though her gut told her it was unwise, she found herself following her friend. As they stepped up onto the boardwalk in front of the bank, she grabbed Samantha's arm. Samantha turned to her.

"Listen, if we see anyone there, we're not going to confront them, okay?" Georgiana insisted in a low voice.

Samantha gave her a look that said, "Do you think I'm crazy?"

"If we even *think* we see someone, we'll run back to the social and get Sheriff Riggs," Samantha assured her, keeping her voice down low as well.

"And we stay together too," Georgiana added.

"Agreed," said Samantha.

The two girls quietly snuck up to the window of the bank and peered inside.

"Do you see anything?" Georgiana whispered.

"I don't know. It's hard to see through the curtains. Now I wish I hadn't insisted Father put them up. It almost looks like there are shadows movin' on the wall, but I can't quite—"

All of a sudden Samantha let out a muffled scream as a large man put his hand over her mouth with one arm and held her immobilized with the other. Georgiana didn't have time to scream herself, for not a half second later she found herself in the same predicament. Try as they might to free themselves, they were unsuccessful. Ultimately, they were both pushed forward and forced through the front door of the bank. Their instinct to cry out as they were thrust to the ground at a woman's feet was sufficiently subdued when they felt the cold, hard guns pointed at their backs. They didn't need the added verbal warning.

"Let out a scream, either of you, and I'll shoot you dead on the spot."

Next they heard the woman speak, but their heads were down low and the bank was dark except for a small light coming from the back office. They could only see the woman from the ankles down. The woman's voice was loud, angry, and brusque, but definitely familiar.

"Gil, Wyatt . . . what are they doin' here?"

"They saw us, boss. They were peekin' in the window. We had no choice," Gil quibbled.

"Yeah . . . and they were 'bout to go get the sheriff too. I heard 'em say so," Wyatt added defensively.

"Well, I guess you best stand them up so I can see their faces. I won't shoot them in the back without first lookin' them in the eyes."

Roughly, the two men grabbed them by the arms and stood them up to face none other than Miss Cordelia Jamison. A smile immediately lit her face.

"Well, well, well. Who do we have here?" Cordelia walked over to them. "If it isn't my dear friend Miss Wallace and the long lost Miss McLaughlin." She stood before Samantha first. "I'm sorry to disappoint you, Samantha, but our little friendship was not genuine. You see, I needed to get close to you so it wasn't suspicious that I was spending so much time hangin' around the bank. I wasn't sure how many things had changed since my father had stopped running it, and of course I needed to find out when the bank runs were. After all, if I'm going to rob a bank, I want to steal as much money as I can." She moved to stand in front of Georgiana next. "And of course your bosom buddy, the high and mighty Miss Georgiana McLaughlin, would be with you. After all, you've become so close again since her miraculous return." She narrowed her eyes at Georgiana. "This is actually your fault, you know, seein' as you had to come back to town. You see, robbin' the bank was really only my backup plan. What I really wanted was that sugar dipped honey-eyed man you stole out from under me. Wasn't one man enough? You already have that puppy, Mr. Alexander, followin' you halfway across the states. Isn't he good enough or is he just *your* backup plan?"

Georgiana's blood was beginning to boil. Her face had turned red, but she forced herself to remain quiet.

"Getting' angry are we?" Cordelia grabbed Georgiana by the face with her hand and pulled her close. "Well, I'm angry too." She dropped her hand to her stomach, giving Georgie a knowing look. "Seein' as now I have no one to be a father to my baby."

Samantha spoke up, understanding at once the insinuation Cordelia had made.

"You're a liar! Ridge would never touch you. He has never loved anyone but Georgiana since the day he moved to Crystal Creek."

"Well, fortunately for Ridge, you don't really have to love a woman, to *love* a woman," Cordelia sneered.

Georgiana was taken aback when Samantha spit in Cordelia's face and equally as stunned when Miss Jamison slapped Samantha, causing her to stagger back. Georgiana reached over to help steady and comfort her friend but was rewarded with a hard shove from Cordelia.

"Tie them up, gag them, and throw them into the back of the wagon," Cordelia ordered Gil and Wyatt. When the two men didn't move right away, she shouted, "NOW!" The boys jumped and headed for the door but stopped when she spoke to someone behind her. It was the first time Georgiana realized there was a third man present. "Slash! Are you done with that safe yet?"

"Almost," a voice hollered from the back room. "Any second now."

"Well, hurry it up!" She turned her attention back to Gil and Wyatt. "Get it done, boys. We need to get out of here before them townsfolk start headin' home from the social. I don't want anyone seein' us leave town. Besides, if we leave real casual like, if someone does see us, they won't suspect anything." She picked up a shotgun that was leaning against the wall behind her, cocked it, and pointed it at Samantha and Georgiana. "Wyatt, you go fetch the rope from the wagon. I'll help Gil watch these two until you get back." The man just stood there, looking dumbfounded until she shouted, "GET!"

Quickly, he scrambled out the door.

When he brought the rope back in, the two men tied and gagged both women. One at a time, they were hauled out to the wagon, and a blanket was thrown over them. The two men climbed in the back of the wagon on either side and laid down low to keep watch.

It wasn't long before she heard Cordelia and the third man coming out of the bank. Several heavy objects were tossed into the back of the wagon in two or three trips. Cordelia swore brashly.

"Someone's comin' up the road. Slash, you go fetch my horse from behind the livery stables. She's tied up at the back gate. Ride her out and meet us just beyond the outskirts of town. We'll head up to the cabin together from there."

"I don't think so," Georgiana heard Slash disagree, his voiced dripping with mistrust. "Forget the horse. I'll hide in the alley there up the street, and as soon as he's gone, I'll join you in the wagon. I'm not takin' my eyes off you and this here wagon until we're free and clear, and I have my share. You may be in charge of this here operation, but no man *or* woman ain't ever gonna call me a fool."

"Fine," Cordelia growled, "but you'd better stay out of sight." She paused to let out a slow breath before she began talking again. "You boys back there stay down and lie low," she warned, "and keep those two women quiet."

Georgiana heard Cordelia climb on top of the wagon seat and slap the reins.

"Yah!" she shouted, and the wagon started moving.

From under the blanket, Georgiana looked into the terrified eyes of her friend. The thought occurred to her that Samantha might be imagining Mitch having died at the hands of similar bandits. *Please God*, she prayed, *at least let Samantha make it out of this alive.*

Suddenly the wagon came to a halt. The two men beside them quickly joined them under the blanket.

"Ridge!" Cordelia sounded surprised.

Samantha's eyes got as big as hers. They were thinking the same thing until they heard the sound of a gun being cocked. Both girls froze. The men were warning them not to make a sound. If they tried anything, Ridge could get shot.

"What are you doing out here, Miss Jamison?" Ridge asked. "I thought you'd left a while ago." Georgiana could tell by his voice that he was not pleased to see her.

"I could ask you the same thing. I thought you headed back into the social hall to rescue your woman in distress." Cordelia's voice was smug.

"Just exactly what did ya say to her, anyway?" His voice was angry.

"Only the truth," she said sweetly. Georgiana cringed.

"And what truth would that be, Cordelia? The real truth or the one that ya imagined in your head," Ridge accused her.

Cordelia didn't answer him but rather changed the subject entirely.

"I'm so glad I'm leavin' this horrid town with all you little men who have such high opinions of yourselves. If I ever see you again, Mr. Carson, it will be a moment too soon."

"That's the second time you've said that tonight." Ridge's voice sounded suspicious, and a long silence ensued. After a while, he simply added, "Well, I agree with ya on that anyway. Good-bye, Miss Jamison."

"You sure you won't change your mind and come runnin' after me the moment I'm gone now, will ya?" she mocked. "You never know. I might have something you want after all."

"I doubt you'll ever have anything I want," Ridge insisted.

"You can never be too sure." Her voice was almost a sneer. Ridge didn't answer this time, and Georgiana heard Cordelia flick the reins to start the horses moving again. "Good-bye, Ridge," Cordelia called back to him. "Have a miserable life."

* * *

Ridge watched the wagon as it pulled away and headed out of town. He was glad to see that woman leave, but for some reason he felt something else pulling away from him. Maybe he was just being paranoid. Just like when he thought he heard a gun being cocked when the wagon first came to a halt. He must have been hearing things. Cordelia had been alone, and she didn't carry a gun.

He turned and walked the rest of the way to the social hall, trying to shake off the nagging feeling that something was terribly wrong. He had started over to Samantha's deciding it would be better to talk to Georgiana tonight rather than wait until the morning. He knew there was more to Samantha's explanation of Georgiana's sudden departure than she was letting on. Something had happened to make her look at him the way she had and then leave so abruptly. Cordelia had said or done something, and he was determined to find out what it was.

When he'd arrived at Samantha's house, there were no lights on. Georgiana must have gone to bed already, and Samantha must have decided to stay, so he'd turned around and headed back. That was when he saw the wagon parked on the street. He hadn't noticed it on his walk past the other direction, probably because he had been so deep in thought. As he watched it, someone climbed up onto the seat, and it started moving in his direction. When it got closer, he could tell it was a woman. When her face came into view, he saw that it was Cordelia.

After the wagon was no longer in sight, Ridge walked into the dance hall. He had no heart to be here any longer, but he had promised Samantha he would stay until she got back. He figured she wouldn't be coming back now, but he felt obligated to stay for a little while, anyway, to make sure. So after dancing with a few more widows, he walked to a corner where he could watch the door, propped himself up comfortably, and waited.

As he stood there, he spotted Dawson. The man looked lost. He probably thought that at least Samantha was coming back. To be courteous, he should go over and explain that he was pretty sure both women had gone to bed, but he couldn't bring himself to do it. So he just waited, not being able to shake the foreboding feeling that something was about to happen.

Not five minutes later, Clyde Pickering burst through the door of the hall and shouted, "The bank has been robbed!"

The social hall was in an immediate uproar. People ran out the door and down the street to the bank. Sheriff Riggs ordered his deputy to start organizing a posse to search for the robbers at first light before he headed over to the bank to investigate. In his wake, Mayor Padderson was attempting to calm everyone down. Still, confusion ensued, and not much was being accomplished. Ridge grabbed a lantern, headed out the door, and hurried up the street behind Mr. Wallace.

When they got to the bank, the door was hanging wide open, and people were crowded around trying to get a look inside.

"Everyone away from the door!" Mr. Wallace demanded. A few people mumbled and stepped back, but most just ignored him. This time he yelled louder. "If you want any chance of gettin' your money back, you'd better get away from the door right now. You're destroyin' evidence!"

At the threat of never seeing their money again, everyone stepped back in unison. It was about that time the sheriff showed up.

"All of you get back to the social hall or go home," he ordered, and his voice meant business. People slowly started drifting way.

"Come on, Ridge," Mr. Wallace called. "I could use your help."

Ridge followed the sheriff and Mr. Wallace into the bank. Mr. Wallace took the lantern from Ridge's hand and set it in the middle of the floor. Ridge froze. There was something small and blue lying on the ground. He knew what it was before he even picked it up.

"They have Georgiana," Ridge announced as he reached down and lifted the tiny blue ribbon off the floor. "There's no other explanation for this . . . and," he paused, "Samantha was with her." When he glanced back up, his eyes looked straight into the stricken face of Samantha's father.

"This changes everything," Sheriff Riggs announced. "The posse must leave tonight. Get home, grab your guns, and meet me back at the social hall," the sheriff ordered before heading out the door.

Ridge didn't move right away. Instead, he stood sifting through his memory. Something important was nipping at the edge of his subconscious, something he knew would lead them to where the women had been taken, but he couldn't pinpoint what it was.

·20·

No Honor among Thieves

GEORGIANA moved closer to Samantha when she felt another violent shiver pass through her. She blew warm air into her friend's tied hands. Earlier she had managed to work the gag out of her mouth and had helped Samantha do the same. The wagon had stopped over two hours ago, and Cordelia and the three men had left the two women in the back of the wagon. Their only protection from the night air was a thin blanket. The night was turning colder, and the blanket did little to keep them warm.

"It's s-soooo . . . c-c-c-cold," Samantha said through the chattering of her teeth. Worse than that though, was the terror evident in her voice. "W-what are th-th-they going t-t-to d-do with us? D-do you think they w-will leave us out . . . h-here all n-n-night?"

"Shhh . . . don't worry about it, Samantha. Just concentrate on keeping warm. I'm sure they will come for us soon." Her friend nodded and closed her eyes.

Georgiana rolled onto her back as best she could and looked up into the clear, starry sky above. *At least it isn't going to rain on us*, she thought. The nights weren't clear like this in New York. It's one of the things she had missed. A shooting star suddenly lit the sky, sparking a specific memory from not long before she had first left Colorado for New York.

She could imagine Ridge lying next to her at that very moment.

"Okay, that half of the sky's yours, and this half is mine." Ridge reached his hand up and drew an imaginary line in the sky. "The person who finds the most constellations in the least amount of time wins."

"But that's not fair," Georgiana complained. "You've got the big dipper and the little dipper both on your half."

"Okay . . . then let's switch sides," he offered, crawling up and over the top of her and then situating himself on her other side. "I'll win anyway . . . I always win," he snickered.

"Did I ever tell ya, Ridge Carson, that one of the things I admire about you most is how humble you are?" she teased.

"That's me!" he shouted affirmatively and turned his head in order to smile at her.

He was so close. She could feel his warm breath as he spoke in the cool night air.

"Well, don't count on winnin' this time. My grandfather taught me all the constellations when I was five," she boasted.

"And my mother taught me them when I was four," he bragged in return.

She smiled and shook her head at him.

"Okay . . . are you ready?" He reached into his pants pocket and withdrew his father's pocket watch. "We each get one minute. You can go first . . . 'cause you're a girl."

"No, you can go first." She turned her head to him and glared. "Because you're a boy."

He turned his head and stared at her for a moment, and she thought he was going to argue, but he just grinned and handed her the watch.

"Okay, ya have ta keep time for me. When the second hand gets to twelve, say 'go,' " he instructed carefully.

"First, ya have to close your eyes . . . and you can't open them until I say so."

"Why?" he asked, puzzled.

"Well, that way ya don't get to start lookin' until your minute begins. It's only fair," she explained.

He rolled his eyes.

"All right, but ya still won't win," he bragged again, turning his face to the sky and closing his eyes. "Okay, I'm ready . . . just say when."

Georgie looked over at him, his dark lashes fluttering softly on his cheeks. A stray lock of hair curled at his temple. She was tempted to reach over and see if it felt as soft as it looked. He was so dreamy.

She almost jumped out of her skin when he opened one eye and peeked over at her. Her face turned red.

"Well?" He looked at her curiously.

"Well, what?"

"Is it time?" he asked impatiently.

She blushed again, immediately realizing she had forgotten that she was supposed to be keeping time. He raised one eyebrow and smiled. This made her blush even more, and she quickly turned away and studied the timepiece in her hand as she began counting.

"Okay . . . five seconds . . . four . . . three . . . two . . . one . . . now!"

Georgiana was brought back from her memory when she heard a door open and close. Shortly, both girls were being forced up and carried out of the wagon.

"The boss says ta bring ya in now, but if you bother her in any way, we'll have ya tied up outside somewhere and you'll just have ta take your chances with the coyotes," Gil remarked offhandedly.

"If it were me, I'd make sure I stayed real quiet like," Wyatt was saying now. "The boss is in a real foul mood, and I don't think she's fond of the two of ya."

They were carried in the door of an old two-room cabin and made to sit on the wooden floor against one of the walls. The wood was hard, but at least they were near the fire. The only furniture in the room was a lopsided table and a pair of rickety-looking chairs. Gil and Wyatt sat down at the table, and Gil pulled out a deck of cards. The third man appeared to be sleeping on a bedroll on the other side of the fireplace. Cordelia must have gone to bed in the other room. Georgiana awkwardly maneuvered herself to sit closer to her friend.

"Samantha," she whispered, "are you all right?"

Samantha nodded her head but didn't say anything.

"I've been thinking. They really have no need for us now that they have their money and are already safely out of town. Cordelia's rotten, but I don't think she's so far gone that she'll let them do any real harm to us. They're probably just planning on leaving us here in the morning and riding on. As long as we don't cause any trouble, we're going to be fine."

Samantha's eyes looked somewhat relieved, and she nodded her head again.

"Listen, we'd better try to get some sleep. We're going to need our strength to get us out of here and find our way home."

Samantha didn't say anything, just closed her eyes and leaned her head on her friend's shoulder. Within a few minutes, Georgiana could tell she'd fallen asleep.

Despite what she'd told Samantha, Georgiana couldn't seem to relax enough to fall asleep herself. Between the dancing tonight and getting jostled in the wagon, her foot was sore and throbbing and would not allow her any respite. She closed her eyes anyway and leaned her head back against the wall. When she opened them again, she noticed the man on the floor stirring. *He must not be asleep*, she thought.

Before the thought had time to leave her mind, he rolled over and began staring at her. She was shocked by the wanton and depraved look in his eyes. She had been frightened by Gil and Wyatt, for they were thieves and as such were greedy and vile in nature. She presumed this wasn't their first act of thievery. But though they had been rude as well as rough in the handling of Samantha and herself, she hadn't felt from them a fear of anything worse. The lecherous way this other man, Slash, was staring at her caused the hairs on the back of her neck to prickle and her stomach to churn. She feared this man's intentions toward them were far more insidious in their design.

To make things worse, she worried no one even knew they had been taken. Everyone probably thought they were home at

Samantha's house in bed asleep. That was why, when she realized they were to be kidnapped, she had discreetly loosened a ribbon from her hair and dropped it on the floor of the bank. She only prayed Ridge or Dawson would see it and realize what it was.

Georgiana closed her eyes to block out the sight of the nauseating man before her and conjured up a vision of Ridge instead, handsome in his suit coat, smiling into her eyes as he led her across the dance floor. *Please God*, she prayed for the second time tonight, *please let me know the feel of his arms around me again. Help both of us to get out of this alive, and keep both Ridge and Dawson safe.*

It was then she was finally able to fall into an exhausted and troubled sleep and block out the frightful man across the room.

* * *

Jake "Slash" Fletcher continued to stare at the delicious young thing as she drifted off to sleep. She was the most beautiful and tantalizing woman he had seen in a long time, and he intended to have his fill of her tonight as soon as those empty-headed simpletons stopped playing cards and went to sleep.

Cordelia had warned the three of them not to lay a hand on either one of the women, but who was she to tell him what not to do? He was through taking orders from that woman anyway.

He had met Miss Cordelia Jamison over in Westchester about three and a half months ago. She'd been working at the saloon trying to help her mother support her lazy father, and she'd been taken with him at first sight. He wasn't too bad looking when he was cleaned up, could even turn a head or two. But his real gift, besides his skill with a knife, was his silver tongue. He'd always had a way with words and had learned early on to use them to his advantage. He could tell from the first time he'd seen Cordelia that with a little effort, she'd be easy pickings. She was vulnerable, and he knew it . . . counted on it.

So he had sweet-talked her and lavished on her his attentions. By the end of the week, she had melted like butter in his arms. After another week had passed, he had tired of her. The look in her eyes told him she was looking for something permanent, maybe a way out even, and it wasn't going to be him. He didn't need the baggage, and he certainly wasn't planning on settling down. So he had quickly skipped town for a couple of months.

He had been back a week when she had approached him, told him what she was planning, and asked if he wanted in. He was skeptical at first. Asked why she'd considered letting him in on the deal if it was as good as she said it was. She'd told him she needed a slick-talking lowlife if her plan was going to work. He could've taken offense, but the truth was it sounded like too good of a deal to pass up. One thing he hadn't counted on, though, was how hard it was going to be taking orders from a woman.

Slash took another eyeful of the treat that was waiting for him before closing his eyes. He could wait. A little while longer, anyway.

❦ ❦ ❦

Georgiana awoke when a hard hand was pressed harshly to her face. Next, she felt the point of a sharp blade in her side.

"Get up!" the man whispered. "You're comin' with me."

Georgiana felt her fear intensify, and she couldn't bring herself to move. The man cut the ropes at her ankles and yanked her to a standing position. Luckily Samantha was no longer lying on her shoulder but had maneuvered onto her own side. She didn't look extremely comfortable, but at least she was sleeping.

"One word out of ya, and I'll run you through with my blade. They don't call me 'Slash' for nothin'." His breath was hot and sticky and his voice rough as he spoke lowly into her ear. "Besides, if that happens, there'll be no one here to protect your little friend from comin' into the same." Georgiana's eyes got wide with fear and worry. It seemed to please the man. "If you satisfy me enough, I might let her be, though I won't make no promises. She's almost as sweet a tart as you are."

Georgiana strained her head to look down at Samantha as the man pushed her into a forced walk. Thankfully, she was still asleep.

As soon as the door was opened, a blast of icy air assaulted her, and she began to shiver as he pushed her down the steps and toward the wagon.

"Now climb up," he ordered.

With difficulty, Georgiana climbed into the back of the wagon, and the man climbed in after her. Her body shook from both the cold and the fear. He forced her to lie down. Taking his knife, he sat down on her legs and cut the ropes from her wrists.

"Now don't be getting' any ideas thinkin' you'll get away and run off. I just can't abide to have you tied up."

Georgiana unconsciously rubbed the rope burns on her wrists with her cold fingers.

"This is not how I usually get my women," the man continued, leaning on all fours now so he could position his face closer to hers. "Despite what you may be thinkin' right now, they usually fall into my arms." Georgiana turned her head to the side to avoid looking at him. He grabbed her chin with the hand that held the knife and forced her to look at him. "If you'd met me at a different place and time, you might be counted among them." Georgiana gave him a disgusted look but held her tongue. "Now, don't look at me like that. I'm usually quite the ladies' man. You might even consider yourself lucky."

Georgiana began to struggle then. The thought of this man thinking he might be doing her a favor caused her anger to thaw the frozen fear and finally release her limbs. She had to get free, for herself and for Samantha.

" 'Course, I never did mind them a bit feisty," he said, a sick smile spreading across his face. She couldn't help the slight scream that escaped her lips as he gathered both of her wrists in one hand. His hand that held the knife slammed down hard over her mouth, cutting a small gash in her cheek. "Now see what you've made me do. I warned you not to make a sound. You'd better hope no one heard that. If you scream again, I'll have to cut your throat, and that will ruin this pretty dress of yours."

Georgiana stopped struggling.

"That's better. Now, I'm going to move my hand. Are you going to try to scream again?"

She shook her head.

"Good."

As he removed his hand, Georgiana quickly took a couple deep breaths. His hand was large and covered her nose as well as her mouth. Had he held it there much longer, she might have passed out from lack of oxygen.

"You'll never get away with this," she threatened when she finally found her voice. "They're going to find you, and this will make it even worse. Let me go and I won't tell anyone you tried to—"

He laughed harshly.

"Nice try, sweet thing. Even if they're lookin' for us, they'll be lookin' for horse tracks not a wagon. Who robs a bank with a wagon? They'll not be findin' us, at least not tonight." He moved his face even closer to hers and put the knife to her neck. "No one's going to save you from me tonight."

Slipping the blade underneath the sleeve of her dress and camisole, he cut through the fabric. The dress slipped away, exposing her shoulder. He groaned, and she felt his lips upon her skin. Georgiana's flesh began to crawl, and she instinctively began to struggle violently. Her efforts to free herself earned her the knife once again pressed to her neck. Fear overtook her then, fear intertwined with hopelessness. The tears finally let loose as she was about to sacrifice all.

No, she would rather die than give in to him.

As she opened her mouth to scream, she heard the hammer of a gun being pulled back. The man froze.

"Lay another hand on that girl, and you won't see the light of day." Though Georgiana could not see her, she could hear it was Cordelia. "Now, get up and get out of the wagon!" Slash stood up reluctantly, his hand gripping his knife viciously. "Slowly, now . . . don't give me any excuse to pull this trigger. You of all people know how much pleasure that would give me."

Slash slowly climbed down the side of the wagon. He was seething. Georgiana could see his breath steaming the air in short, harsh spurts, but he didn't say a word, only glared at Cordelia hatefully. His look seemed to goad her on.

"Oh, come on now, Jake," Cordelia said. "I'm actually quite surprised you resorted to such brutal tactics. You usually pride yourself on being able to sugar-talk a woman into your bed. Are you losing your touch?"

When he answered her, his voice was barely in control. "Watch it, Cordelia."

She did not heed his warning.

"Seems to me, I gave very specific instructions that none of you were to lay your hands on these women. Yet here you are." She shoved the muzzle of the gun closer to his chest.

"I couldn't let a good thing go to waste, now could I? Not just because you're . . . ," he paused and forced a step closer to Cordelia, ignoring the gun, "jealous perhaps?"

Cordelia's eyes flashed with anger.

"Don't flatter yourself, Jake! You're no more than a lowlife, scum-suckin' leach that gets his kicks preyin' on innocent women. I was a fool not to see it the first day I laid eyes on you. Now . . ." Georgiana watched Cordelia instinctively and protectively placed her hand across her abdomen. Immediately she knew. "Now . . ." The mask of anger on the woman's face faltered for a moment, and Georgiana caught a glimpse of hurt and fear, but she quickly recovered. "Now you get back in the cabin and don't ever even think of crossing my instructions again, not if you want your share of the money, anyway." She looked him directly in the eyes. "If you can't live with that," she added, nodding to one of the horses tied up to a nearby tree, "you can get on that horse over there and ride out of here."

"Why you—"

"As a matter of fact," she continued, reaching down, picking up a bag that lay at her feet, and tossing it to him, "you can leave right now whether you want to or not."

"Why you little—" Jake seethed. "This isn't even a fourth of what we agreed on."

Georgiana's heart sped up as the heat of the conversation escalated.

"You're lucky I'm givin' you anything. I've decided you have other things you need to help pay for."

Georgiana knew what she referred to, but the man seemed clueless.

"Why, you greedy little—"

Before Georgiana knew what was happening, she saw a glint of a knife as Slash lunged forward. The shotgun fired, and he slumped to the ground. Cordelia stared at his lifeless body for a moment, not moving.

Abruptly turning to Georgiana, Cordelia shouted, "You! Get back in the cabin!" Georgiana quickly scrambled out of the wagon. "And don't you try anything, or you'll join him." She motioned with her gun to the dead man lying before her.

Hurrying toward the door, Georgiana looked back once more just in time to catch the painful look that crossed Cordelia's face. She had just shot and killed the father of her child. Unexpectedly, Cordelia looked up to meet Georgiana's eyes. Georgiana couldn't keep the look of sympathy from off her face. Cordelia looked puzzled for a moment, and then a knowing look came to her eyes as she realized Georgiana knew her secret.

"It wouldn't have made a difference to him had he known. He would never have changed." Giving the man one last look, she added, "It's better this way."

Georgiana turned away, unable to look at the woman's haunted face any longer, and went the rest of the way into the cabin. Cordelia followed.

When Georgiana came through the door, she straightway looked over to Samantha. Samantha was sitting up straight, eyes wide with fear. Georgiana hurried over to her friend and put her arms around her shaking body.

"Georgiana . . . I thought." Tears began coursing down Samantha's face, and Georgiana tried to soothe her.

"Shhh, it's all right . . . I'm all right," she reassured her friend.

"But your face, your dress—what happened?"

It was then Georgiana remembered the cut on her face, and

her hand went to her cheek. The cut was not deep, and the blood had stopped and already begun to dry. She shuddered involuntarily at the thought of what had almost occurred. If Cordelia hadn't shown up, she would have been far worse off, maybe even dead.

"I'm all right. It's just a surface cut," Georgiana spoke soothingly, trying to calm Samantha down. She couldn't help but look over at Cordelia.

Cordelia was watching them, and when their eyes met, Georgiana mouthed the words "thank you." The woman still had some decency left. Cordelia nodded her head, turned away, and yelled at the two sleeping men.

"Gil, Wyatt!" she shouted. The men did not move. "Get up!" she yelled again. Georgiana couldn't believe the two had slept through the sound of the gunshot. When the men still didn't move, Cordelia walked over and gave each man a swift kick with her boot. "I said, get up!"

Both men sat up groggily and rubbed their backsides.

"What was that for?" Gil complained.

"That's for not gettin' up when I hollered at you," Cordelia shouted angrily.

"Ya know we can't hear hardly nothin' since we did all that dynamite blastin' for the railroad last summer," Wyatt groaned.

"Yeah . . . ya don't need to treat us that way," Gil added. "Uncle Carl's gonna hear about—"

"Quit whinin'. My pa's not here and we've got to get movin'," Cordelia informed them. Straightaway, both men complained again.

"Thought we weren't leavin' 'til sun up," Wyatt moaned. "We still got us a couple of hours."

"Wyatt's right. 'Sides, we've barely been asleep an hour," Gil added.

"Well, we can't wait until sun up. What you boys didn't hear with those deaf ears of yours was the shotgun," Cordelia said, her face a stone mask.

"Shotgun?" Both boys hopped to their feet at once.

"Who fired a gun?" Gil looked around for a moment. "And where's Slash?"

Cordelia ignored their questions, went to the backroom, and then started bringing out bags of money and setting them by the door.

"We've got to get out of here now. Though you may not have heard that shotgun, if the posse did, they'll be after us in no time." The boys were still standing dumbfounded, so she began to give them specific orders.

"Gil, go hitch up the wagon . . . and drag the body into the bushes behind the cabin."

"The what?" Gil asked incredulously.

She ignored him and went on.

"Wyatt, tie up that girl's hands again," she motioned toward Georgiana, "and get them loaded in the wagon. Then come back in and help me carry the money out." She headed to the bedroom.

"How did ya get untied?" Wyatt looked at Georgiana accusingly. Georgiana paid him no heed.

Neither of the boys made any motion to get moving. So Cordelia turned back around and put her foot on the edge of the feeble table and shoved hard, knocking it over to get their attention. Samantha jumped in Georgiana's arms.

"If you boys don't want to find yourselves in jail or hangin' from a tree come mornin', you'd better start movin'!"

"But I thought we were leavin' them here." He looked at Georgiana and Samantha.

"Plans have changed, boys. We no longer have the upper hand. We're going to need those two for insurance purposes." She glared at Georgiana when she said it as if to say, "That's the only reason I came to your rescue." But Georgiana knew the reason had been different. She no longer feared for their lives as long as they cooperated. She just hoped no one else would have to die.

·21·

Money Can't Buy You Love

RIDGE knew they were getting closer. They found the fresh tracks about an hour ago. Once he'd finally put two and two together and figured out who they were chasing, it had been easy. The sheriff and Mr. Wallace had a hard time believing it was a woman who had orchestrated the carefully planned bank robbery, but after questioning them why she'd been hanging out at the bank so much, and why she'd moved back in the first place, they agreed it was suspicious. When Ridge told them how he'd come upon Cordelia leaving town in a wagon and heard what he now realized was in truth a gun being cocked, they had been convinced enough to change courses and look for fresh wagon tracks instead of horse tracks. Most bank robbers would have hauled out of town like hellfire and ridden all night, but Cordelia seemed to have another plan. What really worried him was the time that had been wasted before he'd realized who and what they were lookin' for.

It was dark, which made following tracks difficult. He and Mr. Wallace rode slightly ahead of the others, stopping often and double-checking that they were still headed in the right direction.

When the wagon tracks veered off and headed up a small path toward the mountains, Ridge remembered that Cordelia's father used to own a hunting cabin not too far up the first steep incline. They'd be there before daylight.

Knowing they would come upon the cabin soon, his fear

intensified. What if they had already hurt Georgiana or Samantha? Ridge glanced over at the lines of worry and fear etched into Mr. Wallace's face. He imagined he wore a similar look.

He was glad now that the sheriff had insisted Dawson ride alongside his deputy since he had little experience with such matters as bank robbers and posses. Dawson had been grateful to come along at all. Ridge was glad he didn't have to look into the worried face of Dawson the whole way. Let the sheriff deal with him.

They'd convinced Angus to stay at the ranch in case, for some miraculous reason, they'd been wrong and Georgiana or Samantha showed up there. It was a hard thing for Angus to agree to, and Ridge felt guilty insisting, but Angus's eyesight had worsened considerably over the last few years. He would be worried about the man tracking in the dark, and Ridge already had enough to worry about.

A vision of Georgiana in blue, smiling, came to his forethoughts. He remembered how his heart rate increased by her touch as she had placed her hand on his earlier that evening, thanking him for finding her father's medallion, and again when they'd danced. *Please God, keep her safe,* he prayed, *and help us find them soon.*

He could not lose her again.

When a gunshot went off, Ridge felt a jolt go through his entire body. He looked over to Samantha's father and saw his fear mirrored in the man's eyes. The two men increased their pace dramatically and moved even further ahead of the other men in the posse.

When at last they reached the cabin, it was deserted. Mr. Wallace looked around outside, and Ridge went into the cabin. A fire still burned in the fireplace, and a table lay on its side. The outlaws had left in a hurry. As Ridge walked around the cabin, he spotted another blue ribbon lying on the floor by the far wall. He bent down to pick it up. She was trying to leave a trail to let them know where they'd been. Mr. Wallace entered the cabin and began talking.

"There's another way down the mountain with fresh tracks off to the east, and . . . I found a body in the bushes behind the cabin."

Ridge swung around to look Mr. Wallace in the face as his heart started to pound. Mr. Wallace immediately shook his head.

"It wasn't one of them, but I think I know the man." He paused and shook his head again. "Well, at least I thought I did. A man who looked like him came into the bank last Monday, called himself by the name of Winslow Thurston Applegate III. Said he was plannin' on movin' out this way. Told me he'd sold a very profitable cattle ranch down in Texas and was wonderin' how the banking worked around these parts. He wanted to know whether we kept all our money here or transferred some of it to the Denver Bank. Asked how often the Wells Fargo stage came through. I'm afraid I may have given out too much information."

"Well, what worries me right now is that they're fightin' among themselves. We need to find them immediately!" Ridge hurried out of the cabin and to his horse. Mr. Wallace followed close behind. As the sheriff and the rest of the posse rode up, Ridge announced to Samantha's father, "I'm ridin' on ahead. Show the sheriff the body and tell him what you know about the man and then catch up with me."

Ridge mounted his horse and headed off in the direction the wagon had gone, nodding to the sheriff as he passed by but purposely avoiding Dawson's stare.

He was worried. Who had done the shooting and why? The wagon was less than an hour ahead. If he hurried and caught up to them before the sun came up, he might have an advantage.

He rode hard. Scenes from the previous day flew through his mind: Georgiana's feet dangling in the creek while she ran her fingers though her hair; watching her dance around the deserted social hall hand in hand with Samantha; waltzing as close as he dared at the dance while staring into her eyes. He could stare into them forever. He loved her. He had always loved her—from girlish braids and ponytails with ribbons dangling to the beautiful, full-grown, remarkable woman she was now. Nothing could change the fact that his heart belonged to her. Her memory had never relinquished its hold on him, and when she had returned, only then did his heart begin to truly beat once more.

His thoughts quickly changed to the conversation he had with her grandfather just before he had left for the dance.

Angus had wandered up to the creek, still in hopes of catchin' a trout or two for his dinner. Ridge figured it was as good a place as any to finish the conversation they had begun earlier, so he'd gone after him to talk.

When he spotted Angus, he was sitting on the far side in almost the exact spot that had become Ridge's favorite. Obviously the man had better luck there too.

Ridge made his way up the creek, crossed over the bridge, and meandered his way back down to where Angus sat with his eyes closed leaning up against a tree. For a minute, Ridge considered whether the older man might be asleep, but when he sat down only a few feet away, Angus immediately acknowledged his presence.

"Evenin', Ridge."

"Evenin', Angus."

"Was wonderin' when ye would be comin' around," Angus commented.

"Been expectin' me, have you?" Ridge asked.

"Fer sure and fer certain, I was. Knew ye had a bite to settle with me yet tonight."

"Yes . . . well . . ." Now that Ridge was sitting next to Angus, he couldn't hardly bring himself to chastise the man.

"Suppose I should be apologizin' fer earlier. But I can't bring meself to do it." He opened one eye and looked up at Ridge, then closed it again. "Ya know how I feel about the two of ye."

"Yes, and you know how I feel about you interferin'."

"Aye, I do lad, but I just can't help meself. I'm an old man now, stubborn and set in me ways. Just a lookin' out fer me granddaughter, I am. Wantin' her to have a happy life, like the likes of me and me Shannon, filled with love and lots of laughter. Now that there Dawson fella is a good lad, but I know me girl is not in love with him." Angus peeked out of one eye again. "Just as surely as I know she's powerful in love with ye." He closed his eye again and continued talking. "The lad had a talk with me today. Told me he had already asked me granddaughter to marry him. Said tonight he was goin' to be askin' fer her answer." Angus squirmed uncomfortably. "He up and asks me what I thought she'd be tellin' him." Angus let out an exasperated sigh. "Will ya believe that? Him askin' me such a question? Now how was I to be answerin' that, lad? I may know what's in me girl's heart, but I never know what's goin' to come out of her mouth." Both men chuckled.

"So what did ya say?" Ridge finally asked.

"Told him the same Irish tale I told ye about a month past. Seemed to ponder on it fer a while. Then he tells me if her answer ain't yes or she doesn't give him a bit of hope at least, he'd be leavin' in the mornin' fer town. Thanked me fer me hospitality." Angus was silent for a moment, and Ridge figured he was finished, but he spoke again. "If ye were to be askin' me, I think the lad knows her heart is belongin' to another." He added, "Can't blame him now, fer not wantin' ta give up."

The talk had encouraged Ridge at first, but knowing Dawson was going to speak marriage to Georgiana again had made him nervous. He had watched and waited for them to arrive at the social, and when they had been late, he'd wondered whether they had spoken before they'd arrived. When she and Dawson had danced, he knew the conversation had been serious and intimate in nature. If only he knew how Georgiana truly felt toward the man. Could Angus be right that she wasn't in love with Dawson? If he was right about that, did that mean there was hope for him?

Suddenly, a sound in front of him drew him from his musings and commanded his full attention. He could hear voices less than a quarter mile up the road. He brought his horse to an abrupt halt and dismounted. Tying Storm to a tree, he withdrew his rifle and crept forward in the brush.

He spotted the wagon off to one side of the road. One of the wheels had lost its iron rim, and two men were sitting on the far side of the wagon, desperately trying to repair it.

"You're doin' that wrong," the first man complained.

"Am not," said the second.

"Sure are. When did ya ever learn to fix a wagon wheel, anyway? What makes you so smart?" the first man continued.

"'Cause I saw someone do it once . . . sort of," the second man bragged.

"Here, give it ta me. You're as blind as ya are deaf," the first man said, trying to take over the repair.

Ignoring the two men's bickering, Ridge looked around. He could see Georgiana and Samantha huddled together in the back of the wagon under a small blanket. A huge wave of relief passed over him that they seemed to be unharmed. Scanning the area further, he could not see Cordelia. Nor was he certain there weren't any others around. It made him uneasy. He wished he at least knew where Cordelia had gone.

In the next instant, he got his answer when he felt the barrel of a gun shoved between his shoulder blades.

"Drop the gun, Ridge, and don't think about trying anything stupid. I've already shot one man dead today."

So it was Cordelia who shot the man at the cabin, Ridge thought as he carefully laid his gun down and stood up slowly.

"So who was the man you shot?"

"No one of any consequence . . . at least not anymore . . . now move!" she commanded, shoving the gun deeper into his back to prod him forward.

Ridge watched curiously as the sound of their footsteps went unnoticed by the two still arguing over how to fix the wagon wheel.

"If ya do that, we ain't never gonna get out of here," the second man criticized.

"Well, if ya'd quit lookin' over my shoulder, I might get somethin' done. You're makin' me nervous," said the first, who had taken over.

"Shut up, you two," Cordelia yelled. The two men turned to her and seemed quite surprised to see Ridge standing there at gunpoint. "Can't you boys do anything right? I leave you here to take a look around, and when I come back, look who I find in the bushes aiming a gun at you." She looked from one man to the other. "I'm surprised the women didn't get the better of you two while I was away."

"We didn't hear . . . ," the first man started, defending himself as he eyed Ridge.

"Course you didn't—you're both half deaf, but if you'd stop fighting and look around every once in a while, you might notice a man with a gun in the bushes behind you!" Neither man said a word in his defense as she glared at them. "Just get that wheel fixed so we can get out of here."

"Yes, ma'am," they said together and turned back to the wheel.

Ridge looked over at Georgiana and Samantha. Both girls looked relieved to see him despite his being at the wrong end of a gun.

"Now you," Cordelia said, motioning to Ridge, "sit down right there and keep your hands where I can see them."

Ridge sat down in the middle of the road and laid his arms across his bent knees in front of him. Cordelia stood a few feet away from him, the gun still pointed at his chest.

"Who came with you?" she demanded.

"No one. I came alone," Ridge answered.

"Do you expect me to believe that?" She narrowed her eyes at him.

"Believe what ya want, but I came alone. When I told the sheriff I thought it was you who had robbed the bank and I had seen ya leavin' in a wagon, he about laughed me out of town." He looked Cordelia straight in the eyes and hoped he was believable. "They're off chasing a band of imaginary outlaws on horseback."

By the smug look on Cordelia's face, he knew she believed him. When he glanced over at Georgiana, she turned her face slightly to meet his eyes directly. It was the first time he'd noticed the dried blood on her face. His anger ignited immediately. Who had cut her and why?

"Well," Cordelia began, "you were wise to come alone. If you'd come ridin' up in a blaze of fury, guns firin', as you men so often like to do, there's no tellin' who might have got shot." Cordelia glanced toward Georgiana to make her point clear.

"If she gets hurt," Ridge said, swallowing hard and speaking between clenched teeth, "more than she already has . . ." He paused to get a grip on his anger, then continued, "Or if ya harm Samantha, I can promise you will regret the day ya ever met me, Miss Cordelia Jamison."

"Ooh, is that a threat?" She gave him a pointed look. "For your information, it wasn't me who cut the face of your little lovely, and . . ." She paused, considering whether she should continue, then daringly added, "You might like to know, he had much bigger, more carnal designs for her."

Ridge's heart pounded, and his anger rose again.

"I can tell by the way you look right now, you'd like to kill the man." Cordelia stared at him a moment and gave a hollow laugh. "Well, I already beat ya to it."

"You want me to thank you. Is that why you're tellin' me this?"

"I did it for me, not for you," she spat the words at him. "He had it comin', didn't he, Miss McLaughlin?"

Ridge looked over at Georgiana. He could not accurately read her expression, so he looked back to Cordelia. There was something in her eyes . . . some kind of sorrow mixed with triumph. Not triumphant for killing a man, but rather for overcoming some personal test. He was missing something, some secret she and Georgiana now shared.

"You're not going to get away with this. Think about it, Cordelia. Eventually the posse will come this way, maybe even decide what I told them might be noteworthy. There will be at least fifteen or twenty armed men." He looked over to the two men still not looking like they were making any progress. "Do ya really think you'll hold up in a shootin' match with those two at your side?"

"That's why I have them," she pointed toward Georgiana and Samantha, "and you." She looked down at him. "Someone else might die, but that's a risk I'm willin' to take. Unless . . ."

"Unless what?"

Cordelia walked over and stood behind him. Pointing the shotgun at him with one hand, she took the other and began playing with his hair.

"There is one other possibility," she continued to play with his hair, her voice taking on a dreamy quality. For the longest moment she didn't move or say anything else. Finally, she tore her eyes away from him and glanced at Georgiana. Ridge stiffened, worried what she was planning. Cordelia didn't seem to notice and began speaking again. "I know she's beautiful, Ridge," she continued, staring at Georgiana as she spoke. "And . . . and you're quite taken with her."

Ridge tensed his muscles, preparing himself to act quickly if she made a move to harm Georgiana.

"But . . . ," she said, looking back at him, and he relaxed slightly. "I do have something she doesn't have." Cordelia paused, and Ridge didn't say anything, just waited. "Why, I have all this money," she suddenly blurted out, gesturing toward the wagon. "Just think . . . one bag is enough to live comfortably on for at least two years and there are more than ten in the wagon." Her voice became excited. "We could go someplace, another country, perhaps. I'm supposed to meet up with my father at the Utah/Idaho border. We thought we'd get lost in Mormon territory for a while. They're pretty accepting of outsiders. Who knows . . . maybe they'll even convert me."

She laughed at that and added, "Though Father would be awfully disappointed if I suddenly grew a conscience and gave the money back." She laughed again, almost hysterically. Ridge watched carefully as her hand relaxed on the gun. "But I don't care about my father. He has never cared about me or my mother." Cordelia turned her full attention back to him and once again her voice took on the same dreamy quality as before. "I . . . I know I could make you happy . . . if you'd only let me."

Ridge knew he needed to keep her distracted. If he could, he might be able to get the gun from her without harming anyone. Or maybe he could talk her into leaving with him and get her away from Georgiana and Samantha.

So slowly he reached up with one hand and gently grabbed hold of her fingers that were wound in his hair, bringing her hand down to lie against his cheek. Her breath caught in her throat as he guided her hand further down toward his mouth and with his lips, kissed it softly. He could feel her hand trembling. He felt a pang of guilt, but he knew he had to do something, anything, to keep Georgiana and Samantha safe and to end this all before it became a heated battle.

"Maybe I did make a mistake. Your offer is tempting."

He spoke the words low and seductively, all too aware that Georgiana was watching, listening. It was going to work—she was weakening, becoming even more distracted. Just as he was about to make his move, she abruptly pulled her hand away from his and placed both hands back on the shotgun. When she spoke, her voice was heavy with emotion.

"You're almost as smooth as Jake." Her voice broke. He was surprised to see tears spill from her eyes. "Though you're even more dangerous because . . . I . . . I could more easily believe you," she added. With the back of one of her hands, she swiped at the tears on her face and quickly put it back on the gun. "I may want you . . . or want what you could give me and my . . ." She paused, and her expression turned hard. "But I'm not a fool. I saw the way you kissed her. You wouldn't have kissed her that way unless you were in love, deeply in love." She took a minute to wipe another tear. "You're not going to go anywhere with me. You're just sayin' the things I want to hear."

Georgiana looked sadly over at Cordelia. In spite of everything, she felt sorry for her. Even with her hardened and calloused attitude, she could see Cordelia was frightened. When stripped of her defenses, all she had left to cling to was her anger and her hate. When she'd shot Jake, she'd lost the direction for all those negative feelings. She would not aim them at the child she carried, Georgiana knew that. The protective way her hand went to her abdomen so often spoke volumes. Now, only left with the fear and worry of raising a child on her own, her desperation had culminated. She was looking for a way out but was still not willing to give in.

"Cordelia," Ridge pleaded. "Just give the money back and turn yourself in. They're going to catch ya either way. You're a woman. The judge will go easy on ya."

Cordelia looked tired and desperate. The two were not a good combination. Shaking her head, she looked at the ground for a moment, placing one hand on her stomach. Then they all heard the sound of approaching horses.

Cordelia's head came up immediately, and her eyes turned hard.

"You," she said, motioning to Georgiana, "get down here . . . now!" She pointed the gun at Ridge's head. "Or you can say goodbye to your man."

Georgiana quickly scrambled out of the wagon as best she could with her hands tied. Gratefully her feet weren't tied too. Nevertheless, she stumbled. She fell a second time before she managed to get close to Cordelia. When she did, Cordelia turned the gun on her, just in time for the posse to appear in the bushes behind Gil and Wyatt. The two men were totally unaware of their presence.

"If you come any closer, I'll shoot her."

"Put the gun down, Miss Jamison," the sheriff spoke. "You're only gonna make things worse for yourself."

"I'm not givin' in that easy, Sheriff." She turned her attention to Ridge and ordered, "Mr. Carson, fetch two of those money bags and tie them to that horse over there."

Ridge looked at the sheriff, who nodded his head.

"I suggest you take your orders from me, Mr. Carson, and not the sheriff." She shoved the gun closer to Georgiana. "If you want your woman back still breathin', that is."

Ridge stood quickly, obediently walked to the wagon, and hoisted two of the money bags out. Walking over to the horse, he began securing the bags to the saddle. When he was finished, he stepped back to the middle of the road.

"Now, bring the horse over here."

Ridge walked back, untied the horse, and began leading it toward her. It was at that moment that Gil finally looked up and noticed Ridge walking with the horse, money bags hanging.

"Hey, what's going on . . . ?" Gil shouted. Wyatt looked up.

"Yeah, what's going on?" Wyatt echoed.

The distraction wasn't much, but it had startled Cordelia enough that Ridge was able to lunge toward her, knocking the gun from her hands. The gun went off.

Simultaneously a shot came from the direction of the posse.

Ridge was horrified when Georgiana flung herself in front of Cordelia, knocking her down, and shouted just as he heard another shot being fired. "No, sheriff! She's going to have a baby!"

Georgiana fell limp on the ground.

With Samantha's scream ringing in his ears, Ridge ran to Georgiana, knelt beside her, and lifted her upper body onto his lap. Blood was quickly soaking through her dress, and an immense fear seized hold of his heart. He couldn't lose her, not now!

Please . . . please . . . please! he prayed.

·22·

Home at Last

"MOTHER?"

Georgiana had tried opening her eyes and could have sworn she'd seen her mother's face hovering over her before she'd quickly shut them to avoid the bright light. Someone squeezed her hand, and she once again attempted to open them, this time successfully.

"Mother, is that you?"

"Yes, my dear. It's me."

"But how . . . when . . . ?" Georgiana looked around her. She was lying in her bed at her grandfather's house, so her mother was here, in Colorado.

"Shhh . . . you need your rest. Go back to sleep and I'll fix you something to eat. You must be famished. After you've eaten something, we'll talk."

Her mother bent forward and kissed her on the forehead. Georgiana tried to keep her eyes open, but it was a battle she wasn't destined to win. Despite the slight pain in her head, sleep quickly overcame her.

When next she opened her eyes, she was alone. She couldn't help but wonder if maybe she had been dreaming. How many of the thoughts and memories assaulting her were dreams and how much of what she remembered was reality?

Trying to sit up, she felt a deep pain shoot through her shoulder, knocking the breath out of her and causing her to fall back onto her pillow. Well, the memory of getting shot was real enough. Reaching up, she unbuttoned her nightgown so she could slip it slightly off her shoulder, just far enough to examine the ugly red wound.

Closing her eyes and leaning back against the pillow, she tried to think. Suddenly her eyes flew back open. Ridge! She remembered hearing two shots go off. Had he been wounded too? Then she vaguely remembered seeing his worried face leaning over her, hearing his voice speaking softly . . . the feel of his hand caressing hers as he held onto it for what seemed like forever. He had stayed at her side. She was sure, but where was he now? And where was Samantha?

Just then, there was a soft knock at the door, and her mother entered carrying a tray and smiling brightly at her.

"Hello, again," she said, a warm smile still on her face.

"Mother!" Georgiana's heart was overjoyed. "I was worried I only dreamed you."

"Here," her mother said, sitting next to her and placing the tray before her. Reaching over, she squeezed Georgiana's hand like she had earlier. "Do I feel real enough to you?"

"Yes." Georgiana squeezed her hand back. "You feel wonderful."

"Now, you must eat." Georgiana inhaled the smell of the soup, and her stomach growled hungrily. "I see your stomach agrees."

Although she was starved, Georgiana was starved more for answers.

"But, Mother, when did you arrive, and how long have you been here?"

"Eat first," her mother scolded gently, "then we'll talk. Your body needs sustenance."

Dutifully, Georgiana lifted the spoon to her mouth. The taste was heavenly and filled with memories.

"Nana's stew!" she exclaimed, and her mother smiled.

"Yes, she taught me to make it years ago when I was a young bride."

Georgiana took another spoonful, savoring the taste of stew along with the memories of sitting at the table watching her grandmother chopping the vegetables and mutton while telling her tales and singing her Irish melodies. Before she knew it, she had consumed the entire contents of the bowl, as well as a thick slice of bread. Pushing the tray back, she looked at her mother.

"Mother, tell me, when did you arrive, and how long have I been out?"

"I've been here three days," her mother answered. "I sent your grandfather a telegram almost two weeks ago, telling him we were coming. I wanted to surprise you. Your brothers are going to be very disappointed they weren't here when you woke up."

"William and Aden are here too!"

"Yes, dear, but I'm afraid they headed into town with your grandfather about an hour ago." Georgiana was overjoyed. She couldn't believe they were here. "They've been underfoot all morning. Your grandfather took pity on me. I'm sure they'll come bounding in here as soon as they return."

"How long has it been since I was shot?"

"Nearly five days."

"Five days?" She looked at her mother incredulously.

"Yes, you passed out when the bullet hit you. For the first two days you were in and out of consciousness. You hit your head when you fell to the ground, but Doc Hansen didn't think you'd hit hard enough to cause a concussion."

Instinctively, Georgiana reached her hand up and felt the tender spot on the right side of her head, a few inches above her ear.

"You lost a lot of blood before they were able to get you to him," her mother continued. "He thought perhaps between hitting your head and being shot, your body was just doing the best it could to try and heal itself." Her mother smiled slightly. "The second night you woke up for a few seconds, do you remember?" Georgiana shook her head. "You mumbled something nobody could quite make out and went back to sleep. When you started to run a fever," her mother paused, becoming more emotional, "I was so worried and . . . so afraid." Georgiana reached over and squeezed her mother's hand. It seemed to give her mother courage to go on. "You were delirious most of the time after that. Yesterday the fever finally broke. About all you've done since then is sleep."

"What about Samantha, Mother. Is she okay?"

"She's fine, dear. She's come over every day to check on you, except today, that is."

"What about Dawson?" *Where had he been through the whole ordeal?* Georgiana wondered.

"He's been worried about you too. I'll ask your grandfather to go back to town later and send Dawson a telegram, letting him know you've awakened.

"Telegram?"

"I'm sorry, dear. He had to leave for home yesterday afternoon. The doctor assured him you were going to be fine or he would never have left. Neither would have Samantha."

"Samantha? Samantha's gone . . . but where?" She was getting the feeling she'd missed out on an awful lot while she slept.

"Well," her mother said, looking at her tentatively. "Dawson offered to take her with him to see New York." Her mother smiled knowingly. "Even as a child that girl always dreamed of going to the city."

"I remember." Georgiana pondered for a moment what that all meant.

"He left you a letter." Her mother reached into her apron pocket and withdrew an envelope with her name on it. "Would you like to read it now?"

Suddenly, Georgiana was very tired again. What she really wanted was to know where Ridge was, but she couldn't bring herself to ask. She had only mentioned Ridge to her mother in a few of her letters. Her mother couldn't have any idea of how deep her feelings for him ran . . . or could she?

"Can you leave it on the dresser for me, please? I think I'll read it later. I'm feeling quite fatigued again." Georgiana reached out and took her mother's hand. "Thank you, Mother, for coming. I . . . I've missed you, have wished you were here." Georgiana was on the verge of crying.

"I've missed you too, love. When you wake up, we'll talk some more. We have much to discuss." Her mother's words made her curious, but she was too tired to ask their meaning.

"Mmm . . . ," was all she managed before she was lost to sleep and to the musings and figments of her dreams.

❧ ❧ ❧

Charlotte watched as her daughter drifted off. Gently she reached over and brushed away the wayward strand of hair that had fallen onto her sweet, beautiful face.

Charlotte finally understood why Georgiana had held herself back from Dawson. She cared for him, but she didn't love him, not like a love between a husband and a wife should be, not like she had loved Michael. Why hadn't she seen sooner that Georgiana had lost her heart long ago? Sadly, she knew the answer to that.

For the thousandth time, Charlotte bemoaned the fact that she'd taken her children away from here, from this place so filled with love. As soon as she had walked into the house, she felt it rain upon her, saturating her soul. Why hadn't she realized it then? While being so weak from the sorrow and grief . . . so lost in the loneliness, she had run away from this house and the sound of Michael's laughter that still echoed down the halls. Run from the mountains and from her memories of days spent walking and meandering with him through their majestic beauty. Shamefully, she had even run from the sound of his father's voice, so similar to Michael's own. In that first year, sometimes when Angus would speak or call out, her heart would begin to pound, and she could almost believe it had all been a bad dream. She'd imagine Michael was still here, calling her from the other room. So, yes, she had run . . . run with their children . . . run straight into the arms of her cold and spiteful sister, who for so many years had not owned even an ounce of love in her heart.

When she woke from her grief, it was too late. Cecelia had control over all the family's money, even the little she'd brought with her, leaving her at the mercy of Cecelia's wants and desires. None of them included Colorado or her husband's family. Cecelia was only interested in furthering her own rank and social standing, and unfortunately for Georgiana, Cecelia had decided that she was her surest ticket.

Charlotte's stomach lurched at the knowledge she now possessed, the deceit and the lies her sister had succeeded in perpetrating for so long. She wouldn't be returning to live with her sister, nor would her children. Not ever.

Standing up, Charlotte bent down once again to place a kiss on her sleeping daughter's head and picked up the tray from the bedside table. She still had one more important task she had to accomplish today, and she could no longer put it off.

Once Charlotte finished up the dishes, she donned her hat and cloak and walked toward the far east corner of the meadow. To temper the rising feelings of nervousness and guilt, she busied herself picking wildflowers along the way.

When she came upon the graveyard, she paused at the gate before entering. Only a dozen or so graves decorated the ground; most looked forgotten and neglected. Focusing on where Michael and now his mother lay, she was touched to see that their graves were well cared for—no weeds on or near them, and a bundle of flowers at each that looked to be only a few days old.

With reverence, Charlotte slowly unlatched the gate and stepped inside. This was the first time she'd been back since the day they had placed Michael's body in the ground. Even though they had remained in Colorado a year after his death, she had never been able to bring herself to return.

Taking a deep breath, she first walked over and stood before Michael's mother's grave.

"Hello, Mother McLaughlin." She bent down, lying half of the flowers she'd collected next to the others. Tears wet her cheeks. "I'm so sorry we never came back." The tears fell faster. "I'm sorry you and your grandchildren missed out on so many precious memories together. You were always so good to me, as if you were my own mother. I took so much joy away from you. Please . . . please forgive me."

After another moment, she walked over to her husband's

headstone. Kneeling down, she released the last of the flowers and began running her fingers across the inscription. *Michael Angus McLaughlin 1851–1892 Beloved Son, Husband, and Father.* Drawing her hand back from the stone, she brushed at the profusion of tears with both hands.

She had sought peace for so long, but it had always eluded her. Charlotte now prayed that she might find some solace here at his grave. She had somehow always known this was the only place she would ever find the peace she was seeking, but she had turned away, fearing if she let go of the grief, Michael would be lost to her, forgotten. So she had forced herself to suffer and, in turn, had caused her children to suffer as well.

"Oh, Michael, I have made such a mess of things, not only of my life, but I fear I have caused our children unnecessary pain." Lifting her hand, she once again traced the letters of his name. "It was not fair, you being taken from me the way you were. I was not ready to let you go. Our time together was too short. We were supposed to raise our children, grow old together, and—remember—you were going to take me to visit your homeland."

She smiled for a moment as she remembered how he would gather her in his arms and say, "Charlotte, me love, ever it is when I look into the green of yar eyes I remember the green hills of Ireland. One day, I'll be takin' ye there."

"When you left me, Michael, I couldn't bear it and . . . and I ran. It was wrong, but I was lost without you." Charlotte lowered her hand from the stone and picked up one of the flowers she had laid before it, bringing it to her nose and breathing in the deep, rich scent.

When she heard footsteps behind her, she instinctively knew who it was.

"Hello, Father McLaughlin."

"Hello, lass."

Angus approached his son's grave. He knew she would come. He had prayed for it.

They remained silent for some time before she spoke.

"You know, he was alive that day when I found him . . ."

Angus held his breath. Long had he waited to know the last moment of his son's life. To know whether he had died alone or whether when she had found him, there was still breath in him. He had prayed it was the latter, that his son had died held by the woman he so loved. When she spoke again, her voice was low, wrought with emotion. He knew this would cost her dearly.

"But only barely." Her voice trembled. "I knew before I arrived something was wrong. You remember I had gone over to the Thompsons' to check on Marva. She was near her time and after losing her last child, she was sore afraid. I had just started checking her when I thought I heard Michael call my name. 'That's impossible,' I thought, 'Michael's at home waiting for you.' I looked out the window anyway to see if maybe he had ridden over, but I saw nothing, so I continued with the examination." She paused and took a deep breath. "It was a few minutes later that I heard him call my name again, but this time his voice sounded weak . . . pleading. I immediately began packing my things. Marva begged me to stay a while with her. I could see she was frightened, so I quickly made some tea to calm her and hurried to the wagon. I knew somehow Michael needed me.

"When I got to the ranch, the horses were milling about, acting strange. I didn't see Michael anywhere. Then I thought I heard his voice calling me again." Tears were flowing down her face. "His voice was weak and laced with pain. I couldn't see him, but I knew where he was. I ran to the corral, screaming for him that I was coming, and threw open the gate." Her breath caught in her throat. "Then I saw him. He was lying on the ground, in the middle of the horses, not moving. When I got to him, he was bleeding everywhere. I tried to stop it, but I couldn't. I . . . I tried . . ." She began to sob. It took a moment before she could continue. "He was unconscious at first, and I was afraid he was already lost to me, but then he opened his eyes and looked straight into mine.

"'Char . . . ,' he said, and I could see his pain.

"'Shhh, Michael . . . save your strength,' I said, carefully lifting his head onto my lap.

"'Char . . . I'm sorry.' His chest began to heave hard like he couldn't draw breath. 'I . . . I don't . . . want to . . . leave ya.'

"'Shhh, don't say that . . . you're not going anywhere. Someone will come to help . . . get the doctor.' I prayed it was true.

"'They're calling me, Char . . . the pain is too much fer me, darlin'.'

"'No, Michael . . . don't listen to them . . . stay with me. I need you. The children need you,' I pleaded with him.

"He closed his eyes," Charlotte continued. "I could see his chest rise and fall slowly and hoped he was trying to save his strength. He seemed to be breathing easier . . . I had hope." A deep sigh of anguish escape her lips. "When he opened his eyes again, I knew. I knew he was leaving me." She was sobbing harder now, and her body shook with emotion. Angus dropped to his knees and put his arms around her, his tears mingling with hers. After a few minutes, she was able to continue. "He lifted his hand and placed it on my face. His hand was trembling hard, so I helped him to hold it there.

"'I love ye, Charlotte Anne McLaughlin . . . ever have I loved ye. From the moment I first looked into yar eyes, I have loved ye with me whole heart and with me soul.'

"I couldn't speak. My voice was seized with the fear of knowing he was leaving me.

"'One last kiss, I would ask of ye. One last heavenly kiss . . . so that the last thing I feel on this earth will be the touch of yar sweet lips to mine. Will ye give it to me?'

"The reality of what he was asking released my tongue. He was asking me to say good-bye.

"'Please, Michael, I love you so much. I cannot bear it if you go,' I said.

"'A kiss . . . me love . . . a kiss.'

"And so I kissed him, and he closed his eyes . . . and was gone."

Charlotte collapsed into Angus's arms, her emotions fully spent. For a long time he just held her, his hands too busy trying to soothe her and to wipe away his own tears. Then she sat up slowly and looked him in his eyes.

"If . . . if I had gone to him when I first heard him call, if I had left right then . . . maybe—"

"No, me lass, it was Michael's time to go. I prayed hard after losin' me lad. God granted me the knowin' of it. It has been a little comfort, as it was to Shannon too."

She looked away, doubt clearly visible on her face. He reached over, taking her chin and turning her head back to him.

"It was no fault of yers. It was his time." Angus took his other hand and wiped at the tears trailing her cheeks. "I'm glad to be knowin' ye were with him at the last though. It does me old heart good. He loved ye true, he did—a powerful love. I'll never ferget the smile on his face and the look of pride as he came totin' ye home with him from the city." Angus grinned. "And the love-struck look in yar eyes too." Finally she gave him a small smile. "He would want ye to be happy, lass. You need to start livin' again."

"I still miss him . . . every day."

"I know . . . I know. I miss me lad and me Shannon too. But they are ever with us, in our hearts and in our minds. The memories will never be leavin', even if ye find another to settle with, Michael will always be yers."

Charlotte reached out and hugged him then. When at last she let go, she lifted her apron and dried her tears.

"We should be getting back. Tiny brought me in a bucket of berries, so I baked a pie. It will be done about now. The men will be waiting with plates and forks ready, I'm sure."

"Aye, then we best be hurryin' on back now." Standing quickly, Angus feigned a grin while patting his stomach and helped her to her feet.

"Come, Father McLaughlin," Charlotte said, lacing her arm through his as they headed back to the house.

·23·

Dear Ridge

RIDGE bent down and picked up his hat, dusting it off before placing it back on his head. The wind had picked up again, but thankfully the skies were still clear. There was no threat of a storm, at least not tonight.

Walking over to the campfire, Ridge sat down and began to warm his hands in front of the fire. The nights were getting cooler, but he was glad he hadn't opted to stay the night in town.

As Ridge absentmindedly watched the wind fight with the flames, he conjured up a vision of Georgiana.

He hoped she was awake by now and doing better. He still cringed at the memory of her lying so lifeless in his arms, red blood dominating the blue satin she wore. He had never been so frightened of losing something in his life, had never prayed so hard.

He hadn't left her side for the first three days she'd been unconscious. Angus had tried to convince him to take a break, get some sleep, but he had this immense fear that if he let go, she would slip away. Dawson and Samantha had come and gone, but he had stayed.

Then the sheriff had come to speak with him. They wanted him to help transport the outlaws over to Castle Rock for trial and also to make a sworn statement. He didn't want to leave her, especially not before she'd woken up, even though Doc Hansen swore to him Georgiana would be fine. Ridge knew that his testimony to the judge was needed. So, relying on faith that she'd still be there when he got back, he left with the sheriff the next morning.

Ridge pondered a moment about the questions the judge had asked him. It had been difficult, especially where Cordelia was concerned. He kept picturing Georgiana throwing herself in front of the woman in order to protect her unborn child. He'd recalled the frightened and ashamed look on Cordelia's face as he had held Georgiana's limp body in his arms. He knew somehow, Georgiana's act of pure selflessness had impacted Cordelia deeply. He was actually relieved when the judge decided to give her a second chance. It was her first attempt at robbery, and she had shot the man Slash in self-defense. Cordelia had been sent to live with an aunt in California to bear and raise her child. Ridge truly hoped she would turn her life around with the second chance she had been given.

Thinking of second chances, his thoughts abruptly turned to Samantha and the discovery he had made. After the trial was over, he'd wandered over to the town's restaurant. He didn't have much an appetite since Georgiana was shot. On the way over to Castle Rock, he ate only a few strips of dried jerky. Since they were headed home, he knew should eat something to build his strength to endure whatever he'd find when he returned.

He could only call it fate that he'd caught a glimpse of something familiar when an old weathered man sitting at the table across from him pushed up his sleeves before beginning his meal. Getting up from his table, Ridge walked over to the old man.

"Do you mind?" he asked, gesturing toward a chair. The man shook his head and Ridge sat down. "That wristband you're wearin', I've seen it before."

The man stopped eating, slipped it off his wrist, and set it down on the table between them as a look of profound relief etched across his face.

"Saints be praised!" the old man uttered. "I'd 'bout given up hope."

The old man proceeded to tell him a story. He'd come across a young man on the brink of death almost two years back. He had been robbed, shot twice, and left for dead. He could do nothing for the boy except make him as comfortable as possible. They had taken everything, even his coat and shoes. It was a wonder he had survived the cold night. He'd asked for his name, but the boy couldn't speak. "However, he did manage to slip this here band from his wrist. I knew it must mean somethin' to the boy," the old man said solemnly. "He pressed it into my hand a moment before he passed. Luckily, it wasn't worth much or the thieves wouldn't have left it behind. I asked around a bit when I got back to town to see if any folks recognized it. Since no one did, I hoped if I wore it 'bout my own arm, someone might get a look someday and know who it was belongin' to. I figured I could at least do that much for the boy."

Ridge stared quietly at the wristband after the old man finished his story. It was the one Samantha had given Mitch, he was sure. He had one that was similar in his own trunk back home. After Georgiana had gone, Samantha had made homemade jewelry to relieve some of her boredom. She had actually become good at it. She had given him one on his fifteenth birthday. Though he wasn't much for wearing jewelry, it was plain enough, made of only woven leather. He only wore it a few times. After she and Mitch had become engaged, she had given him one as well. Mitch wore his proudly wherever he went.

Ridge told the man he knew whose it was, thanked him, took the wristband, and left, albeit forgetting his own meal. At last Samantha could have some peace in knowing the truth and maybe, just maybe, she could begin looking again to her own future.

Ridge sighed long and deep. He wished he was already back at Georgiana's side. If she woke up today, he wouldn't be there. Maybe it would be Dawson she would see when she first opened her eyes.

Arrgh! He was driving himself crazy.

Thinking to distract himself, he decided he'd eat the snack that Georgiana's mother instructed Angus to put in his pack. Ridge walked over to his saddlebags and withdrew the bundle wrapped in a cloth napkin. When he did, another bundle fell onto the ground. Ridge picked it up curiously and walked over to the fire with them both. After tossing a few dried apple slices into his mouth and grabbing a hunk of jerky, Ridge unwrapped the second bundle, and a note fell open. He picked it up and began to read.

Dear Mr. Carson,

First, I want to apologize for five years ago abruptly taking my daughter from her two best friends and moving away, so far away. I was wrong in my decision, and now I realize, even to a greater extent, just how wrong a choice I made. I wish I could offer an excuse, but my selfishness could never justify my actions.

Second, I'd like to return some things that belong to you. These letters were written and mailed to you by my daughter. Unbeknownst to her or myself, my sister, Georgiana's aunt, contrived a way to keep these letters from ever reaching you. What mean and wicked design she bore in her heart for such an act, I do not know. However, I do know something of the pain it caused Georgiana being deprived of the communication between her two dearest friends over the past five years.

I have given Georgiana the rest of the letters I found in her aunt's possession, some from various friends, but most from Samantha Wallace. All the letters she wrote to Georgiana were there as well.

These letters I felt, I'm not sure why, should be given to you. Even though I noticed the bundle I gave to my daughter did not contain any letters written from you personally, I felt this was the action I should take. I hope and pray I have made the right decision. I know my daughter cares for you deeply. I suspect in truth that you have feelings for her too. Why else would you so diligently be not removed from her side for the three days following her accident?

For good or for bad, fate has had a hand in our lives for a reason. I pray now that happiness and love will abound and the souls kept apart for so long will find a place to bind and to keep forever.

With Sincerity,
Mrs. Charlotte McLaughlin

Ridge anxiously untied the string that held the bundle of letters together, opened the first one, and began reading. It was well into the night, and he had found it necessary to add logs to the fire many times, before he finished reading all Georgiana's letters. Even still, he picked a few out and reread them.

It was evident that her tender heart had been broken, not by any fault of his, but broken just the same. He ran his fingers over a few smudged words and wondered if the smudges had been caused by her youthful tears. It was lucky for her aunt that he wasn't anywhere near New York. How could a person ever be as cruel and conniving as that woman had been? What made a person's heart turn so stone cold that they would purposely and spitefully interfere with people's lives, causing so much heartache?

Ridge retied the string that bound the letters together and put them back in his saddlebag. As he walked to his bedroll, he pulled the blue satin ribbon from his pocket. He continued to hold it, caressing it with his fingers, as he lay down to sleep. The moment he closed his eyes, she was there at the forefront of his mind: her long golden hair softly framing her face, those gray-violet eyes staring up at his, those soft tender lips longing to be kissed. He knew what he had to do. The only question was how was he going to wait until tomorrow?

·24·

Dear Georgie

GEORGIANA couldn't take her eyes off the box of letters her mother had just laid in her lap.

"But where . . . how did you . . . ?"

"I got a letter three weeks ago from your grandfather. He said you had asked him about some missing letters. It got me thinking, so I did some looking around. I found those hidden in your Aunt Cecelia's room."

"But why would she . . . how? Some of these I took to the post office myself."

"I think Aunt Cecelia was paying Mrs. Schnell, an old school friend who works at the post office, to detain your letters going both directions and bring them to her." Her mother was quiet for a moment, and then sighed deeply. "Your aunt wasn't always this way, my dear." Georgiana's mother told her about the events in her sister's life that had changed her so negatively. "It was devastating," her mother said sorrowfully. "However, that does not excuse or justify her actions. She chose to harden her heart and become the kind of woman who could do such a thing to you . . . to her own sister." Her mother's voice broke. "There is something else I found too." Her mother suddenly looked very saddened, as if she had discovered something profound. "While I was looking for the letters, I found a will."

"A will?" Georgiana didn't understand.

"My parents' will . . . the original one. After they died, Aunt

Cecelia had a new will made. I had it checked. The signatures are false."

Georgiana was torn at the look on her mother's face. She could tell that the sheer depth of betrayal by her sister disturbed her mother greatly.

"Would she really do such a thing?" Georgiana dared ask. Her mother nodded her head.

"When your father and I began courting, my parents were disappointed. They had made other hopeful plans for me, marriage plans which were more advantageous for both me and our family. The first time I saw your father, though . . . the first time he looked at me and spoke in his thick Irish brogue, there was no one else." She smiled. "He was a dream I never thought would come true, in feature, form, and voice, and I knew that I was created to love him.

"Despite the fact that he wasn't who my parents had in mind, your father was very amiable, as well as flattering. He even made my mother blush a time or two, as I recall. I knew they would grow to love him. I could already tell they were beginning to like him. That was why I was so shocked when all of a sudden their attitudes toward him changed. Father refused to give his blessing when Michael asked for my hand, and mother, more often than not, would break out in tears whenever I mentioned his name.

"Your Aunt Cecelia, on the other hand, disliked him immediately from the first time they met and was never found wanting in expressing her opinion of him. I suspected that somehow Cecelia had a hand in the ruination of my parent's good opinion of your father, though I could never find out the truth of it.

"Though my father had refused him, I had already pledged my love to Michael. So I packed a bag and escaped the house early one morning. We were married that same day at the courthouse and headed here to Colorado. I wrote mother and father and begged their forgiveness and explained how deeply I loved Michael, but I never heard from them. Your aunt arrived shortly after we did and insisted I return with her. I'm afraid I had allowed her too much control over my life growing up and thus she felt she could force me into returning. Especially, she assumed, after I realized how uncivilized and impoverished a life I would be living in comparison to my life in New York.

"Truth was, I was never happier than here with Michael and your grandparents, and my happiness and joy gave me the strength to stand up to her. She left swearing I was no longer her sister and I would be cut out of our father and mother's will. I never once regretted my decision." Georgiana reached over and gently laid her hand on her mother's arm as she continued. "When Father and Mother died, Aunt Cecelia sent me a letter, including a copy of the new will. It saddened me deeply. Not because they disinherited me, but because I had somehow hoped they had forgiven me. I had written them often, though I never got any letters in return. Somehow the will was evidence that they were still wroth. It caused me great pain and grief for many years. But now . . . finding those letters of yours and finding the will, I wonder. Perhaps yours weren't the first letters Aunt Cecelia hid away."

"Does Aunt Cecelia know? I mean, does she know you found my letters and the will?"

"Actually, she was out of town on some business when I left. As soon as I realized what she had done, I packed our bags and sent your grandfather a telegram. I knew where she kept her money stash, so I bought the tickets, and we came out immediately. She should be arriving home today. If she hasn't read my letter already, I'm sure she will shortly. She won't be pleased, I'm certain of that. I was quite blunt, I'm afraid, and held nothing back."

"I wish I could see her face when she reads your letter," Georgiana said thoughtfully.

"And so do I," her mother agreed. After wiping the residue of tears from her face with her apron, she stood up. "Well, I best leave you alone. I'm sure you would like some rest or, at the very least, you might like some time to catch up on your mail." Georgiana gave her mother a grateful nod as she turned and walked to the door.

"Thank you, Mother," Georgiana said sincerely.

Her mother smiled warmly and left her room. Georgiana eagerly opened one of the letters from Sammy dated five years previously and began reading.

Dear Georgie,

I can't believe you're not coming back! How will I ever live without you? You're my best friend. It just isn't fair. So for now, I will not think of you as a lost friend, but as a new one living in the city. We will be great pen pals, I will keep you informed of everything that happens in Crystal Creek, including anything and everything about "you know who" and you can tell me all the exciting things in New York.

I am already feeling better. I think this is going to be fun . . .

The letter brought back fond memories, and she eagerly sifted through the pile. There was not one letter from Ridge. He really hadn't written, not once. It was more than a disappointment. It spoke volumes about his true feelings.

Setting the letters aside, Georgiana decided she would rather read them later. Instead, she turned her thoughts to the letter Dawson had left for her. Despite her heavy heart, a smile tugged at the corners of her mouth. His letter had been sweet and his concern for her well-being evident. However, there was something else entirely that had her smiling. Dawson, she suspected, had feelings for Samantha. It was obvious by the way he wrote about how much fun he was going to have showing Samantha around New York. She was happy for him and her dear friend. She realized the night of the dance they were perfect for each other. At least something good had come of all this.

Reaching over with some difficulty, Georgiana managed to extinguish the lamp without hurting her shoulder. She snuggled in the warmth of her blankets. As she drifted off to sleep, she wondered where Ridge was tonight. Again she felt warmth pass through her as she distinctly remembered his presence over the past few days. Where had he gone? Why hadn't he been here when she had awakened? Closing her eyes, she conjured up a vision of him. He was smiling at her, his warm eyes boring into her own as his face descended toward her lips to devour them in a blissful kiss. That kiss would be the fabric of her dreams tonight.

·25·

A Kiss to Remember

JIMMY helped Georgiana down from the wagon.

"Thank you, Jimmy." She smiled warmly up at him, then looked at the worried face of her mother. "I'm fine, Mother."

"The doctor would have gladly come over to the house. I don't know why you insisted—" her mother began complaining.

"Mother, I know he would have, but I needed to get out," Georgiana interrupted. "I'm going crazy lying in bed all day. I haven't had so much leisure time since I've been here! It will be a nice change to be seen in his clinic."

Her mother came over and patted her on the arm.

"I know, dear. It's hard going from being busy and needed to being waited on hand and foot, but still I worry."

Georgiana looked over to Jimmy. He seemed anxious. Jimmy, she had discovered, had been seeing Millie Gunners, the blacksmith's daughter. She could tell he wanted to be excused so he could go visit with her.

"Thank you for your help, Jimmy. I'm sure we can manage from here."

"Thank you, Miss McLaughlin, and you, Mrs. McLaughlin." He nodded his head politely to each of them and was off in the direction of the blacksmith's in a flash. Georgiana turned to her mother.

"Why don't you pick up the things we need at the mercantile while I see Doc Hansen. Mrs. Whitaker would love to hear a tidbit or two from you, I'm sure." Her mother rolled her eyes.

"And I'm sure, whatever I tell her, the whole town will know in a matter of hours," her mother remarked, and they both laughed.

"You must have a good memory then, Mother."

"Where that woman is concerned, I do. She certainly isn't my first choice of persons to visit after all these years, but . . ." Her eyes lit up. "Maybe on second thought I should visit her. Maybe I'll have a little fun."

"Mother, you wouldn't!" Georgiana pretended shock. Her mother's mischievous smile told her she would indeed.

"Well, enjoy yourself," Georgiana called over her shoulder as she headed toward the doctor's office. "I'll see you in a little while."

When Georgiana arrived at Dr. Hansen's office, there was a note posted. It read, *Called out on emergency. Be back shortly. You can wait in the office if you desire. —Doc Hansen.*

Sighing and turning away from the door, Georgiana looked around. She had no desire to wait in a stuffy office. She had been cooped up too long. Nor did she have any desire to go to the mercantile and be subjected to Mrs. Whitaker's endless questioning. Besides, it might ruin her mother's fun. She would just find a place to wait outside.

Looking up the street, her eyes caught sight of the old oak. Suddenly she had a strong desire to see the inscription again that she had discovered engraved into the tree. Casually, she strolled up the street in its direction.

When Georgiana reached its branches, she paused, and as was fast becoming a habit, she looked around to make sure she wasn't being watched before ducking under its cover. She stood motionless for a moment, allowing her eyes to adjust to the dim light.

Instantly, the memories came flooding back, and she walked up closer to the tree trunk and crouched down. As she had done before, she ran her fingers over the inscription.

The thought occurred that he must have at least liked her a little to have taken the time to carve it, even if he had never written. She thought back again to that day, and she was lost in her reminiscing until she heard a sound. Quickly she turned, startled at who might be watching, but there was no one.

Then she saw it. Something hanging from a branch . . . a bundle of some sort, a bundle of letters tied with a ribbon . . . a very familiar blue ribbon. Walking over to it, she untied it and examined the bundle in her hands. She looked around, but she was alone. Was it already hanging there when she had first ducked under the branches? She didn't remember seeing it, but then her eyes had needed to adjust to the shadows. Maybe she had missed it somehow.

Somewhat awed, she sat down, leaning her back against the trunk. She untied the bundle and sifted through the letters in her hand. There were so many, all addressed to her, and all stamped with big red letters that read, *Return to Sender.* Still, Georgiana smiled as she ran her fingers over his childish scrawl.

He had written her! The thought tumbled over and over in her mind. *Practically as many times as she had written him!* Her aunt, though, hadn't just kept his letters but had returned them. It was somehow crueler. Poor Ridge, he must have thought . . . quickly she stood up. She had to tell him. Tell him it wasn't she who had returned his letters, but her horrid aunt. If all this time he thought . . . no wonder! Her gaze was drawn back down at the letters. She wanted to read just one first, then she would find Ridge and talk to him.

Sitting back down against the tree, Georgiana carefully opened up the first one.

Georgie,

Hi. I guess I just wanted to see how you were doin', if you like the city and all. I'm sure there are lots of fun things to do.

It's sure boring without ya around. Samantha hasn't been any fun. If anyone mentions your name, she starts cryin'.

By the way, I went back and caught that huge bullfrog. Told everyone it was yours though. Jonas and Jeremiah were so jealous. Asked what I was goin' to do with it now that you were gone. I told them I was savin' it for ya. You were sure to be back at least for a visit before too long, right?

I guess I'd better say good-bye for now. Still got chores to do, and Schoolmaster Robinson gave me a two hundred word essay to write, and it wasn't cause I pulled a prank or anythin'. I don't break my promises.

Well, I wish you were here. It's going to be a long summer without ya.

Love,

Ridge

P.S. By the way, if you were here . . . I'd steal back that kiss.

Georgiana read the letter two more times before putting it back in the envelope. Taking the pins from her hair, she ran her fingers through it to smooth it out. Then she took the ribbon and tied her hair back as she had done as a child for church or rare occasions. Satisfied, she laid the letters beside her and leaned her head back against the tree trunk, closing her eyes. An unexpected smile suddenly lit her face. *He had written!*

Still exhausted from her ordeal, it wasn't long before she had accidentally fallen asleep.

❦ ❦ ❦

Ridge watched as Georgiana ducked under the branches of the old oak. Sneaking up quietly, he'd hung the letters, tied with her ribbon, to a branch and then snuck away before being caught. He was standing outside the bank talking to Mr. Wallace when Georgiana's mother hurried up to him, a worried expression on her face

"Have you seen Georgiana, Mr. Carson? She went over to Doctor Hansen's place but he hasn't seen her. He was out and has only just returned. I can't imagine where she has gone off too. What if—" Her mother sounded worried.

"I'm sure she's fine, Mrs. McLaughlin," Ridge interrupted. Excusing himself from Mr. Wallace, he took her arm and guided her across the street to where Jimmy waited by the wagon. "I think I know where she is," he admitted. "Why don't you go home, ma'am, with Jimmy here, and I'll go find Georgiana and bring her home myself." Ridge gave her a mischievous grin and winked.

All worries left her face immediately and were replaced by a satisfied expression.

"You found the letters then?" She smiled knowingly.

"Yes, and I'm sure by now she's found mine." Mrs. McLaughlin looked confused a moment, but Ridge nodded in the direction of the oak tree, and a look of enlightenment crossed her face.

"Well then, Mr. Carson, I'll leave her in your good hands. I should be getting home to start supper anyway. Don't want Angus to try anything drastic in the kitchen if he gets too desperate. That man can destroy a kitchen in no time at all, which wouldn't be so bad if what he cooked was edible." She laughed and reached over, laying her hand on his arm. "She loves you, Ridge. Don't let her deny it." Then she let go and walked over to Jimmy, who helped her up onto the wagon.

Ridge turned and looked back to the old oak. She'd been there quite a while, so he headed in that direction. He stopped only long enough to take a deep breath before he moved the branches aside and ducked underneath their cover.

❦ ❦ ❦

Georgiana opened her eyes, awakened by the sound of crunching leaves. The first thing she saw was a pair of boots. Her eyes followed them up until she was looking directly into Ridge's face.

"Hello, Mr. Carson." She couldn't keep the smile from her face.

"Miss McLaughlin." He politely tipped the brim of his hat.

"I must have fallen asleep." As she spoke, he reached his hands toward her to help her up. When their hands met, she felt the familiar warmth surge through her. "Thank you," she said, feeling a slight blush tinge her cheeks.

He didn't respond, just stared at her. Letting go of one of her hands, he reached over and plucked a leaf from off her head that must have fallen as she slept. Self-consciously, Georgiana reached her free hand up to smooth her hair and realized she was still wearing it down, tied back with the ribbon. Embarrassed at how she must appear, she raised her hand again to remove it. Ridge reached out and stayed her hand.

"Leave it . . . please." He smiled so endearingly that she let her hand drop to her side.

Her cheeks warmed again, and her heart began beating madly. She stared into his eyes only for a moment until her gaze fell to his lips. Would she ever be able to stop imagining those lips pressed against her own? Her heart sped up even more. *He won't need to steal a kiss today*, she thought, for she would give him her kiss gladly, if he still wanted it.

Finally, she found the courage to look into his eyes. He *was* going to kiss her. She could tell by his expression. What was he waiting for? Impatiently, she moistened her lips. She wanted nothing more than his kiss, and the silence and the waiting were driving her crazy.

"I . . . I found your letters," she said nervously, breaking the silence. "Thank you. You know I didn't—"

"I know," he said before she could finish and placed his arms around her waist.

"Because I never would have . . ."

"It's okay, Georgie . . . I know." He leaned her back against the tree and leaned his own body against hers.

"I just can't believe my aunt would . . ."

"Georgiana?" Leaning forward, he whispered her name into her ear, and slowly trailed his lips down the length of her cheek and neck, hovering just above her skin. His breath was warm, and the sensation caused an intense delirium to pass through her.

"Hmm?"

"Are you going to be quiet so I can kiss you?"

Instantly her body thrilled. "Uh . . . huh."

"Good, because I want this to be a kiss you'll remember."

"I remember all your kisses, Ridge, even the one *I* stole." Her heart fluttered dangerously as he gave his crooked smile.

"Not like you'll remember this one," he promised, his voice already husky.

He kissed her then, first soft and slow, then, as if his lips were starved for her, he kissed her with a hunger and a passion she'd never dreamt of. Her heart beat madly in her chest. Her knees felt weak from sheer pleasure and longing. She returned his kiss with as much passion as his own, which caused his kiss to deepen further. Reaching up, she lost her fingers in the softness of his hair and he drew her even closer. Never before had she known such bliss. Never had she imagined such a kiss.

Forcibly, he drew his lips from hers.

"Georgiana Anne McLaughlin?" He was breathing hard with restrained passion.

"Hmm?"

"Will you marry me?"

"Uh . . . huh."

"Soon?"

"Today, if you like." She laid her head against his chest. His heart was pounding nearly as madly as her own.

"I think I can give ya at least a week to get ready. Don't want your mother to be angry with me. You're her only daughter, ya know."

"Okay . . . one week then." She looked up into his face, ready to be kissed again.

"If you really need more time, I guess I could wait two. After all, I *have* waited years already." He smiled down at her.

"Ridge?" She removed her hands from around his neck and placed them on his cheeks.

"No longer than two, 'cause I don't think—"

"Ridge?" She leaned in close to his face.

"Hmm?"

"Are you going to be quiet and kiss me?"

"Uh . . . huh." He smiled.

"Because we're standing under the kissing tree, you know . . ." Her heart sped up even more as he leaned in closer, a breath away. "And I'm sure this old giant has witnessed a lot of kisses."

"Well, then." The look he gave her made her knees almost buckle this time. "Let's give *him* one to remember."

Before his kiss could find her, she spoke once more.

"I love you, Ridge Carson . . . ever I have loved you."

"And I love you, Georgiana McLaughlin. More than words . . ." His lips moved closer, "Or kisses . . ." He paused, hovering, his sweet breath mingling with her own. "Can say."

Finally, his lips were hers.

·Epilogue·

THE paint brush froze in Georgiana's hand as she paused to watch her son Michael teasing the little Carter girl, Maggie. At eight years old, he was so much like his father, the same wavy brown hair and brown eyes and the same sprinkle of freckles dotting his nose. Like his father too, he was born with the same predisposition to tease, as well as being known to pull a prank or two.

Looking around her, she quietly observed the families gathered at the Easter Day Picnic. Mrs. Whitaker was talking animatedly to an attentive group of women, no doubt sharing the local "news." She only stopped long enough to scowl when a group of raucous young men, two of them being Georgiana's brothers William and Aden, ran through the center of their huddle.

Suddenly, an old woman waddled by on the arm of Doc Hansen. Could that be old Mrs. Wickers, her former babysitter? *How can she possibly still be alive?* Georgiana thought incredulously. Still shaking her head in disbelief, she looked around again.

Jimmy and his wife, Millie, were sitting with his sister Lizzie and her husband, Reverend Stevens. She watched for a moment as he wrestled with one of his young boys. Millie stared up at him adoringly.

About three years ago, Jonas and Jeremiah had finally found and married two sisters willing to put up with them. Both women sat alone, tending small babes as the twins scoured the refreshment tables in search of food.

Next she looked over to where Dawson and Samantha sat under the shade tree. Dawson bounced their newest son, Nathaniel, on his knee while Samantha washed cherry pie from her daughter's face. She'd missed her friend dearly since she'd married Dawson and moved to live in New York, but at least they both came out once a year to visit. She was grateful they had remained close and stayed in touch.

For a moment she thought about her mother and grandfather so far away. She had received a letter only yesterday and was so pleased they were having a pleasant time. They had been gone two months already, and she didn't expect them back for at least another month. Her mother had plenty of funds now to travel with since her half of the inheritance had been restored. Indeed, this was their second trip to Ireland.

Aunt Cecelia had not even put up a fight. In fact, Aunt Cecelia deeded the house to her mother, even though the will stated it was to be hers, and left New York. No one knew where she'd gone or where she had settled, but after about a year, Mother received a letter. Much to their surprise, the return address was from Sacramento, California. Not one of them could believe it until the second letter came six months later with a wedding invitation. It seemed Georgiana's aunt had fallen in love with a retired Spanish general who had a very large family, and who most ardently returned her affections. Mother had forgiven Aunt Cecelia long before and had traveled out west, accompanied by her father-in-law, of course, to the wedding. Granddad had plenty of time on his hands since he had retired and given the ranch to her and Ridge as a wedding present, although Ridge insisted on compensating him for at least some of its value.

In her letter from Ireland, Mother mentioned that while visiting, Grandfather proudly became a great uncle once again. On their first trip, they learned that Brody, who had returned to Ireland so long ago, had remarried. Her grandfather, much to his great delight, had lots of nieces and nephews as well as even more great-nieces and great-nephews. He wasn't so alone in the world after all. Georgiana was pleased she had a passel of Irish cousins she hoped one day to meet. She was also grateful her grandfather and his brother had been reunited.

There was something else her mother had written though that made Georgiana especially delighted. Mother subtly alluded to the fact that she might be bringing someone back with her. Her mother had been corresponding with an Irish gentleman, secretly, since her first visit to Ireland. Georgiana hoped her mother had finally found someone to love again.

Most of all, Georgiana just couldn't wait for her mother to return. She placed her hand affectionately on her abdomen. She would be needing her before too long.

Her eyes were drawn to where Ridge stood pushing their daughters, six-year-old Shannon and three-year-old Angela, on the swings. As she watched, he glanced up, caught her staring, and waved. She waved back. Smiling, he whispered into Shannon's ear, and she hopped off the swing as he helped Angela down. Shannon took a hold of her sister's hand, and both she and Angela ran over to where Dawson and Samantha sat.

Her heart sped up as Ridge began walking her way. He still had such an effect on her, and when he took her hand and drew her close, she had to fight the goose bumps threatening to break out all over her body. Leaning forward, he whispered into her ear.

"Are you thinkin' what I'm thinkin'?" He smiled his crooked smile, and her heart fluttered.

"Well, that depends. What are you thinking?" She smiled back up at him.

"Well, I was thinkin' it was about time we visited an old friend."

"Old friend?" she questioned.

"Yeah, you know, make sure he remembers us."

A knowing grin spread across her face as she anticipated what he was inferring. He beamed back.

"I'll take that as a yes."

Without warning, he scooped her up into his arms, careful not to upset her easel and paints, and walked up the street toward the old oak. Ducking under its branches, he walked up to its trunk and set her down. Instantly she wrapped her arms around his neck and began playing with his hair. Sliding his arms around her, he pulled her close.

"I was wondering, Mrs. Carson, if I try to steal a kiss, will you slap me or give it freely?"

"Well, Mr. Carson, me dear, I suppose that depends on just what sort of kiss ye were thinkin' of stealin' from me now." She winked at him as she spoke in a feigned Irish brogue.

"Oh, it's that way, now is it? There are conditions." The corner of his mouth turned up slightly. "What if I were to steal a peck, like this?"

He leaned forward and quickly kissed her lips.

"Well then, me thinks I would hardly have time to make me choice because 'twould be over too soon."

He got a devilish look in his eyes.

"What if I tease you a little first before I kissed you?"

This time he slowly and tenderly brushed his lips along her skin, from her ear, down her neck, finally coming to her mouth, hovering above it briefly before finally taking her lips for his own. After a moment, he pulled back and looked into her eyes again. She waited until her heartbeat calmed before answering.

"Well, now," she began, "it's hard to say. Though such a kiss as that might make me forget me very own name," she admitted freely.

He smiled deliciously before he spoke again.

"What if I then take your lips in a madly driven kiss that told tale of how much I want you for my own?"

Her heart began to beat dangerously wild as his lips found hers in a moist, driven kiss of pure passion. It was a masterful kiss that made her limbs tremble. She was entirely undone, and when he broke the seal of their lips, it took several seconds in order to catch her breath before she could speak.

"After that, me dear husband, I could do nothin' but love ye in return, for with that kiss ye own me, body and soul, forever."

Smiling blissfully, she looked deep into his eyes. She was happy and could want for nothing else in this life than the man who stood before her, gazing affectionately back. She could not believe she ever doubted that he loved her as much as she loved him. His next words echoed her very thoughts.

"I love you, Mrs. Georgiana Anne Carson, so much that I never want ya to doubt it." A twinkle lit his eyes. "That's why I'll be kissin' you again, a combination of all three kisses, just so ya know for sure."

"I have been known to be a 'doubting Thomas' at times, so ye just make sure ye convince me good, then I'll never be doubtin' your intentions toward me again."

"You'll know," he promised emphatically.

Once again he kissed her, and she melted in his arms.

About the Author

PRUDENCE Bice has loved writing her entire life. Born in Orange County, California, as one of eleven children, she always felt drawn to stories that spoke to and kindled her romantic heart. Having overcome tragedy in her own life, the inspiration for her first novel was sparked by her desire to ignite true romantics everywhere with a wholesome, feel-good story about the power of love in rising above the pain and suffering from loss.

Prudence resides in St. George, Utah, with her husband, Ray, and their four daughters and one son. Her hobbies include drawing, photography, music, writing, and, of course, reading anything she can get her hands on! Currently she is majoring in English at Dixie State College and loving it. The future is bright, she says. Every day she wakes up with a prayer in her heart and a story in her head. She never thought life could be so good!